Rain and Retribution

By LL Diamond

Rain and Retribution
LL Diamond
Published by LL Diamond

*For my mom, who introduced me to Jane Austen
and never denied me a book to read. I miss you every day!*

Chapter 1

"Into each life some rain must fall..." Henry Wadsworth Longfellow

Wednesday 27 November 1811

Elizabeth Bennet was looking out over the view from Oakham Mount as she thought about how the last few days had become a nightmare. The Netherfield ball, which she and all of Meryton greatly anticipated, had been a series of dreadful, not to mention mortifying, events that had all culminated to become a complete disaster! Mr. Wickham, who she had dearly hoped would request a dance of her, disappointed her by not being in attendance. He had been obliged to travel to town on business the day before, but Elizabeth knew he was likely avoiding the presence of Mr. Darcy.

As the dancing commenced, her cousin, Mr. Collins, petitioned her to dance for the first set. She dearly wished to refuse but she was obligated to accept or she would forfeit the ability to participate for the rest of the evening. He proved himself to be an extremely inept dancer, unknowingly missing steps and treading on her toes, prattling constantly for the duration of the dance. She was extremely fortunate her feet were not bruised from the unfortunate encounter.

If standing up with Mr. Collins had not been enough of a torture, she had been asked to dance by Mr. Darcy, of all people. She could not understand why he wished to dance with her, knowing he only looked at her to find fault. After all, it was he who had said, "She is tolerable, I suppose, but not handsome enough to tempt me." The ensuing argument between the two during the dance did not help to increase her enjoyment of the ball in the least.

4

She had finally returned to her friend, Charlotte Lucas, when Mr. Collins insisted on introducing himself to the nephew of his esteemed patroness. Despite Elizabeth's arguments against the idea, the toadying man ran as quickly as his chubby legs could carry him to prostrate himself before an obviously displeased Mr. Darcy. She was mortified by the event; however, her cousin was very pleased with his reception, babbling on for some time on the subject.

During dinner, there were her mother's raptures over Jane and her eventual marriage to Mr. Bingley when, as of yet, he had not so much as requested a courtship. Elizabeth attempted to rein in her mother's enthusiasm; however, her efforts were in vain as her mother seemed determined to say what she pleased regardless of who heard.

Then there were Lydia and Kitty, who after over-indulging on wine, ran through the dining room brandishing Lieutenant Denny's sword and making spectacles of themselves. Mary's horrible performance on the pianoforte, their father's method of ending it, and her mother's manoeuvring to ensure they were the last to leave the ball.

Her dreadful evening, however, did not cease with the dawn. Early that very morning when she came down to break her fast she found Mr. Jeffries, Longbourn's steward, awaiting her. She had informed her father weeks ago of the need to fix the roof on one of the tenant's homes, praying he would finally take some responsibility for his estate; he had not. Therefore, because she was truly concerned for the people under Longbourn's care, she had grudgingly spent the time she normally devoted to her morning walk making the arrangements for the hole that had since formed to be patched, and providing the steward with the necessary funds for the repairs.

A few hours later Elizabeth's mother cornered her in the dining room, insisting their cousin, Mr. Collins, required a word with her in private. She had begun to suspect her mother was pushing the parson in her direction over the course of the last week, but she had most assuredly not done anything to encourage him! Her younger sister, Mary, would have been a much better match with her proclivity for quoting scripture; however, he had the audacity to continue his pursuit until this morning, when the malodorous little man made her an offer of marriage. Having managed to finally escape his seemingly unending proposals, Elizabeth ran from the house hoping to find peace and quiet, not caring about her mother's wailings for her return.

Unfortunately, she knew while she had been sitting here, her mother would currently be appealing to her father, seeking reinforcements to her cause. Elizabeth hoped that he would support her decision, but she did have her doubts. She was the second of five daughters born to a gentleman whose estate, Longbourn, was entailed to Mr. Collins. In addition to the entailment, Mr. Bennet was an indolent landowner, and had not been financially prudent over the years, leaving very little for his family to live on upon his eventual demise. A marriage to their cousin would at least secure a home for her family when that fateful day arrived.

Elizabeth had vowed long ago only to marry for the deepest love, and she did not love Mr. Collins. Furthermore, there was no possible way that she would ever grow to love him. She could not even respect him, because he was the most ridiculous man she had ever met, and that was saying something! She could not, and would not, do it!

Elizabeth knew she should be returning to Longbourn soon, so she stood and slowly began walking toward the potential tempest brewing at home. As she walked, she contemplated her options should her father try to force her into a marriage with Mr. Collins. Her twenty-first birthday was just around the corner, which meant she would be of age, so if she left, she could not be forced to return to Longbourn. Her Aunt and Uncle Gardiner would surely assist her, but how could she ask such a large favour of them? Was it really fair for Elizabeth to put them in the position of helping her defy her parents? She could only hope and pray that the situation would not necessitate involving her beloved Aunt Maddie and Uncle Edward too deeply.

Entering through the back door of the house, Elizabeth proceeded to walk toward the front drawing room. However, as she passed her father's library she heard him call out to her.

"Lizzy, could you come in please."

Elizabeth ceased walking further into the house and entered the room. Her father, Mr. Thomas Bennet, was seated behind his desk, while her mother, Fanny, as most people called her, stood before it, wearing a triumphant grin. Mr. Collins to Mrs. Bennet's side wore a smug, self-satisfied look upon his face.

"I understand you have refused Mr. Collins's proposal of marriage."

"I have."

"While you may have refused Mr. Collins this morning, I must now insist that you accept his offer," he said, while looking at her over his glasses.

"Father, you cannot be serious. He is ridiculous."

"Elizabeth Bennet! You hold your tongue!" screeched her mother, fanning herself dramatically with her handkerchief.

"I will not hold my tongue, Mother, and I will not marry Mr. Collins."

"Do not tell me what you will or will not do, you ungrateful child. Oh! My poor nerves! Mr. Bennet! That girl will be the death of me!"

"That is enough!" yelled a frustrated Mr. Bennet. "Mrs. Bennet, Mr. Collins, leave us."

"She must marry Mr. Collins," her mother loudly whispered to her father.

"Yes, yes, I know what she must do. Now leave," he stated forcefully, gesturing toward the door with his eyes.

As the two left the room, Elizabeth could hear her mother's continued exclamations, waiting until the door closed to address her father. "I cannot marry him. Please do not make me do this," she pleaded, fighting the tears that were coming to her eyes.

"I am sorry, but I must. If Mr. Bingley had proposed to Jane, I would have had some assurances that your mother and sisters would be cared for should I leave this earth, but he has left Meryton with no guarantee of his return. Through your marriage to Mr. Collins, your mother and sisters will have a home when I die."

"What do you mean Mr. Bingley has left?" she quickly asked before the last words had come out of his mouth.

Mr. Bennet bristled at her interruption, sitting forward angrily in his chair. "His departure is of no concern to you other than that it makes your marriage to Mr. Collins a necessity!"

"I could never be happy with such a man."

"You would be married. You would have a home, respectability, and security," he persuaded.

"But at what cost? To be miserable for the rest of my life, to endure my marriage as you do yours?"

"It is not so bad as that. Your mother provides a source of amusement as Mr. Collins will do for you," he quipped.

"This is not a joke!"

"No, it is not, but the decision has been made. I will brook no further opposition. You *will* wed Mr. Collins, and you *will* be the next mistress of Longbourn."

"I am sorry, Papa, but I will not pay the price for your failure to provide for your family. It is too high," replied Elizabeth, attempting to remain calm. "You sit in here and read your books while you allow your steward to run Longbourn. You do not even do your part; that task has fallen to me. If you had taken the time to handle your own affairs and made an effort to check Mama and her spending, then we would not be in this situation." She felt tears well up in her eyes. "Now I am to sacrifice my dreams so you can atone for the mistakes you have made."

"How dare you speak to me in this fashion!" her father yelled while he rose from his seat. "I will not tolerate your disrespect!"

"I will not marry him!"

"That is enough! You will put a smile on your face and marry Mr. Collins, or you will no longer be welcome at Longbourn!" shouted her father. "Are you prepared to sacrifice your family due to your recalcitrance?"

"You are sacrificing me to make up for *your* neglect. Forcing me down that aisle will quiet Mama and allow you to return to your indolent ways!"

"Enough!" he bellowed, pounding the desk with his fist. "The match has been made and you have no say in the matter! In fact, you are to go to your room, and do not come down until you are able to be pleasant in company and accepting of your betrothed."

Elizabeth turned and stormed from the library, slamming the door behind her. As she climbed the stairs, she wished that things had not come to this point. She had always been her father's favourite, and hoped he would never force her into a marriage as unfulfilling as his own, yet he was attempting to do that very thing—worse actually—at least her mother did not smell.

As she reached the room she shared with Jane, she looked at the place where she had passed so much of her time; the nights spent with her beloved elder sister talking and dreaming about the future and the men they would eventually marry. Of course, those conversations were in the past, but they were still fond memories she would never forget. She pushed the door closed, locking it behind her as she leaned her forehead against it and considered her situation.

Elizabeth was heartbroken that her father had r ˈ˙˙ ᴏiven her an ultimatum. The man he commanded heɪ a ridiculous sycophant, and she knew her fathɛ as foolish as she did. And while she did not knɴ what marital duties entailed, her mother ofteˑ them and she knew it would involve kissing ʃ thought caused a shudder of revulsion to reverberate through her body.

Yet, did she really have the nerve to leave? She would have to find a position as a companion or at the very least, a governess, and prayed her Aunt and Uncle Gardiner would be willing to help. While she gave thought to the actions she felt she must take, a light knock startled her from her thoughts.

"Lizzy," Jane called softly, prompting Elizabeth to take a step back before allowing her sister in to the room. Securing the door once more, she took a seat on the bed where Jane joined her.

"Do not try to make this seem like a good thing, because it is not."

"I know that marrying Mr. Collins is not what you had in mind, but you would be giving security to all of us for when Papa dies."

"You cannot tell me you would marry for those reasons; we always vowed to marry for love," cried Elizabeth.

"I gave up those notions when Mr. Graham left."

"What about Mr. Bingley?" she inquired incredulously. "I have seen you with him. I can tell you love him."

"I think very highly of Mr. Bingley, it is true, but I do not love him."

Elizabeth was aghast, "I do not believe it!"

"It is true. He is what Mama expects me to marry, rich, handsome, and very amiable. I do not require more," affirmed her sister.

"You cannot be serious?" demanded Elizabeth. "Why?"

"Affection eventually causes pain. You would be a fool to give ꭗ the opportunity to be married and mistress of Longbourn."

"You have closed yourself away from affection, so I am supposed to follow your lead for an *opportunity*?" she responded angrily. "At least, if you were to marry Mr. Bingley, you would not be tied to someone you could not even like."

"You have no other option. Whatever choices you had were taken away when Mr. Bingley and his party returned to London today without any expectations to return . . . "

"Papa said Mr. Bingley had left, but I did not believe it," interrupted Elizabeth. "When did this happen?"

Pulling a letter from her pocket, Jane held it out to her sister, who opened and scanned the missive to Caroline Bingley's signature at the bottom. "It was delivered after you ran from Mr. Collins."

Reading the letter, Elizabeth did not necessarily believe all of Miss Bingley's claims, especially those regarding Miss Darcy marrying Mr. Bingley. She knew the woman did not consider Jane a friend, since their family was not grand enough for the social climber. But now she hoped he did not return if Jane was not in love with him. He deserved a chance at love just like everyone else, and she would hate to see a gentleman as amiable as Mr. Bingley fooled into a marriage of unequal affections.

"It is unlikely he will ever make me an offer of marriage, so it is up to you to marry for the benefit of the family, until I can secure a man of wealth who will be able to aid us further."

"Wealth does not buy happiness."

"Love and poverty do not bring happiness either."

"When did money become such a priority to you?" Elizabeth felt as if she were looking at a stranger. This was not the sweet Jane she had known as a child. Her favourite sister had grown cynical and mercenary, and she had apparently been blind to it all along.

"We do not have much to recommend us, Lizzy. It may seem harsh, but I am being realistic.

"If you believe one of us should marry him, why do you not do it? Especially since you do not care to have affection for your husband—the situation seems ideal for you."

"Actually, I told Mama and Papa that I would marry Mr. Collins. My mother would not hear of it, claiming that I was meant for . . ." Jane trailed off, no longer looking her sister in the eye.

"Let me guess, Mama said you were meant for better than Mr. Collins, and neither you nor Papa was willing to put any effort into persuading her."

"It is not as bad as you seem to think," said Jane reassuringly, placing her arm around Elizabeth and hugging her close. "Take your time to compose yourself; I will be downstairs when you are ready."

Elizabeth, who did not wish to hear any more, nodded as her sister left the room; she followed Jane to the door and locked it behind her. Moving quickly to the closet, she searched for the valise her aunt had given her the previous year. As she looked, she thought about her older sister. Elizabeth and Jane had always been very close, but her sister's abandonment by Mr. Graham a year earlier had changed their relationship. Mr. Graham was a wealthy cousin to one of the smaller landowners in the area, who had called upon Jane for months, giving everyone sufficient cause to gossip that an engagement would soon be forthcoming. Then, like Mr. Bingley, Mr. Graham abruptly left Meryton and never returned.

Poor Jane! She had to not only listen to her mother's lamentations, but was also forced to endure the petty gossip and tittering from the ladies of the neighbourhood. Her heart had not only been broken, but also exposed for the world to see.

Nothing was the same after Mr. Graham's departure. The sisters still talked, but Jane no longer confided in Elizabeth the way she once had. She never truly recovered, and Elizabeth had begun to suspect that her sister was protecting her heart. Apparently, Jane hid herself behind her serene countenance more effectively than Elizabeth realised. She had been different during the last year, but it was not as marked as during the conversation they had just had. She gave thought to Jane's advice, knowing many women would approach the situation in the same manner. Of course, her sister did not have to marry or eventually kiss Mr. Collins. That odious chore would fall to Elizabeth.

Locating her bag, she sorted through her belongings, choosing the more practical items, which were mainly the dresses her Aunt and Uncle Gardiner had purchased for her. They were not only the better of her dresses, but also the least used, due to the quality of the material. After packing some of her undergarments as well as nightgowns next to her dresses, she looked sadly at the room she had shared with her sister since they were little girls, and sighed, returning to arrange the final items in her bag. When everything was packed to her satisfaction, she crouched down to lift a small, loose floorboard hidden under the bed, removing her journal, as well as her savings. Having Lydia in the family, one could never be too careful with one's belongings, and most importantly, one's secrets. Finally, Elizabeth removed the garnet cross from her neck, a present from her father for her fifteenth birthday, and left it on the dressing table before donning her pelisse.

Peering out the door, Elizabeth ensured the hall was empty before she quietly slipped out of her bedroom, turning to lock it behind her. As she slid the key into her pocket, she hoped bolting it would provide her some additional time before her father realised she was gone. Jane would hopefully assume she wished for some time to herself and sleep with Mary for the night, as she had done when they argued in the past. Completing her task, she tiptoed to the back stairs, and followed them down to the kitchen.

Mrs. Hill looked up as Elizabeth entered, and noticed the valise she held tightly in her hand. The dear housekeeper had never cared for Mrs. Bennet's ill treatment of her second daughter and her obvious preference for Jane and Lydia. Therefore, Mrs. Hill had always had a soft spot for her; always making sure her "Miss Lizzy" had everything she needed. The older woman put a finger to her lips, imploring Elizabeth to stay quiet, lest other servants hear and inform Mr. Bennet as she led the way out of the house.

As soon as they were a small distance away, Elizabeth turned to face her. "I do not expect you to help me, Mrs. Hill."

"I know, but that greasy little man irritates me to no end, and I happen to believe that you are too good for him."

"I do not wish you to lose your position," worried Elizabeth.

"No one saw us leave the house, besides Mr. Hill has to drive to Hatfield this afternoon. If you hide in the cart, you can catch the post coach from there." Mrs. Hill looked toward the house. "Now you cannot be seen down by the stables, so you run on up to the fork in the road and wait for Mr. Hill there. He will stop for you."

"I am unsure. I would never forgive myself if coming to my aid hurt you in any way."

"Miss Lizzy," Mrs. Hill responded with tears in her eyes, "you were always the sweetest little thing, and as much as I will miss you, I do not wish for you to be our mistress." Elizabeth appraised her carefully, realising that arguing would not accomplish anything.

"Thank you!" said Elizabeth as she reached out to embrace the woman who had taken such excellent care of her during her childhood.

"I just want you to be happy, little miss," wept Mrs. Hill, returning the embrace. "You deserve it just as much as Miss Jane and Miss Lydia."

Elizabeth watched the old woman dry her eyes on her apron before heading back toward the house. Then taking a deep breath, she began to walk in the direction of the fork in the road to Meryton, peering over her shoulder from time to time to ensure no one espied her. At least Mr. Hill would enable her to retain some mystery to her destination, whereas the people at the local post station knew her, and her parents would be able to discover very early where she was travelling. Once she was out of sight of the house, she became so wrapped up in her thoughts that she started upon realising that she had reached her destination, one direction heading to Netherfield and the other to Meryton.

14

Approximately five minutes after she had arrived at the junction, Mr. Hill pulled up in the cart and waited for Elizabeth. She appeared from the trees where she was hiding and climbed into the back.

"Get under the cover Miss Lizzy," suggested Mr. Hill. "We cannot have your Aunt and Uncle Philips seeing you running away. That aunt of yours will run straight to your mother, and the gossip will be all over town." She rolled her eyes, internally agreeing with him; her Aunt Philips was a notorious gossip, just like her mother. She would have the news of her defection all over town by nightfall.

"Oh, and the missus put a small bag of food with a jug of water under there for you."

Elizabeth smiled when she found the sack that contained some bread and apples, which she tucked away with her things for later.

Glancing up at the sky, she noticed that it looked like rain. Hoping it would hold off until she was safely at the post station, she climbed under the cover while the cart lurched forward, beginning an adventure that she hoped would take her as far from Mr. William Collins as possible.

Three miles away, at Netherfield manor, Fitzwilliam Darcy was waiting for his carriage to be readied for departure. His good friend, Charles Bingley, had left for London, and he thanked God that Miss Bingley, his friend's sister, had departed earlier with Mr. and Mrs. Hurst. Miss Bingley would have found any excuse she could for everyone to ride together, and Darcy really did not believe he could be civil for an entire trip to London with that woman. Thankfully, he had not travelled in his coach, which unlike his Landaulet carriage would have had enough room for the entire party.

Since arriving at the estate his friend Bingley had leased, that woman had simpered and fawned at every opportunity; it had become all he could do to remain in the same room with her. He had even heard his doorknob turn during the night a few times during his stay. Luckily, he had remembered to lock his door, and he had reminded his valet to ensure his dressing room was secured every night as well.

Even Georgiana, his younger sister, had already been sent ahead to his estate, Pemberley, due to Miss Bingley and Mrs. Hurst's constant comments about calling on their "dear Georgiana." He did not like their superior attitudes and false sincerity and did not wish his young sister to become what he detested in so many women of the ton.

He could only assume that part of what infatuated him about Elizabeth Bennet was that she was nothing like Caroline Bingley and the other self-absorbed, simpering women of the ton. Aside from her beauty, which was only enhanced by her fine eyes, she was genuine. And never one to say things to garner attention or give herself airs; she even, at times, seemed to be trying to provoke an argument with him. The previous evening at the ball was one of those moments. He could only assume his father's godson, George Wickham, had been spreading his usual vitriol about him to the local populace, and Elizabeth seemed to have heard some of the pernicious gossip. Hopefully she did not believe that scoundrel, because he could not risk his sister's reputation by revealing Wickham's vicious propensities to the people of Meryton.

Darcy climbed into his carriage—very happy to be leaving the local area and the pair of fine eyes that had been haunting him since the Meryton Assembly. As the carriage began moving, he contemplated the danger Elizabeth Bennet posed to his life. She was not only beneath him in consequence, but also brought with her a ridiculous family. If there were a way to take her as his wife without acquiring her feather-brained mother and ill-mannered younger sisters, he would most certainly offer for her.

What had possessed him to actually send a letter to his solicitor in London requesting him to acquire a special license and settlement papers while she stayed at Netherfield to nurse her sister? Having Elizabeth, which was what his heart and mind insisted on calling her for some time now, in the same household had severely interfered with his equilibrium and made him act completely out of character. He had been rash, and was obviously not thinking straight.

Fortunately, the paperwork finally arrived after the Bennet sisters had returned to Longbourn, at which time he decided to wait and see if he could shake the hold she had on him.

As he made his way through town, the inhabitants of Meryton admired the handsome carriage, while Darcy wondered what Elizabeth was doing at that moment. He could not help but notice the marked attention paid to her by his aunt, Lady Catherine de Bourgh's toad of a parson. Miss Bingley and Mrs. Hurst had made several snide remarks pertaining to an upcoming marriage of that man to his Elizabeth; they found it quite amusing actually. It had been difficult to remain unaffected while Miss Bingley happily expounded on the situation over breakfast. She had even gone so far as to say, "Just think Mr. Darcy, you will have the opportunity to admire her fine eyes whenever you visit Lady Catherine." As if Elizabeth would ever consent to such a match! At least he hoped she would not.

"I must conquer this!" he exclaimed as the carriage left Meryton and the rain, which had been threatening all morning, began to fall.

Chapter 2

Elizabeth could hear the hustle and bustle of the people in
Meryton, and was relieved when the noise of the town died
away, leaving only the sound of the creaking cart. Mr. Hill let
her know that she could come out from under the cover since
the road was clear; however, it was not long after when it
began to rain.

Unfortunately, Elizabeth did not have any protection from
the weather, and the cover over the cart did not offer any
barrier from the wet and the cold. As a result, she quickly
became completely soaked through and began to shiver due
to the chill of the late November storm. The rain increased in
intensity and the road quickly became muddy. Without
warning the wagon pitched to one side, causing her to be
thrown off balance into the side of the cart.

"Blast!" swore Mr. Hill. "Oh! I apologize, Miss Lizzy!" he
exclaimed, as he suddenly remembered Elizabeth's presence.

She jumped down, splashing mud all over her dress and
petticoats. Her situation was not good—it was not good at all!
Hatfield was miles away, the rain showed no signs of
stopping, and she was cold and filthy. Mr. Hill quickly
ascertained that the cart had fallen into a deep rut made
impossible to see with the water pooling in the road. Not
only was the wheel stuck, but it was also broken.

They were not too far out of Meryton, and Mr. Hill decided to
walk back in order to find shelter and someone to help, but
he refused to leave her there in the weather. Elizabeth began
to panic; she certainly could not return to Meryton. She
argued that she would find a spot under a tree to wait out the
storm; yet, he would not be moved. She was finally forced to
acquiesce, and was waiting for Mr. Hill to unhitch the horse
for the walk back when a carriage appeared through the
sheets of rain. Elizabeth could not identify the equipage, but
vehemently prayed it was not someone who would return her
to Longbourn.

~ * ~

Darcy had been staring out at the rain, trying not to

contemplate the fine eyes of Elizabeth Bennet, when he noticed a cart to the side of the road that seemed to be having difficulty. As they moved closer to the broken down cart, he thought he saw Elizabeth standing a short distance away from the wreck. He shook his head as if to clear it.

"Good Lord, now I am seeing her everywhere!" he exclaimed, not believing his eyes.

Normally, Darcy would have stopped to help, but Meryton, the last place he wished to be, was still the closest town, so he decided to keep moving. Yet, as they began to pass, he could not help but take a closer look at the young woman standing next to the road. She had a petite frame with a light and pleasing figure, which could only remind him of Elizabeth. However, he could not make out her face, and found himself mesmerized as he watched her peel the soaked bonnet off of her drenched chestnut curls. He was willing to swear that it was Elizabeth Bennet.

"Blast!" he cursed as he beat his walking stick against the roof of the carriage. He had to be sure. If indeed it was her, his conscience would not allow him to simply leave her out in the dreadful weather.

The carriage had barely skidded to a halt when Darcy burst forth before the groom could open the door, striding to the young woman who looked up and startled him to a stop. He could not believe his eyes; he was dumbfounded. Elizabeth Bennet was truly standing before him, sopping wet, her dark curls plastered to her face, her piercing emerald green eyes betraying her shock at his arrival. He took a few hesitant steps to stand in front of her.

"Miss Bennet," he said as he noticed that her clothes were wet through and she was shivering from the cold.

"Mr. Darcy," she replied. She was trying very hard not to be intimidated by his six-foot plus frame, which seemed to tower over her, his vivid blue eyes visible even through the heavy rain.

"I was passing and noticed that you were stranded. May I be of assistance?"

Elizabeth could not believe he had stopped, much less offered his aid. "Mr. Hill was conveying me to the post station in Hatfield when the cart became stuck and the wheel broke. We were just preparing to walk back to Meryton when you happened upon us."

"Please allow me be of assistance. You are cold and need to get out of the rain. We can take shelter in my carriage while we discuss your options?"

"Mr. Darcy, you are perfectly aware that it would not be proper for me wait in your carriage with you," she objected. Although she desperately wanted to be out of the weather, she knew that Mr. Darcy had only ever looked at her to find fault. Jumping into his carriage at the offer he surely felt obligated to make, especially as wet as she was, would most certainly not improve his opinion of her.

"You will catch your death in this rain," Darcy implored, becoming concerned at her increasing pallor and shivers. "I promise you will be perfectly safe with me—unless you think your servant will gossip, because I assure you, mine will not."

His statement affronted Elizabeth and she became defensive. "No, Mr. Hill will not say a word, but I am soaked through, and I really do not believe that you want me in your carriage."

"I would not make the offer, if I did not mean for you to accept."

Elizabeth still had reservations, but she nodded. "Thank you." She turned to remove her valise from its hiding place within the cart and startled when Mr. Darcy took it from her, immediately passing it to a servant before he hurried to assist Elizabeth into the carriage. Once inside, he pulled some rugs from under the seat.

"If you remove your pelisse, you can dry off as much as possible and warm yourself with these."

She nodded just before he turned his back to her, so she could remove the drenched garment without exposing her wet form to him. When she had dried as much as she could with one of the smaller rugs, she wrapped herself in the two largest and turned to face him. She noticed that while he had become wet, he was not as soaked as she was. He had not been in the rain for long in addition to being protected to by his greatcoat, which he had since removed.

Elizabeth was not sure why Mr. Darcy was being so kind to her; he had always been so proud and aloof. After all, he had insulted her at the Meryton Assembly. He practically oozed disdain whenever he was in company with her family, so why would his manner change so drastically?

Upon indicating that she was covered, he turned and regarded her curiously. She was so cold and wet that he did not expect her to refuse his offer, and now she seemed so cautious. Was she afraid of him? Did she think he would become angry if she soaked the upholstery?

"If you tell me where you are going, I can transport you there, so you do not have to venture back into this horrid weather."

"I am traveling to my uncle's house in *Cheapside*," she said, waiting to see a reaction to her destination. "Mr. Hill had to run an errand in Hatfield and was delivering me to the post station, so I could take the next post to London. The rain stalled us."

Darcy pondered his dilemma. He could not strand Miss Bennet here, and he did not feel it was prudent to leave her at the post station alone. However, could he ride in a carriage—alone with her—and not lose his head? He was worried about being in such close proximity to her for the trip to London, yet there did not seem to be much choice in the matter.

"I am en route to London now and would be pleased to escort you."

"Sir, I appreciate your offer, but it would be an imposition. I am perfectly able to travel by post," Elizabeth answered, wondering what he was about.

"I insist. It is no imposition," declared Darcy. "I have the room, and I am already traveling for London. If you are worried about your reputation, you have assured me of your servant's discretion, and I assure you that mine will not breathe a word—no one need ever know."

Elizabeth eyed him warily. She was not sure about travelling all of the way to London, but she was not going to mention that now, since it would only cause further debate. She was resolved to ride with him no further than Hatfield where she would remain behind at the post station when he departed. Elizabeth nodded her agreement causing Darcy to confer with his driver. Mr. Hill was not happy leaving her with the gentleman, insisting on and receiving confirmation of her choice before he left with the horse to return to Meryton.

As the carriage began to move again, Darcy looked at Elizabeth not understanding her trepidation. Deciding conversation was the best way to put her at ease, he tried to think of topics to discuss, and remembering her words from the Netherfield ball, gave a small smile.

"Miss Bennet, we must have some conversation."

She raised her right eyebrow in response to his statement, recognizing her words from the previous night. He was such an enigma; maybe the ride would give her the opportunity to finally sketch his character.

"What do you wish to discuss, Mr. Darcy?"

"I wish to ask you about a comment you made last night, if you would allow me."

"Of course."

"You claimed Mr. Wickham had been so unlucky as to lose my friendship, in a manner which he would suffer from all his life. I was wondering precisely what he told you."

Elizabeth took a deep breath. "Mr. Wickham informed me of his relationship to your family. He told me of your father's wishes, as well as your refusal of the living your father had meant for him."

Darcy was angry to find he was correct in his earlier assumptions. "I suppose he left out the portion of the story in which he informed me that he was resolved not to take orders and compensated accordingly," he declared, without thinking or regarding the tone of his voice; her face flushed and her eyes widened in surprise.

He paused for a moment to gather his thoughts, beginning again in a more regulated tone of voice. "Wickham was the son of my late father's steward. Mr. Wickham senior was a respectable man, and to reward a faithful servant, my father supported the younger Wickham at school and later at Cambridge."

Darcy returned his gaze to Elizabeth's eyes. "When my father died, Wickham turned down the living. He claimed a desire to study the law, so I provided him with three thousand pounds in lieu of the living as well as the one thousand pounds my father bequeathed to him in his will.

However, when the living at Kympton became available, he reappeared, requesting a letter of presentation. Obviously, I refused."

At this point, overwhelmed by what she was hearing, Elizabeth noticed Mr. Darcy take a deep shuddering breath as he returned to looking at the rain, appearing pained, almost defeated. She watched in amazement when, as he turned to face her, his entire manner and demeanour changed. The whole of his body had become rigid, and his face had the stern expression she was so used to seeing him wear.

"The circumstances of my next meeting with Wickham I would wish to forget, and I sincerely ask you to keep this matter between us, as it could have rather dire consequences should this information come to the attention of society."

Elizabeth was not sure what to make of his request, yet she nodded her head in acquiescence.

"Last summer, my sister and her companion, a Mrs. Younge, travelled to Ramsgate. Wickham followed, persuading Georgiana to believe herself in love and consent to an elopement."

Darcy took a deep breath. "Fortunately, I joined them unexpectedly a day or two before the intended elopement, and my sister, confessed the entirety of the affair. His primary object was my sister's fortune of thirty thousand pounds. I also believe he intended to revenge himself on me."

Mr. Darcy's gaze returned out of the window as he said in a softer tone, "His revenge would have been complete indeed."

At the end of his recitation, Elizabeth looked at Mr. Darcy in shock. Oh, how could she have believed George Wickham! She had never questioned how inappropriate it was for him to impart his history with Mr. Darcy so soon after making her acquaintance, and realised with mortification that as a result of his unfortunate comment at the Meryton assembly, she had allowed her prejudice against him to influence every interaction between the two of them.

Elizabeth contemplated the change in his manner prior to relating the tale of his sister; she watched him don a mask that had slowly slipped, revealing the pain of the memory in his eyes. Had he been hiding his true self whenever in company? Why would a man of sense and education hide himself from the world?

"I regret that I attempted to provoke you last night with my uncivil behaviour. I am ashamed to admit that I believed his slander and I whole-heartedly apologize," declared Elizabeth, fighting back tears of embarrassment.

"Please, do not make yourself uneasy, Wickham's easy manners deceive many people. I have not only witnessed but also dealt with the repercussions of his deceptions too many times to count."

Darcy had hoped to warn Elizabeth to be on her guard with Wickham. He had not realised that her generous heart would be hurt by discovering the cad's true character, and found his stomach in knots as he became aware that he was jealous Wickham had gained her regard.

"Now, I only wish I had imparted this information earlier, in order to prevent injury to you," he said sympathetically.

Elizabeth had her brow furrowed in thought until she understood his implication. "Sir, you misunderstand. He had pleasing manners and I enjoyed his company, but he did not injure me."

"Good, I am relieved to hear it," he replied, exhaling in relief. His jealousy and worry subsided as her confession settled within his mind and heart.

Now that he had revealed his history with Wickham, Darcy began to think about how odd it was to discover her on the side of the road, in the pouring rain no less. Why did she not take the post coach from Meryton? Why was she traveling to London with only a valise and not a trunk? He was beginning to think there was more to her story than a trip to visit her aunt and uncle.

"May I ask you another question?" Darcy queried.

"By all means," said Elizabeth, wondering what was causing the suddenly contemplative look, which had appeared on his face.

"I apologize if you find me intrusive, but I was wondering why you did not take the post from Meryton."

Elizabeth, who did not expect the question, coloured and looked away, not knowing how to answer without revealing all.

"I have entrusted you with some very personal information. I assure you, I can be trusted with your deepest and darkest secrets as well," he continued with a mischievous smile tugging at the corner of his lips.

Elizabeth's eyes widened as she looked at his expression; it was so very different from the usual stern manner he used in company. She had never considered him unattractive, however seeing the beginnings of a smile on his face, she realised how very handsome he was.

"I do not doubt your discretion. My story is rather

embarrassing, and I fear you will not think very highly of me when it is concluded," Elizabeth answered, turning to look out of the carriage window. "I would prefer to leave matters as they are. You can deliver me to the post station in Hatfield without any knowledge of my future plans, other than that I was traveling to Cheapside."

Darcy began to worry with her last statement. "I doubt you have heard, but Mr. Bingley and his sisters departed Netherfield today. Obviously, I am leaving as well, and while I do not know if Bingley plans to return to the neighbourhood, I do not." She returned her gaze to him as he continued. "If you are leaving without your parents' knowledge, I will not be in Meryton to be questioned, nor will I offer any information regarding your whereabouts, unless it is your wish."

He had such an earnest look upon his face that she could not help but believe him, but did that mean she could divulge her plans and the reason behind them? She was concerned that taking Mr. Darcy into her confidence would only complicate matters immensely, and complications were not something she could afford at the moment.

"Miss Bennet, if you have chosen to leave home, you will have limited options available to you. I would be willing to assist you should you require it."

"I could not ask that of you, sir," replied Elizabeth softly. She was dumbfounded. *Mr. Darcy* wanted to help *her*. It was inconceivable, yet he was offering. Why would he do that?

"Tell me why you are leaving and let me be the judge of whether or not I would like to help," he implored.

Elizabeth was mortified. She closed her eyes, and attempted to order her thoughts. He had assured her of his discretion. After all, he expected her not to divulge the information he had imparted regarding his sister. She opened her eyes and adjusted the rugs around her body, still trying to warm herself as she decided that she did not have much choice but to trust Mr. Darcy.

Chapter 3

Wednesday 27 November 1811

"I am not sure if what I say will be surprising to you. What occurred this morning was unexpected . . . although I now understand that most of my family as well as our neighbours had some idea." At this statement she watched as Darcy furrowed his brow.

Feeling it was better to get it out and have done with it, Elizabeth closed her eyes in mortification. "This morning, I received a proposal of marriage from my cousin, Mr. Collins." She first peeked through her lashes and finally opened her eyes to see him looking at her with raised eyebrows.

"Since you are in my carriage at this moment, and not at Longbourn celebrating your betrothal, I would hazard a guess that you refused," he stated more calmly than he felt.

"You would be correct . . . several times actually."

"Several times?" he asked in a surprised manner.

"Unfortunately, it was really quite ridiculous. He made a long speech regarding his reasons for marrying, which included boundless praise of his pompous patroness, Lady Catherine de Bourgh." Elizabeth abruptly stopped and coloured. "Please forgive me, sir. I momentarily forgot she is your aunt."

Darcy smiled. "Your description of my aunt is not incorrect. She rather likes to hear herself speak, and has a tendency to issue orders disguised as advice. I am not offended."

Elizabeth's face reflected the relief she felt. "Thank you." Composing her thoughts for a moment, she continued, "I refused him twice. He claimed I was following an established custom of my sex to reject a man on the first application in order to encourage his suit."

At this statement, Elizabeth was amazed to see the

gentleman laughing—a low, sonorous laugh, with the most handsome smile adorning his face. Her breath caught in her throat and a shiver ran down her spine, which she attributed to the cold, and pulled the rugs tighter around her shoulders. Recognizing there was indeed humour in Mr. Collins's farce of a proposal, she began to chuckle as well, continuing her story once their laughter had subsided. "I finally managed to escape, and walked to Oakham Mount for some peace and quiet. I knew he would apply to my father, and my mother would be his most stalwart supporter. I have always fancied myself my father's favourite, so I hoped he would support my decision.

She looked him directly in the eye. "I *know* he finds him as ridiculous as I do. However, upon my return to the house, my father summoned me to his library, and ordered me to accept Mr. Collins's offer of marriage," she said, unable to contain her tears.

When she became discomposed, Darcy produced a handkerchief from his coat pocket. As he handed it to her, he found himself having a hard time containing his anger towards Mr. Bennet. The parson was a buffoon. Elizabeth was entirely too intelligent to be married to that obsequious toad, and too spirited to live under the rule of Lady Catherine. His officious aunt would have made her miserable, would have drained her vibrant spirit. A marriage between Mr. Collins and Elizabeth would have been a tragedy indeed.

"I find it doubtful your parents allowed you to simply leave. Do I need to be concerned that they will run us off the road in pursuit of you?" he asked.

"No, Mr. Darcy, they did not allow me to leave. When I refused to accept Mr. Collins, my father sent me to my room until I was willing to acquiesce to his wishes," she sighed. "I packed my bag, locked my bedroom door, and put the key in my pocket before I crept down the back stairs and into the kitchen. Mrs. Hill, who has always loved me like a daughter, saw me come down with my bag, and quickly ushered me out of the house. Her husband was already preparing to drive to Hatfield on an errand for my father, so she told me where to meet him. I can only assume she informed him, since he stopped when he reached the meeting point, and had some refreshments that she had sent for me." She looked out into the rain for a moment and then back to him. "I rode under the cover through Meryton; at this point, the only people who know I have gone are Mr. and Mrs. Hill, and now you."

He was amazed. A woman running away from home could be quite the scandal, and if she was underage, her father could force her to return to Longbourn to endure his fury. She was taking quite a risk, especially considering she could still have to marry Mr. Collins despite her best efforts.

Elizabeth looked at him and said, "I know what I am doing. I plan on asking my aunt and uncle to help me find a position as a companion, or maybe even a governess. As a tradesman, my uncle often conducts business with men who travel with their families, and I hope to be recommended to one of them."

He blanched at her last statement. Taking a position? Leaving the country? He took a deep breath to calm while he attempted to gather his thoughts.

"May I ask when you come of age?" he asked without considering the reason.

"The first of December," she replied, assuming she knew the reason for his question.

Before he could respond, he felt the carriage slipping in the mud due the deterioration of the roads, which had occurred during their conversation. He realised, however, that while they had not reached Hatfield, they had luckily managed to reach a small village, and the driver pulled up to the inn, descending from his seat to speak with his master.

After conferring with the driver, they decided to stop due to the continued bad weather, as well as the condition of the roads. Darcy asked her to wait within the carriage while he went inside to ensure they would have accommodations for them.

~ * ~

Elizabeth watched him as he ran into the inn. She was not happy to be told to wait in the carriage with the driver and footman standing guard, however, she was still extremely cold and not eager to be in the rain once more. He returned swiftly, calling out orders to his driver and footmen before he climbed back into the carriage.

Darcy did not look forward to telling her the situation with the inn; he felt she would object strenuously, and did not want to spend time arguing. While her shivering had decreased a little, she was still very pale, and her lips had acquired a bluish tinge, requiring him to hastily get her inside the inn and warmed before a fire.

"Miss Bennet, I need to discuss the inn arrangements with you. I do not wish to offend you, but I would appreciate it if you would allow me to finish before you object," Darcy implored, hoping she would not argue over the accommodations.

Elizabeth nodded. "As a result of the weather, they only have one room remaining." He saw her eyes widen and her mouth open, but she seemed to remember her agreement to his terms, and did not interrupt. "Luckily for us, the room is the best one they have to offer, which also has an adjoining sitting room. You may have the bedroom, as I am sure there will be some place suitable for me to sleep in the sitting room." Darcy saw her relax some, and hoped she would accept the remainder of his plans as easily as she did the portion he had already related.

"I have taken the liberty of paying for the room, and giving the innkeeper the name of Mr. and Mrs. Stewart, which was necessary since we do not wish to call attention to our actual status. This will also help prevent gossip which could follow us when we depart." Her eyes had grown large, and she looked upset when he mentioned their aliases but she kept her comments to herself.

"I have looked in the public rooms, and I do not recognize anyone from our acquaintance, so we should not be recognized upon our entry. I have ordered tea to be delivered soon, and dinner to be served this evening in our sitting room. I cannot think of anything I have missed, but I assure you that I will do everything in my power to help you and maintain your confidence," Darcy finished.

While she was impressed with the thought and consideration he put into the arrangements, she did not dare voice her annoyance with his presumption in arranging the accommodations without consulting her first. Even though she understood it was a necessity, Elizabeth also did not like the idea of sharing rooms with him; however, she was chilled and knew she needed to remove her wet clothes and warm soon or she would most assuredly take ill. They also had no idea how long the storm would last, and she could not loiter in the public rooms waiting for the weather to clear, especially later into the night.

Darcy was rather surprised. He had expected her to be angry at his officiousness, yet deep down, he was relieved she had acquiesced without an argument. He stepped out of the carriage, and offered his hand to Elizabeth.

As she exited, she began to leave the rugs in the carriage until he objected. "You are still very cold and wet. Please retain the blankets until we reach our rooms, and you can become warm by the fire."

Elizabeth bristled. "I know very well how cold and wet I am, Mr. Darcy." Suddenly realising how ungracious she must have sounded, she added in a softer tone, "but thank you."

Darcy nodded and helped her down from the carriage, quickly escorting her into the inn and up to their rooms. Once the door was closed, they breathed a large sigh of relief.

~ * ~

Back at Longbourn, Mr. Bennet was furious with Elizabeth's insubordination, and had not left his library for the entire evening. In his present state, he could not handle his wife's nervous complaints as well as Mr. Collins's self-satisfied smile and sycophantic praise. Despite the look she gave him when he asked, he had Hill bring him a tray at dinner; he was, therefore, unaware of Elizabeth's absence at table. It never occurred to him that she would flee; otherwise he would have ensured she remained in her room. As it was, he retired without even the knowledge that Jane had knocked on the bedroom door to retire, only to be ignored. She was irritated to be denied entry, yet decided not to inform their father. Instead, she made plans to scold her sister in the morning as she rapped on Mary's door to stay with her for the night.

Chapter 4

Once they were alone, Elizabeth turned to face Darcy with the intention of informing him she would be going in the bedchamber to dry herself as much as possible, but before she could open her mouth, he began to speak.

"I am sure you would wish to refresh yourself and change into some dry clothes before you become ill. Your bag should already be in your room, and if you will forgive my presumption, I have also taken the liberty of asking my servant to place one of my nightshirts on the bed, in the event all your clothes are wet."

"Thank you," she replied, before turning away from him.

Elizabeth entered the bedchamber, giving him a small smile when she shut the door. As she turned to survey the room, she noted that it was rather small and plain, but was relieved to find that more importantly, it was clean and warm. Unwrapping herself from the rugs, she picked up the nightshirt and strode across to the screen which stood in the corner of the room. She found her bag situated on a chair nearby, and touched the exterior, discovering to her chagrin that it was indeed extremely wet. The items within were not as soaked as she had presumed from the state of the bag, but she would never warm wearing them. So she removed everything and hung her clothes on the screen to dry.

Once the task was completed, Elizabeth noticed there was a ewer filled with warmed water, which she poured into a basin, and washed her face, neck, and arms. She removed her hairpins, the simple action releasing her long curly brown locks and the tension in her neck. Then using one of the towels placed next to the basin, she squeezed the water from her hair. When she was finally satisfied it would not soak any garment she wore, she slipped Darcy's large nightshirt over her head, rolling the sleeves up to her wrists while walking to the fireplace.

It was surprising to her how those few simple actions made her feel so much better. The warmth of the room, combined with the dry nightshirt, soon ceased the shivering she had endured since the rain began. Taking a seat close to the fireplace, she hoped the heat would help her hair to dry quicker than was its wont, and had only been sitting for a moment when there was a soft knock upon the door adjoining the two rooms. As she stood, she noticed an extra coverlet at the foot of the bed, and wrapped it around her before turning the knob.

When the door opened, Darcy was overwhelmed at the sight before him; she was breath taking. Her long curly hair was down around her shoulders, and her toes were peeking out from underneath the blanket she had used to cover herself. In her present state of dress, she looked like the Elizabeth who had been invading his dreams every night since he had first laid eyes on her. Those dreams were sweet torture. A part of him always looked forward to the fantasy, but he always awoke to reality, tangled in the sheets and painfully aroused—the memory of which was not helping his present situation.

"The tea arrived a few moments ago, and I thought you might care to join me for a cup," he said, noticing that she was peering down at her less than proper attire, and deducing that she must be feeling self-conscious. "You look lovely, Miss Bennet."

Elizabeth blushed and averted her eyes, "Thank you."

He motioned toward a chair near the fire, and she sat, tucking her feet into the seat ensconcing them in the warmth of the quilt.

"How would you like your tea?"

"I drink my tea plain, sir, thank you," she answered. He prepared her cup, and handing it to her, took a seat by the fire as well. Deciding they must have some conversation, she smiled as she settled upon a topic. "Last night, I was unwilling to discuss books at a ball, however, we are no longer in a ballroom," she said lightly. "So, what think you of books?"

She was teasing him, and not in the manner she had employed at Netherfield, since here she was smiling sweetly, almost flirting, he would say.

34

"I enjoy a great many books, and read subjects ranging from histories to poetry. Do you have a particular favourite?" he replied, smiling broadly.

"I read a variety of books on a great many topics as well, but I would have to say that I enjoy poetry and Shakespeare the . . ." Elizabeth who had been placing her cup in her saucer paused as she looked at him. She was not yet used to seeing him smile, and the sight still amazed her.

"Is something amiss?"

Realizing she had been caught gawking, and had not finished her statement, she blushed scarlet and desperately searched for an excuse.

"Forgive me, I was distracted for a moment. I was simply saying that Shakespeare is a personal favourite. I particularly enjoy his comedies."

They passed the remainder of the afternoon discussing books, particularly Shakespeare, discovering that they actually shared similar tastes in literature, and had corresponding views of many of the works they had studied. As Darcy had once accused her, she did profess opinions which were not her own, sometimes teasing him and sometimes simply trying to prolong their discussion. With a little over an hour left before dinner, Elizabeth's energy seemed to flag, and she excused herself to rest until their meal was delivered.

~ * ~

At approximately seven, their dinner arrived, and Darcy lightly knocked on the door to the adjoining bedroom. Elizabeth was slow to answer, but when she did, he was struck by how pale she still appeared.

"Are you well?"

"I believe I am just tired from the stress of the day. I am sure everything will be well by morning," she said, not wishing to be more of a burden than she already was. Smiling slightly in the hopes of relieving his anxiety, she proceeded to the small table in the corner of the room, where he helped her with her seat before taking his own.

Although Darcy was pleasantly surprised at the quality of the meal, a hearty stew served with bread, he soon noticed that Elizabeth was not eating much and had been very quiet. Rather than frustrating her with constant questions about her wellbeing, he hoped she was correct and merely fatigued; but thinking about the chill she had taken earlier, he doubted it was that simple.

While they took tea after the meal, Darcy attempted a few tries at conversation, but Elizabeth was not as talkative as she had been earlier. He did not believe her to be angry, but her smile was forced and her eyes were not as animated as they usually were, leading him to worry all the more.

Elizabeth was exhausted. She had tried to eat dinner, but the food did not have much flavour and was so heavy in her stomach. She was thankful that she was able to at least enjoy the tea. Poor Mr. Darcy. He had tried to hold a conversation with her after dinner, even enquiring about her preferences in music and art, but she had a hard time concentrating on what he was saying. She did not contribute much, mainly nodding her head and agreeing with most of what he had said.

"Forgive me, I am not good company tonight," Elizabeth said apologetically.

"Not at all," he replied softly, hoping to alleviate any worry that he was offended. "If you would prefer to retire, I will understand."

"Thank you," she sighed with relief. He had already gone to so much trouble for her today that she had not wanted to offend him by retiring early. As she rose from her seat, she gave him a wan smile and walked into the bedroom.

"Good night."

"Good night," she said, facing him as she closed the door.

Chapter 5

Darcy was having a difficult time trying not to think about Elizabeth in the next room. He longed to kiss her, to touch her, to finally know if her skin was as soft as he had imagined. She had been the subject of his dreams and fantasies for some time, and it was difficult knowing he could not act on those feelings.

A well-connected, well-dowered bride was his family's expectation, and up until recently, they were the expectations he held for himself; however, while Elizabeth had been at Netherfield, those concerns had all but vanished. How could wealth and connections compare to her intelligence, kindness, and beauty? He could not abide the self-absorbed, simpering women of the ton and Elizabeth was a breath of heaven. He had decided to return to London in order to forget about her, to find the "perfect" wife, but he wanted Elizabeth, and not someone like Miss Bingley; marriage to that shrew would be a fate worse than death! Afraid that his conflicting thoughts would keep him awake, he decided to attempt to put them out of his mind, and began to prepare for the night.

Surveying the room, he determined a chaise close to the fire would be the best place for him to sleep. It was rather short for his tall frame, but the bedroom door was nearby, which was convenient if Elizabeth needed him during the night.

Deciding it would be best to sleep in his shirt and breeches, he removed his topcoat and waistcoat, and placed them across the back of a chair. Darcy was thankful his trunk was with him, since Evans, his valet, had been sent ahead to the townhouse. As it was, he would have to fend for himself until the roads improved enough to complete the short trip to London. After removing enough of his garments so that he would be comfortable as he slept, he chose a book, and sat down with the plan to read until he became tired.

~ * ~

Darcy awoke with a start. He was not sure when he had fallen asleep, but he sat up from where he was slumped against the arm of the chaise and retrieved his book from the floor. As he was beginning to drift off to sleep once more, he heard crying from the next room. While not wishing to intrude on Elizabeth's privacy, he was concerned there was something wrong, causing him to rise and knock softly on the door. When there was no answer, he entered the room, and lit a candle, finding her still asleep, but shivering uncontrollably while mumbling and crying.

"Elizabeth," he said, as he touched her arm, feeling the heat radiating from her through the nightshirt. When she did not awaken, he shook her lightly and called her name once more, but she still did not open her eyes. He knew she was ill from simply touching her arm; nevertheless, he put his hand to her forehead to check the severity of the fever, alarmed at how high it had risen since she retired for the night.

He searched the room before rising to retrieve the now cool basin of water he noticed on the opposite side of the room. Grabbing not only the basin, but also the towel she had used earlier, he returned to the side of the bed, placing the bowl on the bedside table. He wet the towel, wringing out the excess water, and began sponging Elizabeth's forehead. She was covered with the coverlet, as well as the blanket, which he decided could not be helping her cool, so he stripped the covers until only the sheet remained to preserve her modesty. Unfortunately, her shivering increased as he sponged her forehead for a second time, and he pushed the sleeves of the nightshirt as far up her arms as possible in order to wipe those down as well.

Wishing there was something more he could do, he considered a doctor, however, trusting anyone of that profession had never been easy for him. He had watched as they bled his father in an effort to cure him only to see their treatments weaken him further, and as a result, Darcy had become very selective. He had a personal physician whom he trusted in London, but sending for him was impossible with the rain. The risk of Elizabeth being exposed and her reputation destroyed would increase by calling attention to themselves, so he decided to continue his ministrations, hoping he would be able to keep the fever at a manageable level.

He continued sponging and keeping watch over her until in

the early hours of the morning, when her fever seemed to lessen, and she began resting comfortably. He breathed a sigh of relief and relaxed into a chair at the side of the bed with the intention of keeping watch over her for the rest of the night.

~ * ~

When morning dawned at Longbourn, Mr. Bennet was dressed and downstairs very early. He had developed the habit long ago to avoid his wife as much as possible. If he rose any later, she inevitably caught him before he could make it to his library, and he would have to listen to the cacophony of her latest nervous complaints while she protested against him breaking his fast at his desk. This morning in particular would be even more of a trial, since he had not taken his tea or dinner with the family the previous day, due to his anger with Elizabeth.

Hill had finally brought him his coffee, and he had just opened a book, when he heard Mrs. Bennet's screeching echoing throughout the house. He tried to ignore the pandemonium brewing outside, but his wife would not allow it. The library door burst open to allow Mrs. Bennet, immediately followed by a toadying Mr. Collins, to enter the room. His wife was shrieking and gesticulating wildly while his cousin sidled up behind her while mumbling some gibberish about Lady Catherine.

"Oh, Mr. Bennet, we are all ruined! That selfish girl has no compassion for my nerves! Now, when you die, we will all be cast out into the hedgerows!"

He looked at her incredulously, wondering if he needed to commit her to Bedlam. "Stop your caterwauling," he exclaimed exasperatedly.

At his pronouncement, his wife stopped and slumped into a chair, fluttering her handkerchief in front of her face.

"Now, you will explain why you have entered my library, disrupting my peace!"

"My dear cousin . . . ," began Mr. Collins before he was

40

drowned out by the lady of the house.

"That ungrateful daughter of yours is gone!"

"She is probably out walking," he said dismissively. "Now leave me to my book and go break your fast."

"My patroness, the honourable Lady Catherine de Bourgh . . .," Mr. Collins continued oblivious to being ignored.

Jane entered into the room with a grave expression on her face, which distracted Mr. Bennet.

"She is not out walking, Papa. Last night, I knocked on the door so I could retire, but she did not answer. I assumed she wanted time to herself, so I slept with Mary. This morning, when the door was still locked, and there was no answer, I asked Mrs. Hill for a key in order to see if she was well. Her best dresses are gone, as is the valise Aunt Gardiner gave her last year." Jane stopped as if she were trying to make a decision before she finally held up her sister's garnet cross. "She also left this."

The irate father's fist slammed down on the desk, causing a sound that reverberated around the room and everyone to jump. "Do Kitty and Lydia know yet?"

"They are not yet awake," replied Jane, turning to see Mary enter the room.

"Come in and close the door, Mary. We need to contain this until I can find that child and bring her back," said Mr. Bennet, trying to concentrate on the task at hand; however, he was finding it very difficult with his wife's fluttering and whimpering. "Mrs. Bennet, cease that noise this instant so I can think!"

He knew that somehow he had to keep Elizabeth's flight from finding its way into the Meryton gossip mill. Hill had a special relationship with her, and would not betray the secret for fear of damaging her "Miss Lizzy." Even so, he would have to talk to the servants to see if they heard his wife's tirade, or perhaps saw his daughter leave.

In the meantime, his two youngest daughters could not discover the truth. They would spread it around the village with no regard for their own reputations, much less the family's respectability. Promising Mr. Collins to return Elizabeth in time for them to be married might quiet him, but the biggest hurdle would be his own wife. He would have to control her if his plan was to work.

"First, if anyone asks after Lizzy, she departed yesterday to visit the Gardiners in London. You can say that she is shopping for her trousseau," he continued, with a dismissing wave of his hand.

"Oh, and do not tell Kitty and Lydia the truth!" he suddenly exclaimed. "This cannot even be discussed within this house. Jane, Mary, do you understand what I am telling you?"

Both girls nodded their heads.

"No sermons about it either, Mary." He looked his middle child in the eyes as she nodded once more. "Good, I need you both to ensure your sisters are still abed, while I finish with your mother and Mr. Collins."

He watched his daughters leave the room, shutting the door behind them. Lydia and Kitty typically slept like the dead and were late risers, so he knew he would not see them for some time yet; however, this needed to be accomplished quickly, so he could talk to the servants, and bribe them if necessary.

"Mrs. Bennet, let me make this perfectly clear to you so that you will understand; you will not breathe any of this to *anyone*. It is not to be discussed! If I find that you have uttered *one* word, you will lose your pin money, and you can forget about any social engagements for the rest of the year . . . *AT LEAST*!"

His wife looked at him with wide eyes, shocked at his vehemence before attempting to reply to his command.

"Mr. Ben . . . "

"Not a word! Nod your head if you understand, but do not

say one word," he exclaimed, attempting to control her latest tirade before it began. Surprised when she obeyed, he ordered her to leave, so he could discuss the situation with Mr. Collins, turning his attention to the ridiculous parson once his wife had closed the door. He hoped he could convince him to be quiet until he managed to find his daughter and return her, presuming, of course, that she had fled to the Gardiners' house, which meant he could have her returned quickly with no one being any wiser.

"Mr. Collins, my daughter was upset yesterday, and made a rash decision. She will adjust to the situation soon enough, and I have no doubts that she will make you a good wife." Before the parson could say a word, he continued, "I assure you, I know where she has gone, and she will be returned quickly. I also plan on having the banns read in the meantime, so as long as I can count on your discretion there should be no further issues."

"Of course, of course," Mr. Collins replied, almost bowing to him as he spoke. "As soon as I inform my noble patroness, Lady Catherine de Bourgh, in full of the status of my engagement and the condition of my fiancée, I am sure she will be more than gracious in her condescension . . . "

"You will do no such thing," interrupted Mr. Bennet. "Informing anyone of this could damage Lizzy's reputation, and by association, your own. As the leader of a congregation, you must guard yourself from the repercussions. Your disclosure would also affect the relationship your future wife would have with her Ladyship, and I do not think you would wish to damage that connection." He looked pointedly at the little man who blanched and began to stammer.

"Mrs. Bennet has already spread the news of this engagement all over Meryton. You are now by honour bound to my daughter. I expect you to marry her."

"Well . . . yes . . . of course, cousin, I admit I had not thought of that, however I always seek Lady Catherine's advice. She would be most seriously displeased to know I have not sought her counsel in this matter," he whined.

"The banns will be read beginning this Sunday, and you will wed Lizzy immediately upon their completion. Once you are lawfully wed, you may consult with Lady Catherine all you wish, but for now, you will not tell anyone. Do I make myself clear?"

The parson looked nervous and displeased, but nodded his head.

"Good, you can go," dismissed Mr. Bennet, prompting the annoying parson to exit the room. He did not close the door, as Mary had returned.

"Papa, Lydia is still snoring, and we woke Kitty when we entered. I believe they slept through everything."

"Well, this is one time their idleness came to our aid," he remarked drily. "Thank you, Mary."

She departed, closing the door behind her, while Mr. Bennet sat back and rubbed his temples. Now that he had hopefully silenced his family, he reluctantly arose from his chair to interview the servants. He was excessively angry with his second daughter. If it had not been raining, he would have immediately travelled to London to retrieve her. As it was, he would have to send an express to his brother Gardiner, and wait until the rain subsided.

~ * ~

Despite his intentions of watching over Elizabeth, Darcy fell asleep from exhaustion, and did not awaken until late morning, when he heard her stirring. Opening his eyes, he found her looking at him inquisitively.

"May I ask why you are in my room?"

"I awoke to the sound of you crying in your sleep. When I came in to see if you were well, you were burning with fever, so I did what I could to reduce it, and remained after the fever subsided, in the event it returned."

Elizabeth seemed to relax at his explanation. She stretched, and he averted his eyes as the sheet pulled tight to reveal the

44

shape of her body underneath. He had been so worried the night before, he had not realised that only his nightshirt and a thin sheet separated them. Trying to put the thought from his mind, he looked up as she sat up in bed, clutching the sheet to her chest. She noticed the coverlet as well as the blanket had been pushed down to the foot of the bed, and she immediately pulled them up to join the sheet.

"I removed those in an effort to help cool you, but I promise you, I never removed the sheet."

Elizabeth studied him as he explained himself, and felt he was in earnest. Although she had slept through the night, she was still exhausted, and assumed it must be due to the fever. Closing her eyes and leaning back against the headboard, she could hear the rain, which had apparently continued through the night, hitting the windowpane. They would be unable to leave today, and while the delay bothered her, she was too tired to let it worry her.

"I would like to have some time to refresh myself," she said, averting her eyes and blushing scarlet.

"Oh! Of course. Due to the rain, I should make arrangements for us to remain here another night, as well as order breakfast to be delivered. Is there anything special you would like?"

"No, thank you, but I would like you to know that I appreciate all of the trouble you have endured to help me."

"It is my pleasure, Miss Bennet," he said as he bowed slightly before departing and closing the door behind him.

She sat staring at the door for some time before she realised that she was smiling. Rising from the bed, she immediately felt dizzy, and needed to stand still for a moment before she could refresh herself and return to lie down once more. She leaned back into the pillows, and must have begun to doze when she was awakened by a knock at the door.

"Come in," she called.

The door opened, and Darcy entered, bearing a tea tray,

which he set on the bedside table before leaving briefly to retrieve a tray of food that he placed on the bed. He fixed her a cup of tea and served her, placing the tray next to her so she could select what she wished to have. She spread jam on a piece of toast and sat back while watching him.

"May I ask you something rather personal?"

He eyed her warily, chewing and taking a sip of his tea as he swallowed. "I suppose so."

"I was wondering why do you not let people see this side of you?"

He looked up, surprised by her question. Most women would ask him about Pemberley or the location of his house in town. Of course, those things would not interest her as they did other women; he had known she was different, seeking knowledge of himself rather than his possessions only served to further confirm her worth in his eyes.

She watched him furrow his brow as he contemplated her question. He had not seemed to take offence, but seemed to be trying to puzzle out his answer.

"I have always been uncomfortable around unfamiliar people, even as a child," he confided, looking down into his tea as he spoke. "When I left home to attend school, I discovered very quickly that I had only a handful of friends who were not trying to befriend me for another purpose. It only increased when I attended Cambridge."

He looked back at her as he continued. "Bingley was one of the few who did not see Pemberley, and connections to my uncle, the Earl of Matlock, when they looked at me. Miss Bingley, however, was a different story."

Elizabeth thought of the times she had seen Miss Bingley excessively complimenting him as she tirelessly clutched his arm, preventing his escape, and could not help but giggle. "Forgive me, but she *is* rather relentless."

"She is actually very much like many women of the ton. They care nothing about a person's character, only their connections, wealth, and how they can benefit from the association." His face was now rigid as he spoke, which she imagined was due to the discomfort of associating with such people. "I became accustomed to the manners of high society, and learned to protect myself accordingly."

"At the Meryton assembly, I heard my name and income bandied about in much the same manner as I did when I first entered society, and sometimes still do when someone is unfamiliar with me. I guess when I am uncomfortable, which is in most social situations, I now react instinctively. My cousin, Colonel Fitzwilliam, has commented many times on my behaviour, teasing me that one day I will offend the wrong person."

"If the majority of your acquaintances are people similar to Miss Bingley, then I can understand why you would hide yourself away," she stated sympathetically. He looked sad, and almost vulnerable, as he finished his explanation, causing her to regret asking the question in the first place. "I wished to understand, but I hope I did not offend."

"Not at all," he said softly, "not at all." He paused for a moment, seeming deep in thought as he took a sip of his tea. "Miss Bennet, it is just the two of us, and I was thinking it might be simpler to address each other less formally—if you have no objections, of course."

"Your given name is Fitzwilliam?"

"It was the name of my mother's family."

"It is such a formal name for a child. Have you ever had a nickname?"

"In school, some of the boys tried to call me Fitz, but I never cared much for it; nevertheless, I would be willing to consider any ideas you have."

She looked at him appraisingly and thought for a moment. "Has anyone ever called you William or Will?"

"No," he answered, smiling. "But if you would prefer either of those, I would not object."

47

"Pay me no mind, I am being impertinent . . . I would be happy to call you by your Christian name," Elizabeth stammered. She had been teasing, not expecting him to accept the names she suggested.

"No, I do not mind either of those names, truly. If you prefer one of them, I would be happy for you to use it."

She appraised his expression, attempting to determine if he was serious. "Actually, I do like Will, unless you have an objection."

"Then Will it shall be."

He did not understand what had come over him. He never allowed people to address him so informally, yet allowing Elizabeth the privilege gave him a contentment he had never before experienced. Not willing to analyse the meaning of such an emotion or its consequences, he dismissed the thought.

As they finished breakfast, Elizabeth's energy was flagging, and she admitted to having a headache, so Darcy cleaned up the dishes and trays, placing them on the table in the sitting room before returning with a few books.

"Would you prefer some quiet, or would you like me to read to you for a while?" he offered. "I have several books with me, including a volume of Shakespeare's sonnets."

She was astonished at how solicitous he had been since they met on the road, however she concluded he must be suffering from a lack of company and decided to give it no consequence.

"Shakespeare would be lovely."

He smiled as he opened the book and began to read. Enjoying the sound of his voice, she lay back into the pillows and allowed the rich, mellow sound to lull her to sleep.

After he had been reading for some time, he looked up to find she was no longer awake. Smiling he marked his place and closed the book. He watched her sleep for a while, studying her every feature, and realising he could not let her abscond into the great unknown. With a new resolve, he rose and returned to the sitting room, allowing her to rest for the time being.

Chapter 6

Elizabeth slept through the noon hour, waking just before teatime. While she had been sleeping, Darcy had ordered their tea, and made arrangements for them to dine in their rooms once again. He returned to find the door to the bedroom no longer ajar like he had left it. Thinking the maid had possibly closed it after tending to the room and replenishing the fire, he gently knocked. Elizabeth responded that she would call for him when she returned to the bed, and he sat on the chaise while he waited.

He did not have to wait long before he heard her lilting voice giving him permission to enter. Quickly rising from his seat, he entered to find her sitting up against some pillows, which she had propped against the headboard. She had slept several hours; however, despite how long she had slept, she still looked tired and he worried the fever had returned as he asked her how she was feeling.

"I believe I felt better this morning," she said ruefully. "The fever from last night seems to have returned this afternoon, and I am afraid that it has stolen what little energy I had."

His face echoing the concern he felt, Darcy leaned forward in his seat. "The tea I ordered earlier has just arrived, and I wondered if you would like to join me for a cup . . . Obviously, you will not need to leave the bed," he added before rising to stand, and gesturing awkwardly toward the other chamber. "I suppose I should just retrieve the tray from the next room."

As she watched him quickly exit, she smiled. Contemplating how different his manner was compared to when he was in Meryton, she toyed with the idea that he almost seemed nervous before he left, but dismissed the notion almost as quickly as she thought it. After all, he had no reason to be nervous with her, since she was not handsome enough to tempt him. Her attention, however, was soon directed elsewhere when he re-entered the room with their tea.

He noticed Elizabeth's brow furrowed in thought, which immediately cleared as he placed the tray on the table.

"Is something amiss?" he asked, as he poured and served her tea.

"No, I was just lost in thought for a moment. It was nothing of consequence." She smiled and took her first sip of tea, which seemed to ease the ache in her body as soon as she swallowed. Refusing the cake that had been delivered with the tea, she relaxed into the pillows, and watched him as he carefully sipped from his cup.

"You are staring."

"I am still attempting to sketch your character, sir," she replied with an impish smile.

The expression she wore made him grin as he took another sip. "I would by no means suspend any pleasure of yours."

She raised that impertinent eyebrow at his retort, and remained silent for a while as she slowly drank more of her tea. He had never been so bewitched by a woman in his life. Since his earlier resolution to pursue his own happiness regardless of the opinions of others, he had become more nervous around her than he had been in all of their prior acquaintance. Knowing that she had not had a favourable opinion of him before yesterday was humbling; he feared she would be as opposed to him as she was to Mr. Collins. He almost snorted at the thought, but fortunately suppressed the sound before it left his throat.

"Would you tell me about your family?" she asked.

Startled by her sudden question, he looked up with a jerk. She must have misinterpreted his reaction because she immediately began to withdraw.

"The question was not to invade your privacy," she said with a hint of worry to her voice. "I only meant to initiate some conversation. If you do not wish to answer, I completely understand."

"Please, Elizabeth, I was merely surprised by the request. I have no objection to discussing my family," he stated, hoping he had reassured her, although he thought she still looked rather apprehensive. "Is there anyone in particular you would wish to hear about, or would you like me to choose?"

"Perhaps you could start with your parents, and we can see where the discussion takes us."

Trying to decide where to begin, he nodded and sipped his tea, stalling for a moment to gather his thoughts. "Unfortunately, I did not know them very well," he said impassively. "My parents had a typical marriage of the ton. He was a very wealthy gentleman. She had money, beauty and connections to an earldom. They did not know each other when they married; I doubt they were much better acquainted when she died."

Elizabeth thought he looked sad as he spoke of his mother and father. She was not unfamiliar with parents who were essentially strangers; although, she was beginning to feel his childhood went beyond her experience.

Taking a deep breath, he began speaking once more. "I was born within a year of their marriage, and raised by nursemaids and tutors, with Mrs. Reynolds, the Pemberley housekeeper, in charge."

She noticed the small smile when he spoke of Mrs. Reynolds, who she guessed was probably the closest thing to a mother he had ever known, and how his face transformed when he returned to the subject of his parents.

"My parents had me brought down only to display the 'Heir of Pemberley' when family visited."

"You had no other contact with your mother and father when you were a child?" she queried softly.

"No, I had tutors until I attended school, and then during holidays, I was sent to London where I had tutors until school resumed. When I was twelve, my mother died in childbirth with Georgiana." Darcy paused for a moment, reliving memories, thinking about the past and how it affected him now. He had been raised to live his life like his parents did before him, however, duty and honour had never made either of them happy. He would catch glimpses of them as he walked to the library or ventured outside with his tutor. They were never in the same rooms, and they were *never* smiling.

"You do not have to finish," Elizabeth suggested gently.

"I am well," he said. "I was remembering how I used to see them in passing, and how unhappy they appeared." He stopped for a moment, looking into his teacup before returning his gaze to her. "My father began teaching me about the estate while I was at Cambridge, but I believe I was too sedate, and he preferred George Wickham's outgoing manner for company. I always saw him as more of a tutor, who taught me how to manage Pemberley, than a father," he confessed. "He died five years ago. The tenants and the neighbouring town of Lambton still speak of what an excellent master he was."

His voice had trailed off by the time he had finished, and she regretted having asked him in the first place. Her attempt to make conversation had backfired, dreadfully. She did not understand why she wanted to make him forget the conversation and make him smile, but she did.

"My mother always wanted a son. I am sure she would be most attentive should you wish it," Elizabeth said with a smile.

Darcy's eyes bulged, and she burst into laughter. He suddenly understood she was teasing him in an attempt to lighten his mood, and a smile slowly appeared on his face. As her laughter subsided, he noticed her grimace and put a hand to her temple.

"You are not well; you should rest."

"I merely have a headache," she replied exasperatedly.

"It would not hurt for you to nap until dinner."

She truly did not wish to rest, but her head ached, so she acquiesced. "Would you read to me as you did earlier?"

"Of course," he responded, as he retrieved the book from the bedside table.

~ * ~

It did not take long for her to fall asleep. He found it touching that she wished for him to read to her again, and probably read longer than was needed to ensure she slept. Picking up a different book that he had been reading for the last few days, he continued it until she began to stir a few hours later, when she awoke requesting a glass of water. After drinking the majority, she quickly returned to sleep, and did not wake until he roused her for dinner. He did not like waking her when she so obviously needed rest, but felt eating was essential if she were to recover. Luckily, the inn brought the soup he had requested for dinner, which, as he had hoped, seemed to be more palatable than the heavy stew from the previous evening. She ate the entirety of the bowl before settling back into the pillows and nodding off once more.

~ * ~

The rain had not let up by the next day, requiring Darcy and Elizabeth to again remain at the inn. She had passed another night sleeping fitfully due to fever, but he was thankful it never became as elevated as it had the previous night.

The day proceeded much as it had the day before; Elizabeth napped for a good portion while he read, and when she was not sleeping, they were discussing whatever and whichever topics they chose, neither giving thought to their prior prejudices, but simply enjoying the companionship of the other. Darcy, once again, happily read to her as she fell asleep, drifting off in the chair not long after her.

Saturday dawned bright and sunny, and Elizabeth was feeling much improved. Now that the weather had cleared, it was only a matter of time before they would make their way to London, which caused her to fret over what would be awaiting her upon her arrival; she hoped her father had been delayed as they had been. They broke their fast in what had become their usual manner, before Darcy cleared the bed of her dishes, returning them to the table in the other room.

She noticed a change in his manner when he returned to her room. Despite her poor ability to read him in the past, she thought he looked nervous when he again took the seat by the bed.

"Elizabeth, I would like to ask you something," he began. "I do not require an answer today, as I understand you may need time to consider what I am proposing to you; however, you *will* need to decide before we travel to London."

Nodding her head, she wondered what he could possibly require of her. She could not think of anything she had which would interest him, and it was making her extremely curious.

Darcy had thought out a speech, but his nerves failed him, and he desperately tried to remember the words he had wanted to say. His hands were clutched in front of him, preventing them from shaking as he tried to choke out the question he needed to ask.

"Will you marry me?" he suddenly blurted.

Not only was she astonished, but Elizabeth was sure her face was betraying her. Of all the questions he could have asked, he chose to ask that one? Why did he want to marry her? She was not wealthy or connected, and she thought she remembered Mr. Wickham saying he was engaged to his cousin, Anne deBourgh.

"You said I was not handsome enough to tempt you," she mumbled, dumbfounded.

Darcy's nerves were forgotten with her statement. He had obviously surprised her, and, after hearing her comment, was silently berating himself for having slighted her at the assembly. It was no wonder she had been so quick to believe Wickham—he had insulted her before they had even truly met.

"I wondered if you had heard me," he said sadly. "Please understand, balls and large social gatherings have always made me extremely uncomfortable, and I only wanted Bingley to leave me alone." He took a deep breath, attempting to calm the butterflies, which still lingered. "Not only was it never meant for you to hear, but it was also most patently untrue. I hope you will forgive me for being so rude."

"Of course I will forgive you," she replied softly.

"Thank you," he responded, relieved.

She nodded, and proceeded to think about the many questions she needed to ask of him. While she was not in love with him, she had enjoyed his company since they had been marooned together at the inn. Options were slim since fleeing Longbourn, and she had to admit friendship was a definite improvement over Mr. Collins.

She thought for a few moments. "Are you engaged to your cousin, Miss de Bourgh?"

At her question, his eyes, which had moved to look at the sun beaming in through the window, returned to her face. His brow furrowed and he paused a moment.

"No, I am not engaged to Anne," he said, as he began to contemplate how best to explain Lady Catherine and Lord Matlock's delusions that he would eventually offer for his cousin, hoping the problems with her father forcing an unwanted marriage to Mr. Collins upon her would help her understand the situation. He decided to explain the entirety of the supposed betrothal. Should they marry, it would not do for her to be caught unawares by a comment made by someone in society, or even in his own family.

"My aunt, Lady Catherine, claims she and my mother planned a union between Anne and myself when we were in our cradles. Of the few memories I have of my mother, I do not ever remember her mentioning that particular desire."

He returned his gaze to his hands as he fumbled with his signet ring. "My father mentioned the matter several times after I had begun Cambridge. By that time, Anne was known to be sickly and frail, and my father was rightly concerned about her ability to provide an heir. He explained I was in no way beholden to her, and I should choose a lady who would add to the stature of Pemberley."

Elizabeth listened thoughtfully to his explanation. She believed him when he said he was not engaged to his cousin, however was concerned a marriage to her would alienate him from his family. Those circumstances could lead to resentment, and poison any kind of a friendship they might have. She had seen the results of bitterness and apathy in her parents' marriage, and she certainly had no desire to live in that manner.

"My uncle, the Earl of Matlock, latched on to my aunt's delusions, and has been promoting the idea since my father died, citing Georgiana's need for a lady of society to mirror. Unfortunately, Anne has grown very spoiled with a demeanour much like her mother's. She has never been in society, and is quite unpleasant to have in company. I do not wish for my sister to emulate her."

"I can understand your reluctance; yet, I do not understand their vehemence," she replied.

Darcy considered for a moment before responding, "I believe my aunt has concerns of Anne never marrying due to her health, causing her estate, Rosings, to revert back to the de Bourgh family. She has never allowed her daughter to have a season in town, so if I do not wed her, she has no chance of marriage elsewhere, and therefore, no possibility of a child to inherit. My aunt also has a tendency to spend beyond her means. Since my father died, I have spent Easter every year reviewing her books and attempting to curb her expenditures. I also have reason to believe my uncle's finances are not much better, which leads me to suspect they have a financial motive as well."

Her eyebrows rose in response to his last statement. Her father was attempting to sacrifice her in order to correct his financial mismanagement, as well as her mother's frivolous spending habits. His family seemed to be attempting much the same thing, with the exception that he had been enduring the pressure for years, as opposed to a few days. Sympathy welled in her heart for his situation, and she wondered if alienation from family such as Lady Catherine and Lord Matlock would be such a hardship.

"They may not accept your marriage to me," Elizabeth

observed.

"No, but I doubt they would accept anyone other than Anne."

"What if they were to sever ties to you as a result?" she asked, not understanding why the answer was concerning her.

"Honestly, I rarely see either of them, and their correspondence is full of orders and inquiries as to when I will marry my cousin. I do not wish to seem callous, but I do not see them as much of a loss." He grimaced. "I have explained repeatedly that I have no desire to wed her, but they do not listen. Even if Anne were to pass from this world, I am sure my uncle would find the spoiled daughter of some political ally from the House of Lords, and shove her down my throat instead."

"I did not intend to upset you," she said softly. "If we were to marry, these could be problems. I feel it is better to discuss them now rather than later."

"I understand, and I agree with you. Anything you would like to know, I will answer."

Darcy saw her nod, and attempted to think of the best way to explain why he wished to marry her without betraying his feelings. While at Netherfield, he had believed himself to be infatuated with her, but the past couple of days in her company had convinced him his feelings ran deeper than infatuation. It was not in love, at least he was not willing to admit that it was—not yet, but he felt her slowly stealing his heart, and there was nothing he could do to stop it. He wanted her to understand; he needed her, and he had never before needed another human being the way he did her.

"When my parents would bring me down to meet visiting family, they always said I would one day do my duty and honour the family," he began. "When I was learning the estate from my father, he pounded those words into my head repeatedly. Recently, I have come to the realisation that while those qualities are not inherently bad, duty and honour never made my parents happy.

"I have been in society for years now, and I have never found

58

a lady of the ton, who I wanted to converse with much less marry. They are scheming, manipulative, and are more interested in my pocket book than my person." He looked up at her before continuing, "A woman of the ton would not have cared if I had cheated Wickham of a living. She would not challenge or question my thoughts. Instead, she would simper and fawn to attract my notice, or possibly attempt to trap me in a compromising position."

Her eyes grew wide at his last statement. "Truly?"

"Yes," he replied, sighing. "There have been numerous attempts actually, which is why I no longer attend social functions without Bingley or Richard . . . Colonel Fitzwilliam, my cousin. They have prevented several . . . undesirable situations."

Elizabeth did not know what to say. She was flattered by his proposal, and she understood his explanations for choosing her, but she was still worried. What about her family? She had observed his reactions to them several times—not that she blamed him—but it was obvious he found them uncouth, and although she did not see herself having much of a relationship with them in the future, she wanted everything out in the open before she decided.

"I wish to know your opinion of my family," she stated.

He blanched and considered his response. "I will not lie to you. I do not always agree with their behaviour, and I am angry at your father for attempting to force a marriage between you and your cousin."

"I do not understand why that would make you angry?"

Darcy suddenly recognised he had said more than he ought, so decided that the best solution would be to tell her the truth, or at least as much as he could without revealing all. "I had considered proposing while you were staying at Netherfield," he replied sheepishly.

She suddenly understood that he had been fighting with this decision for some time, and she had a realisation.

"You were leaving Meryton, and told me you had no plans to return. *You* decided I was beneath you, and intended to leave without making your proposal, but I inadvertently foiled your plan."

"I explained earlier that it was only recently I decided living up to my parent's ideals would not make me happy," he attempted to explain. "I do not believe you to be beneath me, Elizabeth. You have qualities I value which are worth more to me than money and connections." He looked directly into her eyes, willing her to understand. "I admit I *was* intending never to return, but since I found you on the road, I have come to the conclusion that I can not let you go without trying to earn your hand."

Looking down at her hands, she tried to make heads or tails of the thoughts and emotions running through her mind. She could not account for why the idea of him leaving hurt her feelings; after all, they had only recently become friends. However, as she considered his proposal, she also realised that the idea of parting ways with him when they reached London caused her pain as well.

"I want companionship, Elizabeth. I want someone I can talk with, and not someone who will agree with all of my opinions and ignore my concerns. I believe you are that woman." He gazed at her earnestly as he nervously twisted a ring on his finger. "I would like to believe that we have become friends over the last few days."

"We have," she confirmed softly, as he nodded.

"Perhaps it will grow into more. Although, if it does not, I would be glad to forever have your friendship. I think we would do well together."

Darcy observed her contemplative expression. After his last statement, she looked at him, nervously biting her bottom lip. He had never been proficient at teasing, but he decided it could not hurt to try to lighten her mood.

"I could be wrong," he said, trying not to smile. "But I would hope that I am a small improvement over Mr. Collins."

Whatever she had expected him to say next, it had definitely not been that. She began laughing, and noticing that he was chuckling with her, she felt the weight, which had been resting on her heart, lift some, and saw possibilities. Maybe she had never been indifferent to him, and that was why the slight at the assembly had offended her so deeply.

"You asked me earlier why I do not show my true self to everyone. It is true that I am not comfortable in social settings, but I also do not trust people easily, especially with my feelings. And while I cannot explain how it has happened so quickly, I do trust you.

I know this is not an easy decision, but I can promise that you will always be cared for and respected. You and our children will never want for anything, and there will always be places to walk at Pemberley," he finished with a small smile.

She returned his smile as she considered his proposal. He had been very caring and attentive from the moment he had found her. In fact, she could think of no objections other than they were only friends. She had hoped to marry for the deepest love; however, she was no longer in a situation to be picky. By now, her father had more than likely noticed she was gone, and was preparing to leave as soon as possible for Cheapside. He could be waiting for her when she arrived! If she married Will, she would not have to include her beloved aunt and uncle in her scheme, and could not be forced to return to Longbourn to marry the loathsome Mr. Collins.

Looking up from her lap, she began chewing her lip as she perused his figure. He was definitely handsome. He was tall with broad shoulders, curly dark brown hair and piercing blue eyes. As she scrutinized him carefully, she decided it would not be a hardship to kiss him, which made her blush scarlet. She turned her face away from him as she tried to hide the colour rising in her cheeks.

"Is something wrong?" he asked, sounding concerned.

She had a hard time not reddening more as she turned her face to answer his question. "I was just considering your proposal," she said, unable to look him in the eyes.

"It must have come as a surprise. As I stated earlier, you may have some time if you require it. I will, of course, need an answer before we travel to London."

Elizabeth's eyes had wandered to the window; she had not seemed to notice that he had spoken. Suddenly she turned to look back at him. "I appreciate your consideration, but I do not believe I will be able to rest until I have given you my decision."

Chapter 7

Darcy clenched his shaking hands together in an attempt to control the nerves, which had returned full force when Elizabeth revealed she had made a decision. Holding his breath, he waited for the answer that would determine his fate.

"I thank you for the honour of your proposal. I accept."

Two words . . . two little words that relieved his anxiety and allowed him to breathe freely once more. He was ecstatic! She would be his as soon as she came of age, which he remembered was in two days. While packing at Netherfield, he had been tempted to throw the special license he had acquired into the fire. At the time, Darcy had not imagined he would ever again meet Elizabeth Bennet—he was glad he had been wrong.

She watched him as she delivered her verdict, and his face practically transformed. He looked happy, truly happy, which caused her to wonder if he possessed stronger feelings for her than the friendship he claimed. The idea was difficult to credit, but possible. Although if he did, why would he hide them? After reading him so inaccurately in the past, she decided she would not make any rash judgements, and smiled, which only caused him to beam all the more.

"Will," she said, as a thought came to mind. "I was wondering how we can marry? If we have the banns read, they will have to be read in the chapel at Longbourn, and my father will most certainly object. And an application for a common license would have to be posted through there as well. Unless . . . are you suggesting we elope to Gretna Green?"

"None of that will be necessary," he informed her, leaning forward to rest his elbows on his knees. "We can marry by special license as soon as we arrive in London."

She furrowed her brow. "But I have heard they take almost a

week. What if my father finds me during that time?"

"Do you remember when I told you that I considered proposing while you were at Netherfield?" She nodded, and he took a deep breath. "I made the arrangements for a special license then." He studied her expression, and decided she would probably need to see the papers to trust that there would not be any impediments. "If you give me a moment, I will go retrieve it from my trunk."

She watched as he strode out of the room, only to return a moment later with a piece of parchment in his hand. He handed it to her, and she sat stunned as she read their names on the document.

"I plan to have someone marry us before nightfall on the day we arrive in town." She nodded, and he became concerned with how quiet she was. "Are you well?" She started as her eyes left the license to return to his face.

"Yes, I apologize. I was not expecting this." She lifted the papers.

"If you are still willing to marry me, then there is nothing preventing us."

He looked insecure, and Elizabeth realized he would need reassurance that she had not changed her mind. "I will still marry you." She gave him a soft smile, and was relieved when she noticed his shoulders relax.

He studied Elizabeth closely, and noticed how tired she appeared. They had spent all morning discussing his proposal and as a result she had not rested as she should. She had not been as ill during the night, but he wanted her well enough to travel as soon as the roads improved.

"Perhaps I should let you rest," he offered as her smile faltered slightly.

She handed him the license, and settled back into the pillows. "While I admit, I am not my usual self, I feel much better this morning. I truly do not wish to rest at the moment."

He was amused at her stubbornness, and wondered if she would always challenge him the way she did now. He found Georgiana to be a challenge, just not in the same way as Elizabeth. His sister was always so quiet and reserved, although she had always been rather eager to shop, often exceeding her allowance. He had just begun to attempt to rein in her expenditures when she had travelled to Ramsgate, and since the Wickham debacle, she had become resentful, and it worried him. He hoped his sister would come to care for Elizabeth as he did, and perhaps confide in her. However, that time would not be in the immediate future, and as he contemplated the best method to convince his betrothed to nap, he was startled from his thoughts by her voice.

"It seems you are thinking very hard how to make me rest. I would like to offer some advice that might be of use to you as my future husband." Her face pinked toward the end of her statement, and he grinned at her use of his future title.

"I have never responded well to orders, and prefer to be consulted on matters which pertain to me. I do not like to feel as if others are planning my life."

Darcy thought for a moment. He could not say her advice was surprising; however, it was something he had not given much thought to until now. "I appreciate your advice, and I will endeavour to remember it in the future. Although, if I should forget from time to time, I pray you will not be too harsh on me."

He smiled slyly, "In the meantime, perhaps you would like me to read some more of Shakespeare's sonnets? I also have a volume of Wordsworth, if you would prefer it."

"If I did not know any better, I would think you were trying to trick me, Mr. Darcy," she replied mischievously.

He merely raised his eyebrows and smiled in response to her accusation. Realising he would not stop until he had persuaded her to nap, Elizabeth capitulated, allowing him to select the book. After all, it did not really make a difference what he read; she would be fine with him reciting a book on agriculture. She just loved to listen to his voice. She relaxed back into the pillows as he began, and listened quietly while the deep tones of his voice lulled her to sleep.

~ * ~

Grinning smugly when she finally dozed off, he closed the book, and walked to the sitting room. Elizabeth Bennet had agreed to marry him, and he needed to make plans! Digging through his belongings, he placed the license with his important papers, and found the box containing his stationery and ink.

The first letter he addressed was to the housekeeper of Darcy House, Mrs. Thomas. His staff in London would need to prepare the mistress's suite as best they could. It was out-dated, and surely needed some new furnishings, but since there was insufficient time to redecorate, he would leave that chore for his future wife. Therefore, he would simply request that the mistress's rooms be cleaned and aired.

Elizabeth would also require an abigail. As he had always trusted Mrs. Thomas with the hiring of the staff, he hoped Elizabeth would not mind his presumption in this instance, so that at the very least, a maid could be waiting to serve in that capacity when she arrived.

With those plans in mind, he began writing, including that he and Elizabeth would be travelling as soon as the roads were passible. Then concerned about his betrothed's reception by his staff when they arrived at his townhouse without a chaperone, he outlined his plans for them to be married as soon as possible, warning the housekeeper that he would not tolerate any gossip regarding his betrothed or wedding.

Darcy set aside the first letter and began to give thought to the next missive he needed to write. Bishop John Stanton, his godfather, and he had always been good friends. Stanton, as he insisted on being called, had been friends with Darcy's father during their days at Cambridge, but had ceased coming to Pemberley due to a falling out between the two when he was just old enough to remember. Rather than neglect his godson completely, Stanton visited him when he entered school. Darcy treasured those visits; unlike the parents of the other boys, his own father never took the time

66

to come. During holidays, his father would always have him sent to London, where he was under the charge of a governess and tutors. Stanton would also call upon him there. As a result, Darcy and his godfather had continued to have a close relationship to that very day. In the message, he asked Stanton to officiate at his wedding, which he hoped to have at the townhouse the evening they arrived.

When he finished, he left the correspondence unsealed, since he not only wished to consult his betrothed about the arrangements for not only their nuptials but also the trip to London. He had indicated in the letters that their current plans were to leave early Monday morning with them arriving at the townhouse at approximately noon, although he did promise to send word if their plans changed. He had decided to postpone notifying his sister; his cousin, Richard; and Mrs. Reynolds, the Pemberley housekeeper, until he reached London. It would be much easier to take care of any further matters there.

His letters completed, Darcy ensured tea, as well as their meals for the day, would be brought to their suite. He made his way to the bedroom, sitting by the fire so he could keep a watchful eye on Elizabeth while he read a book. Throughout the afternoon, he placed his hand to her forehead several times, attempting to ascertain if her fever had returned. He found her only mildly warm, and was relieved she seemed to be improving so rapidly.

~ * ~

Elizabeth finally stirred from bed about the time their tea was delivered. Since Darcy was in the sitting room at the time, she softly closed the door to the room. Noticing the maid had straightened the room while she had been sleeping and brought warm water for her to refresh herself, she tried to clean herself up the best she could with what she had, while she dreamt of a bath so she could wash her hair. As her clothes were now dry, she changed into one of her own nightgowns, and donned her dressing gown before opening the door to her room.

~ * ~

The maid had knocked on the outer door while Elizabeth was napping, and upon allowing her to enter, Darcy removed himself to the sitting room while she worked. After the maid left, Darcy noticed the door between the two rooms was closed, so he arranged their tea. Elizabeth opened the door soon after, and proceeded to sit in a chair by the fire. Despite how she felt, he thought she should be spending the day in bed, and was not particularly happy to find her exerting herself so soon.

"You should be in bed, Elizabeth," he said with concern evident in his voice.

"Oh, please do not fuss at me. I am so tired of being in that room, and I ache from being in bed for so long."

He feared he would regret not pressing her to return; however, not able to refuse her anything, he yielded to her wishes and brought her a cup of tea. While they were enjoying their refreshments, he consulted Elizabeth about the letters he had written, as well as the tentative plans he had made. She approved of his arrangements, and smiled brightly when she thanked him for thinking of and including her. Right then and there, he decided he would definitely have to find something to ask her opinion about every day, if only to have her look at him the way she was now. Once he had sealed the correspondence, he summoned for one of his servants, immediately arranging for the letters to be sent express as soon as possible.

Darcy returned to his seat, and picked up his cup to continue their tea. "I apologize for the interruption; I wished to have those letters sent as quickly as possible."

"I understand," smiled Elizabeth.

"You have asked me quite a few questions the last few days. Do you mind if I ask you one?"

"Of course not," she replied.

"What were you like as a child?" The serious visage he had been managing to keep faltered when a small smile appeared upon his face.

She grinned. "That is your big question?"

"Yes, were you a model child; or did you try your parents' nerves?"

"If you were to ask my mother, she would say that I continue to vex her nerves." She saw him chuckle. "I preferred boys' pursuits to what my mother deemed appropriate for a little girl. My petticoats were always six inches deep in mud, and I often tore my dresses while rambling in the woods."

"You did not have a doll, or enjoy learning to sew?"

"I had a doll when I was a girl, but she went on my adventures with me, climbing trees and playing in the woods. My mother attempted to teach me ladies' pursuits, but I was not interested until I was almost twelve. Even then, I still preferred embroidery to sewing clothes."

"You are well-read and intelligent," he observed.

"That was my father. He educated me as he would a son, and I would bring books into the woods, hiding in the trees while I read." An image of her reading while sitting on a tree limb came to his mind, and he smiled.

Their conversation moved to Elizabeth's travels to London, the theatre, and touched on some of Darcy's favourite memories as well. They did not realize the time that had passed until a knock at the door heralded the arrival of their dinner.

The maid proceeded to set out their evening meal, and to straighten the room before she departed to her other chores. Due to the girl's presence, they confined themselves to less personal topics; Elizabeth exclaimed her happiness that the rain had not returned, while Darcy expressed his hope that the roads would soon be dry enough for travel. It was not long, however, before the maid departed, allowing them to speak freely once again.

After dinner, Elizabeth still did not wish to return to bed, so they seated themselves before the fire, and discussed plans for when they were able to travel. When they reached the topic of their nuptials, he decided to broach the subject of wedding guests.

"Would you wish for your aunt and uncle who reside in London, to attend?" He was still unsure about Mrs. Bennet's relations, but he knew the Gardiners were important to Elizabeth. The affection was clear in the manner in which she spoke of them, so he was willing to invite them for her sake. After their wedding, he could minimize the connection should they prove to be intolerable.

"If the circumstances were different, I would say yes," she replied. "As it is, I am afraid by the time we reach London, my father will already be there. I know I will be of age by then, and can make my own choices, but I fear Papa will try to return me to Longbourn. I really do not want another confrontation."

"I would not let him take you without your consent, Elizabeth. I hope you know that," he said reassuringly.

Seeing the truth in his eyes, she smiled as she made a decision. "Thank you, but I believe it would be better to simply announce our marriage as a fait accompli."

"I believe that would be best for my family as well," he agreed.

He did not look forward to his Aunt Catherine's vitriol, and he knew his uncle, Lord Matlock, would not be much better. Their reaction did not matter as long as he was married to Elizabeth. Once they were wed, there was nothing anyone could do to separate them. After all, "Those whom God hath joined together, let no man put asunder."* As horrible as the thought was, he was looking forward to the peace and quiet which would come from alienating them.

Over the course of the evening, Elizabeth found she really enjoyed the time she spent talking with her intended. He was intelligent, well-read, and—when he wanted—very witty and charming. She had originally resented the way he had arranged the inn, expecting her to follow along with his plans. She now recognized that he had not done it out of some notion that she was incapable, but because he wanted to care for her—because he was accustomed to making decisions for those closest to him. It could be frustrating, but she also found it endearing.

He had mentioned the many walks around Pemberley, and she asked him to describe his favourite. She had been listening to him describe the walk around the lake when she must have fallen asleep. The feel of strong arms lifting her from the seat caused her to stir, and she felt a warmth, which she attempted to get closer to. There was the sensation of a soft kiss placed upon her forehead, but it was so feather light, she thought she was dreaming.

As she felt herself being placed on the bed and the covers arranged around her, the loss of warmth, in addition to the movement, roused her enough to understand that Darcy had been the source of comfort as he had carried her to the room. She opened her eyes and watched him as he shed his waistcoat, tailcoat and cravat, placing them on the dressing table before taking his usual seat in the chair by the bed.

"Will," she said, still groggy.

"I just brought you to bed," he whispered. "Go back to sleep."

"You are not going to spend the night in that chair again?" After passing the last two days and nights watching over her from that same spot, he appeared excessively tired, and she was not about to permit him to repeat the experience.

"I will be fine."

She pushed over to the far side of the bed. "There is enough space for us both," she said, hoping she could prevent him from occupying that seat for another night.

"My presence may prevent you from resting as well as you should, Elizabeth. Besides, we are not married yet. It would not be right," he claimed, concerned about being in such an intimate position with her.

"I am accustomed to sharing a bed with Jane, who kicks. I assure you, it will not disturb me." She raised herself to her elbow. "We have already thoroughly disregarded propriety by spending so much time alone, not to mention by addressing one another so informally. We may not be married as of yet, but I trust you."

Obviously, she had no idea how much he wanted to be in that bed. Not only did he not wish to offend her, but what if she invaded his dreams during the night. Of course, she did not know of that affliction, and he most certainly was not going to explain it before they were wed.

Elizabeth was attempting to sound collected while she was persuading him to share the bed with her. He looked exhausted, and the chair, as well as the chaise, where he had tried to sleep, was out of the question. She was insistent but nervous—very nervous about sleeping with a man; however, he had been nothing but a gentleman since he had found her. She needed to trust him. After all, she was marrying him.

Noticing his hesitation, she said softly, "I will not sleep until you lay down with me, Fitzwilliam Darcy."

Raising his eyebrows at her ultimatum, but unwilling to argue, he rose from the chair and moved to lay next to her, with the intention of only remaining long enough for her to fall back to sleep. He lay atop the bedding, which Elizabeth protested, insisting he would be cold as she forced him to cover with the bedclothes. Darcy, who was worried he would be unable to extricate himself without waking her, rolled on his side to face her. She smiled and closed her emerald eyes that had not been as vibrant since her illness. Soon, her breathing became even, and he knew she was asleep, although he did not remove himself immediately, but watched her for a short time, unaware of when he fell asleep as well.

~ * ~

Elizabeth slept uninterrupted, not awakening until morning. Initially, she kept her eyes closed, enjoying the warmth of the bed, before she understood that warmth was radiating from the gentleman sharing it. During the night, Darcy had somehow managed to curl up behind her, and was holding her to him with an arm around her waist. As she became increasingly aware of her surroundings, she felt something unusual, causing her to glance downward to find his rather large hand cupping her breast; moreover, there was also something stiff, which she could not readily identify pressing into her lower back. She could feel her face burn, yet was unwilling to wake him, due to the lack of sleep he had suffered over the last few days, so she remained still. Resting until she felt him slowly remove his hand from her breast, she felt him softly kiss her on the neck beneath her ear. The bed shifted as he moved to the opposite side, and threw his legs over the side of the bed, remaining seated on the edge for a while before she heard him rise and walk out of the room.

~ * ~

As Darcy slowly opened his eyes and stared at the braid of curly chestnut locks in front of him, he came to the realisation that he had somehow managed to curl up into Elizabeth's back and had his arm draped over her side. Tensing, he suddenly understood that the soft mass his hand was encasing was her breast. He closed his eyes while he prayed that she was still asleep, so she would not be angry with him. Slowly, he removed his hand as he lifted on his elbow to see if she was awake as well. Her eyes were still closed and she seemed to be breathing evenly. He lightly kissed her, and carefully rose from the bed.

After making his hasty exit, he dressed and made arrangements for breakfast before alerting his driver (who agreed the roads should be much improved) of their departure upon the morrow. If it had not been Sunday, he would have taken a chance with the state of the roads, since they had had a good bit of time to dry, but did not wish to have gossip of a night spent alone in his townhouse to possibly slip out should they not be able to marry upon their arrival. With that thought in mind, their accommodations were reserved for one more night, with plans to leave early the following day.

As he returned to the room, he heard her moving around within the bedroom, and his mind wandered back to waking with her in his arms for the first time, prompting him to smile. He could only hope Elizabeth had not noticed where his hand had roamed, and if she had, he prayed she would easily forgive him.

Once he had begun reminiscing about the feel of her in his arms, he allowed himself to indulge in the memory until she opened the door and entered. Her presence forced him to quickly put those thoughts of her out of his mind in order to regain control of himself, lest she notice the consequences of them.

He was surprised to see she had dressed, and was pleased that he had requested for her gowns to be laundered and pressed. They had been terribly wrinkled from becoming wet while packed within the valise, and he had wanted them to be in good condition before they departed for London.

He noticed the high colour on her cheeks and realised she must have indeed been aware of his hand's indiscretion; he also wondered if she noticed the light kiss he placed on her neck before he rose from the bed. With her hair plaited and resting on the pillow, as well as her shift draped loosely across her bare shoulder, the temptation had been too great for him to resist.

Once again pushing the thoughts of waking with her in his embrace from his mind, Darcy quickly crossed the room to meet her. Taking her hand, he bowed over it, caressing his lips across her knuckles softly before rising to look at her lovely face.

"Happy Birthday, Elizabeth."

She beamed brightly and thanked him for remembering her birthday as she momentarily forgot her embarrassment from the morning.

He took pleasure in her smile for a moment before he enclosed her hand in his and led her to the chaise, where he took a seat beside her. "I must apologize for this morning. In my defence, I was asleep when my hand found its way . . . there . . . and was unaware until I awoke."

If she had been blushing earlier, she was positively scarlet now, averting her eyes as she attempted to speak. "Will, I . . .

74

you had had so little sleep the past few nights . . . I . . . I did not wish to wake you, and while I am unaccustomed to waking in such a manner, it will be well within your rights . . . I mean you . . ."

Realising where her statement was leading, Darcy placed a hand on hers, which were now furiously trying to mutilate the handkerchief she was holding. Startled by his action, she was unsure how to react, when he lifted her chin gently with his bent finger, where she could see his face, as he interrupted her babbling.

"Elizabeth, I will never expect more than what you are willing to give," he said, watching her eyes as he prayed he could relieve her agitation.

Still blushing madly, she began, "I do not mean to say it was unpleasant. I . . . " Suddenly comprehending what she had divulged, and fearing her statement horribly inappropriate, Elizabeth put her hands to her face in mortification; although, Darcy did not allow her to remain that way. He gently pulled her arms down as he cradled her cheek, lifting her face so she could see his. He was smiling. Why was he smiling like that? Hoping that the smile on his face meant her statement was not something scandalous, she relaxed slightly, but was still nervous to his reaction.

"If you enjoyed waking in my arms, I am very pleased." He leaned in closer, and gazing into her eyes, added very softly, "You have done nothing that should make you feel embarrassed or ashamed."

He had had some idea that her innocence had been part of her embarrassment, and based on what most young women were taught, she was probably under the impression that being with a man was supposed to be unpleasant. However, before he could say anything more to further relieve her anxiety, there was a knock at the door, announcing that their breakfast had arrived.

At once, he rose and opened the door, allowing the maids to deliver a tray of food as well as a tea service. Darcy requested the rooms be tidied; and one of the maids immediately moved to the bedroom to clean while the other arranged the food on the table.

Holding out a chair for Elizabeth to sit, he moved around and took his own seat aa they proceeded to break their fast, speaking very little while the maids cleaned not only the bedroom, but the sitting room as well. Elizabeth relaxed some after the maids had arrived, causing him to hope there would not be any further awkwardness related to the events of the morning. When they were once again alone, they chatted about inconsequential matters until they were finished and took seats by the fire.

Elizabeth selected a book and attempted to read, but found she could not concentrate on the words, as her mind was too unsettled. Waking with Darcy's hand on her breast had disconcerted her. She had been truthful when she said his embrace was not unpleasant; but her mother had always bemoaned marital duties—even commenting on several occasions how abhorrent they were. Thankfully she had spoken with her Aunt Maddie about the subject. Her aunt would not tell Elizabeth what the dreaded duties were, but had informed her that in a marriage of affection, it was not unpleasant, and there was nothing to fear, promising to enlighten her further on the subject when she became betrothed. Now she was to be married to someone she had only feelings of friendship for, and she would not be able to speak to her aunt before her wedding. Deciding it was useless to worry about it, she resolved to put it out of her mind, as she would manage with whatever presented itself. After all, her courage always rose at every attempt to intimidate her.

Darcy noticed how pensive she had become as she slowly let her book drop to her lap, and proceeded to watch her, as she obviously was puzzling out a problem in her mind. She stared, not really looking at anything, as she bit her bottom lip, until she suddenly turned to look at him.

"Are you well?"

"Oh . . . yes, I am just finding it difficult to concentrate on what I am reading," she replied. "It seems I keep thinking of other things." She shrugged, and looked down at the book.

He rose from his chair, and walked to where Elizabeth was seated on the chaise. Sitting next to her, he covered her hand with his own. She looked up at him as he began rubbing his thumb in circles over the back of hers.

"Would you like me to read to you again?" he asked, hoping she would. While he was happy just being in the same room with her, he wanted an excuse to be near her.

"It is really not necessary."

"I enjoy this volume of Byron you have selected. If you would like to hear it, I would be happy to read it to you," he pressed. "It would not be an imposition."

She surveyed his expression doubtfully, but nodded her head. "I believe I would enjoy that, thank you."

Darcy took the book from her hand, opened it and began to read. If asked later, neither could tell how long they had sat at that occupation, eventually taking turns reading and then discussing the poems. It was several hours later, when they were startled by a knock at the door, indicating their tea had arrived.

Tea was pleasant, yet upon finishing, Elizabeth found she was rather tired. Hoping he would not notice her fatigue, she returned to take a seat on the chaise. She tucked her feet behind her while Darcy smiled and retrieved the volume of Wordsworth from his trunk before taking a seat next to her to begin to read. He had only read a few pages when she fell asleep against the back of the chaise with her head propped on her hand. He chuckled a bit at her stubbornness, then continued to read until he was sure she was fast asleep.

~ * ~

Elizabeth startled at a knock at the door. She glanced about her, noting that she had somehow lain down, and a blanket was now covering her. As she slowly moved to a seated position, she surveyed the room to find Darcy crossing to open the door. She saw him momentarily turn his head to check on her as she rose from the chaise. They shared a small smile, and Elizabeth walked to the bedroom, closing the door after her.

She returned to the sitting room to find that dinner had been delivered, and they sat down to eat. Their conversation was dominated by a discussion of the weather. The sun had been shining all day, drying the road and making the chance for their travel to London safe and, more importantly, possible.

Darcy left briefly to inform his driver of their plans, returning to the room to find her already dressed and in bed. Not wishing to assume anything after the incident that morning, he proceeded to tell her good night, and sat in his seat by the bed to read, as was his habit, until she fell asleep.

Elizabeth, who noticed where he had situated himself, raised her eyebrow. "Mr. Darcy, I believe we have already discussed your sleeping arrangements."

Chuckling, he knew it was useless to argue, so instead shed his outer layers and cravat, and climbed in to the bed. He smiled inwardly at the opportunity to be so close to her, softly wishing her a happy birthday once more before they allowed sleep to claim them.

* Book of Common Prayer, Cambridge Stereotype Edition. Published 1800. Pg. 187

Chapter 8

Monday 2 December 1811

The day dawned bright and early, finding Darcy and Elizabeth in the same position as the previous morning. Knowing they would more than likely be married by that evening, she endeavoured to curb her natural embarrassment of the situation, and attempted not to wake him as she slowly rolled to face him, gently brushing a stray lock of hair from his face. She was amazed how young he appeared as he slept, and smiled softly, imagining what he must have looked like as a young boy.

He pulled her closer as he rolled to his back and stretched. Lazily opening his eyes, he turned his head to find Elizabeth staring at him.

"Good morning," he said huskily, his voice still hoarse from sleep.

"Good morning," she said with a small smile, suddenly becoming rather shy.

Darcy only grinned wider when he noticed her faint blush. She normally seemed so self-assured and composed that he enjoyed being the only person to see this side of her. Reaching over to touch an escaped curl lying on her neck, he lightly kissed her on the forehead before he indicated that they should rise and prepare to leave.

They packed their belongings themselves, and after the servants loaded them onto the carriage, Darcy checked the common rooms to ensure there was no one of their acquaintance downstairs before he retrieved Elizabeth. They did not dawdle as they descended, meeting the equipage as it pulled around to the front of the small inn. He helped her alight before he climbed in himself, and they quickly departed for London.

~ * ~

Darcy stared at his betrothed, who had been virtually silent since they left the inn, and was currently taking in the scenery outside the window. Covering her hand, which rested on the seat between them, with his own, he watched a small smile grace her lips before she turned to face him.

"You have been very quiet since we left the inn."

Her brow furrowed in thought before responding, "I guess I have." She shrugged a bit as her brow cleared. "I hope you have not been wanting for company."

"I was concerned perhaps something was amiss," he replied, the worry evident in his voice.

"It is nothing, really." Her gaze travelled down to their hands for a few minutes before returning to his face. "I believe I am nervous," she suddenly confessed softly.

He was touched she would confide as much without persuasion, and squeezed her hand gently. "You can tell me anything, Elizabeth. I hope you know that."

As she gazed into his eyes, she felt something stir within her. Since they had met in the rain, he had proven that he was worthy of her trust. While he once had probably felt her situation beneath him, he had obviously changed, and it seemed he had undergone this transformation for her. Elizabeth was flattered, to say the least, and came to the realisation that while they were only friends, she was happy to be marrying him. She did not have doubts about him; she had doubts about herself.

"I believe am just overwhelmed."

Truly anxious that something was very wrong, he put his arm around her shoulders, gently rubbing her arm with his thumb. As she leaned against his shoulder, his heart swelled with happiness. Her trust in him had obviously grown over the last few days, and knowing that, she became all the more dear to him. He continued to hold her for some time before she seemed to completely relax; he almost believed her to be

80

asleep until she began speaking.

"If you are worried I am having doubts about marrying you, I am not," she began. "It surprises me, given the history of our acquaintance, but I do not doubt you." She took a deep breath before continuing softly, "I learned to run a house from my mother and my Aunt Gardiner, but this will be so different to what I am accustomed, and I am afraid I will be a disappointment."

"Elizabeth, you have many qualities that will make you a good mistress. I would not have chosen you if I did not think you would be exceptional," Darcy confessed. "Mrs. Thomas and Mrs. Reynolds have been running the households for years, and they will be more than happy to help with anything you may require."

Elizabeth looked up at him with tears in her eyes, and he was lost. He hoped that she was affected more by his confidence in her than her fears. Raising the hand that was not wrapped around her shoulders, he ran the backs of his fingers from her temple to her chin.

"You are intelligent and kind. I cannot think of any better qualities for a mistress of Pemberley to possess."

Their eyes remained fixed on each other, and Darcy leaned in to softly kiss her lips. Elizabeth thought she had never felt anything more perfect as butterflies erupted in her stomach and she became warm all over. He lingered for a moment before slowly pulling back, once more looking into her eyes. While his hand cupped her cheek, he delivered another kiss to her forehead, and pulled her closer to him. She rested her head upon his shoulder, and remained cuddled to his side for the remainder of the trip to London.

~ * ~

If Thomas Bennet was angry before, he was absolutely furious now. He had left Longbourn before dawn Saturday morning, and had reached London only to find that Elizabeth was not there. In fact, Edward and Madeleine Gardiner claimed to be unaware of where she was, and his brother actually had the nerve to censure him for attempting to force her into a marriage she did not desire, claiming he had brought this upon himself. He had remained and searched until Monday morning, when he could no longer abide his brother's continuous criticism.

He had told that ridiculous Collins that his betrothed would be returned by nightfall, but he had absolutely no idea where else she could be. He had thought it would be so simple. He would travel to London, and bring Elizabeth home. They would then attend church Sunday morning when he would arrange to have the banns read. As it was, he had left strict orders that no one was to venture from home while he was gone, so his family would not have attended church. Mr. Collins was sure to have gone to the service, but Mr. Bennet still felt that his cousin would remain silent, at least until he returned without Elizabeth. Then he was sure that Mr. Collins would refuse to honour the betrothal.

He cursed his daughter for sending him on a wild goose chase, and boarded his carriage to return home. If he checked all the inns along the way, he might find some information as to his daughter's whereabouts. No closer to finding Elizabeth than he was yesterday, he angrily rapped the ceiling of his carriage (causing it to violently lurch forward) and departed London, unaware of the worried Gardiners watching from the window.

Darcy's carriage pulled up to his Grosvenor Street townhouse just before noon. After stepping down, he assisted Elizabeth's descent as she peered up at the edifice of the enormous home. He thought she still looked nervous, but she smiled as he took her hand, placed it on his arm, and led her into the house. They were met by Mrs. Thomas, the housekeeper, as well as Graves, the butler, who took their outerwear and gloves as he regarded Elizabeth with a wary eye.

Darcy noticed his butler's look, and assuming it was due to their lack of chaperone, acted as if nothing was out of the ordinary, and proudly introduced his betrothed to Mrs. Thomas, and the portion of the staff that had assembled upon their arrival. Once the necessary introductions were made, he swiftly escorted Elizabeth upstairs to their suite. The housekeeper followed close behind to ensure all was in order.

As they entered the bedchamber, he turned to face Elizabeth. "The mistress's chambers have not been redecorated since my parents married," he began. "I am sure the maids have aired and cleaned them; nevertheless, I would like you to renovate them however you choose. Mrs. Thomas can assist you with anything you will need."

Elizabeth had noticed the room was out of date, but there was nothing objectionable to it. After all, it was bigger and more opulent than her room at Longbourn, and she did not even have to share it with Jane. The housekeeper's anxiety was rather obvious, and Elizabeth found it amusing that she would be worried about something so trivial; although, she assumed most ladies would not be so understanding, while attempting to think of how Miss Bingley would react in a similar situation.

"I am sure it will be more than adequate."

Darcy grinned. He knew the housekeeper would object to the state of the room, but he was sure that Elizabeth would not mind it in the least. He took her hand and lightly brushed his lips across her knuckles. "As long as you have no objections, I will leave you with Mrs. Thomas."

"I am well, thank you," she said, before he bowed and exited through the door, which led to his rooms. Glancing around the room, she turned and smiled at the older woman.

"Miss Bennet, when Mr. Darcy wrote, he indicated you would require a lady's maid, so I have taken the liberty of engaging Claire, pending your approval, of course." Before she could respond, however, Mrs. Thomas continued, "She is waiting in your dressing room to assist you with your bath."

Elizabeth glanced at the door the housekeeper indicated, and realising she was nervous as well, smiled. "I am sure she will be satisfactory, thank you."

After a brief curtsy, the older woman departed the room, as

Elizabeth entered her dressing room to find a young woman about her age sorting through her valise. She looked up from her duties and quickly curtsied. "My name is Claire, Miss Bennet."

Elizabeth noticed a slight French accent, but it was very muddled. She had never hired staff before, and was sure the housekeeper knew more of what the future Mrs. Darcy would need in an abigail than she did, so she decided she would only request a change if for some reason she did not suit.

"Hello," Elizabeth said brightly. "Since Mrs. Thomas interviewed you, I am unaware of your experience. May I ask how you came to be a lady's maid?"

"Of course ma'am," she replied. "My mother was an abigail before she married my father, and she taught me all she knew. Her sister, my aunt, is also Miss Darcy's modiste, who I have been helping since I was a young girl. When we brought Miss Darcy her latest dresses for a fitting, my aunt mentioned to Mrs. Thomas that I was seeking a position. I believe when Mr. Darcy indicated you had need of a maid; she remembered me."

"Your aunt no longer has need of you?"

"No, ma'am. I have younger sisters and cousins who have learned to assist her, and there is not enough room for us all."

Elizabeth smiled. "I understand. I have four sisters and sometimes the house seemed very small with all of us bustling about."

There was a noise in the adjoining room, and Claire hung the dress she was holding before gesturing toward the door. "I believe your bath is ready, ma'am."

Darcy bathed and donned fresh clothes before descending the stairs to his study. Upon sitting at his desk, his attention was drawn to a letter from his godfather, which had been placed directly atop the rest of his correspondence. He quickly broke the seal, and upon reading the missive, smiled broadly. Stanton would arrive at approximately five o'clock, and he was bringing his wife and son with him, indicating that they were looking forward to meeting the future Mrs. Darcy.

Earlier, his valet had located the special license, as well as the settlement, in his trunk, and the eager groom placed them in his inside coat pocket. He assumed Elizabeth could sign her own settlement papers since, as of yesterday, she was of age. Settlements were meant to protect the bride, but in Elizabeth's case, he did not think this completely necessary; he would always make sure she was protected from this day forward.

A bill set to the side of the correspondence caught his attention. As he perused the figures, he sighed, and was running a hand through his hair, when his thoughts were interrupted by a knock at the door. "Come," he answered.

His housekeeper entered and stood before his desk after executing a brief curtsy. "I beg your pardon, Mr. Darcy," she began. "I would have asked Miss Bennet, but I did not know if the question would offend her."

"Mrs. Thomas, my betrothed does not offend that easily, but I will attempt to answer your question, if you would prefer to ask me first."

The older woman smiled. "Her abigail and I could not help but notice her lack of luggage, and we were wondering if more would be delivered at a later date, sir."

"No," he sighed. "That is all she has at the moment. She will need to make an appointment with Madame duParc very soon." He saw her nod. "I am aware she has very little, but please inform her maid to do the best she can for the moment."

"Of course, sir," she replied, and was about to curtsy and exit his study when Darcy stopped her.

"Mrs. Thomas, I would be interested in knowing if you are aware of the reason Miss Darcy once again needed new dresses?"

He always seemed to be receiving bills from the modiste or some other shopping expense for Georgiana. If she truly required what she was purchasing, he would not mind, but he could not understand how a young woman who was not yet out in society would need so many gowns, gloves and other adornments. She had just bought an inordinate number of dresses a few months ago, and now he was receiving another bill for more. He had forbidden her from shopping during her last stay in London; however, he had been in Hertfordshire, and the evidence before him proved that she had deliberately disobeyed him. His housekeeper had long been aware of the young lady's spending habits, and he hoped she could shed some light on the reason behind his sister's latest excursion.

"I believe, sir," she began, "the dresses Miss Darcy had previously purchased for this fall had become too short. Her maid suggested trying to let out the hem, but Miss Darcy insisted it would not be enough. Mrs. Annesley attempted to prevent her from shopping, but Miss Darcy took her maid one afternoon while her companion was resting within her rooms. In Amy's defence, sir, I believe Miss Darcy threatened to go without an escort, and I had no idea of her attempting to leave, or I would have notified Mrs. Annesley."

Darcy exhaled, running his hand through his hair. He had obtained the information he required, and unfortunately it was not the housekeeper's responsibility to curb Georgiana's spending. He would need to have yet another discussion with her regarding her expenditures—not to mention that she would not be returning to London until she had reimbursed him for her latest purchases.

He looked up, realising he had forgotten to excuse his housekeeper. "Thank you, Mrs. Thomas."

She curtsied and moved toward the door, suddenly turning back to address the master once more. "Sir . . . Miss Darcy sorted through her closet, and pulled the dresses that were supposedly too small. I do not believe she has ever worn any of them." Darcy bristled hearing his sister's wasteful nature recounted to him. "I think they just might be easily adjusted fit Miss Bennet very nicely. They could even be altered to fit the new mistress's preferences."

"I believe you should show the gowns to Miss Bennet, and explain the situation to her," he suggested. "She is one of five sisters, and I am sure she has been required to wear a sister's dress from time to time. In any case, it will make things easier until new garments can be procured for her."

She nodded just before Darcy added, "Miss Bennet is very fair and kind. While I understand the staff's need to impress her, no one need walk on eggshells."

Mrs. Thomas smiled and curtsied. "Yes, sir," she replied before exiting the study.

~ * ~

Elizabeth sat in her dressing gown before the fire, allowing her hair to finish drying. After being sick for the last few days, it had been wonderful being able to wash her hair. She was amazed at how a simple bath could so drastically improve one's spirits after an illness.

Apparently Claire and Mrs. Thomas had prepared ahead for her arrival—not only readying the mistress's suite, but also procuring lotions and various items she may need. Never in her life had she been so pampered. She was very happy with her new abigail, who (in Elizabeth's opinion) had been very adept at her position thus far.

A knock at the door startled her from her thoughts, and she nodded to Claire, who moved to admit the housekeeper, whose arms were filled with gowns.

"I beg your pardon, ma'am, but I noticed you did not bring much with you, and I thought some of these might be of help, at least until you can visit the modiste."

As she laid the dresses on the bed, Elizabeth managed to get a better look at them. She was amazed by the quality of the fabric, as well as the craftsmanship; they were beautifully made. At first glance, there were two or three, which would probably not work with her colouring, but she felt the rest would do quite nicely.

Glancing next to her, she noticed the housekeeper watching nervously, and smiled. "Thank you, for showing them to me . . . may I ask where they came from?"

"Miss Darcy recently noticed she had grown too tall for these, and we had removed them from her closet; although, I had not yet determined what to do with them."

"They look as if they have never been worn," declared Elizabeth, whose gaze returned to the gowns she was inspecting.

Mrs. Thomas's face tensed. "I do not believe they have, ma'am."

At that moment, Claire interjected. "If you would like to try them on, we could plan any alterations they may need, as well as any changes you would care to make to them."

Elizabeth looked at her maid with a questioning look on her face. "What do you mean by changes?"

The young woman smiled. "We can alter the sleeves or the cut on the neckline, as well as add lace or another trim you may prefer. I can make any of the alterations you wish."

Truly impressed with her skills, Elizabeth smiled and nodded.

Her abigail made swift work of her hair, which was quickly styled. She chose one gown that she wished to wear for the wedding that evening, as well as two others that she might wish to wear over the next few days. Although there were fifteen in all, she opted not to keep two. One was a particular shade of orange, which reminded her very much of Caroline Bingley, and the other a shade of chartreuse that she had never particularly liked. Elizabeth recommended to Mrs. Thomas that she might wish to set those aside for the ragman.

Turning her attention to the gown she had selected to wear that evening for the wedding, she ran her fingers through the beautiful ivory silk with delicate roses embroidered upon the bodice. Luckily it only required an adjustment for length, which was quickly measured and pinned. Then she and Claire decided to give the top of the bodice a slight dip in the centre, which reminded her of a heart. Its short sleeves were removed, and the remaining material arranged to make the dress appear almost off-the-shoulder, before the gown was finally prepped, and very quickly removed in order to begin the alterations.

Refreshments were soon delivered, along with a note from Darcy. He wrote that he would be briefly running an errand, and that Bishop Stanton would arrive at five o'clock for the wedding. Smiling at his consideration, she placed the note to the side while she finished eating, and decided to lie down on the bed. She intended only to close her eyes for a moment, but fell asleep instead.

~ * ~

Darcy returned home at approximately half past three in a very good mood. He had visited his solicitor's office, and made arrangements for Elizabeth to be provided for in his will, should anything happen to him. Not that the thought of leaving her made him happy, but the act of making arrangements for her as his wife satisfied him immensely. Final copies were to be completed and delivered to the townhouse for him to sign sometime later in the week. Once finished with his solicitors, he visited a jewellery store to have his grandmother's ring, which would be Elizabeth's wedding ring, engraved, and found two presents for her as well. The first was a choker of pearls with a pear-shaped emerald and diamond accents that he planned to give to her that evening before the wedding. The other present, however, was a necklace for every day. He had noticed her garnet cross was absent from her neck when he found her, and assumed she must have removed it prior to leaving Longbourn. Desiring that she have something from him to replace it, he purchased a necklace with an opal pendant, which he hoped to give her sometime that evening for her birthday.

When Darcy returned from his errands, Mrs. Thomas informed him that Elizabeth was resting until the wedding ceremony. Desiring to see the look upon her face when she opened the pearl and emerald choker, he considered impulsively entering her bedchamber to give it to her, but thought she might wish him to wait to see her until she came downstairs for the wedding. Therefore, he placed the gifts to the side until the time of their nuptials grew closer.

~ * ~

Claire woke Elizabeth at approximately four o'clock. Tea had been brought to her room, and she needed to get dressed. She quickly drank her tea, then Claire unpinned and brushed her hair before arranging it in an elaborate style more appropriate for her wedding. Pleased with the result, Elizabeth thanked her before rising, very curious to view the gown, which had been worked on all afternoon.

She was surprised to learn that during her nap, her maid had been extremely industrious. Her measurements, which had been taken earlier during the dress fittings, had been sent, accompanied by a note, with a maid to Madame duParc, Claire's aunt, requesting several sets of new undergarments, as well as nightgowns. New stockings were procured, and Mrs. Thomas had even found a beautiful pair of slippers in a trunk of the former Mrs. Darcy's things that happened to fit.

Once Elizabeth had put on all of her undergarments, Claire brought the altered dress into the room and helped her into it. Claire's advice about the changes to the sleeves and neckline were perfect. The gown had been beautiful before, but the alterations made it more appropriate for a formal event, and Elizabeth was extremely pleased with the finished product. When she was completely dressed, she stared at herself in the mirror, marvelling how the expensive new silk undergarments, as well as the beautiful gown made her feel every bit the bride.

She was startled from her thoughts by a knock at the door, which Claire answered before returning to give her a small package tied with a green ribbon. An attached note read, 'To Elizabeth, Yours, Will.' Smiling, she opened the package, and gasped when she saw the necklace within the box. It was beautiful, but surely she did not need something so extravagant.

A voice from behind startled her. "Ma'am, would you like me to put it on you?"

"Oh . . . yes, of course," she replied. Still awed by the gift.

"It is very beautiful. I am sure the master will enjoy seeing you wear it."

Elizabeth smiled at Claire in the mirror. "Thank you, I am sure he will."

Believing they were finished, she began to rise before she was stopped. "Oh, I have one more thing. There are several different styles of hair pins in the bottom drawer of the dressing table, which I think included some pearls," she said, opening a bottom drawer and retrieving a small box. "I believe they were never removed after the former Mrs. Darcy used this room."

She opened the box, and held one up for Elizabeth to inspect. "I believe they will match quite nicely."

Hoping Darcy would not mind her wearing them, she smiled and nodded to Claire, who began to arrange them in her hair. When the pins were all in place, she no longer recognized herself as Elizabeth Bennet. She stood as she stared at herself in the mirror.

In Elizabeth's fantasies of her wedding day, her father was always there to give her away, a smile upon his face, but this was not a dream. Unwilling to ruin the reality, she swallowed the disappointment of her father's betrayal, and his subsequent absence from her wedding. The nerves that settled in her stomach made her wring her hands in front of her.

"You look beautiful, ma'am," Claire smiled.

She returned the smile as she turned to walk out of the room, never again to return as Miss Elizabeth Bennet of Longbourn, but as Mrs. Elizabeth Darcy, wife of Mr. Fitzwilliam Darcy of Pemberley.

Chapter 9

Monday 2 December 1811

Darcy was a bumbling mass of nerves. When he first caught a glimpse of Elizabeth coming down the stairs, he was momentarily dumbfounded. He had always known she was handsome, but this evening, she was truly the most beautiful woman he had ever seen. Taking her hand when she reached the bottom of the stairs, he lightly kissed her knuckles as he bowed. After lingering for longer than he should, he finally straightened and put her hand on his arm, leading her to the drawing room to meet their guests.

Stanton, his wife, Helen, and their eldest son, Henry, were waiting for the couple when they entered. Elizabeth was introduced, and they all talked briefly for a moment as the bishop asked them a few questions to determine their preferences for the service. The inquiries were brief, so they soon found themselves repeating the solemn words that would bind them to each other for eternity. Promises were made, vows were exchanged, and as Darcy reverently placed his grandmother's emerald ring on her slender finger, he looked into her eyes, seeing her smile as she returned his gaze. Upon finally hearing them declared man and wife, the new husband breathed a sigh of relief as he grinned widely.

Stanton and his family immediately wished the newly married couple joy, and all assembled were happily chatting when Mrs. Thomas appeared to announce dinner was served, prompting the group to move into the dining room. As Darcy helped Elizabeth with her seat, she turned and smiled as their eyes met. A shiver ran through her body, and she did the best she could to swiftly compose herself lest anyone notice. Her new husband, who had seen her reaction, kissed her softly on the temple before taking his own seat.

She enjoyed the dinner as well as the conversation. Bishop John Stanton had been the second son of an earl, opting for a profession in the church as opposed to the military or a barrister. She felt his happy manner likely aided him in his occupation, and found that he reminded her very much of Mr. Bingley, who like the bishop, seemed to be well-pleased with everyone and everything around him.

His wife, however, was a prim, soft-spoken woman; she did not speak much during dinner, but did enquire about Longbourn as well as Elizabeth's family. Elizabeth did not want to offend Mrs. Stanton, so she answered as briefly, and as neutrally as possible. She could feel Darcy's eyes upon her as she spoke, and looked up to see the concern on his face. He appeared ready to intercede, but the answer seemed to be sufficient for the lady, so they luckily moved on to other topics.

Due to the small number of their group, the party did not separate after dinner, and the men joined the ladies in the drawing room. Darcy, desiring to sit as close to his new wife as propriety would allow, offered Elizabeth his arm, and steered her directly to the sofa to swiftly sit beside her. He noticed the amused grin on his godfather's face when he took his seat, but decided to ignore it.

The conversation that followed was pleasant, until Stanton decided he desired to know how the couple met. The groom coloured and the bride to raised her eyebrow as she chuckled lightly. Darcy, knowing a simple answer would never be sufficient for his godfather, still attempted to disclose as little as possible. "We met at an assembly in Meryton."

"Actually, we were not introduced at the assembly, so that is not where we met," interrupted Elizabeth, in an attempt to tease him.

"That is very true, Mrs. Darcy, however, it is where we first saw one another," Darcy challenged. He saw Elizabeth beaming at his use of her new name before that mischievous half-smile returned, which indicated he would not get off quite so easily. Steeling himself for his godfather's humour, he closed his eyes. "Actually, the first time I saw Mrs. Darcy, I insulted her."

"Yet, she agreed to marry you," Stanton guffawed. "You must have done some grovelling to gain her acceptance, young man."

Seeing Darcy become tense, she interceded before the

teasing became too much for him. "He did apologize; and I must admit that I have since learned that my husband is the best of men." She looked back to find him staring at her with an intensity she had never seen. Having trouble holding his gaze, her eyes dropped to her hands as she blushed scarlet, and attempted to will away the gooseflesh that had appeared on her arms and the back of her neck.

Stanton noticed the looks the newlyweds were exchanging, and decided soon after that it was time for him and his family to depart. Although the Darcys objected, since they had not yet had tea, their company insisted, so the couple rose to walk their guests to the door.

Elizabeth's insides jumped when her husband placed his hand on the small of her back while he escorted her to the entrance hall. She tried to appear unaffected as she managed to smile politely and wish their guests goodnight, but it became increasingly difficult. Not only was his hand resting on her back, but he also began caressing her lightly with his thumb, which was causing a myriad of sensations. Feeling her face flush and her body begin to tingle, she was thankful when the door closed, and the butler quit the room to see to his duties.

Darcy looked down at his wife and noticed her flushed face, which seemed to have appeared in the last few minutes. He grinned broadly at her discomposure. Then he took her by the hand to his study. He helped her to take his usual seat behind his desk, where he brought out the settlement papers he had had drawn up some time ago.

"Normally, your father would sign these. However, since you are of age and he is not here, I thought you might like to sign them."

The new bride was astonished, and not sure what to say or how to react. "But . . . we are already married, would it even be legal if I, a woman, signed?"

"It does not matter if it is legal." He saw her brow furrow in confusion. "I visited my solicitor's office today, and revised my will, as well as made the arrangements for everything in this settlement. I only wished for you to understand that no matter when I die, I have made certain your future is secure."

Darcy saw the tears well in her eyes, and was not sure the cause. He had hoped she would be pleased with the arrangements, but her reaction worried him. Giving her his handkerchief, he rubbed her back as she composed herself. "I hope you are not displeased."

"No!" she quickly declared. "I am very touched at your consideration. It was unexpected."

"My consideration caused your tears?" he asked, somewhat confused by her answer.

She turned to look at his face. "I do not like thinking about you dying," she confessed. Elizabeth quickly stood as she looked down at the handkerchief she still had clutched in her hand. Quickly recovering, she looked back at his face. "It is exceedingly generous of you, especially as I really bring nothing but myself to this marriage."

Disliking her perception of herself as not having any worth, he placed his hand on her cheek and responded, "I do not need any more money. You are worth more to me than any dowry."

"Thank you," she answered quietly. She recognized what he was inferring, and her heart began to beat at the feel of his hand on her cheek. His gaze travelled down to her mouth, and she watched him lean toward her until his lips touched her own. The kiss was soft, like his previous one, but soon his lips brushed each side of her mouth before returning to the centre. As his lips begin to slowly move against hers, she mimicked his movements and returned his kiss. Her heart rate had begun to increase, and she had become very warm when he deliberately pulled back as he gazed into her eyes.

From that moment, Elizabeth had a hard time concentrating on anything, so by the time they left his study, she had signed the settlement papers as he had requested, but did not remember much of what was said. In fact, she was in such a fog that she almost missed the question he asked her when they entered the hall.

"Is there anything in particular you would you care to do this evening?"

As she considered his question, she blushed profusely; she had managed over the course of the evening to put it out of her mind, but it *was* her wedding night. Since the kiss in his study, she had become increasingly nervous, and was not sure how to behave around him. Trying desperately to conceive of an answer to his question, she had become so engrossed in her thoughts that she started when she heard his voice say her name.

"Elizabeth," he repeated, "are you well?"

"Yes, forgive me, I was wool-gathering."

He looked at her sceptically, not sure what was causing her discomposure, but hoping he could find some way to alleviate it. "I would dearly love to hear you play, or we could go to the library and read. I would offer a tour, but I think it would be best to save that for the day."

She nodded, "Perhaps, we could read upstairs," she thought aloud.

"You would like to read upstairs?" he clarified, clearly surprised by her request.

She looked up as she realised she had spoken her thoughts. "Earlier, Mrs. Thomas showed me a sitting room that is attached to both of our rooms. I thought maybe we could spend the rest of the evening there," she said tentatively.

Pleased she wished to spend time alone with him, he grinned broadly before wordlessly taking his new wife's hand and climbing the stairs to their chambers. Upon entering their sitting room, Darcy turned to face Elizabeth, and took her other hand so he was holding both.

At the inn, she had been studying his newest volume of Byron. Not knowing if she wished to continue it, or try something else, he asked, "What book would you like?"

She began blushing furiously at his question and averting her

96

eyes. "I thought perhaps we could change into our nightclothes, and you could read to me like you did at the inn . . . if it is agreeable to you, that is."

It was not the answer he had expected; it was better. The ability to comfort her as he had when she was ill had been special, and he was extremely fond of that memory; however, he had not expected her to continue the practice. He dearly loved those quiet moments they had shared at the inn, and if she wished for them to continue, he would not think to deny her that pleasure.

Cupping her cheek, he turned her face to him. "I would be pleased to do so, if it would make you happy." He looked into her eyes his hand shifting back toward her hair, and his thumb gently stroking her face.

She was caught in his brilliant blue eyes as he leaned in to brush his soft lips against hers. He slowly took her top lip between his, followed by the bottom, before fully claiming her mouth. The hand that was not touching her face rested on her waist before slowly curving around her back. Feeling his tongue brushing along her lips, she opened them, allowing it to caress her own. Elizabeth's heart was beginning to pound in her chest, and she had no idea how long she could remain upright. Their kisses became more passionate, and his hands roamed her body as she shivered in response. One hand made its way up her side until it cupped her breast; she gasped as his thumb brushed over her nipple, and wound its way around her back to pull her closer. Darcy's lips left hers, softly kissing down her neck, leaving a trail of gooseflesh in his wake, and enticing her to press her body closer to his. Elizabeth felt something rigid pressing into her stomach, and an ache begin to build between her legs.

When he reached the base of her neck, he rested his forehead against her shoulder for a moment, breathing heavily. She could feel his heart pounding—as hard as hers was—and she combed her fingers through his hair while he sighed. He raised his head, gently kissed her lips, and rested his forehead against hers.

"You should change," he said huskily, as he pulled back from her body. Elizabeth nodded, confused at the sense of loss she felt as he released her, and turned toward the door to her chambers.

Darcy watched her exit into her bedchamber, and close the door behind her. He took a deep breath and attempted to calm himself, hoping his erection would subside before he went to his chambers to change. It seemed he had been aroused more often than not since he had first laid eyes on her, and it was becoming more and more painful with each occurrence. He had thought to give her time to adjust and hopefully develop feelings for him before consummating their marriage; however, if she kept responding to him as passionately as she was, he did not think he would be able to keep his resolution. Turning, he strode to the door of his bedchamber, passing through to his dressing room, where Evans was waiting to prepare him for the night.

~ * ~

Elizabeth entered her room to find Claire waiting patiently to assist her with her nightly toilette. After changing into one of her new nightgowns, she turned toward the dressing table so Claire could take down her hair and, catching a glimpse of herself in the mirror, she froze in place, shocked. She had been unaccustomed to the thin straps, and the silky, sheer material surprised her. Her nipples were easily discernible, as was the contour of her body, and she was sure the outline of her legs was visible as well. She decided to put aside her embarrassment, since Madame duParc, who was very popular amongst the ton, had sent this for her wedding night, and prayed it was commonplace attire amongst married ladies, hoping she would not offend her husband so soon into their marriage.

Her maid produced a matching dressing gown, which Elizabeth swiftly donned, suddenly very self-conscious of her appearance, and sat before the dressing table. Her hair was released from the pins to fall freely down her back while it was brushed. Claire suggested she leave it loose and flowing about her shoulders, and Elizabeth agreed when she remembered the look on Darcy's face the last time he had seen it in that manner.

Once she had dismissed Claire for the evening, she sat at the dressing table for a few moments, and contemplated changing into one of her usual shifts, provided she could find where they had been unpacked. What would her husband think of her wearing something so revealing?

She looked down at the emerald wedding band now gracing her hand. Carefully sliding it off her finger, she examined the setting and the stone, touched that he would give her an heirloom that had been in his family for so long. She recalled the story behind the ring, a symbol of his grandparents' uncommon love match. Her new husband wished to link their marriage to a loving relationship, instead of the cold union shared by his parents, and had set aside his mother's ring for Georgiana to have when the time was right.

Turning the ring, she noticed it had been engraved. It did not look worn, as an older engraving would, but instead looked as if it had just been done. She brought the ring closer to her face as she attempted to read the small lettering, which encircled the wide band. "I am my beloved, and my beloved is mine," she whispered to herself, recognizing the verse from Song of Solomon that was read at their wedding.

Truth be told, she was very nervous. Her aunt had told her there was nothing to fear when a couple loved one another, but they did not love each other. He had confessed to friendship and admiration, however, many of his actions showed more. How much more, she did not know, but she was beginning to believe that it had to be more than simple friendship.

Her feelings were not any clearer. She knew he was more than a friend, but she could not yet call her feelings love. It was too soon, was it not? Yet, when she was in his arms, she felt safe, protected and as if she belonged there.

Hoping, yet not knowing, if her feelings would ever progress beyond this point, she decided that she would give herself to him fully. He had told her that he would never expect more than she was willing to give, but she was willing, and she wanted to know what it was like to be in his arms, to truly be his wife.

Gathering her courage, she rose from the seat and headed

toward the sitting room. She paused momentarily as she took a deep breath to calm the butterflies in her stomach before she turned the handle to the door and stepped through

~ * ~

Darcy had been sitting before the fire for some time, waiting for his new wife to make her appearance. Attempting to read a book while he waited, he found the endeavour to be fruitless, and soon it lay open in his lap while his mind ruminated on his wife's expectations and feelings about their wedding night. Not wanting her to feel frightened or obligated, he had remained in his breeches and shirtsleeves. The thought of her submitting to him out of duty pained him; he desperately wanted her to love him the way he loved her. His last thought gave him pause: he wanted her to love him *the way he loved her*. When did he begin to love her? He was unable to fix the emotion to a certain time or place, deciding he must have been in the middle before he had noticed he had begun.

Lost in thought, he did not hear her enter, until she was almost upon him, and started from his thoughts, quickly standing when he noticed her. He was mesmerised by her appearance. His only thought was that she looked like a goddess, her chestnut hair falling in soft curls about her shoulders and down her back, the emerald green eyes, which had haunted him even as he stayed at Netherfield, and her fair skin, set against the ivory silk of the dressing gown, that seemed to glow in the firelight.

Distracted from his gawking by her subtle body movements, which indicated her discomfort, he realized he was so entranced by her, he had yet to say something since she had entered the room. "You are beautiful," he said softly.

She blushed and looked at the fire for a moment before returning his gaze. "Thank you."

Taking her hand, he kissed her knuckles, his eyes never leaving hers. He turned her hand and kissed the inside of her wrist before lightly doing the same to her palm. She smiled, and Darcy pulled her toward him. He led her to the sofa and seated himself beside her, tucking her within the embrace of his arm as he kissed the top of her head. Over the last few days, he had discovered that he craved touching her. He did not need it to be sensual, but it was almost as if maintaining some kind of connection to her person would prevent her from disappearing into mist as she had done in so many of his dreams. Luckily, she had not seemed to mind.

Tonight, however, since returning from her dressing room, she seemed tense, and Darcy feared he had pushed her too far earlier. Running his fingers up and down her arm with one hand, he tilted her face up to look at him with the other so he could see her eyes.

"Is there something wrong?" he asked, concerned.

Although her eyes looked unsure, her voice betrayed none of her emotions. "No, nothing is wrong," she responded almost too quickly as she briefly broke eye contact with him. He knew she was avoiding something by her eyes, and became even more worried.

"If I went too far earlier, I apologize. The last thing I would want is for you to be afraid of me."

Surprised at his assumptions, she returned his gaze and noticed the uncertainty. "You did not frighten me," she confided. She hoped he would believe her, and she would not need to confess what was really disturbing her.

"I can tell there something bothering you, Elizabeth," he declared. Whatever he had expected by pushing her, he had not expected her to move away from him and, although he still had a hand resting at the back of her neck, he was hurt by her desertion. She looked into the fire, and he watched it reflect in her eyes as he toyed with the curls of her hair.

"You can tell me anything," he said gently, as he leaned in closer to her face.

Her eyes closed and she took a deep breath. "This is mortifying," she mumbled, still hoping he would let the matter drop.

"Please tell me," he persuaded. "Whatever it is, I promise everything will be well."

"I . . . enjoyed . . . I liked what we did earlier and I am uncomfortable with that."

He could not help but give a small grin at her confession, although a part of him wanted to jump up and down in unrestrained glee. However, once she managed to get past the initial part of the confession, it was as if a dam broke, and the rest came pouring forth so fast, it was almost hard for him to comprehend it all.

"Then I went to my dressing room, and Claire had laid out a nightgown which had been sent over for me to wear tonight. I have never worn anything like it, and I am afraid of your reaction . . . that you will find it improper," she declared, before covering her face with her hands as soon as the last word escaped her lips.

Darcy was still trying very hard to get past her mention of the nightgown. He did not want to seem insensitive, but his mind had begun envisioning possibilities, which were distracting him from the conversation at hand. Attempting to divert his mind from that portion of the statement, he managed to quickly recall the last part.

"You have done nothing improper," he said seriously. He thought for a moment, and moving closer, cradled her face in his hands. "I have no problems with you being wanton," he said with a rakish smile, "as long as you are only wanton for me."

Her eyes became huge and the blush she wore deepened. Taking a chance, he leaned forward and gently brushed her lips with his own before he moved to engulf her in his arms. He kissed the top of her head and soothingly rubbed her back as he felt some of the tension leave her body, and her arms come around his chest. Leaning down, he kissed the top of her ear.

"We do not have to do anything tonight," he whispered. "I told you I would never take more than you were willing to give, and I meant it; however, if you would allow me to hold you for the night, I would like that very much."

She was very still for a while, her only movement an effort to cuddle closer to his chest. He placed an arm under her knees, and lifted her onto his lap, in an attempt to give her the intimacy she required. Sighing, she put her arms around his shoulders and buried her face into his neck as she held him as close as she could.

If it would have been possible, Elizabeth never wanted to leave his embrace; she had never felt so safe, so cared for in her life. The woodsy smell she had come to associate with him was intoxicating to her, and his hand caressing her leg was causing her to shiver. She felt something insistently pressing her bottom, and she wondered if that meant he was as affected by her as she was by him. Wanting to be his wife not only in name, but also in truth, she knew she would eventually have to say something.

"What if I do want to?" she mumbled into his neck. Her warm breath, as well the probable meaning of her words, caused his heart to accelerate. He would not have thought it possible, but he became even more aroused. Endeavouring to control his excitement, he tried to remember his reasons for giving her time, however, her warm body pressed as close as it was to his made it exceedingly difficult concentrate.

He began to comb her hair from her face with his fingers. "I guess I would want to know why," he said gently, hoping she would understand. "I want you to come to me because you care for me, or at the very least, want me." He continued to stroke her hair for a moment, simply enjoying the intimacy of the act. "If I found that you came to me because you thought it necessary, or a duty, I would be hurt," he confided in a whisper.

Touched by his confession, Elizabeth raised her head so she could see his eyes. She did not know how to define what she felt, and she did not want to confess to feelings she did not have, so she decided to let him decide if it was enough. Reaching to lightly brush a lock of hair from his face, she said, "I do want you . . . and I . . . I do care . . . I . . . very much."

He was sure he could see in her eyes feelings she was not ready to admit to herself, and smiled as he reached up to place his hand on her cheek. She leaned towards his face, and he accepted her invitation by closing the remaining distance and kissing her softly. Brushing his lips against hers, he slowly deepened the kiss.

His tongue entered her mouth and Elizabeth touched it with hers. Hearing him groan, she pressed herself to him, and attempted to return his kisses as his hand gently caressed up her body to cup her breast. His thumb brushed over her nipple, and she inhaled sharply, the ache she felt earlier returning as she reached up to grip his shoulders. He moved to kiss along her jaw and down her neck while he began rolling the tip between his fingers, causing her to moan softly.

Encouraged by her response, Darcy stood, lifted her into his arms, and carried her into his bedchamber before standing her next to the bed. Running the back of his hand along her cheek, he leaned in to kiss her again, and Elizabeth did not hesitate to match his intensity. He moaned as he grasped her hips, and pulled her closer to him. His hands were begging to touch every inch of her as they moved to her waist to untie her dressing gown. They then travelled up her torso to her shoulders, where he pushed the garment to the floor.

He broke the kiss and drew back from her body as he viewed the nightgown she had been so nervous to show him. It was easy to understand how, in her innocence, she would be hesitant to wear the gown, yet he had no complaints.

"You are stunning, Elizabeth," he whispered reverently. He ran his hands down her sides to draw her closer. Returning to her lips, he brushed them with his before grazing them down her neck as he untied the ribbons on the front of her gown. When his lips reached her shoulders, he pushed the slender straps from them, revealing her body to his eyes. His breath caught in his throat. "So lovely," he whispered. He ran the back of his hand down her breast to her hip where he wrapped his arm around to caress her bottom.

He began kissing her as he walked her backwards. When the back of her legs touched the bed, she pulled from him and slid on to the sheets, her eyes never leaving his face. Removing his shirt, he lay on his side next to her, gently running his hand from her shoulder to her hip, and felt her shiver as she turned on her side to face him. He spent a few moments just touching her, trying to cool his ardour, lest everything be over entirely too soon.

"Are you afraid?"

She smiled, and gently pressed her lips against his. "Not of you . . . only of what I do not know."

He nodded, and brought his hand up to cup her breast, watching her eyes close and her breathing change. He kissed her cheek as he whispered in her ear, "I believe it is supposed to hurt some, but I promise . . . " Elizabeth pulled back from him, and placed her finger over his lips to prevent him from finishing.

"I trust you," she confided softly, as she looked into his eyes.

Leaning forward, he began brushing her lips with his, pushing her back into the pillows as he deepened the kiss. The feel of her breasts against his chest produced a current that ran through his body; he began to throb with need.

Elizabeth was tingling all over, and the feel of his muscular body against hers only caused the ache between her legs to intensify. He grazed his lips down her neck and along her body until he reached her breast, where he took the peak in his mouth and began to suckle. Initially, she froze, but soon the pleasure overrode the shock, and she gave in to the feelings he was creating. Her breathing quickened and she entwined one hand into his hair while she gripped the sheet with the other, surrendering to the sensation of her body melting into the bed. As she closed her eyes, she felt him release her breast, and trail his tongue across her chest where the other was waiting for him. He repeated the action to that breast, while his hand moved to brush his finger over the nipple he had just relinquished.

When he moved to trail his lips back up to her mouth, Elizabeth eagerly rose to meet him for a searing kiss. As it grew in intensity, she ran her hand from his neck down his torso, combing her fingers through the hair on his chest. She felt his hand roam down to her legs, where he lingeringly caressed her thighs before he parted her soft curls. She whimpered as his fingers stroked her core, and when he dipped his finger within her, she cried out softly as she arched her back. He kissed her neck as her breaths came in quick pants.

She felt as if she were aflame. She needed something, but did not know what; she only hoped it would come soon. Closing her eyes, she lost all sense of time. She felt him kiss his way down her body, dipping his tongue in her bellybutton along the way, until he parted her legs and kissed the inside of her thigh. When she opened her eyes, she saw him beginning to put his mouth on her, and she sat up quickly.

"No," she said softly, attempting to push him back from between her legs.

Lifting himself up, he brushed her hair back from her face and kissed her. "Do you want me to stop?"

She began to become self-conscious once more, as she not only was unsure how to ask, but was also embarrassed. "I thought . . . I thought you were going to kiss me down . . .," she tried to say hoping he would understand.

"You do not want me to kiss you there?"

Shaking her head, she leaned forward to wrap her arms around his shoulders and bury her face in his neck. Darcy wrapped his arms around her and began to rub her back soothingly. "I do not have to, but I thought you would like it," he said softly in her ear.

Pulling her head back, she studied his face as he placed his hand on her cheek, and began to softly trace her lips with his thumb.

"I want you to feel pleasure first," he confessed, as he looked into her eyes. "From what I understand, the first time there can be pain . . . and I wanted . . . to show you what it could be before I . . . I do not want to cause you pain, but . . . ," he
stammered before she stopped him with a soft kiss.

"It is just awkward and embarrassing," she blushed.

"If you do not like it, I will stop. I promise."

Elizabeth was still hesitant and unsure, but she remembered his promise that he would never take anything she was not willing to give. He would stop if she asked, so she decided to trust him, and nodded her assent. He kissed her as she leaned back down into the bed. His fingers returned to her centre, and she sensed the ache she had felt before return quickly. Eventually, he began kissing and licking his way down her body, returning to the point where she had stopped him. She closed her eyes and tried to relax as she felt him lick between her moist folds. When he found her pearl with his tongue, he began to suckle it, and she cried out as she arched her back off of the bed, writhing her hips against him as she tried to get closer, but feeling like she could not get close enough. The ache continued to grow until she began to soar, experiencing an explosion as her body reached its pinnacle. Crying out, she grasped the bed sheets and arched her back as she succumbed to the sensations that radiated throughout her body.

She was unsure of anything around her until he began kissing his way back up her body, once again claiming her mouth and stroking her tongue with his own. He lay atop her, and she instinctively parted her thighs to cradle him between her legs. Her eyes widened when she felt his bare hips against her, and realised he had shed his breeches.

"You are so lovely," he said, as he earnestly gazed into her eyes. "If you wish to stop, we do not have to continue."

His willingness to yield to her wishes made her feel more secure, and she raised her hand to his cheek. "I want to be your wife in truth; not just on paper."

He smiled and kissed her deeply. She noticed something hard rubbing between her legs as she wrapped her arms around his waist to pull him closer. As he began to enter her, she felt herself stretching to accommodate him, but when he broke through her barrier, she gasped at the sharp sting that accompanied it.

He stopped when he heard her gasp, waiting for her to relax before he moved again. She was so tight and warm that it was all he could do to prevent himself from spending right then and there. He spoke softly to her, as he told her how beautiful she was, and how good she felt while he caressed her hip and thigh. When he felt the tension leave her body, he began to slowly move in and out while he watched her face for any sign of discomfort. She smiled softly at him as she reached up to bring his head down for a kiss. The restraint Darcy had been attempting was rapidly deteriorating, and he began to unconsciously quicken the pace as he heard her moaning softly. Suddenly realising she was not yet close, he reached down between them, fingering her sensitive bundle of nerves until he heard her cry out in release. "Oh God, Elizabeth!" he moaned, as he felt her muscles contract and pulse around him. He lost all control and climaxed, calling out her name once more as he spent himself and collapsed on top of her.

When the fog lifted and he was aware of his surroundings, he worried his weight would be too much for her, but before he could move, her arms encircled his neck and she kissed his shoulder. Supporting some of his weight on his arms, he lifted up to look into her face, brushing his lips against her nose as he hovered above her. She smiled softly and brought her hand up to caress his face, which assured him she was well. When he began to lift himself further, she stopped him by embracing his body with her arms.

"Please do not go yet," she said shyly, enjoying the intimacy of the moment, as well as the feel of his body against hers.

"I am too heavy, Elizabeth."

"You are not," she assured him softly.

He nodded, but maintaining some of his weight on his forearms, leaned down to softly press his lips to hers. They lay together for some time before he rose, and walked naked to his dressing room. Covering herself with the bedclothes, she looked up just in time to see his backside as he strode through the door. She had seen statues of men, but she felt what little she had seen of her husband's body was decidedly more attractive, the thought of which made her face feel warm. He returned after a few moments in his dressing gown, and she rolled to her side as he approached the bed holding a damp towel in his hand.

"What makes you smile so?" he asked with a grin.

Although she blushed at being caught thinking about his body, she did not wish to hide anything from him.

"You," she replied, biting her bottom lip, not intending to reveal everything.

Beaming at her response, he sat on the side of the bed and pulled the bedclothes down from her body.

"What are you doing?"

"I intend to clean you," he replied, as if it were a normal, everyday occurrence.

Immediately she sat up in bed and put a hand to his chest. "Will, it is unnecessary. I will do it."

Leaning forward, he softly kissed her. "I know it hurt you when I entered your body. I only wish to be certain you are well," he said tenderly. "Please?"

Unable to say no when he spoke to her so sweetly, she returned his kiss before she nodded softly, and lay back on the bed. The cloth was warm, and felt good as he gently tended to her before covering her with the bedclothes, and returning the towel to his dressing room. When he came back, he disrobed and climbed within the covers. He placed an arm around her to draw her over to where he lay, as she turned on her side so her back was curled into his chest. He held her close, kissed her shoulder and her hair, and wished her goodnight.

• Song of Solomon 6:2

Chapter 10

Tuesday 3 December 1811

The next morning at Longbourn, Thomas Bennet sat at his desk worrying about the predicament of his most wilful daughter. When he had returned yesterday without Elizabeth, Mrs. Bennet had descended into a flight of nerves, the likes of which even he had never seen. She quickly retired to her rooms, yet even from his study he could still hear her caterwauling. His wife's racket was compounded by Mary's sermonizing and Lydia and Kitty's incessant giggles and proclamations of what a good joke it all was—they were truly three of the silliest girls in all of England.

Mr. Collins, however, was a different matter. The normally obsequious man became angry at the insult to his person, and proclaimed himself free of any obligation to marry the "selfish little doxy," loudly explaining how he had been attempting to do them a service by marrying one of their daughters. Affronted by his cousin's tirade, Mr. Bennet vehemently returned the ridiculous man's insults, which continued for well on an hour before Mr. Collins turned and stormed from the room.

Charlotte Lucas, by some quirk of fate, happened to be calling when the entire spectacle unfolded and, never one to miss an opportunity, proceeded to invite Mr. Collins to spend the remainder of the day at Lucas Lodge; Mr. Collins happily accepted. Several hours later, a servant arrived from the Lucases' home to retrieve his belongings. The little toad had not even returned to properly take his leave; Mr. and Mrs. Bennet were in worse states than before.

Elizabeth's father was irate. In fact, internally he was seething. That wilful child would cause a scandal the likes of which had not been seen in the little community of Meryton for some time, and he had no idea how to prevent it. Miss Lucas, who was generally known to be a sensible girl, had no doubt overheard the arguments, as well as his wife's loud lamentations; although she would more than likely not repeat it, the same could not be said for their cousin. Mr. Collins himself must have told the Lucas family the situation for them to invite someone of such a limited acquaintance into their home. Lady Lucas and her youngest daughter Maria were proficient gossips. He had no doubt that all of Meryton would know of Elizabeth's infamous behaviour by nightfall.

The problem was that he had absolutely no idea how to handle the situation anymore. That headstrong girl should have been a son like she was supposed to have been! He had swallowed his bitter disappointment when she was born, and raised her as he would have raised his son; the time he had wasted educating her! Longbourn was being handed to her on a silver platter; Lord knows that idiot cousin of his did not have the common sense and intelligence to run an estate, and she was refusing it as if it were nothing!

He slammed his clenched fist down on his desk before he stood and walked to his decanter of port, pouring himself a generous glass before returning to his seat. It was too early for a drink, but he did not care. He was going to drown away the anger, and hopefully he would not have to think or hear about the situation until the morrow.

Elizabeth awoke to find herself nestled in a cocoon of warmth. Her new husband's arm was draped around her middle, his hand cupping her breast, and she had that same object pressing into her back. She chuckled to herself, remembering how shocked she had been that morning at the inn to find herself in that very same position. Listening to his steady breathing, she attempted to stretch without waking him, relieving the stiffness that had overtaken her since the previous night.

Suddenly there was a familiar sensation, and her eyes widened, as she understood what it meant. "No, no, no," she thought as she slowly moved his arm from its resting place, scooted across the bed and rose to find her dressing gown before running through the door that connected his chamber to hers.

Darcy did not sleep long after his wife left, waking to find her missing. Lifting himself to his elbow, he looked around the room to see if she was still there, and threw back the bedclothes as he got up to search for her. He donned his robe and strode briskly through the door to her chambers, where she was just emerging from her dressing room. Taking her in his arms, he placed a kiss to her forehead while Claire quickly curtsied, and exited back through the door to the dressing room, leaving them to themselves.

"I awoke and you were not there. I was worried"

Elizabeth pulled back from where he had been holding her head to his chest. "I needed to refresh myself."

"Do you require anything else? I thought we could go back to bed for a while."

She looked up into his face, and recognising that he did not mean for them just to cuddle, she blanched.

"I cannot," she said, avoiding his eyes.

"Oh," he mumbled shortly.

As her eyes returned to his face, she noticed the disappointed expression before his mask slipped into place. Suddenly understanding that he had misunderstood, she placed a hand on his cheek, as she blushed scarlet.

"My courses came this morning, and with everything that has happened in the last week, I was caught unawares."

"Oh," he said, feeling a bit ridiculous.

She chuckled at the look upon his face. "I take it I do not have to explain."

He pulled her back into the embrace and spoke softly in her ear, "No, I guess we should begin our day."

She smiled at how disappointed he sounded. "I am sorry if you had other plans for this morning."

"There is no reason to apologize," he said softly. He held her until she realised Claire was waiting for her, promising he would return to escort her to the dining room for breakfast, and left her to finish her toilette.

~ * ~

Darcy was clean-shaven, dressed and passing through his chamber to Elizabeth's when he noticed the necklace he had purchased for her birthday on a side table. Retrieving it, he knocked on the adjoining door, and hearing her call for him to enter, he opened the door and let himself inside. She was seated before her dressing table, where her maid had evidently just put the finishing touches on her hair as she smiled at him in the mirror.

Claire asked her new mistress if she required anything else, requested permission to change the bedding in the master's chambers (which Darcy granted), and removed herself to attend her duties.

Out of the corner of his eye, Darcy watched the maid leave; he was pleased with her performance thus far. When Mrs. Thomas had approached him with Claire's request to send out for some personal items the future Mrs. Darcy might require within the next few days, he had been impressed with her thoughtfulness and initiative to make his wife happy. Now her personal maid was taking on a job that was not her own in order to protect his wife's privacy; as far as he was concerned, her position in the household was solidified.

"Are you happy with your maid?" he asked, curious of Elizabeth's opinion.

She rose and turned from where she was seated. "Very," she affirmed. "She is extremely efficient, and although she has only been my abigail since last night, I do not know what I would have done without her."

He smiled, thinking he would need to commend Mrs. Thomas later for finding such a capable servant to care for his wife, and momentarily forgot he was holding a gift for her.

Elizabeth looked down to Darcy's hands. "What is this?"

Suddenly remembering the box in his possession, he held it out for her. "This is your birthday present," he said, smiling.

"Will, you are going to spoil me! I truly do not require so many gifts."

"But it gives me pleasure to do so, and I did not get to see your face when you opened my wedding present yesterday," he pouted, causing her to laugh.

"I was shocked," she said, still giggling at his pout. "I do not know when I will ever wear it again, but it is beautiful, thank you."

"You will have plenty of places to wear it, I assure you. I have family pieces which you will be able to wear as well," he stated, as he enjoyed the surprise on her face. "However, this is for everyday, and I dearly wish for you to have it."

Lifting her one eyebrow mischievously, she took the small box and untied the red ribbon. When she opened the box and saw the necklace it contained, she smiled brightly. "It is lovely. I do not believe I have ever seen a stone like this."

"It is an opal," he said, taking the box from her and removing the necklace. Placing it around her neck, he clasped it before kissing her shoulder, and viewing her in the mirror from where he was standing behind her. "The ancient Romans believed them to be good luck, while others believe them to be a token of purity. Regardless, it is not nearly as beautiful as you are."

"All this flattery, sir. I will not only be spoiled, but vain if you continue."

She turned to face him with a smile, and gave him a lingering kiss on the lips. Beaming, he took her hand, and kissed it softly before placing it on his arm and leading her down the stairs to the dining room.

~ * ~

Darcy's usual habit included reading the paper during his morning meal, but today—his first day as a married man—he decided to eschew his habit in order to give attention to his wife. He helped her with her seat, placing her directly next to him, since there was no one there to find it objectionable, before taking his own. Once the servant poured his usual coffee, he noticed she was drinking chocolate, which, in the past, the kitchen had only served when his sister was in residence.

"You may wish to inform Mrs. Thomas if you prefer chocolate to tea in the mornings," he suggested. "It is not often brought out unless Georgiana is in residence."

"I cannot imagine having it every morning," Elizabeth said with a smile. "My uncle sometimes would buy some for my aunt and me when I was staying with them, but it was something we drank but rarely."

He nodded, and fell silent once more as he observed everything she did, wishing to know all of her habits, a silly grin adorning his face.

"Are you going to stare at me all day?" She laughed, watching him redden as he looked down to his coffee.

Quickly reassessing his earlier decision, he helped himself to some food and opened his paper. Not really reading, he hunted down a particular item he thought might have been printed. Unbeknownst to Elizabeth, he had sent a wedding announcement to the paper yesterday, prior to their nuptials, actually, which had indeed been printed. Smiling, he folded the paper and turned it to show her the lines printed, which told the world she was his.

Mr. Fitzwilliam Darcy Esq. of Pemberley, Derbyshire to Miss Elizabeth Bennet, daughter of Mr. Thomas Bennet Esq. of Longbourn, Hertfordshire.

Her eyes became wide. "You did not tell me you were placing a wedding announcement," she said. "My father will know where I am."

Fortunately, he realised her worry had more to do with her

fear of her father's response to her actions and possible repercussions, than any shame of being married to him.

"He no longer has any claim to you, you know," he stated with a reassuring tone. "I would never let him take you." Clasping her hand where it lay by the paper, he kissed it before resting them both, still entwined, back on the table. "I also thought announcing our marriage would make your escape from Mr. Collins appear more an elopement. People might assume you had already accepted my proposal, but I had not yet been able to seek your father's consent, which would be why you refused him."

Elizabeth nodded while biting her bottom lip. "You are right, of course. It is preferable to the gossip that could arise from my disappearance; nevertheless, I would have appreciated knowing of this in advance."

"I apologize if I was officious. I only thought of quelling any gossip before it truly began."

"Do you truly believe it will be so terrible?"

"I would rather not speculate on what fodder society will decide to spread. We will manage things as they come, so I truly do not wish to worry over something we cannot control." Not wishing to discuss the unpleasantness of society, he attempted to redirect her to a different topic. "I was thinking that since we have over a week before we must return to Pemberley, we might indulge in a few excursions in town. Do you have anything in particular you wish to do in London before we depart?"

With Darcy's question, the conversation turned to various diversions they could enjoy, attempting to narrow it down to a few possibilities. Elizabeth expressed a desire to see her Uncle and Aunt Gardiner. Truthfully, Darcy was wary of meeting them, since they were Mrs. Bennet's relations, but he was also concerned about fitting it in with his business and the other possibilities they were discussing, so he promised they would make an attempt before their departure. They had been discussing matters for some time when Elizabeth finally took her last two bites of muffin and daintily wiped her mouth with a napkin. Darcy scooted his chair back from the table and rose.

"If you are done with your breakfast, I thought I could take you on a tour of the house," Darcy offered, wanting just to spend time with her. She chuckled softly, and smiled at him as he helped her from her seat by the hand he had refused to relinquish.

Their stroll through the house took most of the morning, and all Elizabeth knew by the end of their trek was that she would have blushed profusely had anyone asked her about it. She had been extremely surprised when her husband pulled her into the first room, closed the door, pressed her against it, and kissed her soundly. Since she most definitely did not find the activity objectionable, it was repeated throughout many of the rooms they had viewed.

As they returned to the hall near the front door, smiling and laughing, Mrs. Thomas happened upon them and requested some time to discuss the meals for the upcoming week with Mrs. Darcy. Watching his wife lead their housekeeper toward the mistress's study he had just shown her a few moments ago, he smiled and turned to enter his office, where he took a seat at his desk. He stared at the large stack of paperwork that had been waiting for him, and sighed; he was not looking forward to taking care of the business that had been neglected since his stay in Meryton.

Deciding there was no time like the present, he valiantly attempted to immerse himself in the documents before him, but he was too distracted thinking about his lovely wife. He wanted to kiss her, to touch her. His eyes closed as he remembered how she had looked last night—skin like porcelain, contrasted by her dark hair and expressive green eyes. She was so trusting and, despite her innocence, passionate.

He had been wool-gathering for quite some time when a commotion in the hall caused him to start and rise from his seat. He had barely taken a step when the door to his study burst open to reveal a very red faced and obviously extremely angry Charles Bingley.

"How could you, Darcy!" he yelled, slamming the door

behind him.

Confused as to what could have made his normally cheerful friend so furious, he furrowed his brow. "Good day to you too, Bingley. Will you not sit down?" he asked, as he gestured toward a chair, only to see Bingley stride forward until he was standing directly before the desk.

"*You* told me the Bennets were unsuitable! All the while you were planning to marry Miss Elizabeth?" Taking a quick breath, he threw the paper down on the desk. "You cannot deny it! The announcement is in the paper! Did you think I would not notice? Or did you just think me a clodpate?"

"Charles, you need to calm down and let me explain," he responded calmly, not wishing to have all of the servants in the house privy to their conversation.

"CALM DOWN! You want ME to calm down! I trusted you when you said Jane Bennet did not care for me!" he shouted. "YOU said Jane Bennet was beneath ME, so how is HER SISTER AN APPROPRIATE CHOICE FOR YOU?"

Tired of receiving Bingley's ire without striking back, Darcy raised his voice, hoping Bingley would listen. "I never said Jane Bennet was beneath you," he said, defensively standing from his seat. "If you think back to every conversation we have had about the Bennets, it was *your sisters* who said the Bennet family was inappropriate. I admit that I never openly disagreed with Miss Bingley and Mrs. Hurst, but the only thing I am guilty of in this circumstance is professing my belief that Miss Bennet is indifferent to you!"

Bingley quieted trying to recount conversations regarding the Bennet family. He eventually pointed at Darcy and said in a less angry voice, "You never approved of the Bennet family, and you can not deny that!"

"I admit that I was never fond of the impropriety shown by Mrs. Bennet, the three youngest daughters, and even occasionally by Mr. Bennet, but I never found anything wanting in Miss Bennet or Elizabeth's behaviour!"

Both men jumped as the door to the study opened to reveal

118

Elizabeth, who stepped inside the room looking at both men anxiously. "Unless you would like the servants to know the entirety of your disagreement, I would suggest you temper your voices, *gentlemen*," she said, looking pointedly at both men.

Bingley at least had the sense to look remorseful. "Yes . . . of course, Mrs. Darcy . . . I whole-heartedly apologize," he responded sheepishly, when suddenly as if he had just remembered, Bingley started, "Please allow me to wish you joy on your marriage."

Elizabeth gave him a beatific smile, which made Darcy's heart swell as he momentarily forgot his anger and beamed at his new wife with pride. "Thank you, Mr. Bingley . . . Perhaps you would care to take a seat, and I can ask a servant to bring you some coffee or tea."

"I think coffee would be perfect, Elizabeth."

"Of course," she replied, "please excuse me for a moment."

"Thank you, Mrs. Darcy," said Bingley, as he took a seat before Darcy's desk.

She opened the door, and after a few words with a servant outside, returned to the study, and sat down in a chair across from Bingley.

"I hope you will forgive me for interfering in something that is obviously between you and my husband, Mr. Bingley. But like the servants, I could not avoid hearing your accusations towards my husband, and I was hoping I could clarify some information for you."

Worried she would confess too much about the hasty arrangement of their marriage, Darcy tensed, praying it would not be mentioned before they could discuss more definitively what they would tell others when they asked.

"A week ago, I would have been extremely angry with my husband for accusing my sister, Jane of being mercenary." She glanced at her husband before returning her eyes to his friend. "However, I learned the day after the ball at

Netherfield, that she does not return your feelings . . . I am so very sorry, Mr. Bingley."

"Miss Eliz . . . I mean, Mrs. Darcy, may I ask how you learned this information?" his friend asked, dejected.

"I would rather not discuss too many of the particulars, but I truly believed my sister had feelings for you. When I said as much the day after the Netherfield ball, she corrected my assumption. She confessed that she would have agreed to a proposal from you simply to secure her future and to make my mother happy."

As Elizabeth made the disclosure, Darcy observed Bingley, whose countenance had transformed until he looked positively heartbroken. That Bingley had harboured some hope that Jane Bennet did have some affection for him was exceedingly clear; her sister had clearly destroyed that hope. Bingley opened and closed his mouth several times, as if he wanted to say something, but in the end decided to remain silent until Elizabeth had completed her tale.

When she had revealed the truth of Jane's heart, Elizabeth began to rise, concerned that she had more than overstayed her welcome. "Forgive me, gentlemen, I have intruded long enough, but when I heard your complaints—I could not remain silent."

Standing up quickly, Bingley quickly halted her exit. "Mrs. Darcy," he started warily, "if you do not mind me asking, why would you tell me this about your own sister?"

"Mr. Bingley," Elizabeth began softly, "you seem to be very amiable and kind. I believe you truly care for my sister, which is why you should know her feelings if you are truly considering marriage to her." She smiled sadly. "I have seen the consequences of a marriage of unequal affections, and I would not wish that pain on either of you."

He nodded sadly. "Thank you for your honesty. Please forgive me for intruding on the two of you so soon after your marriage," he said contritely. "I should be leaving."

At his last statement, Darcy interjected, "Bingley, stay and have some coffee with us." Worried about his friend's state of mind, he wished to ensure he was well before he allowed him to leave. Bingley initially refused before Elizabeth, who shared her husband's concern, insisted, not taking no for an answer.

A maid soon delivered the coffee, and Elizabeth attempted once more to leave the gentlemen to their conversation. However, they compelled her to join them, vowing there was nothing they had to say to one another which she could not hear. Laughing, she agreed to remain for a short time, and took a seat after serving them.

Darcy leaned back in his seat and smiled. "I must ask, Bingley. When did you begin reading wedding announcements?"

Bingley laughed lightly. "Caroline found the announcement," he claimed. "You know I have never read the announcements or the gossip pages."

Elizabeth remembered Miss Bingley's incessant fawning whenever she was in company with Darcy. "I do hope she was not *too* disappointed," she said with a mischievous smirk.

Her husband almost spit out his coffee, and Bingley guffawed at her understatement of his sister's actions that morning. The couple had no idea of the storm Caroline Bingley had unleashed upon learning of their wedding. The self-absorbed woman had ranted and raved, retiring to her rooms, where she began screaming at the top of her lungs and breaking anything within reach, while calling the new Mrs. Darcy names most accomplished ladies would not dare to utter.

Unaware of the story her husband wanted to present to the public of their wedding, Elizabeth was uncomfortable with any questions Bingley might ask. She did not wish to contradict her husband, and trusted him to have a suitable explanation for their unforeseen and hasty wedding; she decided to make one more attempt to excuse herself.

"Well, gentlemen, Mrs. Thomas expressed a desire for me to review the household accounts, so if you will excuse me, I need to meet with her," she fibbed, hoping Darcy would not notice. She smiled softly in his direction before departing through the doors, and asking a footman to summon the housekeeper to her study. The least she could do was ask to review them, so it would not be an out and out lie.

~ * ~

Bingley stayed for another half hour before he finally insisted he should be leaving. After showing him to the door, Darcy went in search of his wife, eventually finding her in the mistress's study reviewing the accounts with Mrs. Thomas. The housekeeper hastily exited, and Elizabeth found herself alone with her husband.

She had been coming to locate her husband when she had heard the yelling coming from his study, and was unfortunate enough to overhear a good portion of the argument before she interrupted the melée. It hurt to listen to the description of her family, although she could not say that it was untrue. At least he had never found her inappropriate and had defended her as his wife, but she was concerned that one day he would get tired of defending his choice.

Noticing her hesitate as she stood, and despite her appearance while in the study with himself and Bingley, he had no idea what she had been able to hear. He dearly hoped she would not be angry with him for things he had said, or not said, in the past. When he approached her, he was relieved that she allowed him to wrap his arms around her.

"How much did you overhear?"

She sighed and stood on her tiptoes to put her arms around his neck, placing her head on his shoulder, "Enough."

"I expected to find you angry."

She took a deep breath and pulled back to look at him. "Hurt—yes, angry—not really. I cannot fault you for persuading your friend against Jane, due to your belief of her being indifferent. I would have probably done the same if she had been in a similar situation. I was also not surprised to find that you found my family inappropriate and beneath you; if you remember, I supposed as much when you proposed to me." Pausing to collect her thoughts, she looked into his remorseful eyes. "It does not mean I like to listen to what you used to say about me or my family."

"I wish I could protect you from the things Miss Bingley or Mrs. Hurst might say to you, but I fear they may employ anything I have said in the past in an attempt to drive a wedge between us," he confessed. "They are extremely spiteful. In fact, I would not put it past them to fabricate something."

She sighed. "It would not shock me. They were rather pointed in their disdain." Pausing, she put her forehead to his chest, dreading the question she did not want to ask. "Did you really say something so terrible?"

"Do you really want to know?" He closed his eyes, praying she would not continue.

"I would rather hear it from you, than have one of them catch me unawares in public," she said softly.

"I would rather not have this conversation," he mumbled.

"Please understand why I need to know the truth."

Darcy exhaled heavily. "I truly regret saying it, but it was just after the assembly. Miss Bingley was criticizing everyone, and I used to say things I thought were rather shocking because she would laugh and leave me alone for a while."

Elizabeth thought about the annoying woman, understanding why he might try anything to make her desist from her attentions. She truly did not want him to tell her; however, she did not want to have it thrown in her face later, where she might give Caroline Bingley the satisfaction of an emotional response.

He had paused for a moment, trying to compose his thoughts, and praying he did not alienate her by confessing something he dearly wished he had never so much as uttered. "I did not mean it," he said softly.

"Will . . . just say it."

He took a deep breath. "Miss Bingley was saying how surprised she was to find you a reputed local beauty," he said softly, as he closed his eyes, bracing himself for her reaction. "I said, 'She a beauty!—I should as soon call her mother a wit.'"

She stepped back from him, separating herself from his body. "Is that the worst?"

He opened his eyes, relieved there was no fury in her features. "Yes, in fact the remainder of my stay at Netherfield, she was constantly making scornful remarks about your fine eyes."

Elizabeth furrowed her brow. "I do not understand."

"I said one night while watching you that I was 'meditating on the very great pleasure which a pair of fine eyes in the face of a pretty woman can bestow'."

"I doubt Miss Bingley cared for your assessment."

"No, she did not. I believe it is why she became so pointed in her attacks against you; she saw you as a threat," he confessed. "After you left the study, Bingley confided that his sister became enraged when she read the announcement in the paper."

Raising her eyebrows, she clearly displayed her surprise. "She honestly believed you would offer for her?"

"I never gave her any encouragement," he said. "In fact, I told Bingley many times that I would never ask for her hand, no matter the circumstances." Worried with how distant she seemed, he reached out to take her hand. Flinching, she backed away, and walked to the window overlooking the garden below.

"Miss Bingley will not be the first to question my suitability as your wife. Are you sure . . . "

Darcy was upon her in a few strides. He turned her softly by

124

the shoulders to face him and noticed the tears, which were welling in her eyes. "No, Elizabeth, I have never wanted anyone but *you*. I do not care if you have fortune or connections, and I do not care if others do—I am in love with *you*."

The blood drained from his face as he became aware of the feelings he had just confessed. He had not meant to reveal his heart so quickly, but had intended to wait until he felt she was ready to acknowledge her own. Although they had been together such a short period of time, he was convinced she was either in love with him, or at the very least falling in love with him. When she looked at him, there was more than friendship in her eyes, and he guessed that she was hesitant to accept the emotions due to the brevity of their existence. If he had not believed she felt more, he would not have consummated their marriage.

"Why have you not told me before?" she asked incredulously.

Dropping into a chair, he raked his hand through his hair and looked at her with a guilty expression, "I did not want you to feel obligated."

Noticeably frustrated, she responded, "Please explain what you mean."

"I was concerned if I had told you, your decisions might be based more on my feelings than your own. I did not wish them to influence you."

"*You*, sir, are infuriating."

A small smile tugged at the corner of his lips. "Does this mean you forgive me?" he asked softly.

After observing his face for a moment, she stepped closer to where he was sitting. "I care for you very much, but I would not yet call it love," she confessed.

"I do not wish for you to profess feelings which are not your own."

Nodding, she regarded him warily. "I do forgive you. I

confess that it hurt to hear it, but I demanded you tell me. I doubt the idea of us one day being married had even occurred to you at the time."

He breathed a huge sigh of relief, rising from his seat to take her hand in his own. "As long as you forgive me."

"You can thank my Aunt and Uncle Gardiner," she confided. "They have an agreement never to go to bed angry, and as we are married, it seemed applicable to the situation."

She stiffened as he took her in his arms, but he kissed her gently on the temple anyway. Her tense posture was more than likely due to her wounded feelings, so he was determined to make it up to her in any way imaginable. However, just as he felt her hands come up to his sides, Mrs. Thomas knocked on the door to remind him of an appointment that afternoon with Madame duParc.

They quickly donned their outerwear, and exited the house in time to alight the carriage, which had just been brought around in preparation for their foray to Bond Street. It did not take long for them to arrive at the modiste's, where they were quickly ushered inside and into a private room. As it turned out, Miss Darcy was a very good customer, and Madame duParc knew having the new Mrs. Darcy as a customer could only help her business.

Elizabeth was noticeably surprised to learn that her husband had sent Claire to the fabric warehouses that morning to select material, and had had it hand delivered to Madame duParc's. Typically, when in London, she would have simply used the modiste at her Uncle Gardiner's establishment, which meant everything was in one location. She was also finding that the time her maid had spent working with Madame duParc, who was the young woman's aunt, was most certainly proving to be beneficial as all of the materials were exquisite, and obviously picked with Elizabeth's colouring in mind.

Before she had arrived, the fabric was examined and patterns had been narrowed down for each sample based on the measurements and description Claire had provided by note the previous day. In fact, Madame duParc was so organized, it did not require much time to choose the styles of dress and trim Elizabeth would like for each fabric before she was escorted to a dressing room to ensure the measurements that Claire had given her aunt were correct. Initially, Elizabeth balked at the number of dresses her husband was intending for her to purchase, but acquiesced to his insistence that not only would she require more as Mrs Darcy than she would as Elizabeth Bennet, but also that the Derbyshire winters would necessitate heavier clothing that she had not required in Hertfordshire.

While Elizabeth was busy with Madame duParc's assistant, Darcy assured everything was in order. He then escorted his wife to the milliners, drapers, and the furriers for everything she could possibly need. They even purchased fur-lined boots, and although Elizabeth objected, since she felt it was a tad bit ridiculous, a muff made of fur.

Once she was fully outfitted for her new role as Mrs. Darcy, her husband brought her to a nearby teashop for a respite. As they took their seats, however, a Mr. and Mrs. Chapman, who appeared to be acquaintances of her husband, approached them. She was immediately introduced, and after her curtsy, allowed him to take the lead in the conversation, which unfortunately was rather stilted. It was obvious to her that they were hunting for gossip; nevertheless she smiled pleasantly, his hand touching the small of her back. Elizabeth found their thinly veiled inquiries and insinuations tiresome. She was attempting to hold her tongue when it occurred to her that Mrs. Chapman looked like she had something with a particularly offensive odour under her nose and had to stifle a laugh. Eventually, the Chapmans decided they needed to finish their shopping, and departed, leaving the couple to their tea.

As they had their refreshments, they chatted about winter and the holidays at Pemberley. With Christmas less than a month away, Elizabeth wished to have some knowledge of what she would need to plan as the new mistress of the house. It was surprising to her to learn that they had never done much for the holidays, which she resolved to correct as soon as they travelled to Derbyshire.

Once they were ready to depart, her husband brought her to

his favourite bookshop, hoping to buy her a book as a treat; however, she declared she had plenty to occupy her in his enormous library, and had no need of anything new. He tried to persuade her to reconsider, but she was resolute. So after enquiring if the shop owner had procured any of the rare books he had requested, they returned home.

Upon their return, they prepared for dinner, after which they adjourned to their sitting room, where they sat together reading until they were ready to retire for the evening, once again spending the night in Darcy's bedchamber, where they lay in bed telling each other stories of their childhood until they both fell asleep.

Chapter 11

Elizabeth did not want to wake up the next morning; it still seemed so early and her bed was so nice and warm. She rolled to her back, and stretched, opening her eyes to see her husband staring down at her.

"Good morning," she said with a small smile.

Beaming, he leaned down to brush his lips against hers in a sweet kiss that she could not help but return. "Good morning, my wife."

She smiled even wider, marvelling at how much she had come to rely on and care for him in the short time they had truly been together. She hoped they would always be this way. Cuddling closer to his body, she sighed as he began to rub his hand in a large circle on her back while he kissed her temple and hair.

"Is there anything special you would care to do today?" he asked. He watched her bite her lip as she considered the question.

"I need to write a letter to my aunt and uncle this morning. I am certain they have seen the announcement in the papers, and I do not wish for them to worry. I should also write to Charlotte Lucas. We have known each other for as long as I can remember, and I would not wish to lose her friendship."

She thought for a few moments about the items the housekeeper had reviewed with her. "Mrs. Thomas also requested I set aside some time for her to begin discussing the changes to my chambers, although it seems a waste, since I do not use them," she finished with an impish grin.

Darcy grinned and brought her closer. "I hope you will always want to stay here with me, but the rooms are yours, even if all you do is dress in them. If you would like, you can remodel the sitting room as well. That room, as well as the master's chambers, were redecorated when I took the rooms after my father died. They are rather masculine."

Touched at his desire to please her, she kissed him lightly before resting her head on the pillow where she could observe his face while she was speaking. "Actually, I like the sitting room. It is very comfortable, and it reminds me of you," she said simply.

He smiled widely and leaned forward to return her kiss before indicating they should rise for the day. Pouting at the idea of leaving the warm bed, which made him chuckle, she eventually conceded, and emerged to quickly depart to the mistress's chambers.

Darcy went to his dressing room, where Evans had him shaved, dressed, and ready for the day with his usual efficiency. He doubted Elizabeth would be ready to break her fast so quickly, so he ventured to his study, meaning to write the letters he had intended yesterday before he became busy with other matters. A letter to Mrs. Reynolds, the Pemberley housekeeper, was soon completed, informing her of the new Mrs. Darcy. He requested the mistress's suite be aired and thoroughly cleaned prior to their arrival late the next week. In addition, he did not want his sister bombarded by his aunt and uncle, so he also included instructions barring Lady Catherine and Lord Matlock from Pemberley, no matter the reason, unless he specified otherwise.

The second, a letter to Georgiana, was much more difficult. Since Ramsgate, she had been different than the quiet girl to which he was accustomed. Belligerent and moody, he had returned her to Pemberley, and placed her under the care of Mrs. Annesley, the widow of the former rector of the Kympton parish. He had hoped the older woman would be able to work a miracle, but his sister was resistant to the efforts of her companion. During his absence, he had written to Georgiana steadily, without receiving a single bit of correspondence in return, and so did not expect a response, regardless of her reaction. He filled his pen and began composing.

4 December, 1811
Darcy House, London

Dear Georgiana,

*I apologize for the delay in writing you this letter. I hope
you have not worried for my safety as I travelled from
Netherfield to London. The trip indeed became quite
eventful, as the weather wreaked havoc upon my plans.
However, I am safely in London, and have been exceedingly
busy upon my arrival.*

*You may remember my making mention of a young woman
in Hertfordshire by the name of Elizabeth Bennet. What you
may not have discerned from my letters was my growing
admiration for the young lady, which soon turned to love,
as well as my determination to have her as my wife. I am
overjoyed to say she accepted the offer of my hand, and we
were married two days ago, here at Darcy House.*

*We wish you had been here to be a witness to our nuptials,
but there were circumstances pertaining to her family,
which necessitated a hasty resolution to our engagement.*

*She is an exceptional lady, Georgiana, and it is my hope
that you will become friends. I know Elizabeth is eager to
meet you, and has asked me many questions about you. She
already has four sisters, and no doubt is happy to include
you in their number—she is truly a very kind person.*

*I am taking my new wife to the theatre Tuesday of next
week, and I am looking forward to enjoying the experience
with her. Due to our current plans, I have scheduled for us
to depart Thursday, putting our arrival at Pemberley on
Saturday evening, should nothing delay us.*

*I hope this letter finds you well, and we look forward to
seeing you next week.*

Yours affectionately,

Fitzwilliam

He had just closed the letter and sealed it, when Elizabeth,
who had been searching for him, entered his study.

"You were not in the dining room breaking your fast, so I
decided to conduct a search."

"What do you have planned for me?"

"Why, to force you to come and dine with me," she said teasingly.

Rising from his seat, he bowed slightly and looked up, smiling. "I believe, Elizabeth, that you shall never have to force me to do anything with you." Enjoying the blush his words created, he offered her his arm and led the way to the dining room. After seeing to it that his wife was seated, he took his own. They served themselves from the dishes on the table before he decided to bring up the explanation of their hasty marriage.

"I was thinking about what we should say when we are asked why we married so hastily," he began, unsure of her reaction to the conversation. He watched her furrow her brow as she looked up from her plate.

"You mentioned a plausible explanation previously. I think it would do nicely, as long as we added a few details."

As this was the reason he had found the most convincing, he nodded. "I confess, it was the story I planned to use, especially since I believe that due to my aunt, your possible engagement to Mr. Collins may be made public," he explained.

"Surely, you do not think she would . . . "

"Unfortunately, I most certainly do think she would, as well as possibly claim I was engaged to Anne. However, my father put a contingency in his will regarding my aunt's delusions—hopefully that will silence her, if not for any other reason than that she would not wish the contents to the fodder for gossip. It would not reflect well on her or her daughter."

Elizabeth was curious, but felt it was more prudent to conclude the matter at hand. "So, you asked me to marry you during the Netherfield ball and I accepted, but you had not yet been able to procure my father's consent," she began, pausing to see if he agreed with her thus far.

"Correct, therefore, when Mr. Collins applied for your hand, you did not feel in good conscience that you would be able to accept, and refused his proposal."

"My father attempted to force my hand, but we left and were married in London as soon as I turned one and twenty," she concluded.

"Precisely," he responded. "It will appear as though we eloped due to your father's misguided intentions, rather than you running away; and while it is still gossip, I believe the explanation renders it not quite so shocking. There have most assuredly been worse scandals amongst the ton, and I do not doubt this will be quickly forgotten," he finished, taking her hand in his in the hopes of reassuring her.

The servant returned to the room and they ceased their discussion, finishing their meal while speaking of more mundane topics, eventually rising to attend to their duties. Darcy had not managed to get any work done the previous day, and desperately needed to finish his business affairs. Once he had completed his work, he would have the rest of the time in London to devote to his wife, and he was eagerly anticipating it.

Meanwhile, Elizabeth adjourned to the mistress's study to write her letters. Mrs. Thomas found her not long after she had finished sealing the missive to the Gardiners, and they proceeded above stairs to discuss the renovations to her chambers, where her husband found her several hours later. She had finished with the housekeeper and had taken up a book to read when he entered, proposing a stroll in the park. Always happy to venture out for a walk, she bounced on her toes as she excitedly agreed. The weather was fine, and warmer than it had been since their arrival in town, so after ensuring she was properly attired, he whisked her out of the door.

They strolled through a rather empty Hyde Park until close to teatime, when they walked back to the house where Mrs. Thomas ushered them inside to warm before the fire. They were sipping their tea when Darcy learned his wife enjoyed chess. The revelation prompted a challenge that occupied them for the remainder of the day.

~ * ~

Jane Bennet was amused watching her Aunt Philips, out of breath and discomposed, practically run up the road to Longbourn as fast as her legs would carry her; a paper clutched in her hand.

"Oh, Jane, the story of your sister's unfortunate flight reached my ears yesterday afternoon. I had planned to come and commiserate with my dear sister today, when I happened across this announcement in London paper. I had to come and show her for myself."

Jane looked at her aunt, clearly confused with what one would have to do with the other, and hoping Elizabeth had not done something horribly stupid. "My mother has kept to her bed since we discovered my sister missing."

"Well, take me to her. I must tell her the news!"

Jane was thoroughly bewildered at what could have brought her aunt in such a mood; it was almost exuberant. The only explanation she could muster in regards to her behaviour was there must be some salacious piece of gossip she was impatient to impart to her sister. Mrs. Bennet and Mrs. Philips were the most notorious gossips in Meryton, but Jane doubted even the most juicy tale would rouse her mother from her self-imposed seclusion.

When they reached the top of the stairs, the older woman stepped around her niece and strode to the mistress's chamber, throwing open the door and entering unannounced.

"Sister, I have something I must tell you!" she cried.

Mrs. Bennet, who had been moaning since Mary had brought her tea an hour ago, immediately sprang up in her seat and began wailing and waving her handkerchief. "Oh, dear sister!" she wailed. "I told you that girl would be the death of me! I have such flutterings in my heart, and pains in my chest . . ."

"She is married!" Mrs. Philips finally yelled over her sister's

134

litany of complaints.

"What! No, sister! She ran away from being married to Mr. Collins! You must have misunderstood!" she proclaimed exasperatedly.

"Then why is it printed in the announcements of the London paper that Mr. Darcy wed Miss Elizabeth Bennet?"

Mrs. Bennet, now certain her sister was incorrect, snatched the paper away from her sister. "You must have been looking in the gossip column, Agatha. That girl would never marry that disagreeable man, even if he is rich."

Jane watched with wide eyes as her mother glanced along the paper until it was apparent she had reached the wedding announcements, due to the expression of shock that came over her face. Taking in the two women at once, she observed her aunt's smile, undeniably proud at being discovered correct, while Francine Bennet gasped and stared at the paper, gaping like a fish, attempting to process the unbelievable information in front of her, until the dam finally burst forth.

"Oh, my goodness!" she screeched. "Leave it to that girl to leave a perfectly suitable man only to marry the most disagreeable man of our acquaintance!"

"But, sister," Mrs. Philips said carefully, "he is rich—very rich."

At hearing her aunt's words, her mother became very quiet, as the meaning penetrated her frivolous mind. The room had been blessedly quiet for the period of time it took her mother to consider the repercussions of her second daughter's folly, but regrettably, her aunt's words had merit—at least as far as her mother was concerned.

"Sister," her mother said with awe, "you are right. Was it not spread around the assembly that he is worth ten thousand a year?"

The other woman nodded smugly, and Mrs. Bennet began screeching an entirely different tune. "Oh! We are saved! Ten thousand a year, and very likely more! Tis as good as a lord! With the rain, they could not have gone to Scotland, so they must have been married by special license!" her mother proclaimed, as if she had complete knowledge of the affair.

Elizabeth was married to Mr. Darcy! Jane could not believe it. Why flee one marriage to a man you found ridiculous only to marry a man you detested? It was too unbelievable to be correct.

"Mama, may I see that please," she asked carefully.

Her mother looked at her, for a moment forgetting her grandiose proclamations. "Of course, Jane, but be sure not to muss it. I will need it to show the entire neighbourhood our good fortune!"

Jane rolled her eyes as she took the paper from her mother, who began wailing for Mrs. Hill to help her dress. The announcement indeed listed *"Mr. Fitzwilliam Darcy, Esq. of Pemberley, Derbyshire to Miss Elizabeth Bennet, daughter of Mr. Thomas Bennet, Esq. Longbourn, Hertfordshire."*

Quietly slipping from the room, she made her way to her father's study, fearful of his reaction to the inconceivable news. She knocked on the door, and her father commanded her to enter.

"I thought you should be aware that Aunt Philips has come bearing news," she began timidly.

He closed his eyes to the squalling above stairs and rubbed his temples. "I have heard," he groaned.

"Then you know what has Mama so excited?"

"Honestly, I cannot make out one word of that racket; only that she has something she wishes to spread all over Meryton."

Jane, hoping to break the news as painlessly as possible, steeled herself before continuing. "Are you aware there is information regarding Lizzy in the third of December's edition of *The Times*?"

Mr. Bennet looked at her as if she belonged in Bedlam. "I read that edition of *The Times*, and there was no mention of her. Your aunt has truly given in to a delusion in this instance."

"Actually, it is not in the news portion of the paper, but the announcements—to be more accurate—the wedding announcements."

"What?" he yelled loudly. "Where?"

Placing the paper on the desk, she pointed to the lines which told of her sister's actions, and watched as her father's face changed from shock to complete and utter fury. "How dare she!" he yelled. "She makes me a laughing stock by marrying that man!"

Truly frightened by her father's unusual display of anger, she approached him, and placed her hand on his arm. "Papa, you must calm yourself."

"Calm myself! She refuses my authority as head of this household, absconding for almost a week with no word, only to turn up married to that rude, disagreeable, and condescending man!" he vented. "I will not calm myself!"

"You must be aware, Mama intends to go to Meryton to tell everyone our good fortune, or so she says."

Mr. Bennet dropped into his chair, seemingly exhausted by his own ire, placing his elbows on his desk as he looked down at the paper. He dropped his head to his hands in frustration. "Do not stop her," he said tiredly.

"Pardon me?"

"The announcement of a marriage is infinitely better than the other gossip which may arise as a result of your sister's actions. This *news* may minimize any repercussions to the rest of you."

"What will happen to Lizzy?"

"I wash my hands of her; she has made her bed, and now she

must lie in it," he said coldly. "You and the rest of the family are forbidden to have any contact with her. Is that clear?"

Unable to believe her ears, she nodded. "Yes, sir."

"Now return this paper to your mother and her sister. They will no doubt need it while gallivanting about Meryton."

As she turned and departed from her father's refuge, Jane wondered if Lizzy had sold her soul for her freedom from Mr. Collins; after all, she had always hated Mr. Darcy. What other reason could she possibly have to marry him? Why would Mr. Darcy, of all people, marry someone he had never shown any preference toward?

Jane could not make sense of it, not at all. She knew she was more beautiful, as well as more elegant. Lizzy roamed the woods, and was not refined enough to be the wife of someone of his income and status. She sighed as she made her way up the stairs, still attempting to understand why someone of Mr. Darcy's rank would marry her sister.

~ * ~

In a modest home in Cheapside, Edward Gardiner was exhausted. He had been shocked when his brother turned up unannounced at his door, frantically searching for Elizabeth, and angrily recounting his disagreement with his now least favourite daughter. His wife had become overwrought at the thought of all of the terrors and tragedies that could befall the young woman travelling alone and unprotected. Given the length of Elizabeth's absence from Longbourn, she had insisted her husband immediately search for their missing niece. Two days had passed, and he had not been able to locate any trace of her. It was as if she had vanished into thin air—until late this morning. He had finally returned home after searching throughout the night, when his wife presented him with the previous morning's paper, which boasted a marriage announcement regarding his niece and Mr. Fitzwilliam Darcy.

They did not know much about the man. Mrs. Gardiner had been raised in Lambton (a small town not five miles from Pemberley), but had only heard tales of the elder Mr. Darcy, who was said to be a good man to his tenants and the poor, although not much of a family man. His wife, upon reading the notice, had written letters to all of her remaining friends in Derbyshire, requesting information on the son.

Frustrated and tired, he had stalked off to his warehouse to reconcile his books, and ensure his business had not had problems during his absence. He hoped Elizabeth was well, but he was irritated that she had not contacted them. She could at least have let them know she was fine, and not in trouble.

As he sorted through the sales of the last few days, he found a receipt for fabric purchased by a Fitzwilliam Darcy of Grosvenor Street. It had been a rather extensive purchase, and when questioned, his employee remembered it had been a maid who had purchased the material for her mistress.

Pocketing the bill, he hurriedly took a hackney coach to the address indicated on the sheet of paper, and applied to the butler to see Mr. or Mrs. Darcy. Although he attempted to inform the butler of his relation to Mrs. Darcy, he was turned away after being informed the couple was not at home to visitors. He had attempted to appeal to the butler, but was again rebuffed; he could not simply barge into the house and demand the return of his niece (who was Mr. Darcy's wife, if the announcement was to be believed), so he left his calling card, deciding to try again on the morrow.

Mr. Gardiner returned home to his wife, informing her of his attempts to see Elizabeth, and subsequent failures, hoping to finally be able to sleep for the first time in days, when their maid brought them a letter. Noticing the return address as Darcy House, they ripped into the missive finding, to their relief, a letter from Elizabeth.

4 December, 1811
Darcy House, London

Dear Aunt Maddie and Uncle Edward,

I apologize whole-heartedly for not contacting you sooner. The last week has been quite the whirlwind, and this has honestly been the first opportunity I have had to write.

I am sure my father has come to your home assuming that I fled there when I ran from an engagement to Mr. Collins that he was attempting to force upon me. My cousin did indeed make me an offer of marriage, which I refused. It was at that time my father informed me that I would marry him or leave Longbourn. Deciding to depart was not a decision I took lightly, however, I could not marry that ridiculous man. Please do not fuss at me for being ungenerous, dearest aunt; you would say the same if you were to meet him.

As I am sure you have seen in the papers, I married Fitzwilliam Darcy on December 2. I know this seems sudden, but he is among the best of men, and although it is still unreal to me at times, I am quite certain of my decision.

I believe we are to depart to Pemberley next week, and I look forward to catching a glimpse of all the places you have described to me in the past, Aunt Maddie. I also hope to see you sometime before we leave London, as I wish to introduce you to my husband. However, if we are unable, I dearly miss you, and I hope you can forgive me for causing you so much worry.

Your beloved niece,

Lizzy

While the letter did much to relieve most of the anxiety they felt in regards to Elizabeth, Edward Gardiner and his wife were still deeply worried about her, but they allowed her words to ease them enough to get the rest they had sorely missed over the last two days. After all, they now at least knew where she was, and that she was more than likely safe, or so she claimed.

One thing they knew for certain; if a man forced Elizabeth Bennet to marry him, she would make him rue the day he ever set eyes on her. Little did they know, that due to Darcy's instructions that they were not receiving visitors, the Gardiners would continue to be turned away from Darcy house for the next several days. A card was left at that first visit, but neither Darcy nor Elizabeth asked if there were any callers, so the cards remained on a tray near the door where they were forgotten.

Chapter 12

For Darcy and Elizabeth, the next few days seemed to fly by swiftly. He managed to catch up on his business affairs, which made him ecstatic, since it freed him to spend with his lovely new wife. Elizabeth had not been idle either. While he had been busy in his study, she completed arrangements for the redecoration of the mistress's suite, began learning the management of Darcy House, and even found some time to practice the pianoforte.

On Sunday, they attended his church, forgoing Darcy's usual pew to sit near the back. They did so with the intention of leaving the minute the service was completed, in order to avoid being detained by people who wished to catch a glimpse of the new Mrs. Darcy.

Elizabeth had noticed some of the women staring in her direction during the service, as well as some of the condescending, sneering expressions of others. She could only assume they felt her beneath them, or that they wished for her position. One thought kept a smile on her face as she felt their gazes on her; he had chosen her. It was not money or connections that made him marry her, instead he had selected her due to her personality and intelligence, and most importantly because he loved her. Those musings helped her to not become intimidated by these so-called ladies of the ton. She felt a certain amount of satisfaction with herself for that.

Monday morning brought a myriad of tasks to be accomplished so that they were prepared to leave for Derbyshire later that week. Darcy needed to attend to some last minute business, as well as visit his solicitor's office in order to sign some personal papers. After he broke his fast, he kissed his wife's cheek and set out—unaware of the tempest brewing in another home, which would soon invade his own.

After Darcy left the house, Elizabeth met with Mrs. Thomas regarding household matters, then began practicing the pianoforte. She had not been playing long when she heard a commotion in the entrance hall. Rising from the bench, she proceeded toward the noise, until she was halted by the French doors flying open to reveal a very stern, ornately dressed woman, who was looking at her with something akin to pure unadulterated disgust. When the woman entered the room, Elizabeth noticed there were two men following her. One was noticeably of a similar station as the woman; the second was none other than Mr. Collins, who was bowing subserviently toward the woman as he sidled up next to her, and whose presence caused her to swiftly realise the identity of the intruders.

"*You* must be Miss Elizabeth Bennet," she declared imperiously.

Elizabeth raised her eyebrow at the woman's tone, determined not to let it fluster her. "I was Elizabeth Bennet, ma'am, but I have since married and now go by the name Mrs. Darcy."

"Miss Bennet, do you know who I am?"

"Since we have not been properly introduced, I can only assume you are Lady Catherine de Bourgh, and that this gentlemen is Lord Matlock. I am already acquainted with Mr. Collins. I am afraid my husband is not home at the moment; however, he is sure to return soon, if you would care to wait for him," Elizabeth offered.

"My nephew is *not* your husband. He was never at liberty to marry a nobody, such as yourself, as he is engaged to my daughter!"

Hearing the woman's voice begin to rise, Elizabeth was praying she could somehow manage the situation until her husband returned, or at the very least a servant came to her aid; surely they would not leave her to fend for herself.

"Mr. Darcy himself informed me he was neither by honour nor inclination confined to his cousin, therefore free to marry as he chose, and I am that choice. As far as I am aware, you have no say in the matter."

"My dear cousin," said Mr. Collins. "You have aspired to a position that far exceeds . . ."

"This is not to be borne!" pronounced Lady Catherine, pounding her walking stick on the floor for emphasis. Mr. Collins clapped his mouth shut and watched with wide eyes. "Obviously your arts and allurements have made him forget what he owes to himself and to all of his family! My daughter and my nephew are formed for each other. They are descended, on the maternal side, from the same noble line; and, on the father's, from respectable, honourable, and ancient—though untitled—families. Their fortune on both sides is splendid. They are destined for each other by the voice of every member of their respective houses; and what is to divide them? The upstart pretensions of a young woman without family, connections, or fortune. Is this to be endured! But it must not, shall not be. If you were sensible of your own good, you would not wish to quit the sphere in which you have been brought up."

With every vitriolic word that spewed from the woman's mouth, Elizabeth found that controlling her ire was going to be more difficult than she had originally imagined. She took a deep breath as she drew herself up as tall as she could manage. "By marrying your nephew, I do not consider myself as quitting that sphere. He is a gentleman; I am a gentleman's daughter; so far we are equal."

"Unfeeling, selfish girl! Do you not consider that a connection with you must disgrace him in the eyes of everybody?" interjected Lord Matlock, finally entering the fray.

Elizabeth was so busy trying to defend herself, that she was oblivious to the servants who were now beginning to filter into the room. Graves, the butler, had, upon being overpowered by the intruders, gone to find help, bringing as many footmen and stable hands as he could muster in so short a period of time. As all of the men slowly stationed themselves around the room to be of aid to their mistress should she need it, a small mouse of a woman came striding into the room as if she owned it.

"Is this she!" she screeched, as she drew near.

144

Lady Catherine immediately turned at the sound of her daughter's voice. "Anne, I told you to wait in the coach!"

"I most certainly will not! This is my home! Fitzwilliam is to marry me, not this little chit, and I will not stand by and let this little nothing usurp my place!"

Elizabeth would not have believed someone so frail looking could move so quickly, but before she could react, Anne de Bourgh strode towards Elizabeth and slapped her—hard. The motion prompted the servants to step forward and subdue the intruder, although they were not fast enough to prevent her hand from connecting with the mistress's face.

Fearful of the master's reaction to the assault on his wife, the remainder of the manservants surrounded Lady Catherine and Lord Matlock as well, preventing any further action against Mrs. Darcy. This manoeuvre began a barrage of demands and insults by the intruders toward their now captors, causing a mayhem of gigantic proportions.

Darcy's carriage was pulling up to the townhouse just in time for him to see his cousin, Anne, exit his aunt's coach, ascend the steps and stride through the front door. Extremely concerned as to what was brewing within, he quickly jumped from the equipage as it was coming to a stop, and bounded up and through the entry, attempting to intercept his cousin. However, as soon as he entered the door, he could hear the melée coming from the music room, and swiftly entered in time to see his wife receive a stinging slap in the face. Immediately rushing to Elizabeth's side, he took her in his arms, shielding her with his body, as his stable hands dragged his cousin away. When he was assured they had a firm hold of Anne, he gently checked his wife's face, which was already beginning to visibly redden and swell.

The intruders, who had suddenly noticed Darcy's presence, ceased to yell at the servants restraining them, but began to loudly insist on their release. Remarkably, Anne was the loudest, demanding her immediate freedom, and insisting she was the rightful mistress of the house.

"ENOUGH!" he boomed, causing his wife to jump within his arms. "John, you and Eli return Miss de Bourgh to her mother's carriage, and ensure she does not leave it!"

"Yes, sir!" they chorused.

"Graves, I need you and the rest of the men to escort Lady Catherine and Lord Matlock to my study, and remain with them until *I* am able to attend them." The butler nodded and swiftly led the way as the footmen forcefully escorted the protesting intruders to the master's study.

"Mr. Collins," began Darcy in a stern tone. "Is there a reason for your presence in my home?"

The parson bowed as much as he was able with servants holding each of his arms. "Mr. Darcy," he exclaimed, "I was asked to attend by my noble patroness, so that I might help show my wayward cousin the grievous act she has perpetrated against you and your most esteemed cousin. Obviously she has entrapped . . ."

"Thank you, Mr. Collins," Darcy interrupted, as he turned to address his men. "Remove him to Lady Catherine's carriage. He can wait with Miss de Bourgh."

"I cannot wait with Miss de Bourgh! It would not be proper!" Mr. Collins had such a look of shock that had Darcy been in a better mood, he would have found his expression humorous.

Exasperated, Darcy took a deep breath. "He may wait outside the carriage, but by no means is he to step foot in this house again."

"But I cannot leave Lady Catherine!"

"Mr. Collins! You will remove yourself from my home! If you do not, I will have my groomsmen forcibly remove you! Do I make myself clear?"

Mr. Collins looked to the men to either side of him and opened his mouth to speak.

"Remove him now!" ordered Darcy.

The Darcys watched Mr. Collins as he was forcibly escorted from the room. However, just before the exit, Mr. Collins tripped and landed flat on his face, prompting the servants to help him to his feet before they managed to close the door behind them.

"Are you well," Darcy asked softly, as he noticed the tears beginning to fall from Elizabeth's eyes.

"I was trying so hard to remain civil, hoping that I could prevent things from escalating until you arrived. Your cousin moved quicker than I had anticipated, and I did not have time to react," she hiccoughed.

"I should have been here!" he cried, closing his eyes and placing his forehead to hers.

"Fitzwilliam Darcy! Look at me!"

Surprised by the use of his name, he pulled back and looked at her as she held his face. "You could not have prevented this from happening. They would have insisted on having their say eventually. There is *nothing* for which you should feel guilty."

In his mind, he knew she was right, yet he still felt responsible. Her protection was not something he took lightly. She pulled his face down, and ever so softly brushed her lips against his before wrapping her arms around his chest, embracing him. He enveloped her in his arms and held her tightly to him as he attempted to forget the altercation awaiting him in his study. A knock at the door caused them to separate in order to bid the person to enter.

"Pardon me for interrupting, sir," Mrs. Thomas said, as she walked through the door. "Claire is waiting for Mrs. Darcy in her chambers with some ice for her cheek."

Looking down at his wife, he noticed that the cheek that Anne slapped had only become more inflamed. "You should go and let your maid tend to your face," he suggested. "I will be there as soon as I am able."

He could see that she was worried; nevertheless, she

hesitantly agreed before following the housekeeper out of the room and up the stairs. Darcy watched her until she was no longer in sight, then walked to his study. He paused with his hand on the knob of the door to take a deep breath in an attempt to calm not only his nerves, but also his outrage over their behaviour toward his wife. Straightening up to his fullest height, he opened the door to reveal the upheaval that was contained within the room. His aunt and uncle were furiously attempting to be released from the confines of the study, in order to attend their nephew, and set him straight as to where his loyalties lay, while Graves and the footmen were endeavouring to keep them there. Slamming the door, he watched as all of the parties involved startled, and the room fell quiet for all of a few seconds before his aunt began her tirade.

"Nephew! I have never been thus treated in my life!" she exclaimed, her face beet red with anger. "How dare you order your servants to assault us in this fashion!"

Lord Matlock, never one to be left out of an argument, stepped up beside his sister. "This is not to be borne! You will not betray your family by taking up with that . . . that . . . little *bunter*!" His uncle however, had no idea the torrent he would unleash with his words.

Darcy rounded from behind the desk and grasped his uncle by the lapels, propelling him roughly against the bookcase in a most threatening manner. "You will desist from speaking of my wife in such a vulgar manner, unless you wish to be called out!" he growled menacingly. "I am my own master, and I may marry as I choose—I have made my choice." After maintaining his stance for a few moments as Lord Matlock stared at him in silent shock, Darcy released his coat and backed away, continuing to glare at his uncle while the man attempted to regain his equilibrium.

"*You* were promised to my daughter, Fitzwilliam Darcy, and you will honour that promise!" Lady Catherine interjected, appalled by the spectacle before her.

Any patience Darcy had had, evaporated into the mist the moment his uncle insulted his wife. "There was never any promise of the sort!" he rebutted loudly before gesturing to the two intruders. "You and Lord Matlock have been spouting off your own fantasies for years, and I decided a long time ago to ignore both of your delusions."

"THEY ARE NOT DELUSIONS!" his aunt roared. "It was the dearest wish of your mother and myself that you wed Anne!"

"Nevertheless, there is no formal marriage agreement. I have never asked for Anne's hand, and my own father told me I was not beholden to my cousin! Whatever you have believed for all of these years has been a falsehood created in your own mind!"

"Everyone in society knows you are promised to my daughter!" she insisted. "You are honour bound to marry her!"

At this statement, Darcy laughed. "Your daughter's frail and sickly constitution is well known amongst the ton," he stated, more calmly than he felt. "No one will be surprised that I have made another choice. In fact, my father instructed me not to marry your daughter. He even included a stipulation in his will, that should I marry Anne, I would be disinherited and Pemberley would be put into a trust for the first male heir of Georgiana's line, provided he take the Darcy name."

He watched as his aunt's face turn a brilliant shade of purple, and she began to huff and puff.

"THAT CANNOT BE LEGAL!"

"Whether it is legal or not, it is a part of his will. You would have known this if you had taken the initiative to learn the contents when he died." Darcy leaned forward on his desk, glaring at his aunt. "I would never take the chance of losing my inheritance for your sickly daughter. Moreover, should you decide to pursue this matter legally, it will become common knowledge that my father would have preferred to disinherit me than accept your daughter as my wife. It will be abundantly clear that there was never any arrangement, and *you* will be the laughingstock of London." He watched his aunt desperately attempted to think of something else to rant at him about. He could only assume she recognized the futility of any further arguments since she snapped her mouth shut, and dropped into the nearest seat with a huff. Meanwhile his uncle, whose eyes had bulged upon learning the stipulations in George Darcy's will, had quickly envisioned another alternative.

"So, you will not marry Anne," he began dismissively, before his demeanour and tone changed indicating he would brook no opposition. "However, we *will* go to your godfather, the bishop, and we will see to it that this travesty of a marriage is annulled as soon as possible. Then, I will find you a wife with not only a fortune, but also connections to the House of Lords."

"I will do no such thing!" Darcy declared.

Lord Matlock turned red with anger, pounding his fist on the desk between them. "I AM THE HEAD OF THIS FAMILY, AND YOU *WILL* DO AS I SAY! A woman with no fortune or connections will not sully the Fitzwilliam and Darcy names! This is one scandal I am willing to endure for the sake of the family. You will annul this marriage, and I will find you a woman with the proper credentials for you to take as your wife!"

Trying desperately to control his temper, Darcy leaned over his desk, and gave his uncle a steely glare. "*You* are head of the Fitzwilliam family. *I* am a Darcy, therefore not under your thumb—*I am not your puppet*," he forced through clenched teeth. "The bishop married us, himself, Monday last, in this very house. My marriage will not be annulled, and I will not be marrying to forward your political aspirations."

The master of the house strode to the door, opening it widely. "I am finished with this conversation. Neither of you are welcome in my homes any longer. And do not bother attempting to contact Georgiana; I have already alerted my staff, and you will not be allowed near her," he stated without emotion before turning his attention to the servants still positioned about the room. "Please see to it that Lady Catherine and Lord Matlock are escorted to their carriage. Should either of them attempt to forcefully enter this home again, you are to notify the magistrate, and have them arrested for burglary."

150

"How dare you! You would never be able to enforce it," Lord Matlock cried irately.

"It matters not," Darcy informed them matter-of-factly. "The gossip sheets and all of society would learn of it, and *that* is something I know you would wish to avoid." Lord Matlock eyes bulged, and he protested as vehemently as his sister while the servants forcefully escorted them from the house.

Relieved to be done with his less than palatable relatives, Darcy proceeded above stairs, praying his wife's face would not bruise, thereby preventing them from attending the theatre as he had planned. Upon reaching her room, he knocked and, hearing her sweet voice bidding him enter, opened the door, and walked directly to where she was seated on a chaise by the fire.

Her cheek was vastly improved from when he had last seen it—thanks to Claire's timely intervention. The swelling and redness was greatly reduced, leaving only a very faint handprint where she had been struck. When the master entered the room, Claire curtsied, and promptly exited through the door to the dressing room, leaving them alone.

"Does your face still pain you?" He took a seat beside her, the concern in his voice echoed on his face.

"No, it is much better," she responded. "Did your aunt and uncle depart?"

"Yes . . . but not willingly, I assure you."

Elizabeth began to look very worried. "You do not think they will return, do you?"

Darcy sighed and took her hands in his. "Honestly, I am not sure what they will do. I believe my aunt has finally come to the realisation that I not only do not want to marry Anne, but also that I cannot marry her. Hopefully she will simply return to Kent." He did have worries of his aunt attempting to sabotage his wife socially, but he remained quiet on the subject. He did not wish to frighten her over a situation, which may never happen.

Sensing his hesitation, Elizabeth leaned in to catch his eye. "What of Lord Matlock?

"As he was removed from the house and escorted to the coach, he was furious, but I do not believe he will attempt anything which could cause gossip or harm him politically. His position within the House of Lords is extremely important to him. Any break in the family—should it come to light—would be scandal enough in his eyes."

She was quiet for a moment as she peered down where their hands were joined. Could they do something even worse? Circumstances such as these, had caused her concern when he had proposed. She had been worried that he might, in time, come to regret their marriage. He had reassured her he would not, but the worry began to resurface within her mind. As he removed his hands from hers, she startled and looked at him questioningly, feeling bereft at the loss of his touch before she realised he was lifting her to his lap in order to hold her closer. An insecurity had surfaced as a result of the day's events, and she found that she needed him to touch her in some manner, to reassure her that his affections were still as strong as they were prior to the disastrous morning. He held her close to him and rubbed her back as she buried her face into his neck, letting his warm embrace and the woodsy scent she had come to associate with him calm her.

"I love you, you know," he said softly in her ear. "They cannot alter my feelings for you."

Hearing him voice his feelings was like a balm to her heart. She had needed to hear the simplicity of those words, the reassurance that he did not place the blame with her. She had married him, despite the concerns over their reception by society and their prior misunderstandings, because she had believed it was the way it should be. If asked, she would not have been able to explain it, but that was the way she had felt, pure and simple. Despite those feelings, she had so far protected a small portion of her heart in the event he regretted his decision—the hurt would not be so overwhelming that way.

But with those last words—that seemed to tumble so effortlessly from his lips—that final barrier came crumbling

152

down, and she unknowingly surrendered the entirety of her heart and soul to him.

They spent close to an hour cuddled together on the chaise, sharing small kisses and talking as he caressed her back and arms, hoping to reassure her of his affections. Since he had no further business to attend, he had offered that perhaps they should spend the remainder of the day within their rooms. Darcy found her in agreement, and they made plans on how they would spend their time. They both rose from the chaise: Darcy rang for a servant and Elizabeth removed to her dressing room in order to dress more comfortably for the evening they had planned together.

The afternoon was spent in varying pursuits; from simply talking to playing chess on the set Darcy kept within his suite, to taking their meals at a small table in the sitting room. Little did they know at the time, but this evening would mark the beginning of many days being spent in such a manner – discovering new activities that they could share with one another.

Chapter 13

Darcy was beside himself with excitement for the entirety of the next day. After checking several different venues, he decided he wished to hear his wife laugh, so he chose Shakespeare's *Much Ado About Nothing*. Most of the gowns Elizabeth had ordered from Madame duParc had arrived that morning, which gave her the necessary attire. Now all that was required of him was to surprise her when it was time to depart for the performance.

He had attempted to make it seem as if nothing was different until after they had a small meal later in the afternoon, which was after the time that they usually took their tea. In the meantime, he had kept her occupied by playing chess, so she would not notice the lateness of the meal. The manoeuver had been a stroke of brilliance, and he gave himself full credit for managing to keep her in the dark.

As they rose from the table, she took his arm, and they ascended the stairs to their sitting room, where he put his arms around her waist and smiled.

"I have made plans for us tonight."

She smiled widely. "What are we doing?"

"It is a surprise." He returned her smile as her eyebrow lifted in response. "Claire knows exactly how you should dress, and do not bother asking her where we are going. She does not know either." He laughed when she pouted, and pushed her toward her chambers. He was enjoying himself entirely too much to spoil the surprise. He watched until she closed the door behind her and headed to his own to change.

Elizabeth was speechless. Whatever she had expected upon entering her room, it was most definitely not what had occurred. Claire brought out her nicest undergarments, and then a gown they had ordered from the modiste almost a week ago. Her husband had insisted she order the gown, so she would have an additional dress to wear with the pearl and emerald choker he had given her. She now knew that he

154

had had an ulterior motive.

When she was in her gown and her hair was styled, she stood before the mirror as she took in her reflection. The gown was exquisite, a white silk with a small border of green ivy embroidered around the neckline, as well as the hem, which was accented by the emerald in the necklace. She chuckled softly as she thought about what her mother's reaction to the gown would be; of course, she would object to the lack of lace, but fortunately her husband had a preference for simple but elegant, as did she. Taking one last look, she turned toward the door to find her husband.

~ * ~

Darcy had dressed, and was having a brandy in his study while he waited for Elizabeth to appear. Impatiently pacing the length of the room, he stopped to consult the time as he decided to check on his wife. After all, he had been waiting for this night for a week, and could not wait another minute.

He strode toward the stairs where he looked up to find her descending, and stood frozen to the spot in awe—she was beautiful. He had finally seemed to regather his wits before she had made it to the bottom of the stairs, where he offered her his hand for the last few steps.

"You look beautiful, Mrs. Darcy," he said softly, as she smiled brightly in response. He loved the way she blushed ever so slightly with his compliment, as well as how her entire face glowed when she smiled. Leaning down, he lightly kissed her knuckles before he turned her hand over to kiss her wrist. He could hear her inhale sharply as his lips touched the delicate skin.

"Thank you," she responded faintly.

As the servants came in with their outerwear, Claire hurried down the stairs. "Ma'am, you forgot your gloves."

Elizabeth thanked her maid, swiftly donning them, before Darcy helped her with her new cloak, the backs of his fingers brushing along her neckline as he laid it across her shoulders. Then, quickly putting on his own gloves and

155

overcoat, he offered her his arm and led her to the coach.

Slightly overwhelmed by how plush and grand the coach was compared to the carriage they had been using, she sat quietly while she waited for her husband to alight. When he took his seat and they began to move, she looked down to where his hand was resting on the seat, and placed her hand over his, causing him to turn it over and lace his fingers with hers. She looked up to find him staring at her with the same expression he had used in Meryton, only now she knew that it was not censure in his eyes.

He smiled, making her heart flutter, before he squeezed her hand gently. "I am glad I persuaded you to order this gown. I wanted a dress you could wear with the pearl and emerald necklace I gave you, and it seems to match perfectly. The green in the dress and the emerald highlight the green in your eyes, which as you know, I have long admired."

"So, you bought me this lovely dress for purely selfish reasons," she said, as she raised her right eyebrow.

Grinning even wider than before, he leaned in closer. "I confess that I did, but I am glad that you like it as well.

She chuckled softly, and stared out of the window to see if she recognized any of their surroundings. His fingers brushed along her cheek, and their eyes met once more. They both leaned in and brushed their lips together lightly as her hand came up to rest gently on his cheek. Elizabeth enjoyed the fluttering sensation of her heart, and the gooseflesh that arose on her body as she responded to his kiss, which ended much sooner than she would have liked. He covered her hand with his before he brought it down to kiss her gloved palm and place it over his heart.

They felt the coach slow as they pulled up to a large building that Elizabeth recognized as Covent Garden from a previous trip to the theatre with her aunt and uncle. When they came to a stop, the groomsmen came around and quickly opened the door. Darcy exited and held out his hand to help her disembark. She smiled glowingly at him as she took his arm, so he could lead her through the crowd and into the theatre where he handed off their outerwear to one of his footmen, who was to be attending them in their box.

As their servant preceded them to their seats, Darcy took her hand and placed it on his arm before covering it with his own; he steered them through the crowd milling around in the lobby. Elizabeth could not help but notice some people staring, and a few women pointing as they whispered behind their fans. But she did not let it bother her as they made their way to the stairs that led to the boxes.

~ * ~

There were many of society in the lobby who were surprised to see the reclusive Mr. Darcy at the theatre with his new wife so soon—none more so than Edward and Madeleine Gardiner. Standing to one side of the lobby, the Gardiners had watched their niece enter with her new husband. Unfortunately, they had happened upon Lord Grenville, an investor in Mr. Gardiner's business, and his wife just prior to the Darcys entrance, and were unable to make their way to the newlyweds.

"So, the elusive Mr. Darcy puts in an appearance with his new wife," chuckled Lord Grenville, amused at the manner in which everyone had gawked at the new couple.

"Oh! How I wish I had gotten a look at her," tittered Lady Grenville. "There are rumours all over town regarding her, none of them very good, mind you. After all, there was gossip for years that he was supposed to marry his cousin. I wager his aunt, Lady Catherine de Bourgh, and uncle, Lord Matlock, are not happy with him abruptly marrying this little unknown. Do you not agree, husband?"

Lord Grenville, who did not seem amused, had attempted to look anywhere but at his wife during her verbose commentary. He closed his eyes when she gave a shrill little giggle at the end. "I have never heard anything so ridiculous," he responded dryly. Lady Grenville, however, did not seem to notice her husband's rebuke as she returned her wide-eyed attention to the people in the room.

The Gardiners were unable to extricate themselves from their company until the bell had rung, when the Grenvilles made their way to their box and the Gardiners to their seats. They scanned the theatre as they took their places, and found Elizabeth quite near them in one of the boxes, which at least allowed them to observe the couple's interactions until the break.

~ * ~

Elizabeth was touched by the surprise trip to the theatre, especially since, despite his preference for Shakespeare's tragedies, he had chosen her preference, a comedy, instead. Seated, waiting for the play to begin, she glanced over where her husband sat next to her looking toward the stage, and thought about everything they had gone through to come to this point. Their courtship had been by no means traditional. However, as she watched him turn to look back at her, she realized with the quickening of her heart that she had fallen in love with him. She had no idea how it had happened, since they had argued more often than not in Meryton. After all, she had only truly gotten to know a small part of him in the last couple of weeks, but the brevity of their relationship had not stopped her heart from binding itself to his. Tears began to well in her eyes, and as his gaze met hers, she could see the concern appear on his face.

"Love, is there something wrong?"

She smiled as he placed his handkerchief in her palm. He took her other hand, bestowing a kiss to it as he held it in his own.

"There is nothing wrong." She dabbed her eyes and smiled up at him. "Everything is perfect."

Grinning broadly, he began rubbing his thumb across the back of her knuckles until he felt her relax and lean against his arm. He did not relinquish her hand when the play began, but continued to hold it for the entirety of the first half, relishing his ability to do so.

As the actors left the stage for the intermission, Darcy turned and kissed her palm as he peered back at her face. "Do you wish for anything during the break?"

She was content, so she entwined her fingers with his and shook her head. They had not been long in that attitude, when their footman interrupted to inform them there was a Mr. and Mrs. Edward Gardiner who wished to have an audience with Mrs. Darcy. Smiling excitedly, Elizabeth quickly agreed, and as she stood the door was opened to admit her aunt and uncle. She felt her husband place his hand in the small of her back, letting her know without words that he was there should she need his support or protection.

Her aunt crossed to her immediately to take her hands. "Lizzy, we have been so worried."

"Did you not receive my letter?"

Her uncle came up to take one of her hands. "We did receive your note, but it was not the same as seeing you safe with our own eyes."

"Elizabeth," Darcy interrupted. "Would you be so kind as to introduce me?"

"Oh, of course . . . forgive me. This is my uncle, Mr. Edward Gardiner, and his wife, Madeleine Gardiner. Aunt, Uncle, I would like to introduce you to my husband, Mr. Fitzwilliam Darcy."

The gentlemen both gave a short bow, while Mrs. Gardiner curtseyed.

"I hope you will forgive our intrusion," said her aunt. "We have been so very worried about Lizzy, since we heard she had gone missing from Longbourn. My husband has been to your home almost daily over the course of the past week, attempting to see her, but was told that you were not receiving visitors."

"My apologies, Mr. Gardiner." Darcy stated earnestly.

"When we noticed the two of you here tonight, we saw an opportunity to see our niece," said Mr. Gardiner bluntly. "I hope you do not mind."

"Of course not, if I had known of your attempts, we would have happily welcomed your call."

Elizabeth could tell that her uncle was upset, but did not want him blaming her husband for their lack of contact. "Uncle, it was not Will's fault. In fact, he asked me if I wished to invite you to the wedding, but I did not know if my father would be at your home searching for me. It also would have put you in an awkward position with him, so I felt it was more prudent to marry before he could attempt to stop it."

Watching as her aunt placed a hand on her husband's arm, she saw him visibly relax, and his face soften as he realised this was no place to air their grievances. "I apologize, Lizzy. Your letter helped—at least we knew where you were, but we still worried and needed to be sure everything was well."

While Elizabeth seemed appeased by this, Darcy recognized the olive branch for what it was, a reprieve, and knew that he would be thoroughly screened as soon as her uncle found the first opportunity. He found it unnerving, but he could not blame the man. If a stranger had absconded with Georgiana, he would no doubt behave in much the same manner.

"Mr. Gardiner, if you would like to stay and watch the remainder of the play with us, we would enjoy having you. I will warn you that we do intend to leave when the play is over, and will not remain for the later entertainment."

Observing the man's face, Darcy noticed his surprise at the invitation, but accepted graciously before they all took their seats as they waited for the next act. There was not much time for conversation before the next scene began, when they all turned to face the stage once more. He felt his wife's small hand take his, and he smiled as he took it between the two of his to keep for the remainder of the act.

As the play ended, Darcy stood and assisted Elizabeth while he turned to face Mr. and Mrs. Gardiner, who had also risen from their seats.

"You are welcome to remain here, if you wish," said Darcy graciously.

"Actually, we had not intended to stay for the later show either," replied Mr. Gardiner. "But, we thank you for the offer."

Darcy nodded, and Elizabeth wrapped her arm around his as she allowed him to lead her out of the box with her aunt and uncle directly behind them. When they had entered the lobby prior to the performance, she had noticed him stiffen slightly, but now he was absolutely rigid as they moved toward the lobby to make their exit. Knowing his aversion to crowds, she placed her other hand on top of his arm. He covered it with his own while she leaned in to whisper in his ear.

"They will not bite." His brow furrowed for a moment before he realised her meaning, chuckled and relaxed a little. They had just entered the crowded lobby, where a few people had heard his low, rich laugh, prompting them to look upon him with shock. Assuming his smile was something rarely witnessed in social situations, she smiled as his mask fell firmly back in place. Two couples, who were obviously attempting to get inside information on the new Mrs. Darcy, stopped them, but after an introduction, her husband politely begged to be excused as their coach was waiting for them, and he ushered her out of the door.

Their transportation was indeed waiting for them, and Elizabeth turned to tell her aunt and uncle goodbye. To own the truth, Darcy had been very impressed with the Gardiners, who could easily have been mistaken for people of fashion due to their manner and dress. The couple was the only part of his wife's former life that she had retained so far, and he felt obligated to maintain the connection for her benefit.

"Mr. and Mrs. Gardiner," he began cautiously. "If you have no other plans, we would be pleased to have you for dinner. I am afraid it is nothing extravagant, but you are more than welcome."

Mrs. Gardiner seemed to be the first to recover from her surprise. "Sir, we appreciate your offer, but we would not wish to intrude."

Elizabeth, who was extremely pleased with her husband's

invitation, proceeded to insist they accept. As they could hardly turn down their favourite niece, they accepted the invitation and agreed to follow the Darcys in their own carriage.

Upon their arrival at Darcy House, Mrs. Thomas easily arranged for the additional couple, and all were quickly seated in the dining room, where they enjoyed the meal as well as each other's company.

When dinner was concluded, the gentlemen agreed to have some brandy while the ladies had some time to catch up in the drawing room. Elizabeth rose from her seat to find her husband offering her his arm, which she took and hugged to her side.

The ladies were escorted to seats by the fire, and after Darcy kissed his wife's hand, were left to talk while the gentlemen proceeded to the study.

"I thought we would be more comfortable in here as opposed to the dining room," said Darcy, as they entered his study and he closed the door. Gesturing to a seat, he poured brandy for the two of them, and handed one to Mr. Gardiner. "I am truly sorry for your inability to see Elizabeth for the last week. I am afraid we have been quite preoccupied in our preparations to leave for Derbyshire, and neglected to ask if anyone had left their cards. We intended to call upon you before we departed. I assure you my intention was not to exclude you from her life, but to protect her from her father, as well as several members of my family, who I felt might be a problem."

Mr. Gardiner nodded and took a sip of his brandy. "I admit not being allowed to see Lizzy did bother me, but I also have serious concerns about this marriage and the manner in which it came about."

"I did not force her to marry me, if that is what you are implying," said Darcy, attempting not to become frustrated. "I assure you she made her own choice."

"I must admit, we did have concerns of that nature, but we also want to make sure she is happy and provided for. Lizzy

162

is special. We do not wish her to be hurt."

"Then we both have the same goal," Darcy replied, bending down to unlock one of his desk drawers. When he rose, he placed the settlement papers on the desk directly in front of his wife's uncle. "Although she had no guardian here when we were married, I have shown her and had her sign these settlement papers. Whether it is legal or not is irrelevant, I will honour it. I may increase some of the amounts as I change my will over the years, but I can swear to you that the numbers on that paper will never decrease."

Mr. Gardiner looked at his new nephew sceptically, picked up the papers and perused the contents. Once he had finished the last page, he peered up at Darcy over the top of the documents. "I am impressed," he said, as the papers rested in his lap. "Thank you, for putting my mind at ease. You understand, with the alienation of her father, it limits her possibilities should something happen to you—I am only looking out for her best interests."

Nodding, Darcy took back the papers, which were handed to him. "I understand, Mr. Gardiner. I would expect no less from someone my wife holds so dear." He paused and furrowed his brow as he looked at the documents in his hand. "Actually, as you are the closest thing she has to a father at the moment, your signature would give the document more legitimacy, if you are willing, that is."

For the first time that evening, Mr. Gardiner smiled at him. "I would be honoured."

Handing Elizabeth's uncle a pen, he watched as the settlement was signed, and after he allowed it to dry, placed it back within his desk before locking it. As he looked Mr. Gardiner in the eye, he took a sip of his brandy and leaned forward.

"I love Elizabeth. I will do everything in my power to protect her."

Mr. Gardiner smiled. "I am glad to hear it. Then we have something in common. I hope you will forgive me for being intrusive, but has she told you that she is in love with you yet?"

"She . . . has not used those words, but I know she cares for me . . . very much."

"Relax, son," chuckled Mr. Gardiner. "It is obvious to us, but she may not know her own heart yet. Be patient, I would venture a guess that you will hear those words before Christmas." Taking another sip of his brandy, he looked back to Darcy. "Most people call me Gardiner, or if you prefer, you may call me Uncle Edward, as Lizzy does."

"I think Gardiner will work for now," Darcy replied with a slight smile curling his lips. "Most people call me Darcy, which, truthfully, I do prefer over Fitzwilliam."

Laughing, Mr. Gardiner watched as his new nephew cringed saying his given name. "May I ask how many people call you Will?"

Darcy's face transformed and he smiled softly. "Only Elizabeth," he responded quietly.

After the gentlemen departed, Madeleine Gardiner turned to her niece and took her hands. "Lizzy, truly, are you well? He did not force you to marry him in some manner?"

"No, Aunt, he asked for my hand . . . it was my choice. I meant what I said in my letter, he is the best of men."

Her aunt smiled widely. "I am so relieved! We were so worried when your father came to the house, expecting to find you there, and related what had occurred at Longbourn."

"I am very sorry for worrying you. When we were delayed travelling to London by the rain, I did not feel I would be able to arrive in London before my father. I was afraid he would attempt to return me to Hertfordshire."

"It is understandable," she replied sympathetically. "I hope you know that your uncle and I both scolded your father for trying to force your hand. We would have helped you, had you come to us."

"I had hoped you would, but I did not wish to put you in the middle."

Visibly relieved after her niece's reassurances, Elizabeth watched as her aunt leaned back in her chair and observed her for a few moments.

"I once told you that I would have a talk with you before you married, although I do not believe it necessary any longer, based on the familiarity between you and your husband."

Elizabeth felt her face burn as her aunt chuckled softly.

"I wanted to make sure you did not have any questions, not embarrass you. You do not have to confide anything if you do not wish it."

Attempting to compose herself, she found it hard to think of any questions she wished to ask.

"Remember, I have heard your mother speak of these things, which is why I agreed to have this talk with you. He has not been unkind, has he?" Mrs. Gardiner asked, concerned about Elizabeth's disquiet.

"No! He has been very patient and attentive," said Elizabeth uncomfortably. "Mama always said it was unpleasant."

"You know better than to trust your mother. Do you find being with your husband unpleasant?" Elizabeth shook her head, and her aunt smiled. "You need to trust in your husband, my dear."

"I do trust him, or else I would have never . . ."

Smiling, her aunt nodded. "I believe he loves you."

"He has told me he does."

"Have you told him that you love him?"

Shaking her head, Elizabeth responded. "Everything has happened so quickly. I did not know for certain myself, until tonight."

"You must tell him, Lizzy."

She nodded as her aunt's hand came around to take hers.

"You and Mr. Darcy love each other, so your intimacy will be different from your mother's. Do not allow her experience to influence how your relationship should be with your husband."

"Thank you," responded Elizabeth.

"Now, will you tell me how all of this came about?"

Elizabeth proceeded to tell her aunt all about her last morning at Longbourn, and her subsequent flight, including their stay at the inn.

"The two of you are married, so I will not lecture you on the impropriety of your actions," her aunt responded. "You were lucky you were never discovered."

Elizabeth nodded, and related to her the "official" story of their wedding. Mrs. Gardiner, who obviously understood the necessity for such a lie, listened intently before she agreed it was indeed the best way to answer any questions that might arise regarding their hasty wedding.

Before long they were re-joined by the gentlemen, who had clearly come to a better understanding of one another, and enjoyed tea while they discussed primarily books and poetry. Darcy was pleasantly surprised to learn that Mrs. Gardiner hailed from Lambton, and after reminiscing about the town and its environs, he invited the couple to Pemberley whenever they wished, which gratified Elizabeth immensely.

The hour was late when the couple showed their guests to the door. Elizabeth was extremely pleased with how the evening had progressed. Her husband seemed to genuinely like her aunt and uncle, and his approval made Elizabeth very happy; she dearly hoped they would visit.

They made their way upstairs to their sitting room, where Elizabeth turned to her husband. "Thank you, for inviting my aunt and uncle for dinner."

"I truly like them. I hope they will take me up on my offer to visit Pemberley."

Beaming, she stepped forward, lifting herself up on her toes to softly brush her lips against his. As she felt him respond, she deepened the kiss, and with some trepidation touched his tongue with her own. Any worry she had dissolved when he moaned in response, and wrapped her in his arms to pull her against his body. She felt as though she was melting in to him; she pressed herself closer, that ache she had experienced before beginning to return. His hands pressed down her back, and cupped her bottom as he rubbed himself against her, which caused her ache to intensify.

Elizabeth grazed her hands down her husband's chest until she was able to unfasten the buttons of his topcoat and waistcoat, then slipped them inside to feel the warmth of his body through the fine lawn of his shirt. He released her, and she pushed his coats down his arms to fall to the floor. As they began to shed their clothes, Darcy started guiding her toward his bedroom. His cravat was the next article to be removed, as she ran her hands along his neck and up through his hair. He held her to him with one arm while his other hand cupped her breast, rubbing his thumb over her nipple. She moaned softly as he began kissing down her jaw to her shoulder to suck on the pulse point at the base of her neck.

Her heart pounded and her body ached with need. She ran her hands over his chest and stomach, reaching the bottom of his shirt where she began pulling it from his breeches. When she finally found the end, she feverishly worked her hands underneath to trace the muscles of his stomach and back.

Darcy had never been so aroused in his life. Her assertiveness was so unexpected after her timidity during their last encounter, that every moment of it was eliminating whatever restraint he had had, and he did not know how much longer he could take it before he began ripping the clothes from her body. Reaching around to her back, he stumbled as he began undoing the fastenings of her dress and petticoats, and they both laughed before he slid them from her shoulders to join his own clothes at their feet.

He brushed the hair back from her face with his hands as he looked into her eyes. He then removed her hairpins one by one while he watched her curly locks fall alluringly about her shoulders. The pins were placed on a side table before he reclaimed her mouth and unlaced her corset. He hastily discarded it as he brushed his lips along her cheek and grazed his teeth along her ear lobe. Hearing her sharp intake of breath, he placed soft kisses across her face until he reached her mouth, and brushed his lips against hers once more before steering her the remainder of the distance to his room.

He stopped when he reached the bed, where she found his mouth for another deep kiss. She stepped back completely from his body, and looking him directly in the eyes, slowly untied the ribbons at the front of her thin chemise before deliberately pulling it from her shoulders to pool at her feet. It was the most erotic vision he had ever seen; lips swollen, hair tousled, wearing nothing but her stockings, garters, and pearl necklace. Swiftly pulling his shirt over his head, he turned her so her back was facing him, and shifted her hair to the side to unfasten the necklace. He placed it on the bedside table before returning his attention to her neck. She arched in response, and he gently ran his tongue along her skin between kisses until he reached her ear, where he licked the lobe. He heard her breathing heavily as he kissed behind her ear, down her neck to her shoulders, when he brought his hands up to knead her breasts. Hearing her whimper softly in response, he turned her to face him, and pulled her close while she cupped his face in her hands to seek his eyes with her own.

"I love you," she said softly.

His heart soared with the three words he had so yearned to hear. He recognised her expression, and suddenly realised what must have made her so emotional tonight. He embraced her and softly brushed her lips with his own.

"I love you, too," he whispered against her lips as he crushed her body against his. Her declaration had been his undoing, and he ached to touch her and make her his own. It was different than before, the last barriers that lay between them had been breached, and he would finally possess all of her, as she had of him.

As they continued to kiss ardently Darcy felt his wife's small hands reach for the fastenings of his trousers. Staying them, he pulled back to remove his shoes and stockings before he allowed her to open the fall to discard the pants as well. He watched as she placed her hands back on his chest to run her fingers through the spattering of hair and down his sides to his hips. When she stepped back into his embrace, she began to trail kisses from his chest up to his neck, and he turned his head to reclaim her mouth when she finally reached his cheek. She was pressed as tightly to him as he could manage. Her breasts were crushed against his chest; her warm body was pressed against his arousal, yet he still needed to be closer.

Lifting her to the bed, he laid her back onto the pillow, and sat back on his heels to remove her slippers. He stroked her leg through the stocking, working his way up until he reached her garters. As he kissed her thigh above the ribbon, he removed it, and lifting her leg, slowly rolled down the stocking as he ran his lips down past her knee until he reached her foot. After he bestowed the same attention to the other, he lay on top of her, relishing the feeling of her supple body under his. Their lips met softly once more before he teased her mouth open and caressed her tongue with his own as he began drawing circles with his fingers on her breast, eventually teasing the nipple to a hard peak. He made a path with his lips and tongue down her neck and shoulders, until he took the tip of the other in his mouth. He suckled while continuing to manipulate its twin, causing her to arch her back off of the bed and moan. Once he had lavished enough attention on the one breast, he ran his tongue in between to the other, tracing circles around her nipple before suckling as he had the first, while his hand reached down to the curls between her legs. He parted her folds to find the bundle of nerves he was searching for, and slowly rubbed her core, kissing her as she began to whimper with need.

One finger dipped inside, and she cried out, clutching his shoulders as his lips returned to the base of her neck. He worked his finger back and forth as she raised her knees to cradle his body between her legs. He could feel how ready she was, and gently kissed her as he slowly entered her body.

"You are so beautiful . . . so beautiful," he said, as she felt him fill her completely.

Unlike the first time, there was no pain, and she immediately felt her body react to the feel of him inside her. When he began to move within her, she matched his rhythm, as she felt something begin to build from where they were joined. The sensation increased with every stroke he made, and instinctively, she wrapped her legs around his waist in an attempt to receive as much of him as possible.

"Will . . ." she cried softly.

"Oh God, Elizabeth, you feel so . . ." he moaned. He did not know how much longer he could hold out. She was so hot and tight, and the feeling of her engulfing him combined with the sounds she was making were about to send him over the edge. Just when he thought he could go no longer, she cried out loudly, the pulsing within her causing him to follow as his body exploded and he spent himself, collapsing on top of her.

He was unable to move for several minutes. Elizabeth brushed her lips against his cheek and he brought his lips to hers. He did not realise how affected she was until he lifted his face from the kiss. She took a shuddering breath, and he became alarmed to find her in tears.

"Elizabeth?"

Reaching up, she cradled his face in her hands as she shook her head. "I am well," she said softly. She knew he would require more of an explanation before he relaxed. "I am happy, that is all."

He looked at her sceptically. "Truly?"

"Truly," she repeated. She lifted her head to kiss him. It was simple yet passionate, and he returned it happily before he rolled them to their sides. He reached down to cover them with the bedclothes, taking great care to ensure she was warm.

"Love," he said as he stroked her face, "were your feelings the reason you were so emotional before the play tonight?"

He saw her nod. "It came upon me all of a sudden that I love you, and I was overwhelmed. Everything between us has progressed so rapidly that I do not believe I have been listening to my heart, and instead, I let my mind tell me it was too soon."

"I believe I behaved very much in the same manner. If you remember, I sent to my solicitor in London for the license and settlement papers while you were at Netherfield."

She raised her eyebrow. "I remember. You were very confident."

"You would have never refused me," he said conceitedly, with a mischievous smile on his face.

"Really?"

"Of course not, I am rich and well-connected. After all, who would turn down connections to the illustrious Lady Catherine de Bourgh and Lord Henry Fitzwilliam, Earl of Matlock."

Elizabeth began to laugh. He chuckled as well, and brushed her hair back from her face, softly kissing her forehead.

"I do not like to think about what your response would have been, if I had asked you then," he confided.

"It is unimportant," she said lightly. "Things are as they should be."

Chapter 14

The next morning, Darcy awoke before his wife, happier than he had ever been in his life. He had opened his eyes to find Elizabeth cuddled up to his side, her head on his shoulder, and his arm wrapped around her possessively. As memories from the night before came back to him, he sighed happily, and bestowed a kiss to the top of her head. The previous night had been wonderful. They had remained awake talking for several hours before making love once more, not falling asleep until the early hours of the morning.

He held her for a while, just because he could, before he carefully freed himself and rose from the bed. An idea formed, and he smiled as he decided how they would spend the day. Making his way to his dressing room, he began a mental checklist in his mind of things he needed to accomplish before his wife awoke.

Close to an hour later, he emerged, wearing his robe. Pulling back the curtain on the bed, he noticed Elizabeth had rolled to her back during his absence. Her arms were thrown around her head on the pillows, and, the sheet at her waist, the entirety of her upper body exposed to his greedy eyes.

He discarded his dressing gown and lay on the bed next to her as he attempted to decide where to touch first. He carefully placed his large hand on her stomach, and softly caressed up to her breast, circling one nipple before tracing his way to the other to repeat the action. He bent over and gently suckled her soft peak.

"Will," she breathed softly.

Elizabeth gradually opened her eyes to find the beaming figure of her husband looming over her chest. She smiled as she ran her fingers through his hair, and brought his face to her own, kissing him deeply. Her hands made their way down his back, where they came to rest at his sides as Darcy rolled her on top of him. They kissed and touched, until in her impatience she began rubbing herself against him.

"Put me inside of you," he moaned. Her eyes widened at his request.

"I . . . that is . . . I do not . . ."

Kissing her softly before she could finish, he patiently showed her and placed his hands on her hips to help her find a rhythm they both found pleasing. Darcy found that he dearly loved watching her above him, her long hair falling about their heads like a curtain, seeing her face slowly transform to bliss before she cried out in release and collapsing atop him. His had followed soon after, and he was rubbing her back as they both recovered, when he heard the door to his bedchamber open and a familiar male voice pervade the silence.

"Darcy! Good Lord man! You never sleep this late—are you ill?"

Elizabeth lifted her head to look at him; silently questioning whom it was as she shifted from on top of him.

"Go away, Richard!" He covered his wife with the bedclothes and donned his dressing gown.

"Get up, Darce! It is not as if you would have a woman in here, you monk!"

Darcy kissed his wife, tied his robe, and parted the curtains on the opposite side of the bed to prevent Elizabeth's exposure. He was extremely annoyed at Richard's intrusion into his private rooms, and the broad grin his cousin was wearing only served to increase his ire.

"Richard, what are you doing here?"

"Well, you are welcoming this morning," he laughed. "I was given leave for the day, so I thought I would visit my staid cousin, which is infinitely better than visiting my parents, as you well know. Imagine my surprise when I was informed you would not be down to break your fast, and I decided you must be ill to remain abed at this late hour."

"I am not ill, but I am not at liberty to entertain you today, cousin. You are welcome to return below stairs. Drink as much of my port as you wish, but I will not be joining you," he stated as he grabbed his cousin's shoulder and began pushing him toward the door. Darcy watched as Richard turned to look at him, obviously surprised by his expulsion, when his gaze was suddenly drawn to the sight of Elizabeth's stockings on the floor. He pulled his arm away to look back at the closed bed curtains.

"You do have a woman in here! My boring monk of a cousin has taken a mistress after all of this time. You do know that you are supposed to set her up in her own house, and not keep her in your own," he finished, laughing hysterically.

"I do not believe I have ever told you what an idiot you are, Richard," he declared. He reclaimed his cousin's arm and propelled him into the sitting room.

"Seriously though, you cannot keep her here when Georgiana returns to London. It would not be appropriate."

Darcy closed the door behind him and turned to his cousin. "I do not have a mistress, you half-wit; I have a wife."

Richard studied his cousin closely for a few moments, and burst into gales of laughter. "That is rich! You, who have never shown interest in any of the women of society, finally picked one to marry. I do not think so. Georgiana's children are more likely to inherit Pemberley than one of yours."

Darcy remained serious as he waited for his cousin to stop laughing. "I assure you; I am serious. We were married Monday last by my godfather, Bishop Stanton. If you would take the time to read the paper, you would have read the announcement published last week."

Richard stopped laughing. "Good God! You are in earnest! Who is she, and why did you marry so quickly?"

"Her name is Mrs. Elizabeth Darcy, formerly Miss Elizabeth Bennet."

"Wait a moment," Richard interrupted. "Is this the young lady you mentioned in your letters with all of the sisters and the ridiculous mother? I thought perhaps you were smitten, but I did not think you would marry her. From what you said, she is nowhere near suitable to be Mrs. Darcy."

"She is suitable. I am a gentleman; she is a gentleman's daughter; we are equal." He regarded his cousin in shock. Contrary to his current position, Richard had never been one to tout social standing or be critical of others. Darcy wondered why he was behaving in this fashion, and hoped to diffuse the situation in the event his wife decided to enter the room.

"And what of Georgiana?"

"What of Georgiana?" Darcy voiced loudly. "She is a child who attempted to run away with George Wickham, the steward's son, for God's sake! As if her opinion on whether my wife is suitable would hold any weight with me. She is most certainly not ready to be out in society, and by the time she is, any talk of the origins of my wife will have dissipated!" He took a deep breath, attempting to calm his anger towards his sister for her actions, and treatment of him as her brother and guardian.

"Do you know that she actually refuses to speak to me? I sent her countless letters while I was in Meryton, without ever knowing if she opened even one of them. I am merely her shopping fund these days," he declared as he grimaced. "Do you know I received another very sizeable bill from the modiste for her? She had not even worn half of the last order of gowns, which had been set aside to give away!"

"The new Mrs. Darcy could only be marrying you for your money as well," Richard interjected, happy his cousin was finally recognising Georgiana's selfish tendencies.

"Elizabeth does not have the expectations of most women of society. She, actually, was happy to take the dresses my sister was discarding, and her abigail is altering them to be more to her taste. I took *her* to the modiste, and she scolded me for buying too much material, insisting she did not need so many dresses. This from a woman who had four dresses to her name when I married her!" Darcy watched as his cousin's eyebrows lifted to his forehead.

"She sounds almost too good to be true."

Darcy relaxed and a small smile appeared on his face. "She is perfect."

"Fitzwilliam Darcy besotted. I never thought I would see the day. I can only hope she truly feels the same way about you."

"She finally told me last night," he confessed softly. Darcy noticed the sudden look of understanding that crossed his cousin's face.

"So, I interrupted your celebration, so to speak. Please give Mrs. Darcy my apologies for my behaviour, and I will leave you two alone, since I see you have yet to break your fast." Richard glanced to the table laden with their morning meal.

"As much as I would like to push you out the door, we do need to speak of Georgiana."

Richard closed his eyes and sighed. "Unfortunately, I agree with you."

Both men turned abruptly toward the door to the mistress's chamber as Elizabeth entered the room, dressed in a simple gown. Her husband stretched out his hand to her, and she stepped forward to take it, allowing him to draw her to his side.

"Mrs. Elizabeth Darcy, may I present my cousin, Colonel Richard Fitzwilliam."

Giving a small curtsy, she observed the colonel as he bowed. She swiftly concluded that while there were most certainly similarities between him and her husband, her husband was decidedly more handsome, although the colonel seemed to have a more open quality to his personality. She was interrupted in her study when her husband began speaking.

"We leave tomorrow for Pemberley, so if we are to discuss Georgiana, it must be now. Why do you not sit with us while we eat, and hopefully we can come to an agreement on what is to be done."

Darcy strode to the table and helped Elizabeth with her chair. He took a seat that he placed directly next to her, as the colonel smirked and brought over a chair from the corner of the room. Richard was only joining them for refreshment, since he had eaten earlier, so once their tea and coffee were poured, the colonel glanced to his new cousin.

"Pardon me for asking, but I assume Mrs. Darcy knows about Georgiana?"

"While I was in Hertfordshire, Wickham became a member of the militia regiment encamped there. Apparently, he has been spreading more of the same rumours there as he has wherever he finds a sympathetic ear." Darcy grimaced. "I found informing her to be a necessity, especially as I have no doubt of her discretion. Frankly, I am hoping her experience of being the second of five sisters may offer us some insight into how to deal with the situation." Watching his cousin's eyebrows lift once more, Darcy wondered if that was the only expression he would see on his cousin's face during the visit.

"I see . . . well, you were ranting about your sister's behaviour earlier, perhaps we should begin there."

"Something must be done about her, Richard, but I have no idea what that would be."

Puzzled, Elizabeth looked between the two men. "You said she was young and naïve, but you never indicated there were other problems."

Sighing, Darcy looked at his wife. "My father was just as dismissive of Georgiana as he was me. Mrs. Reynolds has said that his only interaction with her was to stop by the nursery upon his returns from London, remaining only long enough to gift her with a trinket of some sort. She never wanted for anything. Her nursemaids and governesses always ensured she had what she required materially, but since I did not return for holidays until Cambridge, I do not believe she has ever been close to anyone emotionally."

"I do not understand why he would ignore her, yet buy her gifts. It does not make sense."

"Honestly, I am not sure. I remember that he did not like it when I expressed emotion, and I rarely witnessed him show his feelings. Mrs. Reynolds claims guilt over my mother's death was his motivation for giving Georgiana what he did, but in my opinion, guilt would imply he had feelings for either my mother or my sister, which I do not think he possessed."

"Could he have possibly believed he was buying her affections?" She looked at him doubtfully.

"I attempted to discuss Georgiana with him while he was teaching me to run Pemberley, and he refused. He maintained that she had everything she could need or want, and that she was excelling at her studies. I was then scolded for questioning his duty to his family. He did not appreciate what he considered interference."

"Nevertheless, I find it hard to believe you would continue his negligence?" Elizabeth asked.

"Of course not. I attempted to spend time with Georgiana when I first came home for holiday from Cambridge. I brought her a gift, a trinket really, and I was amazed when she had expectations of more with each subsequent visit. It was then that I realised that the only time she saw my father was when he brought her a present, and those visits were extremely rare.

When he died, I spent a great deal of time with her, as did Richard, who is also her guardian, hoping to reverse the damage. She was forever asking for new dresses or bonnets, whether she needed them or not, but I never indulged her. Her nursemaids and governess informed me of when she required something, and other than holidays, I did not give in to her wants."

Looking between the two men, Elizabeth noticed Colonel Fitzwilliam nod in agreement.

"He really did the best he could, considering how Uncle George treated her," continued Richard. "When she became old enough for school, she seemed much improved, and Darcy enrolled her with the hope that being around other girls her age would be good for her. Only, in the three years she was in school, she became increasingly quiet, so much so that we became concerned."

Her husband enclosed her hand within his own. "That is when Richard and I removed her from school. We placed her in the care of Mrs. Younge, and I began giving her an allowance as opposed to the small amount of spending money she was given previously. She would periodically ask for more, but I told her she would have to learn how to manage what she was given. It was then that she began going to Bond Street, and having me billed for anything she wished to purchase. She favoured the modiste, always giving us the excuse that she had outgrown her wardrobe. She has claimed that twice since this summer. I censured her, hoping it would have an effect, yet it did not."

Elizabeth raised her eyebrows at the audacity of his sister. Not only to claim she had outgrown her gowns twice in almost five months, but also to go to the shops and have her brother charged when he had expressly told her she was required to remain within her allowance.

"By the time Darce brought her to London from Ramsgate, she had stopped talking. She would not speak to either of us. We hoped Mrs. Annesley, her newly hired companion, would be able to reach her, but Georgiana has not seemed inclined to confide in her, keeping herself only to her studies and the piano-forte."

"As soon as we returned to London," Darcy continued. "She went shopping, buying the dresses that Claire has altered for you over the last week. Fortunately, Mrs. Thomas quickly warned me of her intentions to continue her shopping spree, which prompted me to immediately remove us to Pemberley. I had to do something to curb her spending. She had already overspent her allowance strictly from the trip to the modiste, and ignored me when I attempted to speak to her on the subject. Her allowance was withdrawn, and I informed her that it would not be reinstated until she had repaid what she had overspent."

Elizabeth looked at her husband, clearly puzzled. "But, does she not shop when she is away from London?"

"She has spent too much time with my aunt, Lady Matlock, and the Bingley sisters, who see London as the only place to shop. I did bring her with me to town, prior to my trip to Hertfordshire, with the instructions that she was not allowed to go shopping. I wanted to have her closer should there be a problem. I informed her there would be no forays into Bond Street, but she evidently ignored my instructions."

"Your husband wrote me a letter approximately one week before his intended departure from Netherfield," confided Richard. "Miss Bingley and Mrs. Hurst had been speaking of calling on Georgiana, and we had both previously agreed that we would no longer allow their influence. Therefore, he asked that I escort her to Derbyshire before they travelled to London. It was then that I learned that she will still not speak to me—she did not make one peep for the entirety of the three-day trip. By the way, Darcy, Mrs. Annesley felt horrible about Georgiana's last shopping trip, and had planned to pen you a letter when she reached Pemberley. I offered to inform you in her stead."

Elizabeth brushed her hand across her forehead as she thought. "Georgiana's spoiled, selfish nature reminds me of Lydia, with the exception that my sister is bold as brass and extremely vocal in her displeasure, as you well know," she said, gesturing to her husband. "In our situation, however, my mother encourages her while my father makes feeble attempts to control her, preferring to ignore the situation more than anything. As my parents never truly exerted any control over her, it was excessively difficult for Jane or me to temper her behaviour in public, although we did still try."

Darcy nodded, and she listened while her husband and his cousin discussed different ideas for trying to reach her new sister. She interjected her opinions into the conversation on occasion but in the end, there was no real plan to execute. They just had several new possible approaches and methods, but they all depended upon Darcy's conference with Mrs. Annesley upon their return to Pemberley.

After an hour, they felt as though they were going nowhere, and finally retired the topic for more pleasant subjects. By the time they had related the fictional and non-fictional accounts of their wedding to Richard, who was known by

Darcy to be trustworthy, Elizabeth had given her new cousin the privilege of addressing her less formally, and he had likewise offered the same. They were getting along so charmingly that the necessity to warn Richard of his father's visit was forgotten until he rose to depart.

"Before you go, I must warn you," said Darcy. "We have already had a visit from Lady Catherine and your father, which I am sure you can imagine, did not go well . . . at all."

Richard began laughing. "I am sure it did not, and I had already decided to avoid my father and Lady Catherine for quite some time. I do not desire to hear their complaints and demands, which is why I always come here when I receive a day of leave." Darcy raised his eyebrows. "Well, that and your cook," Richard continued, as his cousin's eyebrows lifted even further. "And your port. There, I have admitted it; are you happy?"

"I just wanted Elizabeth to know *exactly* why you come to visit us," Darcy responded, chuckling. Hearing his wife's tinkling laugh, the broad smile remained on his face as he scrutinized his cousin. "Will you come for Christmas this year?"

"I am certain I will still be avoiding my father at that time, so yes, I will most assuredly be there, thank you. However, I have taken up too much of your day already, and I know you have plans, so I will be going. I wish you joy, cousin; you as well, Lizzy."

After Richard bowed to the couple and exited the room, Darcy turned to his wife. "You, love, are wearing entirely too many clothes." He smiled rakishly as she blushed a brilliant shade of red. "The plans I have made for today require your dressing gown, and nothing else."

"Do you wish for me to go retrieve it?"

"No, I do not think we need it right now," he whispered, as he leaned in to kiss her softly. It did not take long before they returned to his bedchamber, not to emerge for the remainder of the day.

~ * ~

Elizabeth awoke very early the next morning to gentle kisses being placed across her face and neck.

"Love, it is time to wake up," her husband said softly. "We need to begin travelling at sunrise, so we can be sure to reach the inn by nightfall."

"Mmmmmm . . . I am awake." Stretching like a cat, she opened her eyes to see her husband's grinning visage looking down upon her.

He brushed his lips softly against hers. "Good morning."

Smiling, she returned his kiss before sitting up to retrieve her dressing gown. As she donned her robe, she watched her husband rise from the bed, and scooted across to stand when he held out his hand for her. She grimaced and clutched her lower stomach when she rose.

"Elizabeth, what is wrong?" said Darcy with worry in his voice.

"I believe I am just sore. I will be fine."

"Perhaps we should not travel today. We can wait a few days for you to feel better."

"It would be quite ridiculous to delay our trip because I am sore," she said, chuckling, unintentionally offending him.

"I am not being ridiculous to worry that jostling about in the coach may cause you further pain," he retorted gruffly.

"I am merely sore because we have been . . . engaging in activities to which I am not accustomed," she said soothingly, as she blushed. "And although I appreciate your concern, it is a trifling thing to cancel our travel over, in my opinion."

"Are you sure?" he asked, as he gathered her close to him.

"I am positive. Claire surely has a warm bath for me, and that has always helped when I was sore from a particularly long walk. It will probably help now as well, so . . . will you come to escort me to breakfast, or shall I meet you in the dining room?"

Darcy indicated he would come for her, and watched her as she left to go to her dressing room where Claire, indeed, had a bath waiting for her. Soaking did help relieve her aches, and she was dressed in her travelling clothes when her husband came for her. They quickly broke their fast before they managed to set off at daybreak.

Their trip was uneventful, and Elizabeth was very happy to be able to stretch her legs whenever they stopped to change horses. Since they had not had much sleep since their night at the theatre, they napped quite a bit, cuddled in each other's arms. During the time they were not sleeping, her husband, who upon discovering she could not read in a coach without becoming ill, read to her from his book.

She found the inns to be clean and very comfortable, but she was mostly amazed by the staff's treatment of them. The innkeepers all knew her husband, and they were more than happy to see him returning to their establishments, ensuring they had anything they wanted or needed. They never required much, since they arrived in time to dine in a private dining room before retiring, only to leave at daybreak again the next day.

The only part of the trip that was not to Elizabeth's satisfaction was her husband's hovering. In a way, it was endearing, but she was becoming increasingly frustrated with it. She did not feel the relatively small amount of discomfort she felt deserved the fuss he was making. Despite her annoyance, she considered his reaction the morning they left London, and decided a confining coach was not the ideal place for the argument she felt her admonishment could cause. She kept her frustration to herself, planning to discuss it with him when they were home.

~ * ~

They reached Pemberley late in the afternoon of their third day of travel. Darcy was anxious to show his wife her new home, and had asked his driver to stop at a particular point on the road, which was not only the first view available from the road, but also the best. He felt the coach slow, and he wrapped his arms around Elizabeth.

"What are you doing?" she laughed, as he covered her eyes.

"Would you like to see your new home?"

She crossed her arms over her chest. "I do not know how you expect me to see it, Mr. Darcy, with your hands covering my eyes?"

He chuckled softly at her impertinence, and brushed his lips along her neck. When he felt the coach come to a stop, he ensured they were in the correct location, and uncovered her eyes.

She gasped in awe as she took in everything. It was a stately home, built of stone, situated on the far end of a valley, backed with woody hills and a natural stream, which swelled to a lake at the front of the property. Feeling his arms wrap around her waist from behind, she was distracted from taking it all in.

"It is beautiful." She felt his lips that were resting on her shoulder curl into a smile. His walking stick hit the roof of the coach, and she jumped as she felt it lurch forward. They remained in that position for the remainder of the drive up to the house, until they separated in order to check their attire.

The groomsmen jumped down when the carriage pulled to a stop. They placed the step and opened the door as Elizabeth tied her bonnet. Watching her husband exit, she nervously straightened her clothes one last time before he offered her his hand to step down as well. Darcy gave her a kiss on the knuckles, and taking his arm, they walked up the stairs toward what awaited them inside the massive house.

Chapter 15

Elizabeth was speechless upon entering the grand foyer of the house. There was a large staircase directly in front of them, and various drawing rooms that she could see as she scanned her surroundings. Eventually she noticed an older woman, who had come to stand directly in front of them.

"Welcome home, sir," the woman said happily.

"Thank you, Mrs. Reynolds," he replied. "Mrs. Darcy, may I present Mrs. Martha Reynolds, Pemberley's most capable housekeeper; Mrs. Reynolds, I would like you to meet my wife, Elizabeth Darcy."

Elizabeth could see her husband's huge grin, and the blush on the housekeeper's face in response to his praise. Elizabeth dearly hoped to meet with the older woman's approval. She had been an important part of her husband's childhood; therefore it was important to her that they get along. Elizabeth was also her new mistress, so she wanted to be sure the new Mrs. Darcy did not make a bad impression.

"Welcome to Pemberley, Mrs. Darcy."

"Thank you," Elizabeth responded warmly. She noticed Claire and Evans coming up behind the housekeeper to retrieve their outerwear. Once she had handed her maid her gloves, she was surprised to see the servants who had lined up to greet the new mistress.

"Mrs. Darcy," the housekeeper said to gain her attention, "I am sure you and the master will be wanting baths?"

Realising she had yet to give instructions since their arrival, Elizabeth gave the woman a rather sheepish smile. "Yes, Mrs. Reynolds, I believe we would both like to have a bath?" The housekeeper smiled and replied, "Of course, ma'am." Mrs. Reynolds curtsied and exited to relay the message.

She glanced up to find Darcy smiling warmly as he offered

her his arm and led her to meet the assembled staff; only a portion were present, as the rest were busy readying the house, as well as dinner. She was amazed at her husband's knowledge of the servants, and listened intently while he introduced her to each of the upper household staff before he finally introduced her to his steward, Mr. Jacobs.

Her husband briefly inquired as to the location of his sister. Learning she had been aware of their imminent arrival and had decided to continue attending her studies, he led his wife up the stairs to their chambers.

Upon reaching their rooms, she startled as Darcy swooped her up into his arms, and carried her into their sitting room. He gave her a brief tour of their suite before he left her in the capable hands of Claire, and returned to his own chambers. Her travelling clothes were quickly removed, and she gratefully sank into the warm tub that was waiting for her. She had only been in the water long enough to wash her hair, when her maid excused herself. Elizabeth heard her husband's voice behind her, and turned abruptly due to the surprise of him being there. He stopped to stand beside the bath to remove his robe. She raised her eyebrow in a silent question as he chuckled, and pushed her forward to step in behind her. Stretching out his legs on either side of her, he pulled her back to his chest, and began to rub her shoulders.

"Mmmm . . . that feels good." She heard his deep chuckle reverberate in his chest. Feeling a soft kiss being placed at her temple, she kept her eyes closed as he began soaping her body, enjoying the feel of his hands on her skin. When he was done, she turned to face him. She soaped his body, helped him to wash his hair, and reclined against his chest once he was clean.

"Elizabeth?"

"Hmmmm?"

"Are you still sore?" he asked very quietly.

"No," she sighed.

Although he was still learning some of his wife's expressions

186

and tones, it was impossible to miss that she seemed irritated. "Is there something wrong?"

"I know you were worried the day we left London," she said, as she turned to face him. "But you took a relatively small amount of discomfort, and began treating me as if I were a child."

"You are exaggerating, Elizabeth. I did no such thing."

"Do you remember the argument we had at the first stop to change the horses?" She watched him furrow his brow. "You insisted that I should not be walking around . . . in my condition, I believe was how you put it. I had to exit from the other side of the coach, and walk away before I became really angry."

"I did not think walking would be beneficial."

"But it was, Will. I ache if I sit in a coach for a long period of time, and I find that getting out to stretch my legs during the stops helps me to feel better. It would have been infinitely worse if I had done what you wished. It was not only that instance. You continually were inquiring how I felt, and attempting to restrict what I could and could not do."

Darcy bristled. "Then why not tell me instead of running away, or keeping whatever has been bothering you to yourself!"

"I did not want to argue during the trip," she answered meekly. Seeing not only his ire, but also the hurt in his eyes, she suddenly understood how wrong she was to let things go on as they were.

"So you did not bother to tell me when I was frustrating you. Did I irritate you this much when you were ill before we married?"

"Once or twice, but I was very sick, and a part of me liked how you took care of me. I recall you were also much more subtle in your coercion as well." She smiled slightly in the hopes of diffusing some of his hurt and anger. He stared at her quietly for a few moments before he rose and stepped out of the tub. He donned his robe as he turned to face her with his mask firmly in place.

"I will see you at dinner."

"Will," she said, as she stood and climbed out of the tub to fetch her dressing gown. "I am sorry I did not tell you sooner, please do not walk away," she finished softly.

"If you will excuse me, I have some business to discuss with my steward."

Although she opened her mouth to speak, he turned and strode out of the door before she could utter the words, leaving her to regret her manner of handling the situation.

Elizabeth dressed, excused Claire and took a seat before the fire to drink her tea, since she found she no longer had an appetite. Once her hair was mostly dry, she paced around her room, attempting to sort out how to repair the rift with her husband. She knew he was hurt, and regretted not being more honest with her feelings. In the past, she had always been able to tell him anything, but had withheld the truth in this situation because she had not wanted to start an argument. As she gave it more thought, she came to the realisation that he must have felt as if she had been lying to him the last few days by pretending things were fine.

Turning, she noticed the door to the sitting room in front of her and walked through. She stopped for a few moments, and glanced around the room before she stepped up to her husband's bedchamber door. She raised her hand to gently knock upon the thick wood. When there was no answer, she tentatively placed her hand on the knob, and turned it slowly as she opened the door to peer inside. She surveyed his empty room as she unconsciously stepped further into his chambers until she was standing directly in the centre.

His bedchamber at Pemberley was very much like in London, only larger. Dark colours adorned the walls, with a huge bed to one side, close to the windows, and a small seating area closer to the entrance. The fire was still lit, and it gave the room a homey feel to it that she had noticed hers lacked, due to the former Mrs. Darcy's rather ornate tastes, which

Elizabeth could not appreciate.

She sat upon the bed for a while before lying down, smelling faint traces of his cologne in the pillows. Although she had only intended to remain for a short period of time, she was rather tired and lonely, so instead of rising to return to her chambers, she inadvertently fell asleep.

~ * ~

Darcy had just finished with his steward. Troubled by his argument with his wife, he had returned to his chambers to change his attire for dinner, when he found her curled into a ball, asleep on his bed. Breathing a large sigh, he crept over to the side of the bed to gingerly sit beside her. He knew she had been hurt and upset when he had left in the midst of their argument. He had also been hurt and angry, and it had made him afraid of saying something he would regret, so he had walked away. She had done something similar when they were traveling, which made his response to her disclosure as unjust as her actions or inactions, in this instance.

The argument had, in fact, been rather silly, and he did not want the gulf between them to remain any longer. Leaning over, he gently kissed her temple and her cheek. He felt her hands reach up to rest on his cheeks as she turned her face to see his.

"I am sorry," he said softly. "I was afraid of saying something I would regret, so I walked away."

She pulled his face down and began kissing him deeply, her tongue immediately seeking his to touch. As she kissed him, she sat up and pulled his body to face hers as she fumbled at the fastenings to his breeches.

"Love," he mumbled between kisses, "we should get dressed for dinner."

However, Elizabeth paid him no heed, and continued in her endeavours. Needless to say, they were late dressing for dinner, although Claire and Evans were efficient, and had them ready on time.

~ * ~

Her husband came to her room to escort her down for dinner, and Elizabeth ensured she was dressed in a deep green velvet gown which he had confided was his favourite. The look on his face upon entering the room was exactly what she had anticipated, and she smiled sweetly while he came to her.

"You are lovely," he said, as he stepped forward to take her hand and kiss it delicately, "but I think this necklace should remain here, as it does not suit this dress." Reaching up, he turned her shoulders and unclasped the opal necklace she had worn daily since he had given it to her. As he removed it from her neck, Claire entered from the dressing room and he held it out to her to put away. He took his wife's hand, led her to his chambers, and disappeared into his dressing room, only to reappear moments later with another necklace in his hand.

"I told you not to buy me any more gifts," she admonished. "I truly do not require so much."

Smiling, he turned her toward a gilded mirror hanging on one wall, and placed the unadorned square emerald pendant around her neck. "I promise, I did not buy it. This necklace, like your wedding ring, belonged to my grandmother Darcy, and I wish for you to have it."

She stared and reached up to touch the rather large emerald now adorning her neck, as her husband observed her reaction with interest. "I know I have said it before, but you truly are going to spoil me," she declared jokingly, as she turned and kissed him on the cheek. "Thank you."

Beaming, he offered her his arm to escort her to the entrance hall, where they found Georgiana waiting for them at the foot of the stairs. She was very unlike her brother in looks. Although they were both tall with blue eyes, where her brother was muscular and broad with dark brown curly hair, she had a willowy figure and fine blonde hair. She reminded Elizabeth very much of her sister, Jane.

Looking up to her husband, she noticed he was smiling at his

190

sister, a hopeful expression on his face. He obviously wished for her to be happy to see him, and Elizabeth's heart ached to see him so desperate for the girl's recognition. Darcy reached out and took Georgiana's hand when they reached the bottom of the stairs.

"Hello, Georgiana," he said tentatively. "I am sorry we did not come to see you sooner, but Mrs. Reynolds informed us you were busy working with Mrs. Annesley."

Elizabeth observed her new sister; while Georgiana stared at Darcy as if she were studying him. Georgiana did not observe him for long, before her face altered to a slight smirk. She quickly decided there was something not right in Georgiana's expression as the girl began addressing him.

"Hello, Fitzwilliam, it is good to have you home," she said in a very controlled sounding voice. "I hope you had a pleasant journey."

"We did, thank you, and we can discuss our trip later, since I would like to introduce you to your new sister." He beamed as he placed his hand on the small of his wife's back. "Mrs. Elizabeth Darcy, I would like you to meet my sister, Miss Georgiana Darcy."

"I am very pleased to meet you, Miss Darcy," said Elizabeth, as she curtseyed. She closely watched the girl's reaction to the introduction, and noticed how Georgiana's gaze travelled up and down, before it fell upon the emerald pendant briefly and returned to her face.

"As I am you," she said in a tone that did not seem quite as genuine as Elizabeth would have hoped.

At first glance, she suspected Georgiana of dissembling, and found herself wary of the girl very quickly. She was practiced, to be sure, however, she had seen the behaviour before in one form or another in her sisters, and at times, some of the ladies she had encountered in town with her aunt. They were normally the wives of her uncle's business partners. She always admired the way her Aunt Maddie would manage the conversation, extricating themselves as quickly as possible in order to finish their shopping. Nevertheless, Georgiana was now her sister, so she invited her to call her Lizzy, receiving a similar invitation in return.

Mrs. Reynolds soon called them to dinner, and Darcy offered both ladies an arm to escort them to the dining room. Elizabeth found dinner to be everything lovely: exquisite room, beautiful table, delicious meal, and her handsome husband sitting across from her. Despite how impressed she was with Pemberley, she could not be pleased with her new sister. The girl wore a sickeningly sweet expression throughout dinner, and answered any question posed to her without offering anything extra in her responses. At one point, Elizabeth realised she was staring at Georgiana as she attempted to decipher her motives for the obvious deception of her brother.

As hard as Elizabeth was trying to discover her new sister's motives, Georgiana was very aware of her scrutiny, and was attempting to ensure she maintained the illusion that she was happy with this new situation, although she was anything but pleased. How dare her brother marry this lowborn little chit! The woman was no better than George Wickham, who Fitzwilliam had adamantly argued was after her dowry and would not allow her to marry. Yet he gave his name to this woman? She had heard all about the Bennet family and Elizabeth's initial betrothal to her aunt's parson, Mr. Collins. She should have become Mrs. Collins, then she would not have been able to deceive her brother into this preposterous marriage, and things could have just gone back to the way they were. Nevertheless, what was done was done, and she wanted her brother to leave her alone. If that meant playing nice with him and his new wife, then so be it.

She looked over to where Fitzwilliam sat staring at Elizabeth with a moonstruck expression on his face, and suppressed the urge to roll her eyes. He was so gullible, it was no wonder this woman could deceive him so. After all, she had been doing it for years, she thought as she plastered her most convincing placid smile on her face. Oh well, why not let him make a fool of himself over the money-grubbing woman he married. It just might make things around Pemberley all the more entertaining.

~ * ~

192

Georgiana retired rather early, after playing a few pieces on the pianoforte, and Darcy and Elizabeth decided to head for their chambers not long after she left. Agreeing to meet in his room once they had both readied themselves for the night, they separated to their own dressing rooms.

When she was in her nightgown, with her hair brushed, Elizabeth entered her husband's room to find him sitting in a chair before the fire reading a book. He glanced up as she entered before he marked his place, and set it on the table next to him as he stood. She removed her dressing gown, and climbed between the sheets, smiling as she watched him remove his robe and nightshirt.

"Do you ever wear your nightshirts to bed?"

"Not for years," he replied, chuckling as he climbed into bed. "However, do not tell Evans. He would be rather scandalized to make that discovery."

"How would your valet not know?" she laughed.

"I have always kept the bed curtains drawn for when the maids come in to tend the fire, and when he has come to wake me in the past, I put the nightshirt back on before I open the curtains. To be honest, I believe he now knows, since he has begun asking me if I require one." He put out his arm, and she cuddled to his side as his smile widened.

"I cannot believe Georgiana is talking," he enthused. "She seems so improved since I last saw her—and her reception of you—I think she is happy to have a sister, and finally succeeding in putting the past behind her."

"Will . . ." she began, worried how he would take her suspicions. She lifted herself on her elbow and looked down at her husband, whose smile faded as he regarded her expression.

"What is it?"

"I . . . do not . . . " she began.

He put his hand up to her cheek and looked directly into her eyes. "I want the truth. No matter what it is."

Sighing, she decided to trust that her husband truly wished for her honest opinion as she turned her face to kiss his hand. "I do not think it is so simple." She watched him furrow his brow. "Please do not be angry when I say this, but I believe tonight was an act." She observed his reaction, truly worried she should not have said anything.

"Why?"

"When whining would not work, Lydia has resorted to misleading my mother and father. Basically, she uses deception, and eventually manages to manipulate one or both of them into doing or giving her what she desires. Looking back on Jane's manner with Mr. Bingley, I have come to realise that she acted much in the same way, by intimating feelings that were not there." She paused before she delivered the blow she hoped did not anger him. "I wonder if Georgiana is doing the same thing. Her happiness not only does not make sense to me, but her sentiments also sound false when she speaks. Think about it, Will, just a few days ago, Richard was telling us that she refused to converse with him for the entire journey here, and now she is happy and talking." Elizabeth watched as her husband rubbed his face with his free hand, finally running it back through his hair.

"I do not understand why though, Elizabeth. Why pretend everything is fine when it is not?" he asked sorrowfully.

"I wish I had an answer, but I just do not know. Tonight, I happened to catch her in a few unguarded moments, and she was not happy. In fact, I would not have even called it sad; she almost looked disdainful, in my opinion."

Darcy sighed. "I just wish I knew why she would play us false."

"Essentially, you have control over her life."

"I would never treat her ill!"

"No, that is not what I am implying. You can withhold things

194

from her and punish her should she behave inappropriately. She might feel that you would be angry if she refused to speak to me."

"I would have been furious."

"She could be seeking attention," she speculated. "Perhaps she wishes to return to London, and believes if she is agreeable that you will allow it."

"I do not care how well behaved she is; she will not return to town until her allowance repays her shopping expenses. The shops will no longer agree to bill me for her purchases either. I took care of that the day we went to Madame duParc's." He sighed as he ran his fingers up and down Elizabeth's arm.

"I sometimes wonder if I will ever understand her. I still cannot conceive of why she would elope with Wickham. How could she support her appetite for material objects married to a penniless man?"

"I do not think she gave it that much thought; she is young, after all. He was close to your father, and probably knew of the gifts he bestowed when he visited. I would be willing to wager that Wickham brought her trinkets of some sort whenever he came to call, and she enjoyed the attention. Regrettably, that is probably her perception of love and relationships, since it is what your father taught her."

Darcy closed his eyes and took a deep breath, embracing her so her head was on his chest. "I cannot think about this anymore. It is all so overwhelming."

"We do not have to talk at all, if you do not wish it," she replied mischievously.

He raised his face to hers, lightly brushing his lips against her own, and gradually deepened the kiss as he reached down to remove her nightgown. As he perused her naked body with his eyes, he decided he had married a very intelligent and beautiful woman, and the only words heard for the rest of the night were her whispers of love as she endeavoured to make him forget all about his sister.

Chapter 16

Life at Pemberley was an adjustment for everyone for several weeks. Once Darcy had given his wife a very extensive and thorough tour, Mrs. Reynolds began working with the new mistress on the daily duties of running such a large house. Elizabeth was happy to find that it was managed very similarly to Darcy House, and she developed a routine of spending an hour or two with the housekeeper, learning and attending to household matters after breaking her fast with her husband. She even began walking, weather permitting, around the paths of Pemberley, followed closely by not one, but two, footmen. The guard, as she called them, had been a point of contention between her husband and her, but she reluctantly gave in to his demands, since the weather was cold, and she did not know the park well.

With Christmas rapidly approaching, Elizabeth and Mrs. Reynolds dedicated a substantial amount of time to discussing decorations and activities for the holidays. According to Mrs. Reynolds, there had never been much of a holiday celebration in the great house, and Elizabeth felt that this was one of the first matters she needed to change. She wished for her first Christmas in her new home to be a joyous occasion. Gardeners were sent to find holly, mistletoe, and greenery to adorn the banisters and mantle pieces. A yule log was procured, and the maids were put to work cleaning and decorating until the house was completely ready. She even ensured Colonel Fitzwilliam's usual rooms were aired and cleaned prior to his arrival.

Despite the cold, Darcy would often ride to look over anything he felt required his attention before breaking his fast with his wife. Then, typically, after the morning meal, he spent the rest of the morning sequestered in his study with his steward as he caught up on the harvest and estate business, as well as the accounts he had missed while in Hertfordshire. After his discussion with Elizabeth, he had decided not to confront Georgiana about the bill from Madame duParc's, in an attempt to see if his sister was indeed seeking attention. His thought was that if he did not confront her, she would eventually search him out, only she never did. As a result, he became increasingly worried, since if she was not trying to garner attention, he was unsure of how to proceed.

Georgiana continued to maintain the busy schedule she adhered to while at Pemberley. She broke her fast daily with her brother and her new sister, but later opted to have her tea with Mrs. Annesley. She would join them for dinner, play a few pieces on the pianoforte when they adjourned to the music room, and retire for the evening. She often spent the bulk of the day attending her studies, and periodically venturing out to ride her horse a few days a week. Darcy took the time to interview Mrs. Annesley the day after their arrival, only she had nothing new to report, which did not help to calm his worries.

The newlyweds did not attend church until the second Sunday after their journey north. Truth be told, Elizabeth found the entire excursion rather diverting. Gossip of the new Mrs. Darcy had obviously been spread throughout the congregation, and all seemed to be attempting to catch a glimpse of her. She even noticed one or two parishioners staring at her during the service. When it was concluded, her husband introduced her to the vicar, a Mr. Matthews, who was very jovial, welcomed her heartily, and expressed his happiness at finally seeing Mr. Darcy married and settled. Her husband endeavoured to maintain his stoic mask, but Elizabeth, better able to read her husband's expressions, giggled, as she could see his mortification.

~ * ~

Richard arrived the day before Christmas Eve, amazed at the change in Pemberley. Accustomed to the usually restrained holidays of the past, he could not help but smile at the life the new Mrs. Darcy infused into the stately old house.

After dinner, the foursome retired to the drawing room; Georgiana played a few pieces before she announced her intention of retiring for the evening, and was wished goodnight. Once a maid had confirmed that she was within her chambers, Darcy excused the servants and closed the door.

197

"Something is not right, Darcy," Richard exclaimed. "She is completely different than when I escorted her here a few weeks ago. You cannot say that after all of this time, she has suddenly moved forward; it is too instantaneous."

Elizabeth regarded her husband with concern as he turned to stare out of the window into the blackness of the night before looking back at his cousin. "As much as it pains me, the more thought I have given to the matter, the more I am inclined to agree with you."

"You do?" he asked, surprised Darcy would agree so easily with his suspicions.

"Regrettably, yes, I do."

Furrowing his brow in thought for a moment, Richard ran his hand through his hair, which caused Elizabeth to smile at his similarity in mannerisms to her husband. "Well, Lizzy, you grew up with a house full of sisters. What do you suggest?"

She sighed. "Honestly, I do not know. I do not think returning her to London is the answer since, I believe, it is ultimately the goal of her behaviour. Mrs. Annesley says that she is truly studying a good bit everyday, and she does not seem to spend her time idly. I do not think she should be reprimanded or questioned for simply being as she is. I do feel that eventually her patience with her lack of spending money, along with the seclusion of Pemberley, should quickly erode, and then we will be able to, hopefully, correct her attitude."

Richard regarded her warily. "That is it? See what she does?"

"Unfortunately, while her solution may not be ideal, she is right," interjected Darcy, who moved to sit by his wife. "We cannot march up there and demand Georgiana open her heart and mind to us—she would never do it. It would only make her more wary of us than she already is, and I think, at some point, the facade she is maintaining will slip, giving us the opportunity to finally understand what is in her head."

"What if she has never been genuine with us?" queried

198

Richard.

Darcy shook his head, not wanting to believe that of his younger sister. "She has always been quiet and reserved—even unsocial could be used to describe her, but I do not believe she has been false with us for so long."

"You did not even come to know her until you came home from Cambridge," Elizabeth interjected. "Richard makes a valid point. She may have never been inclined to accept you."

"So, she pretended?" Darcy was extremely sceptical.

"For the most part, it allowed for her to do as she wished: be in London, shop, Ramsgate," speculated Richard. "I only wish for you to consider it."

"I will keep it in mind," replied Darcy. "I just do not see how it is possible for her to do this for years."

"Not necessarily years," Elizabeth observed. "From what you have said, she was not even remotely friendly, and refused to speak after Ramsgate. She may not have been hiding her resentment for your interference."

Her husband exhaled heavily. "I just do not know what to do with her anymore."

"We will all work through it together," said Elizabeth encouragingly. He looked over to see Richard nodding in agreement.

"Speaking of Georgiana," began Richard, "James Allen came to see me last week. Do you remember him?" Nodding, Darcy waited to see what if anything the man had to do with his sister.

"He recently became father's solicitor. Apparently, my father is having Allen research possible methods to have Georgiana's legal custody remanded to him."

"Why would my uncle trust Allen to do that? It was well known that you, Allen, and I were very good friends."

Richard furrowed his brow. "I have tried to puzzle that out for myself. My father never did pay close attention to my friends and acquaintances. Perhaps, he forgot. Nevertheless, Allen sought me out to warn us."

"Have you heard from your father since the last time I saw you?"

"He has sent a few messages since then, but I tend to throw them into the fire," responded Richard.

"You need to read the next one you receive, cousin. It may be important."

"I had already planned on it. Have you heard from either my father or Lady Catherine?"

"I have received two letters from Lady Catherine," Darcy informed him, "but I burned them both without reading them. I will ensure the next is not important before I relegate it to the fire."

"Well," declared Richard. "It was a long journey, and I would like to retire for the evening. Do not bother rising, I can find my own way."

Elizabeth smiled as she stood, tugging for her husband to rise as Richard closed the door behind him. "I think he has an excellent idea."

Darcy only nodded before she pulled him up the stairs to their chambers to retire for the evening as well.

Elizabeth was excited to awake and find the grounds of Pemberley covered in a thick layer of snow on Christmas Eve. Since walking seemed to be out of the question, she wrapped herself in a blanket, and lounged in a window seat for a while. She watched the white flakes fall from the sky, periodically looking toward her husband, who continued to sleep.

Her aunt and uncle were spending Christmas at Longbourn,

200

and she hoped to receive word soon after the holidays of how her family was faring. She sighed as she thought about how she missed them. Despite the betrayal and hurt that prompted her to flee her home, she could not simply turn off her feelings for her family. She loved them, and yet, she understood them for who they were. Her father had always been one to hold a grudge, and Elizabeth did not believe that he would ever reconcile himself to her disobedience, or her new marriage. As a result, she had not attempted to contact them, instead relying on her aunt and uncle to inform her of the situation, so she would know whether any attempts at reconciliation would even be possible.

She felt a warm arm snake around her middle, and leaned back into her husband as she breathed the comforting scent of his cologne that lingered from the previous day.

"That was a big sigh, Mrs. Darcy."

Smiling, she turned in his embrace, and rose to her knees in order to put her arms around his neck. "I was just thinking about Uncle Edward and Aunt Maddie's trip to Longbourn today."

"It is normal to miss your family, especially as it is your first holiday apart from them," he said, hugging her tighter to him. "In fact, it would be rather strange to me if you did not."

She pulled back from his shoulder and brushed her lips against his. "I love you."

Deepening the kiss, he easily lifted her from the window seat, and carried her back to bed, where all thoughts of Longbourn and the Bennet family were long forgotten.

~ * ~

The couple did not emerge from their rooms until later that afternoon, and although Richard did not rise early himself, he could not help but laugh that he had preceded them downstairs. His chortles and grins earned him a glare from Darcy, who did not appreciate the source of his cousin's amusement. Georgiana joined them soon after for some tea and light refreshments before they were loaded into a sleigh for the ride to the Christmas Eve services, that were trimmed down due to the continuing snow. It was wishful thinking that dinner would have been as brief as church that evening.

Once the last of the dishes had been cleared and the servants exited the room, the cousins exchanged glances. They knew they would have to act if they were to confront her before she retreated to her chambers.

"Georgiana," her brother began. "Richard and I have spent some time discussing matters lately, and we wished to have a word with you before you retire for the night."

Darcy watched as she regarded him warily, and he took a deep breath. "I received a bill from Madame duParc for some purchases you made before departing London—a rather sizeable bill."

"Brother," she interjected condescendingly. "I simply required some new dresses, as I had grown too tall for my old ones."

Angry at her tone, he bristled. "If you did not buy so many that you could not wear them all, I would have had no issue with your expenses; however, you had not worn over ten of the gowns you had laid out to discard. In fact, when I visited the modiste with Elizabeth for her to have some dresses made, I also inquired as to the size difference between your last two visits. Apparently, Madame duParc keeps records with dates and measurements. Did you know that? Do you wish to know what I discovered?" He paused to see if she would say anything at all, yet was not surprised by her lack of response. She even turned her head to the side as if she was staring at something outside of the window.

"The disparity between your last two orders was negligible. Your height had only changed by a half an inch, which Madame duParc assures me could have been let out of the hem." Sighing, he sat back in his chair observing her reaction to what he was divulging, frustrated at her lack of emotion.

"You never needed to buy new dresses," Richard interjected. "Therefore, what we want to know is why you feel the need to waste your brother's money? Do you think you are entitled somehow? Are you angry with him because he does not spoil you the way Uncle George did?"

"My father loved me," the girl responded haughtily.

"Really," Darcy declared, as he sat forward in his seat. "Other than giving you a trinket, and walking out the door, when did he ever spend time with you? Did he ever talk to you, try to discover what you even liked? How about read you a story?"

Elizabeth had been sceptical of the plan when Richard had proposed it that afternoon. But as she observed Georgiana carefully, she noticed that it was becoming increasingly difficult for her to maintain her composure, and she wondered if they might meet with some success.

"You did not love father, but I did!"

"No, I did not love my mother or my father," Darcy confirmed, his volume increasing with his ire. "However, that has nothing to do with the subject we are discussing."

"Uncle George did you a disservice by replacing the time he should have dedicated to you with material objects," interrupted Richard, as he saw Darcy's patience was wearing thin. "Love is not strictly receiving gifts—it is more, much more."

"When our father died, Richard and I became your guardians. Since then, you have become increasingly disrespectful, and you have ceased to adhere to any of the restrictions I have put in place. I informed you *before* you returned to London that you would not be receiving a spending allowance, or be permitted to go shopping until you had repaid what you overspent, yet you defied me once more. I will not tolerate it, Georgiana, and there will be repercussions."

Georgiana opened her mouth to protest, but Darcy quickly stopped her. "You will *not* be returning to London, due to the fact that I cannot trust you. I have informed Madame duParc that I will no longer cover any credit she extends to you, so I do not think she will be consenting to make you any more gowns until I give her permission." He watched as his sister's face became a vibrant shade of red. "Consider your last shopping trip to Madame duParc's your Christmas gift from Richard and me. Do not expect more."

As her brother finished, Georgiana stood abruptly with a furious look upon her face, her chair harshly scraping against the floor. "I hate you! I cannot wait to get away from you all!" she screamed. She then stormed through the door, and directly up to her rooms.

"Well, that went well," Richard quipped. "Do you think she meant the last?"

Darcy rubbed his face with both hands before running them back through his hair. "I have no idea. As far as I can tell, she would have nowhere to go. She does not like Lady Catherine or Lord Matlock."

"Lydia threatens to run away from time to time," Elizabeth offered. "But, she has yet to try it. I am not saying Georgiana will not possibly attempt it, only that we will need to watch her carefully. You will need to tell Mrs. Annesley."

Nodding, Darcy sighed. "Let us discuss something more pleasant, or perhaps you could play for us, Elizabeth?"

Rising from their seats, they removed to the drawing room, where they spent the remainder of the evening, until they retired just prior to midnight.

~ * ~

The snow had stopped falling by Christmas morning. There was a thick layer on the ground, and Darcy, who had sneaked to his dressing room, was returning to his warm bed where his wife was still asleep. He watched her slumber for some time before he began spreading kisses from her cheek to her shoulder.

"Merry Christmas, Mrs. Darcy," he whispered in her ear, smiling widely.

"Merry Christmas," she mumbled. She stretched and opened her eyes to see him hovering over her with a very large grin adorning his face. She laughed and reached up to kiss him on the cheek. "You seem to be up to something."

"I simply wanted to give you your Christmas present before we go downstairs."

"Will," she scolded, "you do not need to give me a gift."

"I bought you a gift because I love you, and it is our first Christmas together. It is truly not much. I promise."

Pulling the sheet over her chest, she sat up in bed as he placed a large parcel in her lap. "If this is not much, I am loath to see what you consider large," she giggled, her eyes wide.

He chuckled deeply as she untied the string holding the package together, and the paper to fell open to reveal the contents within. She was awestruck when she saw the large stack of rather expensive material, and other embroidery equipment.

"You remembered that I embroider."

"Of course," he claimed. "And I knew that you did not have any of the supplies necessary anymore. Since I know nothing about such an accomplishment, I asked Claire to buy you whatever you would need to resume the diversion. I know it is something practical, but I hope you are not disappointed."

"No, I required new supplies. This is truly thoughtful. Thank you!" Elizabeth gushed, as she hugged her husband tightly.

"There is also this." He brought a case up from the side of the bed and placed it beside her. "I thought you might need something to keep it all together."

Smiling, she leaned over, and pulled a package out from under the pillows on her side of the bed. "This is for you."

"You scold me for buying you a present, yet you have one for me as well?" he laughed.

"But you have been purchasing everything I have needed,

due to the fact that I came to you with practically nothing, as well as giving me several gifts since the day we were married."

"And you are worth every bit of it."

Rolling her eyes, she smiled and kissed him quickly. "I love you, too." She handed him the small package in her hand that he unwrapped before smiling broadly.

"Have you read it?" she asked anxiously.

"No, I have not, but I have heard of it," he said. "Byron wrote this in response to the reviews of the work I was reading to you when you were ill." Darcy examined the cover and flipped through the pages a bit. "Elizabeth, this is published anonymously*. Did you know this is a first edition?"

"Yes, my uncle has a friend who deals in rare books. I had asked him when he came to dinner with us to keep a look out for a much-needed Christmas gift for you. I told him some of the authors I knew you favoured, and he sent this to me the evening before we left London, accompanied by a note asking if it was suitable."

"It is wonderful, thank you." He grinned widely, kissed her, and pulled back to rest his forehead against hers. "Is it terrible to wish that we could just stay here all day?"

"No," she sighed, "especially after the confrontation with Georgiana last night. Yet, it is Christmas, and I do not wish a repeat of Richard's chuckling when we finally leave these rooms."

Her husband rolled his eyes, and sat up to throw his legs over the side of the bed, retrieving his robe and handing Elizabeth her dressing gown. It was with great difficulty that they pulled themselves from bed to attend the Christmas services, soon receiving word that Georgiana was claiming illness. Mrs. Reynolds was promptly dispatched to ensure Miss Darcy was not in need of a physician, however, since finding that the young woman was in actuality very well, delivered the message that the master expected to see her downstairs within the hour to attend church with the family.

Georgiana attempted to remain in her rooms while everyone enjoyed their quiet celebration, but she did not get her wish. Her brother required her presence downstairs for the entire day. She mainly played the pianoforte or read quietly while Richard, Elizabeth, and Darcy conducted their own chess tournaments and played cards. Even Elizabeth entertained everyone a few times on the pianoforte. They had been a very merry party, and Richard retired for the night, vowing to spend more holidays at Pemberley. They were far superior to passing them with his parents.

~ * ~

Elizabeth and Mrs. Reynolds had spent a good bit of the holiday planning preparing all of the baskets to be distributed for Boxing Day themselves, laying them all out in the ballroom until they could be delivered. Darcy, who was extremely proud of the arrangements his wife had made in such a short period of time, drove her out in the sleigh himself, since she had not, as of yet, met many of their tenants. While the master and his wife took those closest to the house, Mr. Jacobs and Mrs. Reynolds delivered the baskets to the homes that were farther out, so everyone would be finished by afternoon tea. Richard sadly departed the day after the New Year, and life at Pemberley fell into a routine.

The weather over the next month was intensely cold, even by Derbyshire standards, and everyone was kept indoors for much of January—not that either Darcy or Elizabeth minded. They took long walks through the house and the conservatory, and read, cuddled together under a blanket in the library. Sometimes they did not leave their room at all, which caused a few raised eyebrows amongst the servants. However, no one would ever dare to say a word aloud for fear of losing their position; Mrs. Reynolds had never tolerated gossip amongst the staff, and the housekeeper was known to be extremely fond of the new mistress. Mrs. Darcy loved the master, and that was good enough for the motherly woman, who had known the young master since he was four years old.

As February rolled around, Elizabeth was becoming increasingly frustrated with the lack of post. She had been waiting for a missive from her aunt, and had yet to hear from Charlotte since becoming Elizabeth Darcy. She worried her friend, for some reason, was not allowed to correspond with her. Darcy attempted to calm her, assuring her his correspondence had been affected by the weather as well. Still she fretted.

Apart from meals and church, Georgiana secluded herself during the weeks following the incident on Christmas Eve; but by the end of January, even she could be found wandering the halls for exercise and a change of scenery. Darcy and Elizabeth, who had no idea how to approach her, did not expect her to be talkative or friendly, yet they were hopeful that she would at least remain respectful. They did, however, praise her for the time she was putting into her studies, hoping attention for positive endeavours might meet with some success.

The end of February brought a few warmer days, which were still cold, as far as Elizabeth was concerned, that allowed the snow to melt enough so the post and carriages could travel more freely again. It was then that a letter from Mrs. Gardiner, as well as Charlotte, finally made their long awaited appearance at Pemberley.

Yearning for the news from Longbourn, her Aunt Maddie's letter was the first to be opened as she retreated to their bedroom. She took a seat in the window, broke the seal, and read.

12 Gracechurch Street
London, England
12 January 1812

My dearest Lizzy,

I know that you have been eager to hear what has been transpiring in Hertfordshire since your departure, and I dearly apologize for delaying this letter for as long as I have. In my defence, I have worried excessively as to how to explain the holiday we spent at Longbourn without distressing you. Please do not fret, as everyone is well, it is merely their attitudes, and what they have said in conversation that I am loath to impart to you.

Upon our arrival, we were greeted by not only your mother, but also your sisters, who all seemed very happy to see us; your father was conspicuously absent. Your mother, although she does not understand how you "caught" Mr. Darcy, cannot cease speaking of the excellent match you have made, and will gush to anyone who will listen of her good fortune. Jane is as you have described, and does not seem perturbed by much of anything that transpires. It is just as worrisome as your father's behaviour, which is completely the opposite.

Now, before I write more, I want to say that you are not responsible for this, and I do not ever want to hear you say otherwise! I would not have thought it possible, but your father has become even more of a recluse since you left. Your uncle ventured into his library the night we arrived, only to find him intoxicated and belligerent. He would not listen to anything your uncle had to say, and instead insisted vehemently that he leave him in peace.

Your mother insists that he is pouting because you managed to marry better than he had planned for you, but as your uncle was not allowed back into the study for the remainder of the holiday, and your father never left, it was unable to be discussed.

Mary, Kitty and Lydia are just the same as before you left, as nothing seems to affect them, or change their perceptions. Mary lectures, Lydia is unabashed, and Kitty follows Lydia's every move.

Mrs. Hill had tears in her eyes when I gave her the letter you requested I deliver. She was exceedingly concerned after the gossip of your marriage to Mr. Darcy, but when I told her of your happiness, she asked me to wish you joy. She is so proud of you for marrying above what your parents planned, and although she would love to see you again, she understands why you do not visit.

As for your uncle and I, we are well, and I promise to write more often now that I have managed to finally write this missive. The children are excited to travel to Pemberley with us in July, as it is all they talk about. Please tell your husband again how much we appreciate his gracious invitation, and I look forward to hearing of your first Christmas at Pemberley.

Yours affectionately,

Madeleine Gardiner

Elizabeth sighed. While a part of her knew things would change due to her departure from Longbourn, another part of her had hoped things would have gone on the way they always had, just without her. Her father drinking to excess was unusual; he had never had that habit in the past, and she wondered if the change was due to her.

With one last sigh, she lifted the missive from her friend Charlotte Lucas. Wondering whether the letter contained any new information on Meryton, she quickly broke the seal and unfolded it to see the words written upon the page.

Hunsford Parsonage
Kent
20 January 1812

Elizabeth paused. Why would Charlotte be writing from Hunsford? With a sinking feeling, she pressed on as she hoped her good friend did not do what she was suspecting.

Dear Lizzy,

I must say how surprised I was to receive the news of your marriage, and I must congratulate you for making such a splendid match—I wish you joy. You have truly done well for yourself, and so I hope you will not be too upset with the news I must relate to you. I was married to Mr. William Collins a week ago. I know you, Lizzy. You are wondering about love, and I must confess that I am not romantic. I never was. All I ask is for a comfortable home and security.

I do not have much time, as we are expected at Rosings Park for dinner. Please let me hear from you soon! I want to hear all about how you and Mr. Darcy came to be wed. However, please send your correspondence to me through Lucas Lodge. Lady Catherine is most displeased by your marriage, and though I am happy for you, my husband must not know I am corresponding with you.

Please send your letters to Maria, and she will enclose them within her letters to me.

Please write to me soon!

Mrs. Charlotte Collins

As Elizabeth finished her letter from Charlotte, her husband came into the room. He sat on the edge of the seat beside her, and she handed him the letter from her Aunt Gardiner, which he read quickly.

"I hope you know that she is right. You are not to blame." He wrapped his arm around her, and held her close.

"I suppose I just thought everything would remain the same, despite my absence."

"In a way, it is, only your father has decided to wallow in his mistakes rather than learn from them. *He* made that choice, love." Even though she did not necessarily believe his words in her heart, she nodded her head, not wanting to discuss Longbourn any more than necessary.

"Who is the other letter from?" he asked.

Elizabeth looked down sadly at the letter. "The former Charlotte Lucas."

Lifting his eyebrows in wonder, he could not help but look surprised. "Who did she marry?"

"Mr. William Collins actually," Elizabeth said succinctly.

Darcy, noticing her mood, kissed her temple before whispering in her ear. "You had best not be jealous, Mrs. Darcy." He smiled when he heard her laugh softly.

"No, just disappointed in her choice is all."

"It is actually a good match for her; she may not have married at all if she had not accepted his proposal. She is not exactly a young woman anymore."

"Will!" his wife exclaimed. "How can you say that?"

"I do not mean to pain you. She is your friend, and I know you care about her, but she has to be reaching the age where marriage is less likely, to put it kindly. And, forgive me, but she is rather plain," he finished, desperately hoping she would not become angry. "She will not have to worry about her future, or be dependent upon her brothers when her father leaves this world. There is something to be said for that."

Elizabeth only gave a small snort in response.

"You cannot say that you were in love with me when you accepted me. Do not criticize her for something you, yourself once did."

"There is a huge difference between us, and Charlotte and Mr. Collins. You are not ridiculous, and I felt we had become friends when I accepted you. I was also falling in love with you, although I was unwilling to admit it at the time. They are two very different situations," she replied with a pout.

Darcy smiled at hearing her admit that she had begun to love him so soon. "I loved you already," he whispered in her ear. Her head turned to his, and he saw the brilliant smile that adorned her face. She cupped his face in her hands, and kissed him passionately. It was not long before the subject of Mr. and Mrs. Collins was long forgotten.

*Elizabeth gave Darcy *English Bards and Scotch Reviewers* a satirical poem by Lord Byron that was first published anonymously in 1809.

Chapter 17

The end of February and a break in the weather brought not only the post, but also callers to Pemberley. At first, Elizabeth was excited to meet the ladies of the neighbourhood, but soon she found that hosting these ladies was a less-than-enjoyable activity. Most of her first visitors were friends of the former Mrs. Darcy and correspondents of that lady's sister, Lady Catherine de Bourgh. Those callers often hinted at their so-called knowledge of her husband's supposed engagement to Miss Anne de Bourgh. As unpleasant as those calls had been, a few of the younger women had apparently harboured hopes of becoming Mrs. Darcy, and were rather rude in their allusions that she was not suitable for the position in which she found herself.

She had always been able to laugh at most of the looks she had received, but she was tiring of it. Elizabeth had hoped to leave it all behind in London, so she was initially rather upset by their slights. Her husband, however, assured her he did not particularly care if those women ever called again, and that he would not hesitate to have them refused at the doors of both Pemberley and Darcy House should they insult his Elizabeth. He made his stance clear when he joined her and the ladies during their calls. His presence reassured her; he loved her and would not tolerate any disrespect toward her.

It was also at the very end of February when Elizabeth made the acquaintance of the Greys. Mr. Edward Grey was a friend of Darcy's from Cambridge, and her husband had, by correspondence, invited him to Pemberley for a day of hunting. The gentleman not only accepted the invitation, but having heard that his old friend had finally married, wrote to Darcy suggesting he bring his wife, a Mrs. Esther Grey, and sister, Miss Elaine Grey, to spend the day with Mrs. Darcy. As Elizabeth had no objections to company while her husband was occupied, she consented to the idea, hoping the ladies were different than most of those who had come to call.

Everything was quickly arranged with Mrs. Reynolds, and it was not long before the intended day arrived. As planned, the Greys arrived in time to join the Darcys for their morning meal, which allowed the ladies to acquaint themselves with one another before the gentlemen departed to enjoy their sport. Once breakfast had concluded, the men quickly excused themselves, and the ladies made their way to the drawing room for conversation.

Elizabeth observed the two women as they entered the room and took their seats. Mrs. Esther Grey, who appeared to be about five and twenty years of age, carried an air of disapproval of everything and everyone around her. On the other hand, Miss Elaine Grey, who was closer in age to Elizabeth, seemed very quiet, and was more inclined to allow her sister to do the talking, which intrigued Elizabeth very much.

"We were so surprised when we heard Mr. Darcy had not married his cousin, Miss de Bourgh," Mrs. Grey began in a condescending manner, reminiscent of Miss Bingley. "Wherever did the two of you meet?"

Elizabeth, who had been asked that question several times over the course of the past several weeks, hid her smile before she carefully delivered her standard reply. "We met while Mr. Darcy was visiting his friend Mr. Bingley at his estate, Netherfield, in Hertfordshire. As for Miss de Bourgh, I am sorry for any disappointed hopes; however, my husband was never engaged to his cousin."

"*Really*," the guest exclaimed. "My aunt, Lady Dalrymple, who is *very* good friends with Lady Catherine, has known for years that they were promised to one another. It is amazing to me that you did not."

Looking to Miss Grey, Elizabeth watched the young woman roll her eyes just prior to noticing that she was being observed, she coloured and looked quickly to her hands.

"I can assure you, that although Lady Catherine may have *wished* for the match, there was nothing preventing Mr. Darcy from making his own choice in the matter," she said, smiling rather sweetly. "I would dearly like to know where you met Mr. Grey?"

Elizabeth quickly tired of deflecting the haughty woman's inquiries. For close to an hour, Mrs. Grey had continued to ask questions of Darcy and of Elizabeth's connections until Elizabeth thought she would scream. Miss Grey had remained quiet, surprisingly not contributing to the conversation. Then Mrs. Grey bemoaned how early she had been required to rise, and requested to rest until tea. Mrs. Reynolds showed her to a room she would use for the day, and left her sister in company with Elizabeth.

"Since it is just the two of us, is there anything in particular you should like to do?" Elizabeth asked in a cheerful tone.

Miss Grey looked around the large room before she turned her eyes back to Elizabeth. "To own the truth, Mrs. Darcy, this is my first visit to Pemberley," she began timidly. "In the past, my brother would always visit Mr. Darcy on his own. So, if it would not be presumptuous of me to ask, I should dearly love it if we could walk around the house a little, as long as you do not mind, that is."

Smiling at her lack of artifice, Elizabeth stood and held out her arm as she gestured towards the door. "I do not mind at all. In fact, I typically enjoy a walk in the mornings, but with the weather as cold as it has been, I have taken to rambling indoors."

"I enjoy walking, but I am often unable when the weather turns cold. Esther becomes quite annoyed should I attempt the activity indoors," the young woman said, smiling.

"She seems very different from your brother."

"My parents arranged the match. Edward really had no choice in the matter, unlike your husband."

Nodding, Elizabeth led the way into the conservatory, when Miss Grey stopped and turned to her. "Please do not hold what she said against my brother or me. He would be mortified if he knew how she behaved."

"As you well know, I observed your reaction to her statements, so I am quite certain you do not agree with her opinions. I have no reason to hold you in contempt for the views of another," she reassured the young woman.

Miss Grey giggled. "No, I most certainly do not. But, please, you simply must call me Elaine, or you can even call me Lainey, as my brother does."

"Then you must call me Lizzy." The two women smiled, and continued walking. "I know this is probably a rather personal question, but may I ask why you do not speak when in company with your sister?"

"Oh! Is that all?" she replied with a chuckle. "It is only that she insists that I should remain quiet, and learn to comport myself by her example. If I join in the conversation, I am usually subjected to a lecture on the carriage ride home, so I decided some time ago that I did not wish to argue with her. I am glad that she did not catch me rolling my eyes, or else she would have made me accompany her to her room so she could fuss!"

The ladies continued their extended walk through the house, allowing Miss Grey to view much of the beautiful home that she had wished to see since her brother had become friends with Mr. Darcy years ago. When they entered the music room, Miss Grey indicated she played the pianoforte, and asked if Elizabeth played as well, declaring how fun it would be for them to play a duet. Although hesitant as she had never been one to practice diligently, Elizabeth acquiesced, and the two of them began practicing together. The pair was giggling at a particularly atrocious error Miss Grey had made when Georgiana entered the room, startling them from their occupation.

"Georgiana," greeted Elizabeth, as she and her guest stood. "I believe you have previously met Miss Elaine Grey during a dinner engagement at their estate, Briarwood?"

Elizabeth watched as her sister looked over the young woman now standing next to her. "Yes, of course," she replied cooly. "I hope you and your family are well, Miss Grey?"

"Yes, thank you. It is lovely to see you again, Miss Darcy."

"We were just practicing some duets. Will you not join us?" Elizabeth asked in an attempt to include Georgiana.

216

Georgiana had only remained the same, taciturn and unsocial, and it stumped Darcy and Elizabeth as to how to gain the young woman's trust. Although as she viewed Georgiana's reaction to the invitation, Elizabeth began to comprehend that she did not appreciate being included.

"I do not play duets," she replied disdainfully. "If you will excuse me, I must return to my studies."

Georgiana turned abruptly, exited through the door in which she came, and shut it loudly behind her. Sighing, Elizabeth turned to her new friend and smiled.

"I see you have an Esther in your family as well?" Elaine said lightly.

She did not wish to expose their problems with her new sister to a new acquaintance. "I apologize for her rude behaviour; she is at a difficult age, and we are attempting to get through it as best we can."

Miss Grey obviously became concerned that she had said something wrong. "Please, I do not mean to offend. I only noticed some similar mannerisms to Esther which I should. . ."

"You did nothing wrong," interrupted Elizabeth. "It is only that I am unable to discuss it at the moment, so I must beg you to allow me to change the subject."

"Oh, of course," she said, the relief evident in her tone of voice. "But, if you should ever need to speak of it, I would be happy to listen. I assure you that I will keep what you tell me in the strictest of confidence."

Nodding, Elizabeth checked the clock on the mantle, and after indicating that refreshments should be served in the drawing room very soon, the two ladies strolled back to await them.

Once they had had their fill, Miss Grey claimed fatigue from rising so early that morning, and Elizabeth happily escorted her to a room, which had been prepared for her. She had been feeling a bit tired herself, so she set off to her chambers, breathing deeply. Elizabeth had been frustrated at why, when she was not getting as much exercise as she was accustomed, that she recently would find herself so weary every afternoon. Although today was different, because she had also found herself queasy after the cake she had eaten with Miss Grey. There was a smell that had not been appetizing to her, but she was at a loss to understand why. She had always had a preference for that particular cake in the past.

Upon entering her rooms, she could not hold it in any longer, and made a mad dash for the water closet. She emptied what she was sure were the entire contents of her stomach, and was attempting to rise when Claire came into the room. Her maid helped her up, seated her before the dressing table, and fetched some water and tooth powder, so Elizabeth might refresh herself a bit.

"If you feel ill again, ma'am, you should let me know, especially first thing in the morning, so I can bring you some tea and toast to help settle your stomach."

Elizabeth, who had just finished cleaning her mouth, regarded her maid strangely and chuckled. "I admit that I have felt under the weather lately, but you act as if I should be ill quite often." Handing her the cup and the powder, she noticed the young woman studying her for a moment. "Is there something amiss?" she asked, unsure what to make of her maid's expression.

"If you will allow me to put this away and summon a maid to clean the other room, I will tell you while I unpin your hair, so that you may rest."

She waited patiently as it took a few minutes for Claire to accomplish her task, as she sent for a housemaid to straighten the dressing room and clean the water closet. When she returned to the room, Elizabeth waited impatiently as Claire unbound her hair. She did not speak until Elizabeth's hair was all down and she was brushing out her long curls to plait them.

"Mrs. Darcy, do you know what it means when a woman's courses cease to come?"

Watching her in the mirror, Elizabeth did not need long to remember the teachings of her aunt. Her eyes grew large in shock as she thought back to how long it had been. "But my aunt told me it could take time, and that I may not necessarily fall with child quickly."

"I believe that is true, yet my mother always said it can occur quickly sometimes as well."

Nodding, Elizabeth began biting her lower lip as she thought about what she should do. She stood, and allowed Claire to help her remove her clothes down to her chemise. "Nothing is definite until the quickening, so I would like to keep it between us for now."

"Of course, ma'am. Tea and toast will help when your stomach is unsettled, but you will need to ensure any food you find that does not agree with you is not served for now."

"That is why the cake smelled offensive?"

Claire smiled. "My mother has always loved strawberries. When she was expecting my youngest sister, my father surprised her with some, but she became ill from just smelling them and was unable to eat them at all." The maid's brow furrowed in thought. "If you do not mind me suggesting, ma'am, you might tell Mrs. Reynolds. It may help dealing with some of the food problems you might have."

Elizabeth only smiled. "Thank you, Claire, I will consider it. I think I would like to rest now. Please notify me when either Mrs. Grey or Miss Grey wake, and plan to return below stairs."

Her maid curtsied and left Elizabeth to rest. She ventured into her husband's room, and climbed into his bed, comforted by the scent of his cologne. She only intended to remain until she felt better, but fell asleep and, did not awaken, even when her husband entered the room after his bath.

"Elizabeth," he murmured near her ear and kissed her temple.

"Mmmmmmm," she groaned, not wishing to wake just yet.

"You need to dress for dinner, love." He had noticed lately
that she seemed to be tired in the afternoons. She rarely
admitted to the need for a nap, but she sometimes fell asleep
while they were reading in the library. Elizabeth had insisted
it was all of the late nights they had been having, but Darcy
still worried that she was overexerting, or she was not well.
However, he had hesitated to mention anything after the
debacle resulting from the trip to Pemberley.

"Will," she mumbled groggily. "What time is it?"

Smiling, he leaned over and brushed his lips against hers
before replying. "It is time to dress for dinner."

"What?" she exclaimed, as she drew herself up to a seated
position. "Why did Claire not wake me sooner?"

"From what I have gathered since Grey and I arrived, Mrs.
Grey has not left her room and Miss Grey requested some tea
earlier, but has not left her chamber either."

"Oh, thank goodness."

"Nothing is amiss, love, but are you sure you are well? You
have been more tired lately, and I cannot help but worry." He
watched her close her eyes and smile as he ran the backs of
his fingers down the side of her face. She raised her arms,
wrapped them around his shoulders, and buried her face in
his neck, which made him grin as he enfolded her in his
arms.

"I promise I am well, but Claire is likely to be rather upset if I
do not appear in my dressing room soon," she sighed. "I
would much rather remain here with you."

Her honest confession warmed his heart, and he rubbed her
back for a few minutes before she pulled away. "You must
dress, too, or else I shall have Evans mad at me as well." She
kissed him lightly, and he watched as she rose and quickly
exited the room. He chuckled as he stood to return to Evans,
so he also could also dress for the evening.

Darcy met Elizabeth in her chambers. He complimented her choice of dress, and assisted with her necklace. Once she was ready, he offered her his arm, and saw her smile as she wrapped her hand around it. He escorted her down to the drawing room to await the guests, who joined them and Georgiana not long after. Dinner was pleasant and Darcy was happy to see Elizabeth making friends with Miss Grey. He was not particularly surprised to find Mrs. Grey quiet, and having no interest in his wife, since he knew her to have quite the reputation as a mercenary elitist before she was married to his friend. He could tell she had not changed in the few years since they had been wed.

His sister was very quiet during the meal as well, giving only monosyllabic answers to any questions asked of her. Her behaviour was not any different than when they attended dinner at Briarwood, so he chose to ignore it. He did not wish to fight with Georgiana for behaving the same as she had previously, especially since she was not rude.

Elizabeth enjoyed dinner as Miss Grey was more talkative, and between her and her brother, there was more conversation than that morning. Dinner passed quickly, and the Greys swiftly departed, eager to return to their estate before the hour became too late. Elizabeth was pleased to have made plans for Miss Grey to return in a little over a fortnight to spend the day. They had thought to travel into Lambton to shop, if the weather permitted.

Georgiana visibly let down some of her armour the moment the guests were escorted out of the door, and excused herself to return to her room. As soon as she had ascended the stairs, Elizabeth took her husband's hand, entwined her fingers with his, and led him to their chambers. They did not separate upon reaching their destination, but remained together where Elizabeth lovingly removed her husband's clothes, and then her own. She pressed him back into the pillows against the headboard and straddled his waist.

"I love you, Fitzwilliam Darcy," she said softly.

"And I love you, Elizabeth Darcy."

Smiling impishly, she brushed his upper lip and then lower lip with her own before trailing them and her tongue to his ear, where she gently scraped her teeth along the lobe. He inhaled sharply, and she smiled before she returned to his mouth where she kissed him deeply, running her hands down his sides and back up his chest. She felt him place his hands on her thighs and caress them as she began to make a trail down his neck. She did not stop until she reached his chest, where she touched his nipple with her tongue.

Elizabeth, who had until now not completely taken the initiative when they made love, hoped her husband would not be offended by her aggressiveness as she repeated the action to the other side of his chest. She dragged her breasts along his torso as she came back to his neck and gently bit him at the base. Her hand, trailing down his side, came to his taut stomach where it traced the line of hair down to his erection. She took him in her hand began to stroke him softly. Pulling back to look at him, she noticed his eyes had closed, and his hands were fiercely gripping the sheets below him. She continued to stimulate him as she worked her way down his chest once more, kissing him whenever she got the urge until she was astride his muscular legs.

His eyes had remained closed, and she heard him softly moan as she gently squeezed the tip, in an attempt to discern what he favoured. As she observed his reactions, she thought of how he sometimes used his mouth on her, and on impulse took him in her mouth as far as she could, her hand remaining around the base.

"Oh God . . . Elizabeth," he groaned, as he panted. "You need . . . you need . . . "

Enjoying that she could discompose him to that extent, she gently sucked while beginning to mimic the movements he made when they coupled as his pelvis came off of the bed, and his hands entwined themselves into her hair.

"You . . . need not . . . do this," he finally panted. Taking great care so as not to hurt him, she ignored his statement, and slightly increased her suction. Then she ran her tongue up the underside and across the tip as he moaned loudly, and increased his grip to her head. Elizabeth had thought she

222

would just be giving him pleasure; however, she was becoming increasingly aroused by the sounds he was making. She was just going to release him to take him into her when he abruptly lifted her face to his and reclaimed her mouth. She barely had time to realise what was happening before he had her on her back with her head at the foot of the bed, pinned her with his body, and entered her swiftly.

She gasped as she felt him fill her, and lifted her knees in order to feel him deeper. Her hands grasped onto his buttocks, and pulled him in as far as he would go. He moaned, "Elizabeth," as his hand moved from her hip around to her backside, where he lifted her lower body off of the bed. He quickened his pace thrusting harder than he had in the past. Trying to match his pace, she began to moan as she felt the release beginning to build; she closed her eyes tightly to the rush of light that temporarily paralysed her body and caused her to cry out. She dug her fingernails into him as she barely heard him call out over the roar within her own head. They collapsed back onto the bed with him falling on top of her.

They both lay utterly spent for a time. She felt Will kiss her shoulder, and opened her eyes to find him propping himself on his elbows as he placed small kisses on her eyes, nose, and mouth.

"I love you, Mrs. Darcy."

Smiling, she brushed the curls, which had fallen in his face back she brushed her lips against his. "As I love you."

"Are you well?" he asked.

"I am not made of glass. Besides, it is not as though you were rough with me." The chill of the room suddenly became noticeable, and she shivered in response. "But I have just become cold, and would like nothing more than to cuddle with you under the bedclothes."

Her husband smiled as he carefully lifted himself from her. She crawled up the bed, and burrowed into the covers as he followed. They lay on their sides, facing each other so they could talk with their legs entwined.

"Elizabeth, what made you do what you did tonight?"

She regarded him warily. "I thought about what you do to me sometimes, and I thought you might . . . you did like it, did you not?"

Watching her face blanch, he clasped her tighter to him. "Yes, good lord, yes. But you need not do anything you might find unpleasant to please me."

"It was not distasteful," she said bashfully. "I rather liked it when you became undone."

He chuckled and kissed her lightly. "I understand, as I rather like it when you become undone as well."

Blushing, she smiled, ran her hand through his hair, and brushed her lips against his. As they settled back into the pillows, she briefly told him of her day, and he mentioned that the men's hunting trip was very pleasant, not wishing to bore her with the details of the dogs or the foxes.

Eventually they spoke of their families and dreams of the future. Elizabeth was particularly touched by her husband's vision of their family, and the relationships he envisioned with their children. Those were the thoughts that prompted her to kiss him passionately, and show him her love the best way she knew how. Their encounter was tender and sweet, and when they were both spent, her husband wrapped her up in his arms as he curled up behind her, and they succumbed to their exhaustion.

Chapter 18

While Elizabeth had wished to have a talk with Mrs. Reynolds, the discussion would be delayed, as she had become very preoccupied with her husband over the next several days. Since Christmas, Georgiana came to meals, as she was required, however she ate in silence and swiftly returned to her rooms. Darcy attempted to speak with her daily, often seeking her out when she was with Mrs. Annesley. He tried to discuss her studies with her and even offered for them to go riding together, but to no avail, so he left her to her bookwork. Instead, he hunted down his wife where she was reviewing the accounts or writing her letters, and spent the entirety of the day with her cuddled in the library, reading and playing chess.

The couple proceeded to happily spend the next few days ignoring their responsibilities. They found places to hide and spend time together all over Pemberley, even going so far as to lock themselves in the conservatory with a picnic that they did not emerge from for several hours.

By the end of the week, Darcy's steward ensured his employer knew of business that required his attention, and so, after breakfast, they each departed to their own study to finally attend to their duties.

"Mrs. Darcy, I was wondering if I might have a word with you," Mrs. Reynolds called from the door.

"Of course," Elizabeth replied. "Please come in and close the door behind you, I have something I would like to discuss with you as well." She saw the housekeeper nod before she closed the door, and stepped in front of her desk. "Now, please take a seat, and tell me what it is that you feel requires my attention."

"Well," the older woman began. "One of the upstairs maids had commented that you were ill the day the Greys came to visit, and you have seemed more tired as of late. I wished you to know that if you require anything, please do not hesitate to ask."

Elizabeth chuckled at the irony of the situation. "It is funny you should mention it, actually, because it is the matter I wish to discuss with you." She watched as Mrs. Reynolds raised her eyebrows. "Claire and I have both come to suspect that I may be with child, and although I am waiting until I am certain before I tell my husband, my maid suggested I confide in you."

"So that things might be handled around the house in a more discreet manner for the time being?" the housekeeper interjected.

"Precisely," responded Elizabeth. "Especially as I have found myself rather sensitive to certain smells and foods, including the cake that was served the day I was ill. Please understand, I have liked the cake since I first came to Pemberley, but I cannot stomach it for some reason right now."

Seeing the mistress's worry that she would offend, she smiled. "It is not a problem, Mrs. Darcy. I will simply suggest to the cook that perhaps we should begin making the cakes we serve around Easter. The season is growing close, so I do not think it would be too suspicious."

"Thank you, Mrs. Reynolds."

"Just let me know, or have Claire inform me of any last minute menu changes you may need to make," she replied, smiling. "You do understand that it will be smothering when he discovers."

Elizabeth giggled and looked to the housekeeper, who was laughing as well. "I know, which is why I have not said a word thus far."

"Well, if you will excuse me, Mrs. Darcy, I need to make some arrangements in the kitchen, and adjust the menu for the coming week."

"Of course." She smiled as the housekeeper turned and exited the mistress's study, leaving Elizabeth to resume her review of the accounts.

~ * ~

Saturday 29 February 1812

In the parlour at Longbourn, Jane Bennet stood in front of a window as she contemplated how her life had come to this. Everything could be traced back to her sister, Elizabeth, and her flight from a betrothal to Mr. Collins, as well as her subsequent marriage to none other than Mr. Darcy—it was still incomprehensible to Jane how she had accomplished that.

Her father had barely left his study since his return from London. He had imbibed all of the brandy and port Hill had placed within the room, and then demanded more. Initially, she had thought he was merely upset that her sister had disobeyed him. That was until a fortnight ago, when Jane entered his study to retrieve a book, and heard him muttering as he swayed back and forth in front of the window. As it turned out, he had never planned for his favourite daughter to leave home.

Mr. Bennet had intended to propose that upon Elizabeth's marriage to Mr. Collins, the parson would resign his post in Hunsford, and he and Elizabeth would move into the small dower's cottage down the hill. The arrangement was not only to keep her sister close to him, but also so she could continue to run Longbourn. The marriage he had planned was not as much to save the family from being cast out upon his death, but a way to give his estate to his favourite daughter! That knowledge alone had begun to stir resentment within Jane. After all, she was the eldest; if she had been a boy, Longbourn would belong to her.

And if that was not bad enough, it was not only her father who had changed dramatically since her sister's defection, but her mother was a different person as well. Mrs. Bennet was always heard to be saying how Jane was the most beautiful and Lydia had such an agreeable personality, but recently, all her mother could do was laud Elizabeth. 'How clever Elizabeth was to snare Mr. Darcy and his ten thousand a year!' 'How rich Mrs. Darcy must be—the pin money, the jewels!' 'Lizzy shall save us from the hedgerows!' Her mother's effusions infuriated her father, and had deepened the newly formed resentment she felt toward the sister she had been so close to all of those years.

Jane heard voices growing closer, and schooled her features before anyone could see the discord within written upon her face. Once again appearing serene, she turned to find Lydia and Kitty entering the room.

"I am so tired of hearing about Lizzy," said Lydia scornfully. "What difference does it make that she married that irksome Mr. Darcy? La, he is such a prig—and boring to boot!" She gave a giggle. "Of course, Lizzy was always rather dull. She forever had her nose stuck in a book." Lydia looked over to Jane who had not moved since her sisters entered the room. "At least you managed to get your own room with Lizzy having left. I still have to share with Kitty," she pouted. "Oh well, with Lizzy gone I no longer have to compete with her for Mr. Wickham, and he has been so attentive lately."

Kitty giggled annoyingly, and Jane rolled her eyes as her youngest sister continued her silly rant. Jane was always amazed by how quickly Lydia could go from bragging to pouting and whining and back again. She tuned out her sisters' voices as her view returned to outside the window. She was tired of her parents' differing attitudes, and there was no way she would continue dealing with the neighbours' gossip regarding Mr. Bingley. The speculation over why he had left without making her an offer of marriage left a bitter taste in her mouth. She refused to go through that nightmare again.

Leaving the window and sitting at the writing desk, she decided to pen a letter to her Aunt Gardiner, requesting to stay with them in London until things returned to normal at Longbourn—if only she knew how long that would be.

~ * ~

Friday 15 March 1812

"When do you expect Miss Grey," Will asked casually, while breaking their fast.

"In her letter, she indicated it would be shortly after the morning meal, so I would imagine she will not be much longer," Elizabeth said, smiling. After spending a fortnight returning the calls she had received upon the weather

228

clearing, she was ready to spend some time with a friend. The calls were not all bad, but at least she was done with the chore, since she did not expect most of the women to visit her again.

"When do you plan on travelling to Lambton?"

"I would prefer to go this morning, but I will wait to see what Lainey prefers before making the final decision."

Darcy was rather anxious about his wife taking a trip into Lambton. While the village was not a great distance, he had noticed her fatigue during the last fortnight, as well as her change in eating habits. His wife adored chocolate, but he had not seen her drink it in weeks. In its stead, she was drinking tea with dry toast, and not only at breakfast, but also several times each day. Why dry toast?

He had been trying not to hover or question her excessively—he knew she did not appreciate that—yet he wished that the ladies would find things to amuse them around Pemberley. He did not want them to venture off where he could not keep an eye on Elizabeth.

"I want Matthew and Samuel to escort you around to the shops . . . and bring Claire with you."

His wife raised her eyebrow at his order. He had been scrutinizing her quite a bit lately, and she was concerned that he had noticed something was different. His demands annoyed her, but she decided to humour him for now as the nausea had only become worse in the last week. If she refused to do what he wished and something happened, he would never let her forget it.

"I will see if Claire is busy, if you would not mind informing the footmen?"

"Of course." He stood and offered Elizabeth his hand to help her stand.

Her maid, as it so happened, did not have anything pressing to do, and as Miss Grey agreed with the idea of shopping earlier in the day, Claire was sent for to accompany them.

229

Lainey chuckled upon their arrival to town when Elizabeth's escorts disembarked from the coach, and followed behind her at a small distance.

"Do you always have this much of an escort when you shop?" she giggled.

Elizabeth sighed. "This is the first time I have been without my husband, and I think he is a bit uneasy."

"Maybe just a bit," she replied, holding her fingers up and about an inch apart.

Laughing, Elizabeth looked up and down the street. "Where would you prefer to begin?"

"Why not begin here by looking at ribbon, and we can work our way down to where the shops end at the chapel?"

The ladies agreed, and entered the first shop where they both purchased some ribbon. As they wandered through the shops, Elizabeth found herself purchasing materials to make baby clothes. While she was still not certain that she was with child, in her last letter, even her aunt seemed to agree that it was very likely, given the way she had been feeling as of late, and she felt that it could not hurt to begin preparing. She had noticed her friend looking at her purchases with an inquisitive eye, but she acted as if nothing was out of the ordinary and continued shopping.

They were in the last of the shops when Elizabeth, who had been perusing some knitted items a local woman had on display near the front window, spotted someone familiar passing by the window. Holding a pair of booties in her hand, she carefully walked closer to the glass to observe the man walk toward the chapel and across the street, where under the chestnut tree by the smithy was none other than Georgiana Darcy, holding her horse by the reins.

She felt Miss Grey brush her arm as she came up beside her, but never turned from what had so captivated her attention.

"Is that not your sister?"

"Yes, unfortunately, I believe it is," Elizabeth replied softly.

"Do you know the gentleman?"

"I do. Would you be so kind as to ask one of my footmen to come over here please?"

Nodding, Miss Grey crossed the store to where the servants were standing as they waited for the ladies to make their purchases, and soon Samuel, as well as her friend, were standing next to her.

"Did you need something, ma'am?"

"Yes, Samuel. Do you happen to recognise the man by the chestnut tree with Miss Darcy?" whispered Elizabeth. Turning to watch the young man, she saw his eyes widen as he identified the man in question.

"That there is George Wickham, ma'am. He has some nerve showing his face here in Lambton after all of the debts he left the last time he came to town," he declared, as his eyes scanned the area. "But where is Miss Darcy's groom? She is not to be riding without an escort."

Observing the surprised look on her friend's face, she turned back to the footmen. "I need you to keep an eye on Miss Darcy, but do not let her know she is being watched unless she is in danger. Once she has left to ride back to Pemberley, you can return, since you do not have a horse to follow her. Do you understand?" she asked. He seemed hesitant, so she turned to look in the direction of Matthew and Claire. "I have Miss Grey and the rest of my escort. Mr. Darcy will wish to know exactly what happened between his sister and Mr. Wickham. He would be very upset if someone did not ensure her safety."

"Yes, ma'am," he replied quickly. "I will return as soon as I am able."

Elizabeth watched him stride swiftly out the door and cross in front of the window to the alley between the church and the shop before her eyes returned to the couple down the street. She was just in time, too—she saw Wickham take

Georgiana's hand, and lean over to kiss it. However, he did not bestow just a simple kiss on the hand.

"Did you see that?" Miss Grey asked incredulously.

"He passed her a letter," Elizabeth said under her breath. She was thankful the store was not busy that day, so that no one would notice why they were tarrying in front of the window as they watched the smithy.

"Who is he?"

"His name is George Wickham. I cannot go into particulars, but I would appreciate it if you would not say a word about this to anyone, as it could. . ."

"You do not need to ask, Lizzy," she replied. They saw Georgiana lead the horse around so she could mount as Wickham held the reins. A few more words were exchanged before she turned the horse and rode out of town. Elizabeth, who was busy watching her sister, did not notice Wickham cross the street, and walk directly towards the storefront, until her friend grabbed her arm to pull her away from the window.

"Turn around; you do not want him to be aware that you witnessed their meeting."

"Thank you," said Elizabeth. She returned to the knitted items she had been studying earlier, while Miss Grey kept an eye on the window.

"He has passed, but in the event he is staying here in town, we should think of heading back as soon as your footman returns, so he does not discover us."

Elizabeth nodded and selected the baby blanket and booties she had already been holding to purchase before they loaded themselves into the coach to wait for Samuel. He showed a few moments later, and they quickly set off for Pemberley.

~ * ~

232

Upon their return, Miss Grey, understanding that Elizabeth would need to speak with Darcy, expressed the need to refresh herself. Claire, who was heading to the mistress's dressing room, offered to show Miss Grey to the guest room that had been prepared for her. Elizabeth motioned to Samuel to follow her as she proceeded to the master's study, and knocked on the door. She heard him bid them to come, and proceeded to enter.

Darcy gave a brilliant smile as she stepped through the door, that faded when he saw the look on her face, and the footman who closed the door behind them.

"Did something happen?" He swiftly crossed the room to take his wife's hands to assure himself of her safety.

"I am well, but there was an important occurrence in Lambton that you should be made aware of." She watched as her husband's eyebrows lifted, obviously curious as to what could be so pressing that not only would she immediately seek him out after returning home, but also bring Samuel with her. Deciding it was better just to say it and be done, Elizabeth steeled herself for the reaction she was sure would follow.

"While Miss Grey and I were in the little shop adjacent to the chapel, I witnessed your sister meeting George Wickham by that chestnut tree near the smithy." As she carefully stated her disclosure, she regarded warily the myriad of emotions that crossed her husband's face, beginning with curiosity, followed by shock, and finally anger.

"You are sure," he responded in a very tightly controlled voice.

"I am positive, which is why I brought Samuel with me to inform you of what happened. I had him watch them from a closer vantage point. When their meeting concluded, he followed Georgiana, as she rode out of town until he was assured she was returning to Pemberley, and met the coach where we awaited him."

"You were not alone, were you, Elizabeth?" he asked abruptly. "Wickham would not think twice about trying to hurt me through you!"

"I was not alone. I had not only Miss Grey, but also Matthew and Claire, who remained in the shop when I sent Samuel to spy on them. When Mr. Wickham passed the shop after their rendezvous was completed, Lainey pulled me back from the window, and quickly told me to turn around so he would not see me."

When Elizabeth was done, her husband closed his eyes and nodded. "Will Miss Grey keep this in confidence?" he asked, seemingly wary.

"Lainey has assured me of her discretion, and based on her help today, I have no reason to doubt her sincerity," said Elizabeth in a reassuring tone. "There is something else you should know."

Opening his eyes, they focused back on hers as she took a deep breath.

"There was a point when he took her hand to kiss it," she said, as his eyes widened. "I am certain he passed her a note."

Darcy turned to the footman and addressed him. "Is there anything other than what my wife has told me?"

"I was not close enough to hear what they were saying. They talked for a while. Then as the mistress said, he passed her the note, and held her horse while she mounted. I stayed kind of far back, and followed her from within the trees until I saw her cross into that trail near the beginning of Pemberley woods. Then I returned back to Mrs. Darcy."

"She was riding alone?" he wondered aloud.

"I was wondering the same thing, sir," the servant declared. "Because I know she is not supposed to walk or ride without some sort of escort."

Casting an eye to Elizabeth, he watched her for a few moments while he thought of his next move. The situation had become a tricky game, since he did not know exactly who

234

all of the opponents were. There was definitely Wickham, but how exactly did Georgiana fit into the puzzle? And what of the groom who did not ride out with her? Had his sister or Wickham influenced him?

"Samuel," he said, causing the young man to stand a little taller, "I need you to gather your elder brother and a few of your cousins, and find George Wickham in Lambton. I want him put on the first post coach out of town; it does not matter where, just make sure he leaves Derbyshire. If he has the money, have him pay for his own passage, but if he does not, then I will cover the trip—only the trip. He will receive no other money from me."

The footman nodded, prompting Darcy to continue. "I also want you to discover who was supposed to be riding with Miss Darcy this morning. Make sure everyone involved today knows they are not to breathe a word of this to anyone, and you will report back to me when the task is completed."

"Yes, sir," Samuel responded. The footman bowed, turned, and exited the study, closing the door behind him.

As soon as they were alone, Darcy strode over to Elizabeth and took her in his arms. "I was so worried something would happen today."

"But, Will, I am fine," Elizabeth assured him. "I was never alone, and I sent Samuel to watch Georgiana in the event that there was trouble that she could not resolve on her own. Matthew could have assisted him, and I still would not have been alone."

"I know, but I do not know what I would do if you went missing or you were hurt."

A knock sounded upon the door, and after separating, Darcy bade the person to enter. Claire moved in to admit a maid carrying a tea tray.

"Excuse me, sir," she said hesitantly. "I thought the mistress might wish for some tea."

Elizabeth looked to see her husband's eyebrows rise in a

silent question, but she returned her gaze to her maid.

"Yes, thank you. If you would place it on the table, we shall manage it on our own." Inspecting the tray, she could not help but smile at the cunning of Claire and Mrs. Reynolds. There was obviously tea on the tray; however, there was also a plate that not only contained her dry toast, but also some of her husband's favourite biscuits. They were apparently hoping to make it seem as if it was for the two of them, and not a necessity for her. She heard the maids leave the room as she sat on the small sofa, and began to prepare their tea.

"I do not know what to do about Georgiana," Darcy finally pronounced, as he came to sit beside her while she worked. "First, I must know which groom was supposed to be following her, or if she managed saddle her horse without anyone noticing, but I do not know how that is possible."

"Regardless, we must attempt to retrieve that letter," asserted Elizabeth. "You should know the exact nature of their meeting, as well as the contents of the missive." Seeing him almost absentmindedly nodding his head in agreement, she raised her hand to touch his face. He started, and returned his eyes to her face once more.

"I heard you, love," he began softly. "The mention of the message prompted me to wonder if somehow she has been receiving mail from him. It is very probable that Wickham knows women who would be willing to address the letter, so it would not look suspicious to the staff."

"Perhaps you should check her mail before it is delivered to her, but I would not let her know. Otherwise, she might somehow warn her correspondent."

"I will notify Mrs. Reynolds to ensure she and Roberts are aware that all mail should come through me, whether it is coming or going," he said. "That way it will not be noticeable to the bulk of the staff that I am keeping an eye on Georgiana."

"It will be necessary to confront her. As much as I understand your hesitance, it must be done," Elizabeth stated empathetically. "She must understand that she is accountable for her actions, and what she did could ruin her reputation should someone prone to gossip notice her. We do not know if there was anyone else who caught a glimpse of her with that man."

She took a bite of toast and chewed slowly, dearly wishing the nausea would subside. The drama of the morning was not helping to settle her stomach in the least. She closed her eyes, took a deep breath, and opened them to find her husband studying her intently.

"Are you sure you are feeling well?" he asked, cupping her cheek and running his thumb along her face. "I could not help but notice that you seem to be partaking of quite a bit of tea and toast recently."

Swallowing her last bit of toast, she took a sip of tea before replying. "I confess, my stomach has been a bit off for a little while, but I am quite sure it will return to normal very soon."

"Elizabeth, it has been for a few weeks, which is more than a 'little while'. If it does not at least improve soon, I will send for the family physician to examine you."

"Yes, dear," she replied, smiling sweetly. Her Aunt Maddie had informed her in her latest letter that the queasiness should subside soon. Elizabeth hoped she was correct.

Darcy placed his empty teacup on the tray, and scooted himself closer to his wife, who had just done the same with hers. He placed his arm around her shoulders, and pulled her to his side. He heard her sigh as she leaned against his strong frame while he kissed her on the top of the head. They remained that way until her breathing became steady, and she began to slump against his body. Cradling her as he slowly moved, he gently laid her down on the sofa. He covered her with a blanket, and carefully brushed the hair back from her face.

He was amazed that she could fall asleep this deeply in such a short period of time. Desperately attempting to quash the worry pervading his heart, he attributed her fatigue to the trying events of the morning. He kissed her softly on the cheek as he stood, and slightly opened his office door to prevent people from knocking, which would wake his wife, while he sat at his desk to work.

He had become so engrossed in his papers, that he almost missed the footsteps approaching the door. Looking up to spy Samuel returning to his office, he waved him in, and gestured to where Elizabeth slept, indicating he should speak as quietly as he could manage.

"We were just getting ready to go find Wickham," he began, almost whispering. "But I wanted to tell you that Smith was supposed to be riding with Miss Darcy. He usually rides out with her, but I wanted to be sure it was he that was supposed to go today before I told you."

Furrowing his brow, he nodded. "Jed Smith? He has been here almost two years, has he not?"

"I believe so, sir."

"Thank you, Samuel. Let me know how things go in town," he said, giving the footman a meaningful look.

"As soon as we return, sir."

With a final nod in acknowledgement, Darcy returned to his work, although he had too many thoughts and suspicions running through his head to give the documents before him much consequence.

Chapter 19

<u>15 March 1812</u>

Samuel did not return until much later that evening. Georgiana had returned to her chambers as soon as dinner had concluded, leaving Darcy and Elizabeth to await him in the library. They were cuddled together on the sofa near the fire, reading, when Roberts announced the footman, and his older brother, Jarod, who worked in the stables.

"Pardon me, sir, but you wished to see me upon our return."

"Yes, Samuel, please close the door." As the footman did what he was asked, Darcy stood. "Now, tell me what occurred."

"It was not hard to find him, sir. He had taken a room at the inn, that he had paid for in advance. Mr. Ellis was not going to be taken in by Wickham again."

"Well, at least I will not have to pay for his rooms," said Darcy with disdain in his voice, pacing while he listened.

"We knocked on the door to his room, and forced our way in when he opened it a bit to see who it was. He was not alone; Jed Smith was with him."

"What?" Darcy exclaimed, as he stopped abruptly. Given the events of the day, he did not know why the news shocked him, but it did.

"Yes, sir. They went to arguing once we made it in, and Smith—he was right angry with Wickham—began yelling. Smith struck him, knocking him to the ground, but just before he did, he said he was Wickham's cousin," Samuel revealed with a bewildered tone. "His name is not even Jed Smith—it is Jack Wickham."

"Jack Wickham?" Darcy cried. "I did not even know that he had a cousin!"

Samuel looked to where Jarod was standing quietly behind

him. When the master acknowledged him, the older man stepped forward. "Yes, sir, their fathers had a falling out when they were young, and Jack's parents left Derbyshire. I do not remember what the fight was about but as I recall your father had to get involved. It was a long time ago, I was a young lad at the time and Samuel had not yet been born. I reckon that is why I remember his name, but I did not know his face when he came to work in the stables."

"That Jack struck his cousin but good, and put him out cold. Then he tried to get to the door, but my cousin, Peter, took care of him." Samuel turned toward Elizabeth. "It did not take much, my cousins are pretty large boys," he said, as he stifled a snicker. "We hauled them down to the post coach and loaded them in. Between the two of them, they had enough to pay for their trip, and we used the money you gave us to pay the driver to keep quiet and not ask questions. His next stop was somewhere in Nottinghamshire, as I recall."

"Good," Darcy replied. "Did you discover any information other than what you have already told me?"

"No, sir," the men replied in unison.

"Wickham was knocked out too quickly, and Smith . . . I mean Jack was too busy trying to escape, so we did what you asked," Samuel clarified. "We went through the belongings that were in the room before we loaded them, but we did not find anything."

"Of course, thank you," said Darcy. "Jarod, I will ensure Mr. Turner is notified that you are now the groom who is to ride with Miss Darcy. She is not to be without an escort at any time, and if she manages to elude you, it is to be reported immediately. Is that clear?" Darcy saw the stable hand nod in acknowledgement. "Now, if you and the remainder of the group go to the kitchen, Mrs. Reynolds is to see to it that you get something to eat."

"Yes, sir, thank you." They bowed and exited the room, shutting the door behind them.

Darcy watched the door close before turning toward his wife, who had remained quiet during the entire exchange. "What do you think?”

“I do not think there is a coincidence to any of this.”

“What worries me is Smith was typically the groom who rode out with Georgiana, which I am now positive is not happenstance. I do need to know something before I confront her, that I did not think to ask earlier. Did she seem surprised to see Wickham today, or did she seem to expect him?”

“I had not considered it before now,” Elizabeth replied thoughtfully. “I watched him cross the road to where she was standing, so I did not see her initial reaction, but Will, when I did notice her, she was smiling at him.”

“Blast!” he cursed, and ran his hand through his hair. “Forgive me, love. I am just so frustrated with the entire situation. Wickham has something planned, else he would not have been here to see Georgiana, and although after Ramsgate I believed that she trusted me when it came to that wastrel, I was obviously mistaken.”

“I doubt she will tell you the purpose of their meeting,” she stated matter-of-factly. “She has thus far refused to tell us anything of consequence, and I do not foresee that changing because of what I witnessed. Unfortunately, I think the only way we will know how she is involved with Wickham is to watch her closely.”

“I am loath to admit it, but I believe you are probably correct. But I still have to make an attempt to reach her.” He watched his wife as she rose and walked to him, placing her arms about his neck and claiming his lips softly with her own.

“You try to ascertain what Wickham, and possibly your sister, have planned. I will be waiting for you in our rooms.”

Smiling softly, he kissed her temple. “I will not be able to concentrate well enough to interrogate Georgiana thinking about that, Elizabeth,” he said softly next to her ear. A frisson passed through her, and he pulled away to offer her his arm. He escorted her to their suite where he stopped before the door to brush his lips against hers. Then she watched him stride to the very end of the hall to his sister's room and knock upon the door.

Darcy waited for Georgiana to answer as he glanced back down the hall to see Elizabeth's skirts disappear into their suite. He had to knock a second time before Amy, her maid, answered the door.

"Yes, sir?"

"I need to speak with Miss Darcy," he declared in a tone that brooked no opposition.

"I am sorry, but she is unable at the moment. Perhaps on the morrow?"

"No, I will not wait. You tell her that she *will* see me now. It is not a request—do you understand?" He observed the maid as her eyes grew wide, and she closed the door. He heard voices; although, he did not understand them until he heard his sister become angry.

"You had best be dressed, Georgiana, because I am coming in!" he called through the door while firmly grasping the handle. He entered to find his sister sitting in a chair by the fire, still as impeccably dressed as she was for dinner, with her wide-eyed maid standing next to her.

"You will leave us, Amy."

"How dare you, Fitzwilliam," his sister complained. "You have no right to dismiss my maid."

"I have every right, dear sister; I pay her wages. You do not have any money to pay her, remember?"

She stood as her eyes bored into him. "Then what do you want now? Make haste, I have things I would rather be doing."

Swallowing the anger her words were creating, he stepped forward, so that she had to look up at him. He had decided any advantage he could use certainly could not hurt.

242

"What were you doing meeting George Wickham in Lambton today?" he asked, observing her carefully in the event she let her guard down. He saw her eyes widen a bit in surprise before she quickly schooled her features to hide the emotion.

"And what makes you think I would be meeting with him?" she questioned in a snide tone.

"You were sighted. Do not play your games with me—I have had enough of them! You were also seen receiving a note from his hand. Where is it?"

"I have no such thing."

"Then you will not mind if I relocate you to another room in the guest wing while I have yours searched? Or maybe it is on your person?" He watched her eyes dart to the fire, and assumed she had burned the correspondence as he clenched his fists in frustration.

"What were you doing with George Wickham?" he asked once more, hoping to obtain some kind of response. However, he was disappointed when she returned to her seat, turned her face to the side, and stared into the fire. He was furious at her dismissal, but instead of losing his temper, he maintained his mask, and moved to stand in front of her, which prevented her from ignoring him.

"George and Jack Wickham have been put on a post coach, and are currently on their way to Nottinghamshire. In the future, Jarod will be the groom who escorts you while you ride, and Georgiana, there will be no substitutions for someone you would prefer. If you decide to walk around the grounds, Samuel and Matthew will accompany you as they do Elizabeth, and if she is out walking, then you will wait until she returns. Do you understand?" The expression on her face was positively furious as she stood with her hands clenched at her sides.

"I hate you!" she screamed, as she strode toward him, stopping a few steps short of him. "You are a hypocrite! You and your penniless, low-born wife!"

Darcy was visibly surprised at her statement regarding

Elizabeth. He had understood since their prior confrontation that she resented him, but it was the first time she had ever brought Elizabeth into the fray.

"You informed me that you hated me at Christmas, but I would be interested to hear how I am a hypocrite, and why you seem to have a problem with my wife. She has done nothing to deserve your anger. Elizabeth has only tried to save you from yourself."

"She was supposed to marry her cousin until the two of you eloped to London! Where are her fortune and connections, Fitzwilliam?" she asked disdainfully. "Your duty was to marry someone to elevate our status, not raise hers!"

"Our parents, although I barely knew them, married for wealth and connections, yet they never seemed happy. I will not live my life as miserably as they did. Let me inform you of something: you have a lonely life in store for you if you continue to look down upon everyone, as well as manipulate anyone who happens to fall in your path."

"As if you would ever have any idea what my life is like," she cried. "You are so gullible, that woman has fooled you, and you fell for it."

"Enough! You have not even taken the time to acquaint yourself with my wife, so you have no room to judge her. You will not so much as roll your eyes at her, or I will send you to Rosings to live with Lady Catherine."

"You would not dare!"

"Try me," he responded, holding her gaze with his own before she glanced to the side unable to continue. "If you decide you wish to speak, I will listen, but I am your guardian, and despite whether you like me or not, I will be treated with respect."

Striding from her bedchamber, he ventured downstairs, where he asked Roberts to find Mrs. Reynolds and accompany her to his study. They entered the room, and he turned from where he was staring at what was left of the fire in the grate.

244

"Please close the door," he began. "What I tell you right now is to be kept in the strictest of confidence." Seeing them nod their heads, he sat down behind his desk. "Jed Smith, who up until today was working in the stables, is none other than Jack Wickham, George Wickham's cousin." He watched as their eyebrows rose while they waited for him to continue. "Both men have been put on a post coach to Nottinghamshire, and hopefully, will not wake until they have made the majority of the trip. I am concerned that they are slipping letters to Miss Darcy through the post in some way. From this point on, all incoming and outgoing letters are to come to my desk before they are delivered or posted. Is that clear?"

"Yes sir," they chorused.

"Thank you. And now, I would like to retire for the evening."

"Of course, Master," said Roberts.

Darcy rose and went to his dressing room, where Evans was waiting to prepare him for the night. As he entered his room, Elizabeth was there as she had promised—well almost. She was seated provocatively on his bed, wearing her dressing gown, which was arranged to show that she wore nothing underneath it. Wearing a silly grin as he made his way to her, his expression caused her to laugh before she made him forget all about the Wickhams and his sister for the rest of the night.

~ * ~

The next morning, Darcy had awakened at dawn and, after he had kissed Elizabeth gently on the neck, had left her slumbering peacefully. He wished he could remain, but rang for Evans instead. Shaved and dressed, he informed Evans to please ask Mrs. Reynolds to accompany Amy, Miss Darcy's maid, to his study as he wished to have a word with the two of them. His valet had never been a man of many words, but the raised eyebrows on his face upon the master's request spoke volumes.

"What is the talk below stairs?"

"Sir, there is the normal tittle tattle, however yesterday there was some mention of Miss Darcy. I believe a few of the maids have noticed the strained relationship between you and the young miss."

"Is there anything that should concern me about what they are saying?" he inquired, worried.

"No, sir, I believe the talk at the moment is that the problem has to do with Miss Darcy not getting along with the new mistress."

Nodding, Darcy contemplated the situation. "When you inform Mrs. Reynolds, please do so discreetly. I do not wish to add more kindling to the fire, so to speak."

"Of course, sir." Evans replied, as he bowed and exited.

Leaving his dressing room, he strode downstairs to his study, requesting a pot of coffee from a chambermaid on his way. He had not been there long when a knock sounded, and Mrs. Reynolds opened the door, followed by Amy carrying the tray of coffee.

"Thank you for being so prompt," he began. He watched his housekeeper pour the coffee and place it next to him on the desk. "Amy, I need you to answer some questions for me. What I ask you—as well as what you tell me—is not to leave this room. Do you understand?" he asked, studying her reaction. Wide eyed, she nodded.

"I want to warn you now that if I ever discover that you have lied to me or reveal to anyone, even Miss Darcy, what was discussed this morning, you will be dismissed without reference, and escorted from Pemberley property." She nodded once more as he placed a sheet of paper in front of himself, prepared in the event he needed to write down anything of importance she might say.

"Now, are you by chance helping Miss Darcy to correspond with someone outside of Pemberley?"

"No, sir . . . I would never," the young woman stammered.

"Do you know of any unusual post she has received?" he asked, watching her furrow her brow as she thought.

"She often reads letters, except I do not think all of them are new. She does not receive much post. But when she is not studying with Mrs. Annesley, she often has what looks like a note that she is holding. Though, I only see her take it out within her rooms." She regarded him warily. "Sir, she will be extremely angry with me for saying any of this."

"It does not matter if she is angry. I pay your wages, and I wish answers. If she discovers we had this conversation and she begins to treat you ill, inform Mrs. Reynolds. We can find you another position within the house, or if you wish to seek employment elsewhere, I can provide you with a recommendation. Is that clear?"

"Yes, sir," she replied, appearing somewhat less agitated than before.

"Do you know what she does with these letters? Where she might keep them?"

"I do not know for certain," she said, as Darcy to looked at her doubtfully. "Honest. She has never put them away with me in the room."

"Is there anything that you can think of that I should know?" He hoped she would offer some information he had not thought to ask.

"No, sir."

"Thank you, Amy. If you should learn something, anything that you think would be important, I will reward you for disclosing it to me."

"Yes, sir," she said with wide eyes.

"You may go attend to your duties, and remember, you are not to say a word about this." He watched her nod once more and depart the room.

"What do you think, Mrs. Reynolds?"

"I believe we can trust her. She was hired at the same time as Mrs. Annesley, so she has not been her maid for long. I do not believe Miss Darcy confides in her."

Nodding his head as he considered everything he had learned since the day before, he took a sip of his coffee.

"Thank you, Mrs. Reynolds, that will be all for now," he said, as she curtsied and departed the room, leaving Darcy to ponder his next move.

He picked up the pen he had placed to the side, and wrote a letter to Richard. In the missive, he informed him of the events of the previous day, and the subsequent argument with Georgiana. He read over the letter when he finished, and noticed that his words were devoid of any feeling, and wondered when he had disconnected himself from any emotion when it came to his sister. Yesterday, he had been frustrated and angry at the situation and at her stupidity, but he had not been as hurt by it as he had been by the incident at Ramsgate. The lack of feeling was disturbing, to be sure, but he did not think he could endure much more of her manipulation or vitriol. Deciding that as long as things remained the way they were, he would have her come out in society when she turned seventeen, she would marry, and that would be it. His family would be the one he created with Elizabeth. That was to be his top priority, and by maintaining Georgiana's reputation at the present time, he was preserving the reputation of the Darcy name for the benefit of his children. That was all that mattered.

Chapter 20

Late March, 1812

Life at Pemberley continued as spring began to show hints of its arrival. Aside from practicing her pianoforte in the music room, walking and riding as weather permitted, Georgiana remained primarily in her rooms. She began requesting trays for breakfast and tea, taking her meals with Mrs. Annesley while she studied; however, she was still required to come down to dinner. She did not speak, so Darcy and Elizabeth merely conversed between themselves, not letting her surly disposition affect them.

While they chose to treat meals in this manner, they had not given up on her. Both had attempted to reach her, but to no avail. She simply ignored her brother, and stared at Elizabeth with nothing short of disdain when, in the vain attempt of having an affect on the girl's attitude, Elizabeth ventured to Georgiana's rooms. Nevertheless, Darcy still tried daily. Since they spent so much time dealing with a spoiled child, they did make a point of enjoying their time alone. After all, things were much more pleasant without a moody and brooding girl in attendance.

The end of March brought Easter, and plans for spring. All of the Darcys attended the Maundy Thursday, Good Friday and Easter Sunday services, followed by a formal meal and time in the library bundled together under a blanket on the sofa. Georgiana always excused herself immediately following the meal.

Despite spring showers, April bloomed and the Greys returned the Darcys' hospitality by inviting them to spend the day at Briarwood. The couple happily accepted, while Georgiana was informed she would remain at Pemberley; her brother did not wish to offend their hosts with her less-than-pleasant demeanour. As a result, the day was enjoyable, and the couple returned home late that evening exhausted, falling asleep the moment their heads touched the pillows.

~ * ~

Monday 20 April 1812

One rainy day, about a fortnight after their dinner at the Greys', Elizabeth finally felt the sensation she had been waiting so long to experience. Her aunt had informed her in one of her letters what she might expect, but it still did not prepare her for that light flutter in her lower abdomen as she was planning the menus for the next week. She sat stock still in shock at first, and then in an effort to see if it would re-occur. It was not until after she had completed her task and was writing a missive to her aunt that it finally happened once more. Beaming, she bit her lip while putting her hand tenderly on her belly.

"Well hello there, little one," she crooned softly.

Since she was almost finished, she completed the note and sealed it before she set off to her husband's study to surprise him with the news. Striding briskly to her destination, she knocked, and upon hearing him bid her to enter, she walked into the room and closed the door behind her.

She had not noticed anything was amiss until she stepped further into the room. Once she saw the expression on his face, she froze.

"Will, whatever is the matter!"

He appeared furious, and his expression was not softening as it usually did when she entered the room.

"What is this?" he immediately demanded, brandishing what appeared to be a letter.

Elizabeth looked at the paper and shrugged her shoulders. "I do not know? Why do you not tell me who wrote it, and then maybe I can help you."

"It is correspondence to you, from Wickham!"

"What! You must be joking! I have neither written to, nor received a letter from that man in my life, and I would never deign to accept one!"

250

"You must have, because I found these on the dressing table in your chambers!"

Elizabeth was incredulous. The only thing she could think to do was to attempt to control her emotions. She needed to calm him so they could speak about not only what he had discovered, but also where it possibly came from, since it most certainly did not come from her.

"I have never received anything from that man. The only time I have laid eyes on him since we left Meryton was when he was in Lambton, and I was accompanied by not only Miss Grey, but also Samuel, Matthew and Claire at the time, if you remember." Her husband was beyond angry, as he ceased to hear anything she said.

"Did he somehow plan our meeting, or even our marriage? How do I know you have not been deceiving me this entire time?"

The last accusation tore her to the quick, causing her to retaliate, stepping forward and slapping him fully across the face.

"How dare you, Fitzwilliam Darcy!" she cried, as tears poured down her cheeks. "I have *never* lied to you. When would I have supposedly received this letter, or even met with the man? The few times I have been out of your sight, you have had someone watching me for you. The day I went shopping, not only did I have to have two footmen, but I also had to have my maid accompany me. When the weather is nice enough for me to go for a walk, Samuel and Matthew are always with me! The only time I am alone is within the house!"

Taking a deep breath, she frantically attempted to wipe away her tears with her hands, since she forgot the handkerchief that resided in her pocket.

"Do not even mention that I could have received them in the post! Who would have sent them to me? My Aunt Gardiner? Charlotte Collins? Or maybe my newest correspondent, Miss Grey?! Please enlighten me! After all, you have been sorting my mail as you open your sister's for the past few weeks. I have even sat in this very room with you, and opened my letters. Why would I do that if I had something to hide?"

Trying with every fibre of her being not to collapse and sob at his feet while he stared at her with a clenched jaw, she once again took in a large breath before weakly uttering, "How dare you." With that, she could no longer look at him, and turned as she fled from the room. She did not stop until she reached her chambers, where she collapsed on the bed sobbing into her pillow until she cried herself to sleep.

Darcy slumped down into his seat, and thought about Elizabeth's reaction to his accusations. It had been an accident when he had found the letter on her dressing table. He had simply gone to her room to leave a few roses from the conservatory around the house where she would find them throughout the day: her dressing table, her desk in the mistress's study, her case of needlework. Her room had been the first place, since he knew she was not there. He had been shocked to see a piece of paper with George Wickham's handwriting gracing the surface of his wife's dressing table— where she sat when her hair was styled each morning and brushed out each evening. Her vanity was such a personal space. And Wickham had invaded it. Seeing that missive had caused a fit of jealousy he had never experienced before, and he had no idea how to deal with those unfamiliar emotions.

Darcy had immediately grabbed it, and rushed down to his study, where he read his contraband as quickly as he was able. As he read, he seethed and became increasingly angry at the blatant familiarity within the message. He then paced for some time after, his ire increasing the longer he had to contemplate the issue. By the time Elizabeth had come through the door, she had looked so happy, and he had not even given her the chance to explain why she had sought him out.

As he sat there reviewing the argument in his head, he had to admit that she was right. She had either been with him or someone he trusted implicitly since they had been married, and she did have a very limited acquaintance. Her aunt, Charlotte Collins and Miss Grey were her only correspondents, none of whom would have ever included a note from another man in her letters. Charlotte Lucas had always seemed a very level headed woman, at least until she had married William Collins, but she was not even in Hertfordshire anymore. She was in Kent, and had obviously posted her correspondence directly at the post station in Hunsford.

"Why did I not just ask first?" he mumbled to himself.

As he did not know where the letter originated, he was still hesitant about trusting her, especially after all of the recent issues with Georgiana. Darcy had never been one to trust easily; he had had too many people in his life that had never lived up to the faith he had inherently bestowed upon them—his parents, his aunts and uncles, Wickham, and lastly, Georgiana. But the look on Elizabeth's face—he could not erase the heartbroken expression she wore from his mind.

He headed up to his room a few hours later, and sat down to try to clear his head so he could think. Looking toward his wife's room, he crept toward the door, and listened to see if he could hear her before carefully turning the knob. She was curled up on her side, sleeping, and he tiptoed closer until he reached the edge of the bed. He brushed the backs of his fingers down her cheek, which was still damp with her tears, taking a deep breath before exiting back out of the room.

A few hours later, he dressed for dinner, and made his way to downstairs. A part of him expected to find his wife waiting for him; however, he was to be disappointed as there was only Georgiana. Once he escorted his sister in to dinner, he took a seat.

"Is your wife not joining us?" she asked with affected amazement.

"No, I believe she was feeling a bit ill."

"Oh?"

Looking up, he studied his sister intently. She had been silent at meals since the last argument over her meeting with Wickham in Lambton, yet she chose tonight to actually ask about his wife. The coincidence was a bit much to ignore, but he decided that he would have to keep to himself until he determined the truth of the situation.

He was desperately worried about alienating Elizabeth, but he was not sure what to do. He had hoped to speak with her before dinner, but she did not come down. The problem was that even if she had come down, he did not know what to say to her. He had never felt so strongly for another human being, and the pain of finding that letter had been acute. That Georgiana might have been responsible for the letter had not entered his mind until after he had confronted Elizabeth; in hindsight, he should have considered her probable involvement immediately. A part of his heart was telling him that Elizabeth was not telling him a falsehood, but he was scared, and was not sure he could move forward without proof.

Brother and sister ate their meal in silence, while Darcy glanced at Georgiana from time to time. She almost appeared pleased with herself, a small smirk remaining on her face for the entirety of the meal, which made him more resolute in his decision to ascertain if she was in any way involved (or Heaven forbid, *responsible*) for the day's catastrophe. By the end of dinner, he knew that he must unearth the truth quickly, before his relationship with his wife became irreparably damaged. He could only pray that it was not already.

Elizabeth had napped until around dinner, awaking to a headache and queasy stomach. Claire helped her change into a shift, and requested some toast and broth from the kitchen. Once she had gingerly eaten the tray, she lay back down, and quickly fell back to sleep.

By the next morning, her stomach had settled, but the headache had not abated. When she broke her fast in her room, she fully expected her husband to come and question why she was not leaving her chambers. He never came. The thought of another confrontation caused her dread, but she was disappointed wholeheartedly that he did not care enough to inquire whether she felt poorly.

Picking up her needlework, she contemplated the

circumstances of the previous day. She would wager that Georgiana was somehow behind the letter, which meant that the girl had been in her private rooms. She rose and quickly checked to see if her journal was where it was supposed to be, worried that perhaps she had tampered with it in an effort to find some other manner in which to manipulate her or Darcy.

Once she had ensured the book was still within her writing desk, she stared at the cover for a while. Eventually, she flipped to the last entry—dated yesterday morning—scanned her words, brushed a tear aside, and made a decision.

~ * ~

It was near mid-day, as Darcy sat in his study going over different scenarios in his mind. He was attempting to decide what to do about the entire situation with the letter, when there was a knock at the door. After calling for the person to enter, he looked up, surprised to find Claire standing before his desk, holding out a book he did not recognize.

"Excuse me, sir," she began cautiously. "But the mistress asked me to give this to you."

"Thank you," he paused as he took the book. "She was not at dinner last night or breakfast this morning. Is she well?"

"She was a bit queasy, and had a headache last night, but her stomach was improved by this morning."

"Good," he replied absentmindedly, disquieted by the thought that she had been unwell.

As Claire stood there waiting to be excused, Darcy had an idea.

"Would you please go get Mrs. Reynolds and Miss Darcy's maid, and bring them here?"

She nodded as she dropped a curtsy, and strode out of the door. Turning his attention to the book, he flipped through it, only to realise Elizabeth had sent him her journal. However, before he could give it his attention, Claire returned with the two women in tow. The three regarded him curiously as they stood in front of his desk. He closed the book while he definitively decided to implement his plan.

"I believe that Miss Darcy is currently attending her studies with Mrs. Annesley?"

"Yes, sir," Amy replied. "They are currently in Mrs. Annesley's sitting room, working."

He nodded, quietly contemplating the list of things that would need to be accomplished in his mind.

"Mrs. Reynolds, I would like a room aired and cleaned in the guest wing for Miss Darcy's use," he began, watching the housekeeper's eyebrows lift in surprise. "I want her current suite locked, and I want a footman posted outside of the door. Under no circumstances is she allowed back inside that room. Do I make myself clear?"

"Yes, sir," they chorused with surprised looks on all of their faces.

"She is not to leave the house without escort, and she has an assigned groom that is to ride with her should she choose to go out on her horse.

Mrs. Reynolds. Amy. Once you have the maids preparing a room, I want the two of you to begin with my sister's gowns and dresses. All of the pockets and reticules are to be checked, and anything out of the ordinary should be brought directly to me. Then they can be moved down to the new room for her use. Obviously, Mrs. Darcy is your first priority, Claire, but if you have the time, I am sure they would appreciate your assistance."

"Pardon me, Mr. Darcy," Amy began timidly. "What should I tell Miss Darcy?"

"I will take care of her. You just do as you are told."

"Yes, sir," she said quickly, with wide eyes.

"When you have finished, please notify me."

256

Mrs. Reynolds nodded, and after ushering the two maids out of the room, she closed the door. Darcy took a deep breath and left his study striding up the stairs to the portion of Mrs. Annesley's suite that was used as a schoolroom. Halting before the door, he sighed and ran his hand through his hair before knocking and stepping through.

"Pardon me for interrupting, Mrs. Annesley." he began sincerely. "May I have a word with you in the hall for a moment?"

"Of course, sir," she replied with a concerned expression. He noticed his sister frown as her companion followed him out of the room and into the empty hallway.

"If you remember, almost a month ago, Miss Darcy met with George Wickham in Lambton. At the time, he slipped her a letter, and I am beginning to suspect they are corresponding. Since she will not speak to me, I will be conducting a thorough search of her rooms. Arrangements have been made for her to be relocated to different chambers, and we will be searching her belongings before they are moved."

"Sir, if she is corresponding with that man, I have not seen any evidence of it."

"No, I did not think you would, but I do need you to pay attention to what she is doing when she is with you. If she happens to be reading a letter, or you find one in her possession, you are to confiscate it and bring it directly to me. Is that clear?"

"Yes . . . yes, of course."

"Good, I wish to have a discussion with my sister, but I would like you to remain." He noticed her nod in recognition, and returned to the room where he focused his attention on Georgiana, who looked up from her book.

"Is there something you wanted, Brother?" she said in a happier tone than he had heard in some time.

"Actually, there is, *Sister*," he responded, with some disdain. "I would like you to empty your pockets first."

"What?" she replied, losing some of her composure.

"And if you brought any books with you from your room, I wish to see them."

"What is the meaning of this?"

"I do not have to tell you a thing. Do as I say, or I will do it for you," he said through his teeth, as he leaned toward her, staring into her eyes. He smiled inwardly as she paled, and reached down to turn out her pockets, which only produced a handkerchief that was placed in his outstretched hand. Once he was sure there was nothing concealed within the thin material, he returned it to her, observing her expression as she hastily stuffed it into her pocket.

"Did you bring any of these books from your rooms?"

"No," she replied disdainfully. "These remain within Mrs. Annesley's rooms."

As he watched the thinly concealed contempt crossing her face, he looked to her companion, who nodded in confirmation before delivering the coup de grace. "At this very moment, Mrs. Reynolds and your maid are moving your belongings to a suite in the guest wing, and your former rooms will be locked until I have searched them thoroughly. When my search is complete—and not a moment before—I will decide if you may return to the family wing, or if you will remain in the guest wing."

He was unconcerned that his sister regarded him with pure and utter loathing. He was unconcerned that his actions might damage their relationship for the rest of their lives. He was going to discover the truth one way or another, and she was just going to have to remember that he could make her life a living hell.

He knew she would not respond further to him, so he turned and strode out of the room to his sister's dressing room, where he checked on Mrs. Reynolds's progress. They had gone through the majority of her clothes, but to no avail. Passing through her dressing room, he sat before her desk and began sorting through the contents. Once an item was determined to be unimportant, he placed it in a crate next to the desk that would delivered to Georgiana's new room.

He went through her desk twice, filled the box, and had it removed to the guest wing. He had found nothing. Disheartened and hungry, he went downstairs for a small repast, and then returned to Georgiana's room to search her bedside table. He carefully sorted through his sister's belongings, repeating the process he used with her desk. Frustrated because he did not know exactly what he was seeking or what was important, he decided prepare for dinner.

Georgiana did not come down to dinner, but Elizabeth did. Her eyes were red rimmed, and although she nodded at his reserved greeting, she did not speak throughout the meal. In fact, other than greeting him, she did not even look at him. She barely touched her food, pleaded a headache as soon as they finished, and stood to leave the room. He stood and asked if she was well, as she rose from her seat, but she only mumbled something unintelligible while she nodded then quit the room.

Upon entering his study later that evening, he glanced around the room, missing Elizabeth as he contemplated the events of the last day. He felt he was on the right course, but was truly worried about how long it would take to find evidence of the truth, so he could trust his wife with his whole heart once more. Remembering her journal, he opened it to the beginning; reading from where Elizabeth had began almost a year prior.

Meanwhile, Elizabeth had returned to her rooms after dinner. She swiftly concluded her evening toilette and fell asleep the moment she laid her head on the pillow. The stress of the situation combined with her condition had caused a headache, which had worn her down, and she slept through until morning.

Chapter 21

Friday 24 April 1812

The remainder of the week progressed in much the same
fashion. Elizabeth's nights seemed to alternate. One night
she would cry herself to sleep, slumbering fitfully, and the
next pass out from the exhaustion of the night before.

Darcy was not sleeping well either. He was meeting with his
steward after breaking his fast every morning, and then
when he was not having his meals, he was searching his
sister's rooms, frantically trying to find anything to absolve
Elizabeth. He would usually fall asleep in the early hours of
the morning as he was reading her journal, only to repeat the
process the next day. The end of the week, however, finally
brought the breakthrough he was seeking, when a letter fell
into his lap as he opened a book from the small library his
sister kept on some shelves next to the fireplace. Setting
down the book, he picked up the note and glared at the
handwriting.

"Wickham!" he seethed through clenched teeth.

Unfolding the paper, he dropped into a chair as he read.

Dear G,

I recently found London to be no longer to my liking,

"Which means that you gambled away whatever money you
had," he mumbled.

*so I have joined a militia unit stationed in Hertfordshire.
You had told me he was here, but imagine my surprise to
catch a glimpse of your brother in passing on the very day I
arrived.*

Darcy's eyebrows lifted. Wickham was following him, and
Georgiana was helping? Eager to know more, he began to
read once more.

He and his friend Bingley were riding through Meryton while my friend, Lt. Denny, was introducing me to some of the locals. Bingley stopped to speak with one of the daughters of a local gentleman. It was apparent in your brother's expression that he did see me, but simply rode past—he did not even have the courage to face me.

Darcy snorted and continued.

Last night, the officers were invited to a party at the home of a Sir William Lucas, where I was in company with many of the families of the neighbourhood. I have begun warning people with whom I have become acquainted of your brother's infamous treatment of me. He is already not favoured by many due to his haughty attitude, which has caused several to believe my side of things for a change, and not side immediately with his money and connections. Hopefully, no one will be taken in by his false sense of decorum.

So this was the source of Georgiana's information regarding his wife. The scenario made sense, since Wickham would have been in Hertfordshire during the aftermath of Elizabeth's escape and subsequent marriage.

Let me know when you next make it to London, and we can arrange another meeting in Hyde Park. Do not forget to call me the name we agreed upon, otherwise we might clue in your companion as to who I truly am. I miss you desperately and look forward to seeing you again.

Yours,

G.W.

Darcy lifted the book and flipped through the pages. He found two more letters before he turned it upside down and shook it to ensure he had found them all. Then he suddenly thought of the night he had confronted Georgiana about meeting Wickham in Lambton, and remembered the manner in which she quickly looked towards the fire when he mentioned the letter. She was not looking at the fireplace, but the bookshelf next to it!

Grabbing one of the crates next to the door, he pulled the

chair up to the fireplace, and began sorting through the books, one at a time. Not all of them had letters, but he checked every book, especially her novels, which seemed to be her preferred hiding places.

He was tired, and it was time for dinner by the time he had sorted through all of them. There were approximately twenty letters hidden within the contents of the shelves, beginning just after Ramsgate, and ending with the correspondence she had received when she had met him in Lambton. As he had gone through them, he placed them in chronological order, then read them, attempting to find any hidden meanings, but failing miserably.

He was relieved that none of them were love notes, or made reference to anything of that nature. He would have found it excruciating to read something like that about his little sister, no matter his current feelings toward her. Instead, they seemed to be more of an accounting of Wickham's life, and the people he met. The lengthiest of letters, which was written after their wedding announcement, even chronicled the Bennet family, Elizabeth's refusal of Mr. Collins and subsequent disappearance, as well as Wickham's reaction to the news of their wedding.

The final missive, however, was different and a bit more detailed. It indicated that there was a letter enclosed that Georgiana should, after some period of time, place in a noticeable spot in the mistress's chambers. Cursing himself for questioning his wife's loyalty, he rose from his seat as he placed the last of the books into the crate.

He instructed a footman to take the box to his sister's chambers, then asked Mrs. Reynolds to bring his father's miniature of Wickham from the case downstairs. She returned quickly, carrying the likeness and wearing a puzzled look on her face as he asked her to accompany him to Mrs. Annesley's room.

They were admitted to the companion's sitting room, and the lady regarded them carefully as she became worried she had done something she should not have.

"Mrs. Annesley," Darcy began. "I need to know if you have

ever seen this man?" he asked, holding out the miniature. She took it from his hand as he watched her reaction carefully.

"Of course," she replied, smiling. "This is Mr. Simpson."

"No, *that* is George Wickham." The woman's eyes became round as saucers, and she blanched when she came to the realisation of what she had unwittingly allowed.

"Mr. Darcy, I would have never knowingly . . ."

"I understand. I should have shown you this portrait when you became Georgiana's companion, but I thought the matter was resolved. I did not think he would continue contact her. That was my mistake. But now I need to know how many times since you began as my sister's companion that you have seen him. I also need a full accounting of what happened at each instance."

"It always seemed accidental. We would take a walk in Hyde Park, and we would just happen upon him. Miss Darcy introduced me. She said he was a good friend of yours," she continued worriedly, wringing her hands as she spoke. "There was never anything of consequence said. They would each inquire as to the other's health, and he would always ask about you."

"What information did my sister give him?"

"It was all rather general. She would usually inform him of your wellbeing and your whereabouts, Pemberley; London; or Hertfordshire, at the last meeting. Then usually they said their goodbyes, and he would bow over her hand."

"I need you to think carefully about anything that was said that might not have seemed important at the time, but could possibly have meant more than it seemed. By what you have said, he was using Georgiana to keep track of my location. However, just in case there was more, please try to write an accounting of each meeting, if you can," he requested seriously, as she nodded in agreement. "In the meantime, do not trust my sister. Other than when she is in her rooms, she is to be supervised at all times. Is that clear?"

"Yes, sir," she replied.

They left the room and separated—Mrs. Reynolds to attend her duties, and Darcy to his sister's room. He walked in to find her frantically searching through the crate of books.

"Are you looking for these?" he questioned, brandishing the letters he had discovered.

"You have no right!" she exclaimed. She charged toward him, yet stopped just before him.

"I have every right as your brother and guardian to ensure your reputation remains intact, which compels me to confiscate these. Now, Wickham always has a plan, and I want to know what it is this time."

"I do not know," she said, sitting in one of the chairs by the fire and turning away from him.

"I have had enough of you turning your back on me! Face me, Georgiana, or so help me, I will turn you around myself!" Darcy stood with clenched fists while she slowly rotated her body to face him once more, a livid expression on her face. "Let me explain something about Wickham. Our father always enjoyed his company. And Wickham was his godson, so he wished him to have a living when it came available. *He did not want the living, Georgiana.* He requested and was given three thousand pounds in lieu of the position. In addition to the one thousand our father left him outright in his will. He gambled it away in less than three years, and then returned requesting the position when it became available." It was difficult to discern if she was even listening, as her face was impassive.

"I refused at that time, and I did not see him again until Ramsgate. Whatever he has told you is a lie. All he wants is your dowry, Georgiana, and if he were to receive it, it would be gambled and wasted away. You would then be left somewhere, probably with a child or two, to fend for yourself, unless you managed to find your way back to me. I must tell you though, after your attempt to interfere with my marriage, I am not sure I would allow you back into my home." He watched as Georgiana's eyes widened.

264

"You should also be aware that it takes both Richard *and* me to approve your marriage and dispense your dowry, which we will not do if you wed Wickham. That alone will make you worthless to him, and he will have his way with you, leaving you stranded somewhere within a fortnight. I would stake my life on it." He paused to see if she would have some kind of reaction to his disclosure, but he was disappointed. She had quickly masked her earlier response, and now exhibited no emotion whatsoever.

"You should also know that Lord Matlock and Lady Catherine would refuse to take you in as well. They would not wish for the scandal you create to touch them, and would send you away to live in exile for the remainder of your life. As I see it, you need to decide where your loyalties lie." He ran his hand through his hair as he scanned the room. He remembered Wickham and himself as boys, scaling the trellised climbing rose bushes on the family wing of the house. They were all over the stone walls of that wing, which included the terrace of her old chambers.

"Due to the fact that this bedchamber does not have a balcony, you will reside here indefinitely." She looked up at him, her eyes once again widening as he spoke, yet she remained mute. "You will not return to London until you come out, which will be as soon as it is socially acceptable. I may even hand you over to Lord and Lady Matlock and let them find you a husband. They will not care about your preferences, and will choose someone according to rank and wealth, which frankly, I am seriously considering as well."

He took a deep breath as he ran his hand through his hair. "You attempted to sabotage my marriage, Georgiana. You entered Elizabeth's private rooms without permission, and planted a note to make it look like she married me for ulterior motives. I cannot understand why. Why would you wish to take away one of the few people who truly loves me?"

He did not expect an answer, and since he knew there would be nothing further coming from her, he turned and left her there. As he exited, he nodded to one of Samuel's younger brothers who was stationed in the hall. He had hired them during the last week, in the event she attempted to sneak out. He was thankful for the footman's large family, long time tenants, who had always been immensely trustworthy. He had hired the two youngest siblings to keep tabs on his sister when she was not with him or Mrs. Annesley, and had every confidence in them.

He dressed for dinner, met Elizabeth in the drawing room and escorted her to the dining room. The footman who stepped forward to help his wife with her seat was waved off, and he pulled the chair out himself before taking the seat next to her. She looked at him curiously, yet remained quiet, as she had since the confrontation he whole-heartedly wished he could forget. He was not surprised that his sister did not come down for dinner.

"It appeared to be a lovely day. Did you take a walk?"

"Yes, Samuel and Matthew accompanied me around the lake," she answered cautiously, glancing over to see him nod.

"Mrs. Reynolds commented to me yesterday that you visited a few of our tenants?"

Elizabeth did not know what to make of her husband. She had been extremely hurt when he had accused her of being in collusion with Wickham. Claire, however, had kept her abreast of everything, from his inquiries over her health to his sister's removal to the guest wing, and the subsequent search of her rooms. Georgiana's guilt had always been the obvious conclusion in her eyes, although, he seemed to need tangible proof. He had not spoken much at meals, with the exception of household matters, but now he seemed to want to have a conversation.

"Yes, Mrs. Smith had her baby, and Mrs. Reynolds prepared a basket for me to deliver to her. Then Samuel brought me to check on his mother. She has been ill recently. I brought her a basket as well, and arranged for the physician in Lambton to come pay her a visit, so hopefully she will be up and about soon . . . It . . . was good of you to find a small job for the boys to share. The extra bit of money will help them out quite a bit." She watched as her husband swallowed his bite, now seemingly uncomfortable.

"They are a good family, and have always been excellent in

whatever capacity I hire one of them. The two eldest have never worked for me, because they worked with their father until they took on farms of their own, but the three daughters work as maids within the house, and now the two youngest sons are working here for the time being."

"Yes," she replied with a small smile. "Mrs. Ellis never ceases singing your praises." She noticed him blush, and as he was obviously uncomfortable with the praise, she changed the subject, continuing with small talk for the remainder of the meal.

As soon as they were finished, Darcy offered her his arm, which she took hesitantly, but instead of escorting her to the drawing room, he began walking in the direction of his study. He had longed for her so much during the week (not to mention the lavender and rose scent she was wearing was driving him to distraction) that he did not want to make small talk. He only wanted to be alone with her in the closest place available.

Elizabeth was confused as they entered the office, but did not have time to inquire, as her husband turned abruptly, pinning her body to the door with his own and kissing her. She had missed him so much that while she was hurt by his accusations, she pushed the circumstances of the past week to the far recesses of her mind as she attempted to lose herself in his embrace.

She felt his hand begin caressing her breast as his tongue parted her lips to taste what he had missed so dearly. He curved his other arm behind her to grasp her rear, and pull her as close to him as possible. Manoeuvring her to his desk, he lifted her to the top as she parted her legs, and pulled his body to hers. She could feel his heat penetrating through her clothes to her skin.

However, reality could not be kept at bay for long, and began to intrude in her mind as he was pushing her skirts to her waist and unbuttoning the fall of his breeches to release his length.

"No . . . Will, stop!" He released her, and she put her hands to her cheeks. They were wet with tears she was unaware she had shed.

"What is it?" He looked at her, bewildered, as she quickly slid from the top of his desk, and adjusted her skirts.

"Are you crying?"

"I am sorry," she said quietly, as she unlocked the door and ran from the room. She did not stop until she reached her bedchamber, where she leaned against locked door as she wept.

Darcy stood in place, still staring at the door she slammed. Suddenly realising that he was only partially dressed, he hastily pulled up his breeches from where they had been pushed to his thighs and closed the fall before swiftly following his wife.

Worried she would refuse him access to her room from the hall, he went to the door that adjoined the sitting room to the mistress's bedchambers and knocked. He waited for some time, yet although he could hear movement, she was not answering.

"Elizabeth, please!" he finally implored through the door. Noticing after a moment the knob turning, he watched as the door slowly opened to reveal her tear-stained face and red-rimmed eyes. He had felt like a heel as she ran from the room, and while he did not think it was possible, he now felt even worse. How could he have not noticed that something was wrong?

She moved aside as he entered her bedchamber, regarding him cautiously as he paced back and forth.

"You ran from my study crying, Elizabeth, and just now you did not want to let me in. Why?"

She looked at him aghast as he spoke, and found it hard to control her emotions. "Why?!" she began angrily. "Why? You really do not understand why I would be upset?" She observed his expression incredulously as he seemed surprised by her ire. "I came to your study to speak with you, and you accused me of betrayal—of even lying to you from

268

the beginning of our marriage in the harshest manner you have ever used with me," she began, unable to control her emotions as tears of hurt and anger began to fall down her face once again. "You then ignored me for a week, only asking of the most menial of household or estate business that for some reason you required during our meals, which were otherwise eaten in silence until tonight, when you show up acting as if nothing has happened. Am I supposed to just instantly forget how much you hurt me?"

Darcy stood before her, knowing that he should not be shocked by her fury, but he was.

"I missed you so much this week that it was painful. Did you think it was easy for me to be in the same room with you while you mostly pretended that I was not there?" Taking a deep breath, she wiped her eyes with her hands. "Tonight, I just wanted so badly to feel close to you that I tried to push away the hurt to be with you, but it was impossible. It felt like we were a thousand miles apart."

"But I was not far away, love. I have missed you desperately as well, and I was feeling possessive," he said, as he pulled her into his arms. "I was right there."

Elizabeth allowed him to hold her close. She inhaled the woodsy smell of his cologne that always made her feel secure, at home, before pushing herself back from his body.

"What has changed?"

"I do not understand, Elizabeth," he said, feeling physically bereft from her withdrawal.

"You have avoided or barely spoken to me for a week!" she cried. "What has changed?"

Suddenly understanding the meaning of the question, he ran his hand through his hair. "I cannot imagine that Claire has not told you anything."

"It does not matter what she has told me. I want to hear it from you. I *deserve* to hear it from you."

He thought about the situation for a moment. If he had been in her place, he would have wanted an explanation as well, so he could not find fault with her for that. "I found letters from Wickham to Georgiana hidden within her suite," he admitted sadly. "He orchestrated all of this to drive a wedge between us."

"So you needed proof that you could trust me, and now you have it?"

"Elizabeth, please," he implored. "I do trust you, but I was so insanely jealous and hurt when I read what was in that letter, that I reacted without thinking. He alluded to you meeting on your walks in Hertfordshire, not to mention the day when you would be together again, for God's sake. Every bit of time I have had since, I have spent in my sister's chambers searching for something to confirm the suspicions I formed after thinking about it with a clearer head."

Reaching out, he attempted to take her hand, which she pulled back as she stepped further away from him, the pain of the past week etched all over her beautiful face. She walked over to the window, and stared out at the lake reflecting back in the moonlight.

"And I am supposed to instantly forget this past week, your accusations, the lack of trust and the callous disregard, simply because you have decided that I am innocent," she said softly, with a mournful expression on her face. "I do not wish to argue with you anymore tonight. Please leave me."

Darcy felt like he had been stabbed in the chest, yet she was correct. He had expected her to just forgive and forget, without so much as an apology, all because he could not bear to admit that he had been wrong. Her feelings were not unreasonable; nevertheless, he still found it difficult to say what he now realised he would have to tell her.

He watched as she sank heavily down into the window seat. She curled her legs up underneath her as she stared at whatever was outside of the glass. She looked so small and fragile, not weak, though. His wife was definitely not a weak woman. She situated herself, and he noticed that she placed her hand on her stomach, carefully cradling the small swell that he had not noticed until that moment.

Suddenly, like pieces to a puzzle, everything from the last few months fit together: her sporadic illness, her fatigue, and even tonight, how emotional she was. When had she planned on trusting him with the news? After all, he had every right to know.

"Elizabeth, when were you going to tell me that you are with child?"

Chapter 22

She turned her head to stare at him with wide eyes. "How did you . . . who told you?"

"You did," he said, as he pointed to her abdomen. "When you placed your hand on your waist. I would think you have known for some time; so when were you going to inform me?"

"I did not wish to tell you until I was certain, which was a week ago, when the babe quickened. I immediately went down to your study to surprise you, but you had other things you wished to . . . discuss," she replied with a cold edge to her voice he was unaccustomed to hearing.

Darcy was stunned as her meaning became clear and his eyes widened. Good God! She had come to tell him she was with child when he hurled those atrocious allegations at her. If he had realised before that he owed her an apology, he now understood that he should be grovelling for mercy, and he was not even sure that was sufficient.

He looked up to where she had returned to staring outside, and crept quietly over to the window, sitting on the edge of the seat facing her.

"Elizabeth," he said softly. She turned to look at him, bringing to view her tear-streaked face that only reinforced what an ass he had been. "I am so terribly sorry for hurting you the way I did. When I found the letter on your dressing table, I did not think to question where it came from, other than the obvious, and I became insanely jealous and irrational. While nothing can take back what I said to you or how I behaved, I swear to you that I do trust you. I know that by my actions, it seems that I do not, but I doubted my rash assumptions as soon as you slapped me. Everything I have done since that morning has been to prove that my trust in you was not misplaced."

He watched as her eyebrow rose in a silent challenge to his

272

statement, and understood he had probably not phrased his thoughts in the best way; he quickly continued. "I know that it is *not* an excuse, but I have had very few people in my life who I could trust. I do not do so easily, and my sister's betrayal has not helped. The letter Wickham gave Georgiana in Lambton was the instruction for all of this mess," he said, as he held out the letter, allowing her to take it from his grasp. "He wanted to drive us apart, and Georgiana implemented his plan."

Pausing a moment so she could read the majority of the missive, he took a deep breath before continuing with a mournful expression. "I am truly sorry that I did not trust you, and that I caused you pain; this past week has been a torment for me as well. I will never forgive myself for the way I have treated you, especially now that you have told me why you came to see me that day."

"Have you confronted Georgiana about finding the letters and intruding into my rooms?" she asked. "I can tell you now that if you have not, I will." Attempting to control her tears, she studied his expression as he began his response.

"I challenged her about the letters, as well as the intrusion into your rooms, but she said very little." He sighed as he nervously ran his hand through his hair, worried she would reject any attempt he made to touch her. "Her motivation is a mystery to me, but I swear to you that I will not let her come between us again.

She finished the letter and looked up at him warily. "I cannot go through this again," she stated softly.

"I know, love. Never, I promise." He waited as she scrutinized him, with tears still trailing down her face. Cautiously he reached for her hand, and stroked her knuckles with his thumb. When she did not protest, he gathered her into his lap as she began to sob, stroking her back while he held her as close to himself as possible. "I love you so much," he crooned into her ear until she quieted. He had not realised she had fallen asleep, until her body relaxed in his arms. Then he carried her into his room to put her in his bed, where she belonged. Carefully, he removed her clothing down to her chemise, marvelling at how soundly she slept before creeping to his dressing room, where Evans helped him prepare for the night.

She was sleeping on her side when he returned, and divesting himself of his robe, he gingerly entered the bed, curling up behind her as he wrapped her in his embrace.

~ * ~

Elizabeth was surprised when she woke late the next morning to find herself in her husband's room, but as she remembered the events of the prior night, she understood how she had come to be there. She gingerly lifted her head from his shoulder and watched him sleep until he stirred and opened his eyes.

"Good morning, love."

"Good morning," she replied, suddenly uncomfortable.

"Selfishly, I did not wish to sleep alone again last night. I hope you do not mind that I placed you in my bed. I have not slept well without you—I missed you."

"No," she replied. "I have missed you as well, but I cannot just forget instantly that you did not trust me, that you abandoned me. It is going to take time."

"As long as you let me prove to you that I will never do it again," he replied, caressing her cheek with his hand.

She looked at him appraisingly. "Did you read my journal?"

"Very little," he replied. "I was so busy searching Georgiana's rooms that I did not have much time until I was in bed. I would begin to read, but exhaustion would usually claim me soon after. Would you mind if I finished it now that I have more time?"

"No, I do not mind. I had used the last of the pages a few days before I gave it to you. Fortunately, I purchased a new one when I was last in Lambton." She studied him for a few moments. "Since you were searching your sister's rooms all week, you must have a good bit of work waiting for you."

274

"More than likely, I do. Perhaps we should begin our day," he said reluctantly, not wishing to force anything between them. "Shall I come to escort you downstairs?"

"I would like that," she answered with a small smile.

Over the next week, Elizabeth learned that if one thing could be said for Fitzwilliam Darcy, he was certainly adept at grovelling. From that day forward, he found some manner of surprising her daily. He placed flowers throughout the house in rooms that she frequented for her to find, he planned surprise picnics by the lake, and conspired with Mrs. Reynolds to have her favourite desserts worked into the menu without her knowledge. Elizabeth was beginning to think that she should be upset with her husband more often.

~ * ~

Friday 22 May 1812

The feeling of something soft tickling down her bare back made Elizabeth squirm just before she felt her husband's body cuddle up behind her. She felt him begin kissing across her shoulder and up her neck until his warm breath behind her ear caused her to shiver.

"Mmmmmmm," she moaned, as she rolled to face him.

"Good morning, love," he smiled. She opened her eyes, and saw the rose he was now trailing down her face.

"When did you rise?" she asked, noticing he was dressed in a shirt and breeches.

"I have been awake for an hour or so, working up here at the writing desk," he said softly. Since they had reconciled, he had begun working some in his rooms while she napped or slept late, one of which tended to happen daily. "I like being able to keep watch over you while you rest."

A month had passed since the end of the letter fiasco, and with the passage of that time, Elizabeth to returned to her old self. However, true to herself and her marriage, she did not hold back, and they had spent the time since rarely leaving the side of the other.

They had spent the entirety of the day before in their rooms, playing chess and reading, giving Darcy reason to be ecstatic. He felt they were finally back where they had been prior to Georgiana and Wickham's interference. Praying she felt the same, he had planned for them to break their fast in their rooms before they spent the day together doing whatever she wished.

Elizabeth watched as he pulled down the sheet to examine her stomach. Rolling her eyes despite her very large smile, she laughed at the silly grin adorning his face as he studied the now bump that graced her abdomen, and leaned over to kiss it softly.

"How is my child today?" he asked, since he knew from her that the babe tended to be pretty active in the morning. He splayed his hand over her stomach, waiting. Since he had discovered she was carrying their child, he had wanted desperately to feel the baby move, but had had to settle for his wife's descriptions. While he was thrilled with the prospect of being a father, he was still unhappy over Georgiana's reaction to the news. When they informed her at dinner a fortnight ago, she simply raised her eyebrows and looked as displeased as ever.

"Moving around a little," she replied. "Aunt Gardiner said in her last letter that it would probably be another few weeks before you could feel anything." He pouted like a child and she giggled.

"I know. It does not mean that I cannot hope that it happens sooner."

"Will, what would you like for your birthday?" she asked. Although he had told her his birthday during one of their late night chats early in their marriage, Mrs. Reynolds had gently reminded her that he would be eight and twenty on the last day of the month. Elizabeth, who had chuckled at the not so subtle hint, had not decided what she wished to do, and thought he might have some preference.

"Your forgiveness and our child are my gifts. All that I could ever want is right here, unless you can get him to move on command for me," he finished with a smile. "I simply wish to spend the day with you."

"But there is nothing unusual in that. We have been doing that every day."

"Then why do anything different?"

She growled softly at his stubbornness, and he chuckled. "You, sir, are impossible."

He ran kisses up from her stomach to her face, claiming her lips passionately. "I would say I am very easy."

She laughed, and he silenced her with a kiss, parting her lips to stroke her tongue with his. Her ardour began to build as he left no part of her untouched. Her breasts, legs, and back all received long massaging caresses as his lips and tongue kissed and suckled all over her body. Desperate to feel him touch her, she thought she would cry in relief in when he parted her soft folds to stroke her with his tongue, bringing her quickly to her peak.

"Will, please," she begged. Seeing his rakish smile, she sat up to push him down to his back and straddle his waist, slowly taking him inside her. He groaned, and she sighed as she began moving with him, skimming her fingers across his chest and arms while he watched her intently. The heat between her legs spread throughout her body as she succumbed to the sensation. When her second climax began, she bit her lip, closing her eyes until she could no longer remain silent and cried out.

"God, I love to watch you," he moaned just before he gave in to his release as well. She collapsed atop him, and he rolled them to their sides, brushing the curls back from her face.

"You are so beautiful." She blushed and kissed him softly. They both laughed as her stomach growled loudly.

"Come," he said, rising and holding out his hand to help her. "I had breakfast brought to our sitting room." As he held out her robe, he gave thanks that she was no longer ill, as she had been when she was first expecting. Instead, she would awaken hungry, so he had begun having their morning meal delivered to their chambers, allowing her to eat as soon as she wished.

She pulled him around and brushed her lips against his before he led her through to where their meal had been laid out. They had taken their seats and were just beginning to eat when there was a knock. Darcy rose from his chair and went to the door. He returned shortly with a stack of post, which he began to sort. She noticed his expression change as he paused to stare at a letter, contemplating it for a while before glancing up at his wife.

"Elizabeth . . . you have a letter from Longbourn."

"What?" she choked out. "May I?" She held out her hand as he handed her the missive, observing her closely for any upset.

As she studied the letter, she recognised the handwriting immediately, and groaned before opening it to see what it contained.

15 May 1812
Longbourn, Hertfordshire

My daughter Lizzy,

Six months! Six months and we have not heard a word from you, young lady. If Mrs. Lucas had not mentioned that you have been writing Charlotte, I would not have known where to send this letter! I had to request the direction from her and I am sure I will never hear the end of it!

Now, you should have told us that you were betrothed to Mr. Darcy, and I would not have tried to force Mr. Collins on you. For shame child, when you were engaged to someone so rich, as if I would have turned away someone with ten-thousand a year and very likely more! 'Tis good as a lord! Although why he would want you and not Jane or Lydia, well I guess that does not matter now. How you vex my nerves!

278

Jane has been very out of sorts and I believe Mr. Bingley's departure is to blame. I expect you to fix this, Lizzy. As the wife of Mr. Bingley's dearest friend, you are in the perfect position to reunite them. My sister Gardiner, has plans to match her with a business associate of my brother, who is worth three-thousand a year, but she is too beautiful to settle when she should have Mr. Bingley. He is not only worth more, but also attempting to buy an estate to become a true gentleman. It would be exceedingly agreeable to have my most beautiful daughter close and so well settled— Mistress of Netherfield—how well that sounds!

You must write immediately to tell me when you will travel to London, so that you may rectify the situation with Jane and Mr. Bingley. Then you will take your sisters shopping and to balls in order to throw them into the paths of rich men. I am sure Mr. Darcy must have some friends who would suit. After all, Lydia is so agreeable. She is bound to attract someone even more prestigious than your Mr. Darcy, perhaps even a peer of the realm! Harriet Forster has invited her to Brighton when the regiment leaves, but what are officers, when she can be in London with you being introduced!

Your father vexes me greatly by staying in his study all day and all night. He has gone through all of the port in the cellars, and has actually had the audacity to order more. He will drink himself into an early grave. Although with you so well married, at least we will not have to worry about starving in the hedgerows when Mr. Collins comes to throw us out!

Do not disappoint me, Lizzy!

Your mother,

Fanny Bennet

Cringing, she folded the letter with the intention of disposing of her mother's offensive words as soon as she rose from the table. She did not expect her husband to grasp it as soon as he saw the look upon her face.

"No, Will, please do not. I am going to burn it as soon as I am done eating," she cried, as she reached for the missive. She could tell it was too late when she saw his jaw clench. "I do not intend to answer it."

"She asks nothing of how you are after so long, only demands." His eyes narrowed while he read the closing. "I guess after she and your father attempted to force you to marry Collins, I should expect no less, but I had hoped it was more. I am so sorry that I even gave it to you."

"You were right to give it to me; I do not wish to have my mail censored as if I were a child. I was always my mother's least favourite, and the contents of that letter do not surprise me at all. Did I ever tell you that Jane offered to marry Mr. Collins?"

"No," he replied, surprised.

"She had decided that since Mr. Bingley had left, that she was willing to marry for the family. My mother would not allow it. Jane was worth more, she said," recounted Elizabeth with bitterness in her voice.

"Oh, love," he said, as he pulled her out of her chair to sit across his lap. "Your mother may feel that Jane is more worthy, but she never drew my eye. I believe when Bingley praised her at the assembly, I told him that she smiled too much." He grinned as he heard her soft chuckle.

"You were not in the best of moods that evening," she said, raising her eyebrow.

"No, but you did draw my eye, despite the unfortunate comment I made. The more I saw you, the more I was drawn to you – your intelligence, your wit, your beauty—I was addicted." He was surprised when she suddenly kissed him ardently.

"Thank you."

He smiled and brushed his lips across her temple. "Now, I have received a letter from Bingley. It seems, if I am reading this correctly, that he, his sister and the Hursts will visit sometime around the beginning of August. With you being so close to your confinement at that time, I believe they will need to move forward their plans or postpone the visit. I apologize for not mentioning it sooner. I had invited them before we left Netherfield, and it had slipped my mind until now."

"I think you should write to him today. My Aunt and Uncle Gardiner are expected at that time, and while I do not mind their presence, I do not wish to deal with Miss Bingley and Mrs. Hurst so close to when the babe is to arrive."

"I am sure Bingley will understand," he said soothingly, since he had felt her tense up when he mentioned the visit. He rubbed her back and held her closer. "I will pen the letter as soon as we are done here. Would you care to go for a walk when I am finished?"

"Mmmm," she replied, enjoying his hand's massaging. "That sounds lovely." She was about to close her eyes, when she spotted something familiar on one of her husband's letters. "Why does that say Rosings Park? Are you still receiving correspondence from Lady Catherine?"

"Unfortunately," he replied, grimacing. "Since Richard mentioned his father's plans, I have read all of her letters before burning them, but they are nothing but baseless demands. She has not threatened me since I informed her of the stipulations in my father's will, but she has commented that she is having a solicitor research whether they are valid." He rolled his eyes. "I believe she will eventually give up. That letter is probably the same as all of the others. Do not let it worry you."

"What of Lord Matlock? Have you heard anything additional from Richard?"

"I received a letter from Richard a week ago. He says his father has been busy with something else, and has not had the time to devote to challenging our guardianship of Georgiana." He shrugged.

She leaned her head back on his shoulder, and closed her eyes. "You should ring for Claire while I write the letter to Bingley. I will finish dressing, and meet you in your rooms when I am ready." Darcy watched as Elizabeth rose and lit her mother's missive on the candle, placing it quickly in the fireplace. She watched it burn to ash before she turned and held out her hand to her husband.

As he entwined his fingers with her own, Elizabeth led him back to his rooms, where they were delayed in their plans for the day—not that she noticed her husband was complaining.

~ * ~

Jane Bennet looked across her aunt and uncle's table at Mr. Mason, a London tradesman who had a small investment in her uncle's warehouse. He was a widower, whose wife had died five years ago, leaving him childless. Since Jane's arrival in Cheapside, he had been calling on her almost daily.

She could just hear her mother rant. She would scoff at Mr. Mason with his paltry three-thousand pounds per annum. He was not exalted enough for her dear girl. After all, Jane had attracted Mr. Bingley, who had reportedly been worth five.

However, Jane was more than willing to settle for a tradesman of lesser means if it meant that she did not have to return to Longbourn. She wished, in hindsight, that she had not been so blunt with Lizzy before her departure. Then perhaps she would have reintroduced her to Mr. Bingley, but her sister's face when she informed her of her lack of affection for him was evidence enough that she would not.

So, she painted a serene smile on her face when Mr. Mason came to call, in the hopes that she could endear herself enough that he might ask for her hand. He was at least forty, and unattractive, not that Mr. Collins was a handsome man, and she had been willing to marry him. All she could hope was that he would settle enough money on her that should she be widowed young, she would never have to return to Longbourn. After all, when she travelled to London, she had already vowed to find some way to never return, even considering the position of a companion. If only she could manage to become his wife before her aunt and uncle journeyed to Derbyshire. They had invited her to accompany them on their trip, to help with the children, but she hoped she could marry from Cheapside prior to their departure. Then she would not have to journey to visit Elizabeth as well.

Jane pulled herself from her thoughts in time to look up as Mr. Mason smiled in her direction. "Miss Bennet, I was just requesting your uncle for a moment to speak with you privately after dinner, if you would do me the honour, that is?"

"Of course, Mr. Mason," she said demurely, smiling to herself.

~ * ~

Sunday 31 May 1812

Elizabeth crept back into the master's suite and to the bed as quietly as she could. She did not know how she had managed to awaken before her husband, but luckily she had, or all of her morning plans would have been for naught.

Taking off her dressing gown, she looked down at her belly and smiled. She knew that just recently, the baby's movements were beginning to be felt from the outside, but her husband had not felt it as of yet, because she had wanted to wait for today, his birthday. As she crawled onto the bed, she carefully began to make her way over to him, when she heard his voice.

"Where have you been, love?" he chuckled, his voice still husky from sleep. He rolled over to see her frozen on all fours, and laughed even harder. "So, what have you been doing?"

"Happy Birthday, Will," she said with a small smile on her face.

"Oh, so that is what you have been doing? You could have told me you had gone to the water closet and I would have been none the wiser," he said still smiling, and guffawed when it was obvious that she realised how easily she could have deceived him.

As she attempted to rise once more from the bed, he stopped her before she shifted back towards the edge of the mattress, caressing his hand across her abdomen. "We have not had our morning discussion yet."

Giggling, she watched as he settled on his stomach and began to talk to her bellybutton. It was not long before she felt the baby become active, and took his hand as he looked at her questioningly. She placed it on one spot, and gently pushed his fingers into her skin.

"Elizabeth, what are you doing?" he said, afraid of hurting her or the baby. Seeing her smile, he looked down to where his hand was pressed against her tummy, when suddenly he felt something roll under his fingers. "Was that?" he asked, his eyes wide.

Nodding as she smiled at him, she watched as he beamed at her, and reverently kissed and covered her stomach with his hand before he crawled up until they were face to face. "Happy Birthday," she said softly. "I love you."

"I love you, too."

"I was actually returning to bed to wake you," she began in a suggestive tone. "But if you are done conversing with our child, there is something in the sitting room that I need." She began to sit up, and Darcy grabbed her arm.

"You stay here while I go get it," he said, beginning to rise when she stayed his movement with a hand on his chest.

"No, it is your birthday, and besides, you do not know what it is," she said.

"Then tell me."

"No," she giggled, as he rolled his eyes.

"Then I will follow," he said stubbornly.

"Why can you not just let me surprise you?" she asked pleadingly.

"Elizabeth, you walk all over this house every day, and you take your walks on the grounds, and I do not say a word. Forgive me if I do not want you exerting yourself more than you already do on my account."

"You do not fuss since it will make me angry," she said seriously. "Do not pretend that it is by your own initiative."

"Tell me why you are going to the next room."

Sighing, she looked at him wearily. "To bring you breakfast." She watched as he smiled softly at her.

"It is very sweet, but I would prefer to eat at the table. Perhaps you could sit in my lap and feed me strawberries?" he asked with a rakish grin.

As she chuckled at his request, something occurred to her. "How do you know that there are strawberries?"

His eyes widened, and he ran a hand through his hair. "I may have been spying earlier."

"Fitzwilliam Darcy!" she said sternly, trying to hide the smile on her face. "Oh well, I suppose there is nothing for it, and I am sure the last of it has arrived since I returned to bed."

"Love, do not be vexed with me," he said, as he helped her rise. "I did not want you to go to a great deal of trouble today. After all, you are already carrying my birthday present. I truly do not require anything but the two of you." He placed his hand on her belly once more, and she covered it with her own.

She could not stay cross with him when he said such lovely things, and placed her hand on his stubbly cheek as she kissed him softly. "Very well, but I am famished, so let us go eat," she responded, hearing him chuckle. Ignoring it since she knew he was laughing at her recent voracious appetite, she led the way to breakfast.

He had been surprised to see all of his favourites laid out, including scones and clotted cream, and in honour of his birthday, Elizabeth did sit in his lap and feed him strawberries. They loitered within their rooms for most of the morning, emerging just after noon to take care of a few menial tasks they both were required to attend. Darcy had a brief meeting with his steward before he checked in on Georgiana, who had never acknowledged his birthday in the past, and did not bother once again; Elizabeth consulted with Mrs. Reynolds to ensure that the remainder of her plans for the day were being prepared to her specifications.

An hour later, Elizabeth sought him out in his study to inform him that he would be accompanying her on a walk. With a smile, he excused Mr. Jacobs, and taking his wife's hand, entwined his fingers with hers, escorting her from the house and out to the grounds.

They wandered on the path around the lake until they reached a small trail that ventured from it; Darcy did not remember the path being that distinguishable in the past. His wife veered in that direction, pulling him to follow with a mischievous tug at his arm. After walking for almost another quarter hour, they came to a small clearing where a stream that fed the lake passed through the woods.

"I have not been here since I was a child," he said, turning in a circle as he recalled the area. "I can remember playing here as a boy."

"I found the path about a month ago, much to Samuel and Matthew's dismay. They did not like fighting their way through the branches that had invaded the trail. I have been coming back here to read sometimes when you do not walk with me."

He smiled as he imagined her curled up on the grass with a book, biting her bottom lip like she did as she read. He startled from his reverie when he heard a rustling behind him. When he turned, he found the very footmen she had just mentioned with a basket and blanket.

"Thank you, if you would just set them on the grass, we can take care of the rest, and you may return to the house."

"Yes ma'am," they chorused, as they deposited the items and departed back in the direction they came.

Elizabeth reached for the rug, but her husband swiftly grabbed it away before she could bend down. "Where would you care for the blanket, my lady?"

"I was thinking on the grass by the willow, if that suits," she replied, as he also moved the basket to where she had indicated. "I hope you do not mind, but Mrs. Reynolds had told me how much you dearly loved picnics as a child, and although you are now an adult, I thought it might be diverting."

"I did love them, and Mrs. Reynolds always ensured that my governess would take me for one a week as long as the weather permitted. I tried to take Georgiana, but she did not seem interested. As soon as we had set up everything and eaten, she had some errand or important lesson that necessitated her return to the house." He furrowed his brow as he reconsidered many of her past actions.

"What is it?"

"It is just that now that I know what she is, I see so many things differently."

Crossing to where he had spread the rug upon the ground, she placed her hand on his arm. "Your father created her, and you have tried, but you cannot blame yourself. It is also your birthday, so no more talk about your sister. I do not wish for you to be upset today."

He gave a half-smile and kissed her softly. "Your wish is my command."

She rolled her eyes and took a seat as he set the basket next to her. She laid out their luncheon while he placed himself beside her. They chatted while they ate, and packed away what they were no longer using, creating enough room for Elizabeth to recline with her head in her husband's lap.

He had laughed when she pulled his volume of Shakespeare's sonnets from the basket, but happily read from it as he stroked her hair, which she had unpinned. They took turns reading for a while, until he heard her softly snoring as he turned a page. He chuckled silently at the noise she had only begun to make in the last fortnight. When he had first told her that she had begun snoring, she vehemently denied it, insisting "I do not snore, Fitzwilliam Darcy!" He gently removed her head from his lap, and lay beside her to watch her sleep, only to succumb to dreams himself a short time later.

Elizabeth awoke a couple of hours later to her husband staring down at her with a large smile on his face.

"Is there something wrong?"

"No, I was just listening to you snore," he said, chuckling.

"I do not snore! I have never snored!" she cried.

Leaning forward, he captured her lips and heard her sigh. He deepened the kiss as he ran his hand down her back and pressed her back into the blanket. Soon, he was running his hand up her thigh when she stopped it with her own.

"Will, someone might come," she said, not wishing to be discovered.

"You said yourself that the trail was obscured when you found it. No one will intrude upon us; I promise," he breathed as he slipped a finger inside, causing her to moan. She reached up and pulled his mouth once more to her own to continue what he had begun, delaying their return to Pemberley until it was time to dress for dinner.

Chapter 23

Tuesday 16 June 1812

"Love, I have at long last received a letter from Bingley," Darcy said as he strode into the dining room. "If you remember, he, Miss Bingley, and Mr. and Mrs. Hurst were to visit in early August. However, due to the letter I sent requesting they change the time frame of their visit, they have altered their plans and will arrive in a fortnight. They will break their trip here as they travel to Manchester, where Bingley still owns the family home not far from his father's mill."

"Thank you for writing to Mr. Bingley. I will let Mrs. Reynolds know and make the necessary arrangements for their stay as soon as we are done eating. Did he say how long they would visit?"

"Honestly, Elizabeth, I was lucky to decipher that much," he sighed, as he held up the letter for her to view all of the ink blots obliterating the message. "Apologize to Mrs. Reynolds, but what I have told you is all I could ascertain from his attempt at handwriting."

"My goodness," she exclaimed, laughing. "And here I thought it was a joke at Netherfield when they said Mr. Bingley's penmanship was atrocious, but I would say the assessment of yours was correct."

"Pray tell, madam, whatever do you mean?"

"Well, I do remember a lady who commented on the evenness of your hand and how charmingly you wrote," she said mischievously. "Although, do you truly search for so many words of four syllables?"

"I have never given it much thought. You have received notes from me," he taunted. "Do you find that they are filled with such long words?" He laughed heartily at the blush that spread from his wife's hair to the neckline of her gown. Since they had been married, even the simplest of notes to tell her where he had gone for the day not only included declarations of love, but usually an erotic element as well, and he was enjoying immensely the effects of reminding her.

"Very well, Mr. Darcy, I forfeit," she replied. "Would you care to have the Greys over for a dinner party during the Bingleys' visit?"

"I do not think they will come. Perhaps Grey may come for a day of sport with Bingley and me, but I do not foresee his wife wishing to associate with a tradesman and his family, despite the fact that he is trying to become landed."

"No," she sighed. "I do not think she would consent either."

"Perhaps you could invite Miss Grey to visit for a few days while they are here," he suggested, wishing for her to have an ally against Miss Bingley and Mrs. Hurst.

"I will admit it would be nice to have a friend here. Miss Bingley never liked me, and I doubt will have improved in civilities since I hold the position she so coveted."

"She will no longer be welcome if she is rude to you, Elizabeth," he stated matter-of-factly. "I will not have you mistreated, and I indicated as much in my letter to Bingley."

"Since you offered, I will write to Lainey today and invite her to visit during that time. I wager she will accept, if only to have a respite from her sister."

"Yes, well, speaking of sisters, I do not anticipate the ire I will receive from Georgiana when I inform her that she is confined to her rooms for their stay."

"Do you truly think that is necessary?"

"I do not trust her," he said softly. He glanced around to ensure the servant he excused as he entered had not returned. "She has shopped and visited with Miss Bingley in the past, and I fear what Georgiana might say, even if it is only lies. It only takes one letter from Miss Bingley to the right person in London to begin the rampant spread of gossip. I prefer to stay out of the rumour mill, if I can prevent it."

Nodding in understanding, she thought for a moment. "Although Georgiana is in a guest wing, from what Mrs. Reynolds has told me it is the portion typically reserved for family, and where Lady Catherine and Lord Matlock have stayed in the past. I am unaware of where she has previously placed the Bingleys, but I could place them in the actual guest wing that is on the opposite side of the house, allowing your sister to be confined to that wing instead of just her chambers."

"In the past, we have used the rooms near where Georgiana is now for all guests, since it has only been the two of us, but I think placing them in the actual guest rooms is a splendid idea," he said thoughtfully. "There will be less chance of accidental meetings that way. Some of those chambers need to be redone, so you may want to inspect the rooms to choose which are used."

"Actually, I believe Mrs. Reynolds and I have already altered enough of the rooms to accommodate everyone, although I believe I will place Lainey within the wing Georgiana is currently occupying."

"When did you accomplish this?" he asked, genuinely surprised.

"When I made arrangements to purchase papers and materials for my rooms, I also ordered some to redo several of the guest rooms as well."

"The bill was not high enough for that, Elizabeth."

"Do you remember where I purchased the materials?" she asked, laughing.

"Of course, from your uncle's warehouses."

"He shipped us everything at cost. He insisted it was a belated wedding and Christmas gift. I did not ask him to, and I did ask my aunt to find out the difference, so I could pay him out of my pin money. She would not help me."

"I should send him a letter of thanks," Darcy said thoughtfully. "I wish you had mentioned it sooner. I feel remiss waiting so long."

"You are welcome to send him a note," she replied happily. "I am sure my uncle will be glad to know that you appreciate his gesture."

Darcy nodded, turning his mind back to the rooms in question. "I would think some of the furniture would need replacing as well, though." He looked up from his food to find Georgiana entering the room. She moved to the buffet and began preparing herself a plate. "Good morning, Georgiana," he said. She turned and nodded in their direction while Elizabeth greeted her, before returning to their conversation.

"No, the furniture is rather ornate, but when paired with a sparsely decorated paper and fabrics, it looks nice," she commented cheerfully. "Honestly, once we had changed the walls and the coverlets on the beds we did not have to recover any chairs. It was just a matter of reducing the decoration and the plethora of rugs on the floor. I have ordered materials for the nursery, but after that, I will wait until next year to finish that part of the house." She paused for a moment, considering a question she wished to ask. "There is one thing I have wondered, why is it that the main rooms of the house are not as ornate as the mistress's chambers or those guest rooms were?"

"I believe my father asked Mrs. Reynolds to oversee the redecoration of most of the public rooms after my mother died." He could not help but notice his sister's surprised expression that his father would order rooms redecorated. Her expression was short-lived, since as soon as she became aware of her unguarded expression, she feigned indifference to the conversation. "My chambers and the master's study, I had renovated before I moved in after my father's death, and I continued with a few rooms a year, as you plan to do."

Since he was finished with his breakfast, Darcy stood to attend to some work in his study. He questioned whether he should leave his wife alone with Georgiana, but his study was not far; surely he would hear any commotion that might occur. Looking to Elizabeth, she smiled and nodded. She seemed to understand the reason for his hesitation, and he took her nod as permission to tend to his business, so he departed. He took one last glance at the ladies before he walked out of the door.

Elizabeth looked to her sister, who was quietly eating across from her. She had not yet confronted the young woman about her intrusion into the mistress's chambers, feeling that she did not have enough control over her emotions so as not to cry in the attempt.

"John," she said to the servant, who had returned and resumed his post to the side of the room. "I do not think we will require anything else this morning. I will send someone to the kitchens to notify you when we are finished."

"Yes, ma'am," he replied. He bowed and exited through the servants' door.

"I assume you would like to speak with me in private," said Georgiana, as she sighed.

"Of course I do. You entered my rooms without permission and attempted to shatter my husband's trust in me," Elizabeth responded, setting down her utensils forcefully. "Did you expect me to never say a word?"

Georgiana shrugged her shoulders as she continued to eat.

"Your brother has had so few people in his life that he could truly trust—Richard, his godfather, and now me—I do not understand why you would take that away from him, especially since he has found lately, in the most painful fashion, that he cannot trust you." Elizabeth examined the girl across from her, searching for any displayed emotion, but was unable to find anything.

"About four years ago, my sister, Lydia, entered my room at Longbourn and stole my journal. She was angry with me for scolding her, and hoped to embarrass me in some fashion." She looked up to see Georgiana watching her carefully. "Since Lydia was the only one of my sisters who would steal, I knew who it was immediately. When I confronted her, she refused to return it as she laughed. She taunted me that she would give it to the Lucas boys, so I grabbed her by the hair and I blackened her eye. Needless to say, she returned my journal." Elizabeth watched as the young woman continued observing her with wide eyes.

"Step one foot in my room again, and I will have no problem doing the same to you." Rising from her seat, Elizabeth paused before walking out of the door. "We will expect you at dinner," she said, as she left for her morning meeting with Mrs. Reynolds.

~ * ~

Miss Grey quickly responded to Elizabeth's invitation, and consequently the next fortnight was spent planning for their guests. They were expected to stay several weeks, and Elizabeth hoped that the Bingley party would not attempt to extend their visit.

Elizabeth was excited to have her friend visit as she sat in the front drawing room with her needlework awaiting her arrival. Darcy had needed to take a ride around the estate, and was expected back in time to be dressed for dinner, providing the two of them some time before he returned.

She had been quite engrossed in the pattern when Roberts, the butler, showed Miss Grey into the room. Elizabeth began to rise while her friend quickly came over.

"Lizzy, do not bother trying to stand. I think we are friends enough to overlook such formalities, especially right now," she said, giggling. She looked down to Elizabeth's belly and leaned in to give her a kiss on the cheek.

"You are as bad as my husband, who only lets me out of the house for a walk because he fears my wrath should he not." She gestured for her companion to sit.

Picking up the small gown Elizabeth was stitching when she entered, Lainey ran her fingers along the delicate embroidery. "It is lovely, although I thought you said that you were not very accomplished at needlework."

"I like embroidery, but I detest making clothes. My seams were never sturdy enough to hold, and my sister Jane would

294

always have to re-stitch my chemises when we were younger. Claire has been helping me though. She makes the garment, and I do the trim and decoration, so my baby's clothes will not unravel as they are worn."

They laughed as Miss Grey handed her the tiny garment. "So, tell me about your guests. You have not divulged much in your letters."

"Well, Mr. Bingley has been a friend to my husband since they were at Cambridge together. He is amiable and has very happy manners, while his sisters are actually quite the opposite." Elizabeth looked at her friend guiltily. "Miss Bingley and Mrs. Hurst are very much like your sister in some ways, with the exception that they make barbs and titter. In fact, Miss Bingley wished nothing more than to be mistress of Pemberley, and we were told that she took the news of our marriage very poorly."

Giggling, she took a long look at Elizabeth. "In other words, I am here so that you are not alone with the harpies. And I thought I was going to escape Esther for a few weeks."

"I would not have put it that way," Elizabeth said dryly.

"Very well," she responded. "There was another gentleman, if I recall correctly."

"Yes, Mr. Hurst. He enjoys cards, port, and a ragout to a plain dish."

Chuckling, the ladies were startled suddenly when Darcy entered the room. "Forgive me, ladies, for the interruption. Miss Grey, we are very happy you could be here." He gave a small bow.

Miss Grey rose and executed a small curtsy. "Thank you, Mr. Darcy," she responded cheerfully.

"Perhaps I should show you to your room so you may dress for dinner," said Elizabeth, as her husband rushed over to offer his hand for her to rise. "I have actually placed you in the guest wing on the same side of the house as the family rooms, so it will not be too far out of my way."

She smiled at her husband, who recognized that he was being dismissed until she reached their chambers. "Then I will see you momentarily, Elizabeth," he said in a softer tone he hoped only his wife heard.

Nodding, she led her friend out of the room, and glanced back before they headed toward the stairs to find Darcy watching her leave. She blushed as she turned back to Miss Grey.

"He always seems so formal. Does he not call you Lizzy?"

"No, he never has," she responded. "My family has always called me by that name and a few people have called me Eliza, although I heartily dislike that name at times. You will notice that Miss Bingley enjoys using it." Her brow furrowed for a bit as she contemplated her husband's use of her name. "I have never thought to ask why he prefers it, but I think it may be because he is the only person who calls me by my name. Why do you ask?"

"I have not heard anyone else use it."

"I gave you permission to call me Lizzy. In fact, his cousin, Colonel Fitzwilliam, uses Lizzy, and to be honest, I like that Will is the only person to call me Elizabeth."

"I wish Edward had been allowed to marry for love," Lainey confided sadly. "Perhaps things would be different if he had."

"I was under the impression that you and your brother got along very well," Elizabeth exclaimed in surprise.

"We do! It is only that he is not happy. Esther makes him miserable, and it pains me to see it as I do not know how I can help."

"I do not think there is anything you can do, but to be there for him should he need to speak of it, which I believe you already are."

"Yes, we have always been close," she responded with a small smile. "If you do not mind me asking, how is your new sister?"

"That is a long story," Elizabeth sighed. "Things have not gone well, and while we have guests, she is confined to the wing of the house where her chambers are located. If you see her somewhere besides that north east upstairs corner of the house, please let us or Mrs. Reynolds know."

"Of course!" she exclaimed. "I am terribly sorry that it has been so difficult. You never indicated that it was in your letters."

"I do not desire the problems with her to become common knowledge, if possible. I know that you will keep a confidence, yet should the letter become misdirected or someone else happen upon it . . ."

"It is understandable," she said.

Nodding, Elizabeth gestured around the room they had just entered. "The dressing room is through there, as is the water closet, and you have a sitting room through the door behind you.

"Georgiana is residing just down the hall at present, and the Bingleys are in the guest wing on the other side of the house. I did not feel it was proper to place you in the same part of the house with the Bingleys, since Mr. Bingley is unmarried. I believe him to be a gentleman, but I felt it would be better to place you closer to us."

"My brother will appreciate it. He has done similar when Esther has had unwed friends visit the estate at the same time he has a hunting party. He would always have to change their room assignments after she made them. She does not consider such things . . . " she trailed off, leaving Elizabeth to infer the rest.

"Indeed! She sounds a little like my mother," Elizabeth laughed.

"How so?"

"Well, when there are five daughters, no sons, and an entailed estate, a woman as silly as my mother would throw us into the paths of unmarried men as soon as she knew of their existence. If they were rich, it was even better."

"But you are not that way," she said, surprised.

"No, but I always found her embarrassing, and when she forced me to come out at fifteen, I resented it. I wished to be roaming the woods and climbing trees, not attracting a husband. She always said that I would be the death of her." Elizabeth laughed as she turned to look at the clock on the mantle. "I should leave you to dress for dinner. Should you need anything, just ask myself, Mrs. Reynolds; or even Claire, my maid, may be able to assist yours."

Turning once more before she closed the door, Elizabeth declared, "I am so glad you could come."

The day before the Bingleys and the Hursts arrived, Darcy asked to speak with his sister after dinner, so Miss Grey would not have to endure a meal with the attitude Georgiana was likely to exhibit. Therefore, while the ladies adjourned to the drawing room, Darcy escorted his sister to his study, where he asked her to take a seat as he closed the door.

"I have been pleasant when in company, and I have done nothing wrong. I do not understand why you are insisting on speaking with me again."

"The Bingleys and the Hursts will be here tomorrow, and I have decided that you will not be in company with them," he stated clearly, preparing himself for her anger. "I expect you to remain in your rooms or study with Mrs. Annesley. You and Miss Grey will be the only two residents in that wing, so you can take exercise by walking in the halls. If two footmen are available, they can escort you down the servants stairs for a walk outside."

"You cannot be in earnest!" she exclaimed in fury. "I am friends with Miss Bingley and Mrs. Hurst."

"You have other friends. I do not find Miss Bingley and Mrs. Hurst to be acceptable role models, Georgiana, and I will no longer allow their influence. They are both manipulative and cruel, and you have exhibited enough of those tendencies recently," he said, maintaining a controlled voice. He watched her face redden in anger and her hands clench at her sides.

Sighing, he leaned forward. "I care or else I would leave matters as they are. It breaks my heart to think of you becoming like Miss Bingley." Georgiana gave a small humph and opened her mouth to speak. Her brother interrupted her before she could make a sound. "Before you begin yelling, I am your guardian, and you will do as I say. This conversation is over. If you cannot be pleasant company for the remainder of the evening, I would recommend retiring." He gestured toward the door, and when she left with a huff, followed her to the drawing room, where she said goodnight before she ascended the stairs to her rooms.

~ * ~

Friday 3 July 1812

Darcy was in his study working, while his wife and Miss Grey attended their needlework in the front drawing room, when the Bingleys and the Hursts entered the gates of Pemberley. As soon as he was notified that their coach was seen entering the park, Darcy hastily finished what he was doing in order to be there at the time of their arrival.

He strode into the room as the coach pulled up to the door, waiting until he could hear them in the entryway before helping Elizabeth to stand so that she would not have to struggle before Caroline Bingley. As they were shown into the room, one look at the lady, although he hesitated to call her such, told him that she was sharpening her claws. Scanning her environs, her eyes lit upon seeing Elizabeth in her condition before they narrowed, and Darcy began to worry about allowing her into his home.

However, he was not the only person in the room to catch the malevolent look upon Miss Bingley's face. Elizabeth and Miss Grey both caught her expression, and although both found amusement in her jealousy, Miss Grey was already wary of the woman. She had seen too many women of so-called high society, and she knew all too well that this woman was not here for a leisurely vacation, but to cause trouble.

When everyone had stepped into the room and curtsied or bowed, Darcy stepped forward.

"Bingley," he said, as he took his friend's outstretched hand. "It is good to see you. I am sure everyone remembers my wife, Mrs. Elizabeth Darcy, Miss Elizabeth Bennet as was, and this is her friend Miss Elaine Grey of Briarwood, which is just north of here. Miss Grey, may I present, Mr. Charles Bingley, Mr. Reginald Hurst, his wife, Mrs. Louisa Hurst, who is also Mr. Bingley's sister, and Miss Caroline Bingley."

Once everyone had been acknowledged, Elizabeth glanced around the room. "I am sure everyone would like a chance to refresh themselves, so Mrs. Reynolds will show you to your rooms. We are having tea in here in an hour, and dinner will be served at seven."

"It sounds splendid, Mrs. Darcy," Bingley replied jovially, as his sisters nodded uninterestedly before they all departed to be shown to the guest wing of the house.

The door closed, and it seemed that everyone in the room let out a large breath. Elizabeth was just about to sit when Miss Grey turned to her.

"Lizzy, do not dare let your guard down around *that* woman!"

Startled by her vehemence, Elizabeth paused a moment before she finished sitting. "I do believe she is jealous, but I do not think it is anything to worry about. I fully expect a few well-placed insults, insinuations or barbs, but other than that, she is harmless."

"I disagree," Darcy interjected. "I do not like the way she looked at you when she came into the room, and while I do expect her to be shrewish, I would not put it past her to try something."

Laughing, Elizabeth looked at him incredulously. "What could she do? Slap me? Your cousin already did that. I think the two of you are panicking over nothing, but I will be careful, if it makes you feel better."

Leaning over in front of his wife so that they were eye to eye, Darcy gazed at her imploringly. "Please, promise me."

"I promise."

A servant appeared not long after to tell them that Miss Bingley, as well as Mr. and Mrs. Hurst were exhausted from their trip, and wished to rest instead of coming down for tea. So, Darcy and Mr. Bingley had refreshments in the library before they adjourned to play billiards, while Miss Grey and Elizabeth took tea and refreshments in the mistress's sitting room so that Elizabeth could rest comfortably.

Miss Bingley was very late to dinner that evening, and although Elizabeth was willing to delay the meal until she arrived, her husband as well as Mr. Bingley, both insisted that the food be served as scheduled.

"My sister is aware of the time of the meal," Bingley stated resolutely, while the first course was placed before them. "She should have been on time, and not show such a lack of courtesy to everyone else."

"Charles, I am sure she will be down very soon," Mrs. Hurst offered, seemingly offended by the idea that they would not wait for her sister. "I honestly do not know what could be keeping her. She was dressed when I left her."

Bingley looked at his sister incredulously. "Which only means she is being more inconsiderate than I had believed earlier. Please serve the meal as planned, Mrs. Darcy," he implored earnestly.

Ten minutes and one course later, Miss Bingley was shown into the dining room by one of the footmen, the surprise on her face evident upon entering the room.

"I see you have all started without me," she said with a falsely cheerful voice, eyeing Elizabeth with a glint of malice in her eyes.

"You knew what time dinner was to be served," Mr. Bingley

informed her as the footmen helped her with a chair and a plate placed before her.

Ignoring her brother's remark, she surveyed everyone seated at the table and frowned. "Where is *dear* Georgiana? I was so looking forward to seeing her."

"She has been very busy with her studies, and unfortunately, will not be in company with us during your stay," Darcy responded in a tightly controlled manner. "I apologize for any disappointment you might feel as a result, but I assure you it was unavoidable."

"But surely she will be able to spend some time with Louisa and me," she began in an even more shocked tone. "We have missed her company since she returned to Derbyshire. She will be coming out within the next few years, and she must learn to how to behave in society, especially since she has no one to help her in that regard."

"Miss Bingley, we are in complete agreement that it is very important that Georgiana learn to comport herself as a lady, and I can think of no better example than my wife," he said sternly, as he looked Miss Bingley directly in the eye. "I can assure you, I am aware of my sister's needs, and I will not be swayed. She will not be a part of our party."

Elizabeth happened to glance back at the woman in time to see a rather disdainful look that was aimed directly at her. Her attention was then diverted as the plate in front of her was removed and replaced with the next course. The remainder of dinner that evening was uneventful, although Darcy and Miss Grey both noticed the hostile looks Miss Bingley was giving Elizabeth, and were finding the entire situation worrisome. Darcy reiterated his warning to Bingley when the ladies separated to the drawing room after dinner, making it perfectly clear that his sisters would be ejected from Pemberley should they continue Miss Bingley's behaviour from dinner. He even went so far as to ensure Bingley, as well as Hurst had been privy to the looks their sister was sending his wife's direction. Elizabeth was indeed aware of the nature of the woman's glances, and while she would never admit it to her husband and friend, she was beginning to understand their concern. The next fortnight could not pass quickly enough!

Chapter 24

True to Elizabeth's predictions, Miss Bingley did not attempt anything untoward in regards to the new Mrs. Darcy . . . at least for the first few days. Little did Darcy or Elizabeth know, but the disagreeable woman had been internally seething since the day she had arrived. While she had managed to control her disappointment during her time in London, setting foot into Pemberley was an entirely different matter, and it had unleashed a torrent of emotions that had long been suppressed.

The upstart had no idea how to run a home as grand as Pemberley! After all, even Mrs. Reynolds knew that they were always placed within the guest rooms closer to the family wing. Her menus were ridiculous and lacked sophistication, and the rooms the housekeeper had indicated were newly remodelled were terribly plain. To make matters worse, in the past, Darcy had always offered her his arm to escort her to dinner, and he was instead escorting that Miss Grey into the dining room. In her delusional mind, she did not think of Miss Grey as a gentleman's daughter whose brother was master of an estate, but as competition and the usurper of her place.

Over the course of the week, Elizabeth had planned a picnic at the lake as well as several other diversions that were all in all very entertaining, and helped to quickly pass the first week of the visit. Miss Grey even remarked how Miss Bingley was even managing to be on time for not only these events but also the meals following that first evening. However, while she had been fairly well behaved at the beginning of the visit, the longer Miss Bingley was at Pemberley, in company with the new Mrs. Darcy, the more incensed she became, until she began unleashing small barbs and insinuations in order to vent some of her ire.

Those instances gradually became more and more frequent, until an evening about a week into the stay on a dreary and rainy Friday night that the spiteful woman went too far.

Dinner had been very pleasant. Elizabeth had ordered a lovely menu, even including a ragout to suit the tastes of Mr. Hurst. The conversation had flowed and was not stilted, although Elizabeth and Miss Grey had a difficult time taking their eyes from Miss Bingley's bright chartreuse gown. Miss Grey did not understand how someone could pick a colour so at odds to what would suit them, and Elizabeth was marvelling at the similarity to the shade of Georgiana's gown that she had sold to the ragman when they were last in London.

As soon as all of the ladies had taken a seat in the drawing room, Miss Bingley's first attempt was to comment on how different Pemberley was from Longbourn, which made Miss Grey roll her eyes, and attempt to disguise a snort as a cough. Elizabeth, however, maintained her composure.

"It is truly not such a great difference, Miss Bingley, since as the daughter of a gentleman, I was raised on an estate, and my mother ensured I understood a mistress's duties." She observed Miss Bingley as she reddened at the subtle reminder of her roots in trade.

"Yes, you were so fortunate as to marry Mr. Darcy when your family had already arranged your marriage to your cousin, Mr. Collins. I particularly remember your mother exclaiming at the Netherfield ball over your future role as mistress of Longbourn. Such a change in circumstances," she continued disdainfully.

Elizabeth glanced to her friend, since they had never discussed any of the gossip or circumstances surrounding her marriage. Finding Miss Grey to be visibly unresponsive to the barb, she turned her attention back to her adversary.

"Well *Miss* Bingley," responded Elizabeth, "my mother was mistaken on a betrothal to my cousin. Mr. Collins did not propose to me until the following day. As I had already accepted Mr. Darcy's offer of marriage at the ball, I did not feel that I could, in good conscience, accept my cousin's proposal," she continued. Elizabeth attempted to remain unaffected as the men filed into the room behind Miss Bingley, who was too preoccupied to notice.

"And it is so odd that Mr. Darcy would desire to wed you. I remember one night after your family had dined at Netherfield, we were discussing how amazed we were to find you a local beauty; and I particularly recollect him saying 'She a beauty!—I should as soon call her mother a wit.'" She and her sister finished in a cascade of titters still not noticing the men standing behind her, their brother's countenance particularly furious.

"Yes, Miss Bingley, but that was only when he first knew me," Elizabeth spoke quickly. "I believe that for some time now, he has considered me one of the handsomest women of his acquaintance. Is that not true, love?" she finished in an almost sickeningly sweet tone, looking toward her husband. She could see him hide his amusement, as well as noticing out of the corner of her eye, Miss Grey, stifling her laugher while Miss Bingley turned and paled, a horrified expression upon her face.

"Far be it for me to contradict my wife, but I do believe she is the handsomest woman of my acquaintance," he said in a very serious tone, although to Elizabeth, his eyes gave him away. His expression did change quickly as he turned to address his friend. "Bingley, I believe I mentioned repeatedly that I would not tolerate any disrespect towards my wife. Miss Bingley has become increasingly rude to Elizabeth for the last few days. She has made some rather thinly veiled insults that I have not failed to notice, and this episode is the end of my tolerance—she leaves first thing tomorrow morning."

"WHAT?" Miss Bingley screeched. Her brother had informed her of Mr. Darcy's letter and threats, yet she never believed he would actually evict her from Pemberley.

"Miss Bingley, I have only ever tolerated you for the sake of your brother. I never gave you any encouragement, and I informed Bingley repeatedly that I would never offer for you—no matter the circumstances."

Blanching and looking toward her brother, who gestured towards the door, she gripped her skirts in fury. "Caroline, I think it is time you retired, and you should take Louisa with you."

"I did not say a word, Brother," Mrs. Hurst exclaimed.

306

"No, but you were laughing, and made no attempt to censor Caroline even though you knew the consequences."

"I will escort them to Manchester tomorrow, Bingley," Mr. Hurst volunteered, rising from his seat and offering his arm to his wife. "And you can meet us there in another week as you had originally planned."

Bingley had an obviously surprised look upon his face as he regarded his brother. "Thank you, Hurst."

Mr. Hurst nodded as he took his wife and Miss Bingley each by an arm, and forcibly escorted them from the room as both complained of his unusually officious manner.

"I apologize, Mrs. Darcy," Mr. Bingley said contritely, "by the time we had left London, it had seemed as if she had accepted your marriage. I truly did not believe she would attempt anything."

"Please do not think on it another minute. I am unharmed, after all," Elizabeth responded graciously. "However, I am rather fatigued tonight, so if you do not mind, I think I will retire early and allow you to visit with my husband."

Darcy rushed forward to help her stand, as Miss Grey stood and also offered her an arm.

"I will escort you upstairs, Lizzy, and perhaps we can chat once you are done with your maid," she offered, as Elizabeth chuckled at her husband's forlorn expression.

"Go play billiards with Mr. Bingley. I will be upstairs when you are finished."

"Very well." He kissed her hand and watched her as she left the room. Gesturing to the door, he and Bingley walked silently to the billiard room. They each selected their sticks, and once Bingley had racked the balls, began to play. As soon as Darcy broke, Bingley surveyed the table.

"I cannot apologize enough for Caroline's words tonight," he said sincerely. "You have said for years that you would never ask for her hand, which I indeed told her, yet she never would listen. She has no one to blame for her disappointment but herself."

"Just as long as she is gone in the morning. You are always welcome, provided your sisters are not with you." Darcy took his shot then surveyed the table.

"I envy you your happiness," his friend began. "You have a lovely wife, who obviously adores you, and a baby in a month or so, not to mention everything to go with it." He looked around the room as he made his last statement, his eyes landing on Darcy as he finished.

Darcy successfully made his next shot and glanced at the man before him. "Bingley, we have been friends for years now. During that time, you have asked my advice many times, and I have always been honest. Your father left you a large sum of money to fulfil his dream of buying an estate, which you have been considering the last few years, leasing Netherfield as a precursor to ownership, but I have never asked you what you want. Do you even know?"

Staring as he watched Bingley furrow his brow in thought, they played in silence for a time as he pondered Darcy's advice. He completed a difficult shot, and looked up.

"I think before you do anything else, you need to decide what you want from life," Darcy continued. "Disregard what your father, your sisters, and society expects, and figure out what you desire."

"That is a pretty radical statement coming from you," Bingley replied with his eyebrows raised.

Darcy looked his friend in the eye with a steady gaze. "You said you envy my happiness, yet do you understand what has truly made me happy?" Bingley furrowed his brow. "I struggled at Netherfield to accept Elizabeth due to the expectations of society and my family. Once I decided that I would live my life the way I wished, without regard for anyone else, it was as if a weight had been lifted from my shoulders." He paused to observe Bingley's confused expression.

"I could have done what society and my family expected, and married my cousin, Anne, or another woman of the ton, but I would have been miserable. I would not have wished to spend any time with them, since their personalities make me grit my teeth. I would have been as alone as I was prior to the marriage." He saw Bingley's eyes widen in comprehension.

"But what if I make the wrong decision?"

Sighing, Darcy put his hand on his friend's shoulder and looked him directly in the eye. "If it makes you happy, Bingley, it is not the wrong decision."

With a contemplative look upon his face, Bingley walked around the table and attempted his next shot, watching it miss before he looked back up.

"My father's godson, a Mr. Clarke, is a respectable and very wealthy manufacturer in Manchester," Bingley explained. "Not long after Caroline came out, he requested her hand in marriage and she refused, probably hoping that she could ensnare you. Since my sister would not have him, he married another young woman, who unfortunately died in childbirth just over a year ago. A few months ago, I received a letter from him. He inquired as to whether Caroline might be more amenable to him now."

"If you do not mind me asking, why is he so determined to have her?" Darcy asked, as he surveyed the table.

"I believe he wants to expand his business, and sees Caroline's dowry as a means to that end. He owns his business outright, which he inherited from his father, along with a large home in the city. He once told me that he had been saving all of the interest from his wife's dowry, and now that she is gone, he no longer needs to save it. I believe he will use that to expand once he has my sister's money."

"She refused before, what if she were to do so again?"

"Nevertheless, I will not be returning to London with her, and I will make it clear that Hurst will not facilitate her return either," he said with more conviction than Darcy had heard in years. "No, either she marries Clarke, or she sets up her own establishment and lives off of her dowry. I have been considering this since I received his letter. She has been an obstacle to everything I have ever tried to accomplish, and I will need to do this before I can even attempt what you suggest, and decide my future."

"It is a start, Bingley," Darcy commented, as he stood from sinking the winning shot. "I hope you will forgive me, but my wife is waiting for me. If I do not retire soon, I suspect she will fall asleep."

The men shook hands as Bingley chuckled, departing the room and heading up the stairs. Separating when they reached the top, Darcy did not stop until he reached his chambers, where he immediately went to his dressing room to find Evans waiting for him.

~ * ~

Once she had changed into her nightclothes, Elizabeth and Miss Grey visited, until they heard the door to the master's chamber close. Wishing each other good night, Miss Grey departed for her room as Elizabeth entered her husband's room. She took a seat in a chair in the far corner of the room that she had found particularly comfortable as of late.

Closing her eyes and sighing, she was surprised when she heard the knob to the hall door quietly turn and the door open. Elizabeth, whose eyes were adjusted to the dim light of the room, watched curiously as the unmistakeable form of Miss Bingley slipped into the room, quietly closing the door behind her.

Elizabeth was excessively angry at the woman's presumption, yet wanted to know exactly what she thought she was going to accomplish in this manner. She also understood that her husband would be furious if she attempted to confront the woman alone, so she remained in the shadows. Elizabeth glared as Miss Bingley removed her dressing gown, which she threw haphazardly across a chair closer to the bed.

Elizabeth stared at Miss Bingley, and prayed her husband would not be long. She knew it was more likely that she would be noticed if he tarried. Thankfully, it was only a few

310

minutes after that thought that light filtered in from the opening door to the dressing room, where her husband was entering the chamber. Elizabeth watched as Miss Bingley attempted a provocative pose at the edge of the bed and her husband physically recoiled at the sight.

"Miss Bingley, what are you doing in my chambers?" he asked sternly.

"I have come to the conclusion that your statement in the drawing room was due to the presence of that woman. I know that you did not mean it." She began removing one shoulder of her gown. "You must know by now that you made a terrible mistake marrying that little nobody from Hertfordshire—after all, she keeps poor Georgiana locked in her room." She slinked forward a step and Darcy took a step back. "It must be dreadful. I have no doubt you are secretly seeking to rid yourself of her, and I am here to offer myself to you when you succeed."

Darcy was furious. He knew she had always wanted him, or more precisely, she had wanted Pemberley. She had attempted to put herself in a similar position in the past, but he and his valet had been very careful to prevent such an occurrence. Now he was married, and she had finally succeeded to find her way into his rooms. He could only hope his wife would understand.

"I married Elizabeth because I love her. I will not send her away, and I will never have any kind of relationship with the likes of you," he seethed, barely controlling his anger as Elizabeth watched spellbound.

"She will ruin you socially. You should end your marriage to her while you still have time to save *dear* Georgiana's prospects. I can be the perfect wife—everything that she is not." Miss Bingley said the last in what he could only assume she meant as an alluring tone. She trailed her fingers from her chest down to her hip in an evident attempt to draw his attention to her figure.

"You have yet to understand me, Miss Bingley, I do not *care* about society," he said fervently. "I only care about Elizabeth and our child." Darcy was repulsed by her attempt at seduction, but he was more concerned with her machinations. He had attempted to rein in some of his fury in order to ascertain whether she was an immediate threat to his wife and was thankful she had not mentioned anything of that nature.

"I assure you I was in earnest earlier tonight when I told you that I would have never offered for you, and I will never be unfaithful to my wife. I suggest that you remove yourself from this room immediately. Not only do I wish you out of my sight, but you will stay away from me, my wife, and any children we may have, or I will ruin you in the eyes of London society. Do you understand?"

The woman before him blanched and began to stutter, "But . . . Mr. Darcy. . . I . . ."

"No more!" he boomed, effectively silencing her. "I married Elizabeth for many reasons, the main one being that she is nothing like *you*! If I wanted a simpering, fawning, over-indulged, manipulative woman, I could have taken my choice of any woman in society." Stopping abruptly, he peered around to where he felt a small hand touch his back. He found Elizabeth, who upon hearing the beginnings of his rampage, emerged from her place in the shadows to calm him.

"How long have you been here?" he asked, clearly surprised to find her there.

Elizabeth noticed Miss Bingley's head jerk to where she was standing just slightly behind Darcy, her eyes narrowing. "I was here when she entered the room, but I knew you would be upset if I confronted her on my own." Miss Bingley gave a rather unladylike "humph," and Elizabeth moved to see the woman turning her head to the side as if she were admiring the view of the room.

He nodded, closed his eyes, and took a deep breath, endeavouring to calm himself. A moment later, Bingley's familiar voice could be heard through the door to Darcy's dressing room.

"Evans, I came without question, man, but what has

happened?" he asked, as he stepped through the door. Miss Bingley's brother paled as he saw his sister in her less than proper attire. "CAROLINE!"

His sister swiftly righted the shoulder of her chemise, grabbed her dressing gown and put it on. She was fumbling with the tie when she found her arm yanked roughly by her brother toward the door to the hall. He rounded on her, his finger pointing directly into her face before she could open her mouth to protest his treatment of her.

"Do not utter one word, Caroline. I know *exactly* what you were up to, and I will no longer put up with it. As of this moment, you can consider yourself engaged to Mr. Jeffery Clarke."

"What! That tradesman who was the godson to our father? I refused him before, and I will not marry him now!"

"It is too late; I have already discussed it with Hurst, and he agrees," he declared. "You will not be returning to London. You will either marry Mr. Clarke, or if you refuse, I will set you up in your own establishment in Manchester, and you will have to live off of the interest from your dowry. As for our father, he would be proud to see you married to Mr. Clarke. I cannot say the same about your behaviour for the last few years."

"But . . . but, Charles!"

"No, Caroline, we will all be leaving tomorrow, and we will call on your intended the day after our arrival to inform him of the good news. Now, I will escort you back to your chambers and request that a footman be posted outside of your doors to ensure you remain until we depart on the morrow."

Darcy nodded to Evans, who departed the room quickly, as he watched Bingley take his sister by the arm and almost drag her out of the door, which slammed shut behind them.

"Dare I ask if anything else might arise?" laughed Elizabeth, as she turned to face her husband.

"I do not know," sighed Darcy wearily. "I do know that I really do not wish to think about it anymore, and I would dearly like to sleep in the mistress's chambers tonight."

Wrapping her arms around his middle, she chuckled harder. "I think that can be arranged," she said, as she pulled back to look at his face.

"I love you," he said softly before kissing her passionately.

"I know," she said with a smile, as she laced her fingers with his and led him through the door to her room.

~ * ~

Saturday 11 July 1812

Elizabeth had not been there as the coach carrying the Hursts and the Bingleys pulled away from Pemberley early the next morning. Miss Bingley was the first person loaded on to the coach, followed closely by the Hursts. Mr. Bingley, who had decided to accompany them so he could quickly arrange for his sister's marriage to Mr. Clarke, lagged behind.

As they said goodbye, Darcy offered a place for him to stay when he came back through on his return to London.

"I do not know when that will be now," Bingley said. "Caroline has overspent for so long that I will not allow her to plan an elaborate ceremony. She has so many dresses and gowns that I refuse to buy her wedding clothes, so hopefully I can get everything accomplished quickly and return to London when I had originally planned."

"Good luck," said Darcy, as the two shook hands.

"Thanks, I will need it."

Darcy chuckled at his friend's comment as he watched him alight the coach, and held up his hand when it began to move before returning to the house. Striding up the stairs, he entered the mistress's chambers and removed the clothing he had donned to see Bingley off. He slipped back under the covers, cuddling up to his wife's back.

314

"Will, please," she mumbled groggily.

"What is it, love?"

"I am so hot," she whined. "I love you, but you only make it worse."

He laughed as she began trying to remove her leg from the covers. As her condition had progressed, she had begun to complain of being warm, and finally with the addition of summer, she had found the heat unbearable. Helping her to remove the bedclothes, he put an arm around her and kissed her where her neck and shoulder met.

"Better, love?" he asked, barely containing his laughter when he realised that he would not receive an answer. She was once again asleep; the sound of soft snoring coming from her as she breathed.

Chapter 25

Life returned to a relatively normal pace once the Bingleys had left Pemberley. Georgiana was happy to be released from the confines of her room, and Miss Grey remained a visitor, as Elizabeth had asked her to stay for a week longer than the fortnight the Bingleys had planned to be there. She was an easy guest, since she did not expect anyone to go out of their way and was simply there to enjoy her friend's company.

The Monday after the Bingleys' departure, Colonel Fitzwilliam appeared unannounced, arriving on horseback early in the afternoon.

"Richard!" Darcy called out jovially, as he strode down the front steps to greet him. "You should have let us know you were coming."

"I apologize for that," said Richard. He dismounted and shook his cousin's hand in greeting. "I have been wanting to come, but circumstances prevented it. Since I did not know when I would be able to make the trip, I was unable to send you warning."

"You are always welcome, as you well know. Come inside, and Mrs. Reynolds can arrange for some refreshments for you. I am sure you could use them."

"Always," Richard laughed, as they made their way into the house and to the master's study.

"What brings you to Pemberley?" Darcy asked, while he took his seat behind his desk. "And do not tell me this is just a visit. If you were coming for a rest, you would have taken the time to write to me of your intentions."

Smiling, his cousin began to chuckle. "You know me too well."

"Well?"

"Father contacted me just after Christmas, requesting my presence at his house in London. If you remember, I was initially ignoring his messages, since I thought he wanted to vent his spleen about your marriage. But he did not relent, so after several weeks of messages being delivered to the barracks, I finally went to Park Lane."

Darcy stared, wondering what could be so important that his uncle would send so many letters to his son while he was busy with his regiment. "Is he finally pressing his suit regarding Georgiana?"

"No, he has actually been too busy to pursue custody of Georgiana. And frankly, after this, he will probably be afraid of the scandal and scrutiny such a legal action would precipitate." Richard took a deep breath. "I cannot say that it was a complete surprise. I have been saying for years that something like this would happen."

Darcy raised his eyebrows, waiting for Richard to elaborate.

"My elder brother, Philip, has the French disease," he said gravely. "He and my mother did not say anything at first. They hoped that the mercury treatments would cure him; however, when it became clear they were not even helping, my father began sending for me."

"I am sorry to hear about your brother," said Darcy in a sympathetic tone.

"Yes, well . . . you remember the way Philip was. It was only a matter of time." While Richard replied flippantly, there was a look in his eye that belied his tone of voice.

Darcy suddenly sat up as if startled. "Richard! There is no reason for you to remain in the Regulars! You must make..."

"Darce."

"...haste to London and resign your commission..."

"Darce!"

"before they send you back to the continent!"

"Darce!" he exclaimed for the third time, finally succeeding in interrupting his cousin's exclamation. "It is already done; that is why my father had sent for me. As not only am I the next in line, but also since the physicians do not expect Philip to live much longer, he did not wish me to lose my life on the peninsula when I will be the next earl."

"I wish it was not at your brother's expense, but I am very happy for you, cousin," said Darcy, as a knock sounded at the door. "Come!"

Mrs. Reynolds bustled in with a tray of sandwiches and a pitcher of lemonade. "Here you are, Colonel," she said cheerfully, placing the refreshments on a clear spot on the desk.

"Actually, Mrs. Reynolds, I am just The Honourable Richard Fitzwilliam now."

"You say that as if it were a bad thing, young man," she replied. "As much as I respected your role as an officer, I will be glad to see you not return to war."

"Thank you," he said with a grin.

"Now, if you boys need anything else, you be sure to let me know."

"Yes, Mrs. Reynolds," Darcy said, suppressing a laugh as the older woman exited the room.

"Why do I always feel as though she sees us as little boys?" Richard chuckled once the door was closed.

"I think I could have grandchildren running through the halls of Pemberley, and she would still see me that way."

After laughing a bit more, Richard surveyed the room before returning to his cousin. "Say, Darce, where is Lizzy? I am surprised she has not come to greet me," he asked before taking a bite of food.

"She has taken to napping for a few hours every afternoon these days."

"She is well?"

"She is very well. Some nights when the babe is active, she finds it difficult to sleep, and I believe that happened last night. The heat has not helped, as it adds to her discomfort."

Richard nodded as he finished chewing, and swallowed. "How much longer before her confinement?"

"The midwife estimated the beginning of September."

Finishing his food, he placed his plate back on the tray, and leaned back in his chair. "I know that things will be very busy around here for a while, but I was hoping you would not mind allowing me to follow you around while you manage Pemberley. My father never bothered teaching Philip, and I am sure the accounts of his estate alone are a disaster. I do not even want to think about Matlock's finances at the moment. I would prefer to be sure of what I am doing when the time comes."

"Has Philip's condition progressed to that point so soon?"

"Father has somehow successfully managed to keep it quiet, despite the fact that he has apparently been infected for some time. The physicians have attempted everything from bloodlettings to multiple sessions of mercury, the last of which weakened him excessively. He has since become ill with fever," Richard confided. "Father has had him moved to Matlock, so that mother can spend time with him until he passes. Oh, and father is demanding you show yourself at the funeral; he does not wish for anyone to question why you are not there."

Rolling his eyes, Darcy leaned forward onto his desk. "Do you have any knowledge of Ashworth's finances?"

"I travelled there on my way here, and met with the steward, Mr. Morris. There was some debt due to Philip's lifestyle, however a large portion of that has been repaid while he has been ill and in treatment. I am unsure of how much remains."

Did you bring the account books with you?" asked Darcy.

"Perhaps we could review them, and try to gain a better understanding of the situation."

"No, I meant to, but in my haste to depart this morning, I forgot them." Richard sighed. "But, I would definitely like to take you up on that offer."

"I will be happy to examine the accounts as soon as you can send for them. You need to understand exactly where Philip has placed Ashworth financially." Darcy sighed at his cousin's frivolity. He was known for his gambling and womanizing, which, by the state of things, had finally caught up with him. "You may stay here and work with me as long as you like, and I am sure Jacobs will be happy to assist you as well. I am surprised your father is simply allowing you to leave right now."

"He agreed when I stated my wish for you to help me. Whether or not the two of you see eye to eye, he does respect your knowledge and success with Pemberley. Although he feels that a week or two should suffice, and he is already pestering me about visiting some of his friends in the House of Lords with the intention of meeting their daughters."

"And how do you feel about that?" laughed Darcy. He was extremely thankful he did not have to deal with his uncle's machinations anymore.

"Honestly, I do not know how you dealt with it for so long." He sighed and ran a hand through his hair. "Not only do I have father, but Aunt Catherine has somehow learned of Philip's condition. She has begun writing me letters, insisting that I come to Rosings and marry Anne. At least my father agreed with you that it was highly unlikely she would be capable of carrying an heir, and has forbidden her from spreading any rumours that I am engaged to her daughter."

"If you happen to find the right woman, then by all means propose, but do not marry to forward your father's political ambitions. Do you really want to be married to someone for the rest of your life that you do not even like?"

"Do not worry, Darce. I informed him that I would make my own decision, which made him angry," he chuckled.

"However, I reminded him that I am the only remaining heir, unless he wished to leave Matlock to you, of course, and he ceased his arguments."

Darcy sat back in his chair as he laughed loudly. "I have always admired your manner of dealing with your father."

~ * ~

"I had heard a rumour that you were here, Richard," Elizabeth said, as she entered the drawing room before dinner that evening.

As he turned, his eyes bulged as they reached the swell of her abdomen. "You have grown, Lizzy!"

"That I have," she laughed. She stroked her belly through her dress before turning serious for a moment. "Will told me about your brother. I am sorry he is in poor health, but we are always happy to have you here."

Miss Grey entered the room, and Elizabeth turned. "There you are. Miss Elaine Grey, I would like you to meet Mr. Richard Fitzwilliam, Mr. Darcy's cousin." She paused while the two bowed and curtseyed, as was the custom, before continuing, "Miss Grey was visiting during the Bingleys' time with us, which was cut short due to some unforeseen circumstances, and I decided to keep her here for at least what would have been the original duration of her stay."

Richard looked inquiringly to Darcy, who closed his eyes and shook his head. "I will tell you after dinner while we have our brandy. The fortification will be necessary to relate the tale I fear."

Giggling, Miss Grey looked back to Elizabeth. "You act as if staying is such a chore, and going home presents such a temptation," she joked before turning to Richard. "Actually, Mr. Fitzwilliam, I believe I have made your acquaintance, but it was about two years ago."

"Are you related to Edward Grey?" he asked, surveying her carefully.

"He is my elder brother," she smiled.

"You were preparing for your come out, as I recall."

"Yes, I was," she responded with a small blush.

"And how is your brother? It has been some time since I have seen him. He, Darcy and I were rather good friends at Cambridge."

"He is well, thank you," she replied, turning as Georgiana joined them. Richard regarded his young cousin warily. He had visited her earlier with the intention of attempting a discussion, but came away immensely disappointed. Unsure if she could be trusted, he only told her of the viscount's illness, expected demise and his resulting change of status. She did not say much, mainly responding to any queries with a yes or no—if she deigned to answer at all.

Mrs. Reynolds soon entered to inform them that dinner was served, and they moved to the dining room. Overall, the meal was pleasant and the evening was spent enjoyably in conversation with the exception of when Elizabeth and Miss Grey performed. Miss Darcy remained quiet during the meal, only answering one or two questions posed to her by her cousin; however, she did surprise everyone when she took her turn to perform at the pianoforte. Nevertheless, due to Richard's travel that day and Elizabeth's condition, everyone retired a little early.

~ * ~

"Where is Miss Grey, Elizabeth," said Darcy. He was striding up to his wife, who was comfortably seated on a chaise under a tree by the lake, her fan folded in her lap while she enjoyed the light breeze.

"She is walking on the lake path with your cousin." Elizabeth smiled, and glanced to where she could see the pair strolling along. "Samuel has been standing just over there, ensuring I am well, dear."

He chuckled at her resistance to his protective nature, and sat beside her as he took her hand. "I know. I just did not

322

expect you to be here by yourself."

Leaning her head back onto the seat, she regarded him with concern. "How has Richard fared with learning to run an estate?"

"Very well actually," he answered. "Considering his father never took the time, he seems to understand a good portion of the duties that we addressed last week, so this week, I have been reviewing what I do during harvest, since he may have to return to Ashworth to oversee it. If Richard implements some of the newer farming techniques, he may be able to raise the estate's income. I had made the recommendations to Philip, but he never wished to be bothered."

"Were you ever close to him?

"Philip?" he asked. She nodded and he looked out over the lake as he spied Richard and Miss Grey walk over the footbridge near the edge of the wood. "No, he was always a great deal like his father, and frankly I think he saw me as quite a bore. I did not spend long hours at the club, gambling, and I would not visit the brothels with him."

"Was Richard close to his brother?"

"No, Richard always preferred my company. I believe that my uncle doted on Philip, and took more time with him than he did Richard, which did not promote friendship between two siblings." He pointed to a missive in her lap. "Is that a letter from the Gardiners?" he asked, clearly wishing to change the subject.

"It is," she smiled. "She sends her usual advice, and word that my uncle can not leave due to his business for a fortnight, so they will not be travelling until late July."

"Will they have to shorten their visit to Pemberley?" he asked, concerned, since he knew that his wife had dearly missed her aunt and uncle.

"No, they have decided to forgo their trip to the lakes, and only venture as far as Derbyshire. She asked if it would be acceptable for them to stay here, and perhaps make a few day trips to wherever they wish to go.

"I think that sounds like a splendid plan," he declared, happy his wife would have more time to spend with the only family she still retained. "You should write them today, and let them know that they are welcome. Have you given thought to the children? Mrs. Reynolds may know of a young woman or two from among the tenant families who might help with them while they are here."

Elizabeth knew that he had liked the Gardiners when they had met in London, yet he had had so little contact with them, that she was well aware that he was being so solicitous because of her, which made her smile. Even though he had been so proud and disagreeable when they first became acquainted, she was sure that if he had just shown a portion of the person he was now in Meryton, she would have fallen madly in love with him. Smiling, she thought that it was probably a good thing that he was so disagreeable then, or else she would have had many more women who would have been competing for his hand. One thing she could have never denied was how attractive she found her husband.

"What makes you smile so?" he asked with a grin. As she began to turn a brilliant shade of red, Darcy began to chuckle. "Should I be escorting you upstairs for your nap?" he continued in a husky voice.

"I was not thinking of that!" she cried, embarrassed.

"It was very similar to the expression when you do think of *that*, Mrs. Darcy," he laughed. "So, are you going to tell me, or am I going to have to tickle it out of you?"

"Oh look, here are Richard and Lainey!" she exclaimed, as the pair came closer. "How was your walk?"

"It was lovely, thank you for escorting me, Mr. Fitzwilliam," Miss Grey replied, a small smile on her face.

"Yes, thank you for accompanying me, Miss Grey," responded Richard. "But I am afraid that I told Mr. Jacobs that I would ride out while he attended some duties in a quarter of an hour. I should really be off to the stables and have my horse readied." With a quick bow to their guest, Richard turned and began to stride off in the direction of the stables.

"You are not needed, Will?"

"No, my steward offered for Richard to shadow him as much as he liked, and when Jacobs told him of his duties this afternoon, my cousin wished to go," he finished, explaining. "I came out to escort you upstairs for a rest."

"Did you?"

"Yes," he smiled.

"If you two will excuse me," Miss Grey chimed in. "I believe I would like to practice the pianoforte for a while, if that would be acceptable to you, that is."

"Lainey," said Elizabeth in a frustrated tone. "I have told you before that you need not ask. You are more than welcome to play anytime you like."

Giving a giggle, Miss Grey curtsied. "Then I shall leave you. Have a good rest, Lizzy."

After shaking her head at her friend, Elizabeth turned to her husband and stretched out her arms. "You wish to escort me upstairs, you say?" She laughed as he pulled her to a standing position, bringing her close, so he could lean in next to her ear.

"Very much so," he whispered into her ear as he felt her shiver. He pulled back, offered her his arm, and led her into the house. Once they had made it upstairs and into his chamber, he closed and locked the door behind them. As he turned to her, he saw her eyebrow rise, and stepped forward to take her in his arms, leaning forward to brush his lips against hers. He felt her hand snake up through his hair while she deepened the kiss and stroked his tongue with her own. Elizabeth untied his cravat, removed his coats, and fumbled, looking for the bottom of his shirt, running her hands up his chest when she managed to work them underneath the fabric.

Moaning, Darcy spread kisses down her neck as he turned her around so he could reach the fastenings on the back of her gown. She began to pant as he suckled the base of her neck while he opened the dress, and allowed it to drop to the floor where it was quickly joined by her petticoats and chemise. Her corset and stockings were gladly absent due to the heat and how uncomfortable they were in her condition.

He hastily stripped his shirt before he began ardently kissing Elizabeth once more, walking her back until her legs came into contact with the bed. She took a seat and scooted back onto the mattress as he sat down and removed his boots. Her arms embraced his neck and she pulled herself to her knees, spreading small kisses across his broad shoulders.

Once he had removed everything but his breeches, he stood to strip them off as well, before he crawled toward where she was shifting back toward the head of the bed. After kissing her once more, he moved down to take a nipple in his mouth, gently sucking and nibbling until he could hear her breathing coming in sharp pants, only to move to its twin.

"Will, they are too sensitive," she said breathily. "Please, I want you to come inside me."

"Are you sure?" he said. She had not been very comfortable the last time they had tried. As she nodded, he kissed her belly as he ran a hand around its circumference before returning to her lips. He loved her body enlarged with his child. He would not have believed it was possible, but he was just as attracted to her now, as he was when they had first married.

"Trust me?" he asked, as he helped her roll to her side, facing away from him. She nodded and he ran his lips up her back, leaving small kisses in their wake until he reached her shoulder where he lightly bit her before suckling her ear lobe. He wrapped his arm around her, and fingered her folds. She was ready, so he gently pulled her top leg back to ease himself inside.

Elizabeth inhaled sharply at the feel of his large girth filling her, and arched her back in an effort to take him in further.

"Are you well," he gasped out.

"Yes." She wrapped her hand behind her to grab his hip. As she heard him moan, he began moving within her. The position, which they had never tried before, seemed to be perfect. Not only did her back not ache as she lay on her side, but he was eliciting a response from her physically that had not been achieved since she had grown so large. She felt herself reaching climax very quickly, calling out his name loudly when she hit her peak while he gripped her tightly and groaned as he spent himself a minute later."

He rubbed her belly softly as they both caught their breath, and gave her a soft kiss on the shoulder.

"You are well?" he asked, watching as her head nodded.

"I promise," she responded. "I know I should have told you last time, but I did not wish to disappoint you."

"Well, we will just have to figure out other ways," he said with a mischievous grin as she slowly turned to face him.

"I am sure you will rise to the challenge." She laughed at the expression on his face.

"Now, I want to know what you were smiling about down by the lake."

She covered her face with her hands and grimaced. "Oh no, we are not back to that!"

"Do not make me tickle you, Elizabeth."

"Very well, I should have never told you that I hate to be tickled," she said, sighing. "I was only thinking how fortunate it is that you are so bad in social situations."

Giggling at his obviously affronted expression, she caressed her hand up his side to his face. "It is only that if you were more amiable in public, I would have had much more competition, because you are so handsome," she revealed, as she blushed anew. He placed his hand on her belly, and caressed the spot where his child was safely carried.

"I still would have wanted only you." He stared earnestly into her eyes as he pulled her close and kissed her. "You must be tired. Would you like me to rub your feet and ankles for a little while?"

"That would be wonderful," she breathed as he sat up. He took her foot in his hands and kneaded her skin with his strong fingers.

Soon he heard the sound of soft snoring, and looked up to find her sound asleep. Smiling, he placed the foot he was holding back on the bed, and rubbed the other. When he was finished, he pulled the sheet up over her and located his dressing gown. Her petite frame not only made her belly seem so large, but he was also sure that it contributed to her swollen ankles and aching back. Determined to keep an eye on her, he decided to remain there while she rested. So he grabbed her journal and sat next to her on the bed, reading until she woke, just before it was time to dress for dinner.

Chapter 26

Thursday 23 July 1812

Darcy walked into the music room as he looked for Elizabeth, only to find her sitting on a chaise by the window with her needlework in her lap. Laughing when he heard her soft snoring, he quietly crept over, and carefully removed her embroidery from her grasp. He placed the materials in her basket, but as he returned her hand, she opened her eyes.

"I am sorry," he said softly, taking a seat next to her. "I did not wish to wake you." He stroked her cheek, leaned in and kissed her soft lips gently. "How are you feeling?"

"Hot," she said, still groggy.

Chuckling, he placed a hand on her abdomen, rubbing in circles. A swift kick made him and Elizabeth smile before he glanced back to her eyes. "Why not go up to our chambers, and you can sleep in your chemise with the doors open for the breeze?"

"I was waiting for Lainey to return from her ride with Richard," she said wearily. "I did not think they would be gone for so long."

"They went riding together again?" She nodded, and with his free hand, he took hers. "Did Mrs. Annesley accompany them?"

"Yes, I think she has rather enjoyed it, since Georgiana prefers to ride on her own. I am just concerned for Lainey."

"She will be safe with Richard, love," he said to reassure her. "He knows better than to play with her feelings."

Sighing, she peered outside before she looked back at her husband. "But, I think she already cares for him. She has always been very open about everything, but when our cousin's name is mentioned, she is evasive, and I am worried. I do not wish to see her hurt."

"Well," he replied, holding up a letter, "if it makes you feel any better, I received a note from her brother. He is coming tomorrow, and he will depart with her the following day. I let Mrs. Reynolds know when I passed her in the hall a moment ago, so she can have a room prepared for him."

"I can still carry out my duties, Mr. Darcy," she responded with a raised eyebrow.

"I am well aware of that, Mrs. Darcy. I only thought to help." He lifted her hand for a kiss to her knuckles.

"I apologize," she said. "I am tired and hot, and I guess I am in a foul mood." She began to stand, her husband helping her before offering her his arm.

"Then let me escort you to our chambers, where you can rest, and if you would like, I can rub your feet and your lower back until you fall asleep."

"What did I do to deserve you?" she said with a small smile.

"You ran away from Mr. Collins," he replied, making the two of them laugh as they ascended the stairs.

~ * ~

Edward Grey arrived approximately an hour before dinner the next day. Darcy and Richard greeted him in the foyer, inviting the guest to the library for a glass of brandy once he had been able to refresh himself. As soon as Darcy handed around drinks, Grey looked to Richard curiously.

"It has been a long time, Fitzwilliam," he said carefully. "I must say, I was quite surprised when my sister informed me in her letter that you were here at Pemberley. Did you resign your commission?"

"Yes, I did," Richard answered in a guarded fashion. "My brother is in very poor health, and they do not expect him to survive the year. Father did not wish me to be sent back to

330

the continent, when I would be needed at Ashworth."

"I am sorry to hear of your brother's condition," Grey replied earnestly. "Is there truly no hope?"

"No, every known treatment has been attempted, and the physicians believe he is beyond that now. It is just a matter of time."

Nodding, Darcy watched the two men as his friend furrowed his brow, and took a sip from his glass.

"Lainey mentioned in her last missive that you wished to have a word with me?" Grey asked. "I must say, I have been very curious about what you could possibly want."

Richard looked up to find Grey's eyebrows raised, and peered at Darcy, who had his eyebrows lifted as well in silent question. "You are not going to make this easy for me, are you?"

"No," Grey said, as he smiled into his glass. "I am not."

Narrowing his eyes, Richard gripped his drink. "You already know what I wish to discuss."

"Maybe . . . maybe not, my sister and I have always been very close. Imagine my surprise when she included in a letter all of the attention you have been paying to her since you arrived."

Richard almost choked on his brandy. "She told you everything?"

At his cousin's shocked expression, Darcy guffawed. "Mrs. Darcy was concerned with the time you and Miss Grey were spending together," he said, when he had finally managed to stop laughing. "She was afraid you would create certain expectations, and did not wish to see her friend hurt."

"You know that I would never do such a thing, Darce," Richard responded, offended. "I discovered very quickly that I truly enjoyed her company, and I wished to get to know her while she was here."

"Nevertheless," Grey continued with a serious expression, "while she did not say as much in her letter, I believe you have engaged her feelings, but I have yet to speak with her on the matter. I want you to know that I will not give her away in marriage unless she loves the man and he loves her in return." Sighing, Grey looked to the fire before he looked back to Richard. "I will not have her in a marriage like mine. I care too much for my sister to give her away for less."

"I have asked if I may court her," Richard approached carefully. "She has accepted me. I only wish for your approval."

"Why?"

"Pardon?"

"Why do you want to court my sister?" he asked gravely.

"I enjoy her company," said Richard, averting his eyes out of the window.

"Not good enough."

Richard sighed and stared into his glass. "She is vibrant and happy; she tells me exactly what she thinks or feels without artifice. I have found in the last fortnight that I anticipate being in her company, and I do not want her to leave tomorrow." He ran his hand through his hair, and dropped his hand to his side before looking over to his cousin, who was smiling broadly. "What?"

"Nothing, I am just enjoying this immensely."

"You would," grumbled Richard as Darcy chortled.

Grey was smiling as he looked down into his glass of brandy. "You must understand, Fitzwilliam. My parents saw to it that I married my wife, just before they were killed in that carriage accident. I was fortunate, as a younger son, that my mother had an estate as a part of her dowry set aside for me; it was that and my marriage that enabled me to immediately become my sister's guardian when my brother did not wish for the responsibility."

He looked up into Richard's eyes as he continued. "Unlike my parents, my brother, or even my wife, Lainey and I have come to care little for connections and wealth, yet I was forced to marry with those considerations in mind. I do not wish for that for my sister. I want better for her."

"My father has already begun to push me toward the daughters of his political allies. I have no desire to be married to someone conniving and insipid," Richard said in earnest.

Grey studied him for a few moments before he stood. "Very well, you have my permission to court my sister," he responded, as he held out his hand for Richard to shake.

Clasping his friend's hand, Richard gripped it firmly, a wide smile on his face. "Thank you!"

"You act as though you have already earned her hand, Richard," Darcy chimed in, amused at his cousin's behaviour. "You still have to court her."

"I may need some advice there. I have no idea what to do."

"I would ask my wife's advice," Darcy smiled. "I was so inept at showing her my preference that I shocked her when she realised I had feelings for her."

Grey chuckled. "Based on my sister's letters, I do not think you need any help."

Turning quickly, Richard exclaimed, "What exactly did she write?"

The question was never answered, since there was a knock on the door to the library, which opened to reveal Elizabeth and Miss Grey.

"Dinner is ready," Elizabeth announced, peering around the room. "Miss Darcy is not down yet?"

"No," replied Darcy. "Perhaps . . ." His statement remained

unfinished as his sister strode into the room, and stood before everyone assembled.

"I apologize if I am late," she almost whispered.

"Well, then we are ready when you are, gentlemen." The men had decided earlier not to adhere to formalities for the evening, so Darcy offered his arm to his wife as she smiled demurely at him. Presenting his other to escort Georgiana, he watched as she hesitantly accepted. Richard took Miss Grey's arm before she turned to loop her arm through her brother's as well, so he was not left to bring up the rear alone.

Dinner was a pleasant affair and the Greys remained for a portion of the morning, giving Richard time to make arrangements to call on Miss Grey, and allowing everyone to visit a bit more. They departed close to the noon hour, leaving Richard to the mercy of his cousins until circumstances necessitated him returning to Ashworth the next day.

~ * ~

Saturday 1 August 1812

A week later, the Gardiners arrived at Pemberley. Elizabeth was ecstatic to see her beloved aunt and uncle, and hugged them both tightly when they entered the drawing room, the children all gathered around, attempting to greet their favourite cousin. Georgiana, who was introduced upon their guests entering, politely greeted them and excused herself to return to her studies.

"Look at you!" Mrs. Gardiner gushed, as she placed her hands on Elizabeth's abdomen. "How are you feeling?"

"I am well," she replied. "My husband would never allow anything that might render me any other way."

Madeleine Gardiner smiled as she attempted to rein in her three children. "Let Elizabeth sit down, and then you can each give her a hug and a kiss," she reasoned, as her niece sat on the sofa. The youngest daughter, Brenna quickly climbed up and hugged her before the others could wrestle free from their mother.

Darcy and Mr. Gardiner stood to the side, the former worried that the children might overwhelm his wife.

"She will be fine," Edward Gardiner laughed when he noticed his nephew's tense posture. "Maddie tells me the baby should arrive at the beginning of September?"

"Yes," Darcy replied. "Elizabeth has been so uncomfortable the last month. I do not know how she will manage for another at least."

Mr. Gardiner grinned. "It is always more difficult during the summer. Michael was born in early August, and I never thought I would hear my wife cease her complaints about how hot she was."

Smiling, Darcy turned to glance at Elizabeth's uncle. "Elizabeth does that." He then turned back to watch his wife as the two remaining Gardiner children greeted her before they were whisked upstairs by their nursemaid while tea and refreshments were brought into the room.

"Aunt," Elizabeth began, appearing confused. "Where is Jane? When you wrote that she came to stay with you, I had hoped she might travel with you?"

"Lizzy . . . Jane was married a fortnight ago," Mrs. Gardiner stated carefully.

"What? To whom?"

Mr. Gardiner, who saw that his niece was not only curious, but also upset, placed his teacup on the side table and leaned forward. "Do you remember my business associate, Mr. Mason?" Elizabeth nodded. "He began calling on her shortly after her arrival in London."

"But he is so much older," Elizabeth said, bewildered. "And I thought she would want to come see me. I was certain she would write when she came to stay with you—since my father was not there to forbid it—but she did not.

"I am sorry, Lizzy," her aunt replied. "She made it perfectly clear when it came time to set a date, that she did not wish to return to Longbourn for any reason, and she preferred not to travel here with us. As a result, we considered not bringing the children, but Jane would never have agreed to watch them. And since you and Jane are no longer at Longbourn, I will not entrust them to your parents' or sisters' care."

Elizabeth found that she could not control the tears that were beginning to fall from her eyes. "I admit that I was upset and disappointed with her when I left. She knew my dreams and expectations of marriage, and was still persuading me to marry Mr. Collins. But she is my sister, and we used to be so close." She felt the cushion sink as her husband sat beside her, and placed his handkerchief in her hands before putting an arm around her shoulders.

"Lizzy," her aunt reached over from her seat to take her hand, "since we spoke in London, I have tried and failed to understand her behaviour towards you on the day you left. I also could not appreciate her manner during her stay with us, so I confronted her shortly after she became betrothed." Elizabeth noticed her aunt take a deep breath before she continued. "I am afraid I was rather hard on her, but she finally told me—well, yelled it at me is probably a better description."

"What do you mean?"

"She resents you, Lizzy. It is very petty, and I hope you do not give her feelings any credit." Observing that her niece was only more confused, Mrs. Gardiner finally relented. "Do you remember how I told you that your father has been drinking a bit more than he has in the past?"

Elizabeth nodded. "He has actually been drinking until he is intoxicated daily for some time now. While he was in this state, Jane entered the study, I do not recall why, and heard him ranting to himself about why he wished for you to marry Mr. Collins."

"I do not understand, Mrs. Gardiner," Darcy

interjected. "Collins could have proposed to any of the Bennet sisters, so are you saying that Mr. Bennet planned for Elizabeth to marry him?"

"We believe that he steered Fanny to recommend Lizzy rather than Mary, who would have been a more suitable choice for Mr. Collins, and who would have more than likely accepted him." Mr. Gardiner stated.

"Lizzy, he wanted to give you Longbourn," her aunt finally confided. "He did not believe that Mr. Collins had enough intelligence to run an estate, and that you would be able to not only control him as your husband, but also make Longbourn prosper. He had planned to renovate the dower cottage for the two of you until he passed."

Everyone watched as Elizabeth's eyes widened in shock. "I am not insensible to the compliment in that, but that was also a plan for him to continue his indolent behaviour. He never wanted me to leave because I ensured the steward had what he required and tended to Longbourn's books; it is why he was always so eager for my return when I would visit you."

"I am sure that is part of it, Lizzy," her uncle confirmed.

"You must understand that Jane has been listening to your mother rave about your marriage and how you have saved the family," Mrs. Gardiner continued, obviously disgusted with her sister's behaviour. "So, when she heard your father make the remarks that he did, she became jealous and resentful."

"She has had Mother fawning and fussing over her since we were little. I was always told how I would never equal Jane in beauty or temperament, and she resents me now because of this?" Elizabeth's voice was incredulous. "She should read Mama's letters to me. All they consist of are demands and criticism."

"I was unaware Fanny had written you," commented her aunt.

"She has written two virtually identical letters, and they were both awful—I burned them."

"For what it is worth," Mrs. Gardiner replied sympathetically, "your mother was incensed by Jane's betrothal. She has made no secret that she felt her eldest deserved better than Mr. Mason, and I do not think she will ever forgive Jane for marrying from London."

Elizabeth's eyes grew wide. "She did not even return to Longbourn to marry?"

"No, she refused, and your father gave Edward permission to act in his stead. She wished to marry as soon as possible."

Elizabeth furrowed her brow as she felt her husband's thumb rub in circles on her shoulder, and attempted to take comfort in his presence, suddenly realising how weary she felt.

"Aunt Maddie, Uncle Edward," she said, as she looked over to where they were sitting. "I apologize, but I am fatigued, and cannot discuss this any longer. Please take your time with your refreshments. Mrs. Reynolds can show you to your rooms to rest or change, should you need to."

"Lizzy, are you sure you are well?" her aunt asked, concerned.

"I am well," she said smiling as she stood.

"As soon as I see Elizabeth upstairs, I will return," Darcy informed them.

"Do not hurry back on our account," Mr. Gardiner replied softly. He watched his niece slowly walk towards the stairs and dropped his voice. "See to your wife's comfort. We will be fine."

"Thank you," he responded gratefully before he strode quickly forward to offer his wife his arm and escort her up the stairs.

Elizabeth remained resting in their rooms until it was time to dress for dinner. Her husband attempted to get her to talk before she lay down, but to no avail, so he remained working within their rooms, keeping watch over her until she was ready to return downstairs. He tried several times to return to the subject, worried that she was restraining her emotions, but she resisted. She insisted she only wished to put it out of her mind.

~ * ~

Wednesday 5 August 1812

Several days later, Elizabeth awoke late to find her husband fully dressed and seated beside her on the bed.

"Good morning."

"Good morning," she said with a groggy voice.

"Love, I have a question I need to ask you." He paused until she nodded for him to continue. "May I ask what happened to your garnet cross?" he asked once she had stretched and slowly raised herself to a sitting position.

Crinkling her forehead, she looked at him questioningly. "I left it on my dressing table the morning after the ball at Netherfield—the morning I left. Why do you ask?"

Darcy nodded and reached into his coat pocket. "You may remember that I began checking all of the post as it arrived?" She nodded to indicate that she did, and waited for him to continue as he pulled a few letters from the same pocket. "There was nothing unusual at first, but about a month ago, Georgiana received a letter supposedly from a Miss Rebecca Greer."

She raised her eyebrows. "It was not from the lady?"

"Indeed, it was not," he replied. "It was from Wickham." Elizabeth inhaled sharply.

"I do not understand why I am shocked," she replied.

"Since the arrival of the first, there have been several addressed in the same manner. The latest was on my desk this morning, and it contained this. He had attempted to conceal it by placing it behind the seal, but it was poorly

339

done," he stated as he held up the necklace she had not seen since the day she left Longbourn. Her eyes widened and she reached up to take it, turning it over to study the back of the pendant.

"It is mine," she confirmed, holding it out for her husband to see the small "E" etched into the back of the pendant. "I was named for my grandmother Bennet, and she etched the letter so she could tell hers from her sister's, which is why my father gave me the cross."

"But how did Wickham get it?"

"I do not know," she shrugged. "You have said he is without morals—perhaps he stole it. I suppose my father could have sold it."

"Your father would sell an heirloom that once belonged to his mother?" he asked doubtfully. She furrowed her brow and rubbed her swollen abdomen.

"At one time, I would have never believed it of him; however, I would have never believed him capable of the behaviour he has reportedly exhibited as of late. Have you questioned Georgiana in regards to any of these letters?"

"I have tried to talk to her almost daily since the day we arrived at Pemberley together, whether she wished to speak to me or not, but she will not talk to me," he stated, wearily. "I have not confronted her about any of the letters. It had been a hope that perhaps she would comment about not receiving them, but she has not said a word. I will admit that I probably have not tried as hard as I should to get through to her. At this point, I think I try more out of familial obligation than feeling. I do not think I can ever forgive her for attempting to sabotage our relationship." He looked so forlorn that Elizabeth reached out and took his hand, rubbing her thumb across his knuckles. "Is it horrible that I am relieved that she has been on her best behaviour this week?"

"No," she replied. "But I think she does not wish to be restricted as she was when the Bingleys visited." Elizabeth ran her hand along his cheek. "I am sorry that it turned out this way—truly I am. If you need information about the necklace, perhaps my aunt and uncle may know, since they visited Longbourn on the journey here."

"I am not sure," he said apprehensively.

"They can be trusted, Will, and they may know something that will explain how Wickham came into possession of it."

He agreed, although, he was still wary while he waited for Elizabeth to complete her toilette before escorting her downstairs to break her fast. The Gardiners, who were thoroughly enjoying being on holiday, were already in the dining room when the Darcys arrived, and immediately greeted them.

"Lizzy dear, how are you feeling this morning?" her aunt inquired.

"I am well. I have just been so tired lately, and when I attempt to sleep at night, the baby moves so at times, that it keeps me awake."

Her aunt smiled knowingly. "It will soon be over, and then you will be fatigued due to night time feedings."

Elizabeth smiled at her aunt's comment before becoming serious. "Aunt Maddie, when I departed Longbourn, I left my garnet cross on my dressing table. Do you perchance know what became of it?"

As soon as the words were out of her mouth, her aunt and uncle looked at one another; Elizabeth did not miss their expressions. Her husband must have also observed their reaction, since she noticed the servants who were attending them depart to the kitchens and the door close behind them.

"Lizzy, I...," her aunt began.

"Please do not try to spare my feelings. It is very important that we discover what happened to it." She noticed their perplexed faces and glanced toward her husband, only to receive a grim nod, giving his permission to trust them. Elizabeth began the long tale, beginning with

Ramsgate and ending with the discussion that morning and the unveiling of the garnet cross from Darcy's coat pocket.

The Gardiners seemed somewhat shocked, but Elizabeth watched as they looked toward one another in an unspoken agreement. Her uncle then turned his head toward them and sighed. "Your father had it on his desk just prior to Christmas when I visited him in his study."

"The next time we saw it was Christmas Day when your mother gave it to Lydia," continued her aunt, "who—you can imagine—was flaunting her acquisition of something that once belonged to you, her father's favourite."

Elizabeth rolled her eyes in response to the narration of Lydia's behaviour before thinking back on her most imprudent sister's relationship with Wickham. "Lydia always did find Wickham to be so pleasing and handsome," she pondered aloud, as she looked toward her husband. "If he charmed her, I have no doubt that she would probably give him anything for which he asked." Elizabeth noticed as Madeleine Gardiner closed her eyes, obviously mortified by the more than likely imprudent actions of her youngest niece.

Edward Gardiner sat forward in his seat. "At this juncture, I am unsure how to handle the situation. Normally, I would write to Thomas and inform him of Lydia's actions, but I do not believe he would so much as read the letter."

"And Fanny believes Wickham to be so very amiable," her aunt continued. "She believes a story he has been spreading throughout Meryton of being denied a living by your husband, and is beginning to believe that Darcy is somehow preventing you from contacting them or helping the family. She had not mentioned her letters. Perhaps she did not want to take a chance that your father would discover she wrote you." Mrs. Gardiner sighed. "The militia did move to Brighton for the summer, but unfortunately Lydia was invited by the wife of a Colonel Forster to be her particular companion and your mother allowed her to go."

"I can only imagine what Mama would say," Elizabeth exclaimed.

"I never denied Wickham a living," Darcy began as he explained his history with Wickham. When he was finished, he sighed and looked to his wife. "As for contacting her family, that has always been Elizabeth's prerogative."

"In my mother's letters, she wrote that she did not understand how I married Mr. Darcy when Jane was so much more beautiful, then she insisted that I invite her and my sisters to town to take them shopping. I am also supposed to persuade my husband to escort all of them to balls and the theatre—to throw them into the paths of other rich men." She paused as she closed her eyes, embarrassed by her mother's callous disregard and abrasive manner. "I lived with her telling me for years that I would never be as beautiful as Jane or as amiable as Lydia, and I am finally free of that, and I am happy. I do not care if she brags about me incessantly to the neighbourhood. I will not respond to her demands any longer."

"You do not have to explain to us," her aunt soothed. "It is one of the reasons we tried to have you with us as much as your father would allow. Unfortunately, in regards to Lydia, I do not believe there is much we can do at the moment. Perhaps we can attempt to talk to your father and mother when we stop at Longbourn on our return to London, but I do not hold much hope that they will heed our warning, especially since we cannot tell them about the necklace and Miss Darcy."

Darcy nodded. He was beginning to understand that at times there was nothing that could be done. "Thank you for giving me the information I required. I appreciate you keeping what you have been told regarding my sister to yourselves. I am loath to admit it, but if things do not change, she will be married as soon as she is out, to a suitable match. I will not allow her to continue to wreak havoc in my life."

The Gardiners regarded Darcy sympathetically. "I believe I understand," responded Edward Gardiner. "While my father never said as much, I believe that is why he married Fanny off to Thomas Bennet as quickly as he could. She was always silly and demanding like Lydia, and my mother, while not like her daughter, indulged her. When he saw Bennet admired her beauty, it did not take him long to forward a match between the two."

Darcy sat for a few moments before rising from his seat. "If you will excuse me, I need to go have a word with Georgiana."

"Would you like me to come with you?" Elizabeth asked worriedly.

"No, love," he replied. "I do, but I think she will behave worse with you in the room, and I do not wish you upset."

"I do not give any importance to what she may say. My only thought is to be there for you should you need it."

Smiling, he held out his hand, which she took as she rose from her seat. "Very well, then I would be pleased for you to join me." He entwined his fingers with hers as he led her from the room.

Chapter 27

When they arrived at Georgiana's door, Darcy paused and took a deep breath before raising his hand to rap on the hard wood. Amy answered and stood aside to allow them to enter, then departed to the dressing room, leaving the three of them alone.

"You have been receiving letters from a Miss Rebecca Greer," Darcy began. He watched as his sister went from staring at the wall as if he were not there to staring at him agape with wide eyes. As he held up the open pieces of paper, her face began to crimson. "Obviously you know very well who truly sent these."

"How dare you!" she exclaimed. "You have no right!"

"I have every right!" he bellowed. "You are going to ruin your reputation, and quite possibly your life, associating with Wickham!" Taking a deep breath, he tried to calm himself. "I have never lied to you about his intentions, Georgiana, yet you refuse to believe me. It has been a struggle to keep you from harming your own reputation, especially as of late, yet I have endeavoured to do just that."

"You should not have read those," she retorted. "Why should I believe you anyway? You have never cared for me."

"That is not true. I would not have done as much as I have if I did not care."

She gave a rueful laugh. "You are a liar."

"Let me tell you about the liar, little sister. His latest letter contained this," he said, holding up Elizabeth's garnet cross. "Would you like to learn how he obtained it? Because I believe I know. He most certainly does not have the money for a pendant like this, much less a gold chain." Georgiana's eyes flitted to his hand and then back to his face. "You see, I recognized the chain and the cross, because it belonged to Elizabeth. She left it behind, in her room, when she came to

345

marry me. Her parents gave it to her youngest sister, Lydia, for Christmas. From there, one of two things happened; he either stole it, or he charmed her and she gave it to him. If I were to wager on it, I would pick the second."

Elizabeth watched with fascination as the young woman attempted to pretend the information did not bother her. She was not very successful, as her eyes kept darting back to the necklace hanging from her brother's hand. He must have finally hit a breaking point, because she stood and rounded on him with her hands fisted at her sides.

"George told me what a little whore your wife is. Did you know that?" she cried. "He told me all about how she flirted shamelessly, attempting to seduce him, and she probably gave him that necklace then. She should have married her cousin, like she was supposed to! Although given George's description of him, I cannot say that I blame her! Only she discovered that she could marry you, and decided that neither a lieutenant in the militia nor the future heir of her father's estate were worth her time! I bet that child she carries is not even yours!"

It was a split second reaction, and before Darcy knew what had happened, his hand was whipping around when he felt small fingers grasp his arm and pull. He stared in horror as he realized he had been about to strike his sister before his wife had intervened. Georgiana was no less affected. Her eyes were as wide as saucers as she gaped at him. He did not say a word before he turned and strode from the room.

Elizabeth was torn as she watched him leave. She wanted to go comfort him; however, another part wished to set the record straight with the naïve little girl who had sunk into her chair. Stepping forward, she set her hand on the back of the chair as she looked down upon its occupant.

"I never flirted with Mr. Wickham. He told me a falsehood about his history with your brother, and I believed him, until Will finally told me the truth," she said before she sighed. "I pity you." Georgiana's face jerked toward her, surprise evident in her features. "Your brother has so much love to give, while all you seem to desire is material objects. He is one of the gentlest men I know, yet he lost control and

346

almost slapped you. Does that not give you cause to think that your behaviour is beyond the pale?"

"This is none of your concern," Georgiana seethed through her hands.

"You upset my husband, so yes, it is," Elizabeth replied simply. "I do not pretend to know what there is between you and Wickham, but you have proven yourself to be a very selfish and stupid little girl. You have bestowed your trust upon the wrong man."

"And you should have stayed where you belonged; although, I guess it really does not matter. George will come for me, we will leave, marry, and I will never return. I suppose it really does not matter if you ruin my brother's life. He deserves it after attempting to ruin mine."

"You believe that if it gives you comfort, but you know in your heart that it is a falsehood." Elizabeth turned to Georgiana's dressing room and exited through the door. As she paused to take a deep breath, she recognized the sound of crying coming from within, which gave her cause to hope. Amy was visibly surprised to find the mistress standing in the dressing room until Elizabeth informed her that Miss Darcy would need some cool cloths for her eyes. Praying to find her husband, Elizabeth then made her way to the master's chambers.

When he was not there, she made her way to his study and the library, and having no success, found her aunt and uncle in the front hall, preparing for a walk with the children.

"Lizzy dear," her aunt said sympathetically. "Your husband looked ever so upset when he strode out of the front door a short time ago."

Elizabeth thanked her aunt as she walked as briskly as she could outside. Scanning the front lawn, she did not see him, and began to think where he could be as she moved toward the stable. For the first week of August, the weather was stifling, and she realised that he was probably not riding, as it was nearing noon, and it was already hot; at least to her it was. She had stopped momentarily when a thought struck her; she strode purposefully in the direction of the trail around the lake. Due to her slower gait, it took a bit longer to reach the small trail, and she had to tread carefully, however her persistence paid off when she reached the small pond, where he stood staring into the water. She began to creep quietly toward him, until she stepped on a twig; the sound of it breaking startled him and caused him to turn around.

"Elizabeth?" he said incredulously. "Please tell me you did not walk the entire way here."

"I am only with child, not helpless."

"Matthew and Samuel did not insist on you returning to the house?" he continued.

"I just exited the front doors looking for you. I did not consider requesting an accompaniment," she replied, as she watched his eyes grow large.

"You walked out here by yourself! Elizabeth, what if something had happened! You could have fallen or the baby could come early, and no one would know until it was discovered you were missing!"

She took the last few steps and stood before him, placing her hands on his chest. "I am fine and I am here with you. I wanted to ensure you were well."

Darcy closed his eyes and rested his forehead to hers. "I have never struck a woman, and I am appalled that I nearly did so. The fact that it was my sister horrifies me all the more."

"She has defied you and resisted your efforts, pushing you until you just could not endure it anymore."

"I did not even think about it; you stopped me before I even realised what I had done. I think that is what scares me the most."

"You would never hurt me, and I do not truly think you would have done any lasting harm to Georgiana," she

348

replied. "In fact, I have wanted to thank you for asking me about the necklace this morning."

"I promised you my trust. I cannot say that I did not fight a wave of jealousy when I opened the letter, but I do trust you," he said with an earnest expression. "I hope you know that."

"I do," she replied. "Do not distress yourself about your sister. Perhaps the threat of a slap might make her easier to deal with in the future."

"It still does not make what I did acceptable," he said forlornly. "I know what she was saying was patently untrue, but I let her affect me. I should not have." He pulled back from Elizabeth's face and looked down at the forest floor.

"Will," she declared, cupping his face in her hands to ensure he was looking at her. "You are human, and we all make mistakes. Though I cannot say that slapping Georgiana would necessarily be a mistake." She smiled mischievously as her husband regarded her incredulously. "I myself would not have minded striking her at the time. I just knew you would never forgive yourself if you had done it."

He chuckled. "Are you to be my protector then?"

"As much as you are mine," she answered earnestly, before a contrite look happened upon her features. "However, at the moment, I would dearly love to begin walking back."

"Are you tired?"

"My feet are beginning to ache, but I believe if we leave now, I will be able to make it to the house before they become worse." She observed his reaction, thankful that he had not seen fit to say 'I told you so,' when he took her hand and began to stroll slowly back toward the lake. As they reached a large shade tree by the bank not far from the house, Elizabeth stopped and turned toward Darcy, smiling softly at him.

"I do not want to return inside just yet."

"You do not?" he questioned, unsure of her meaning.

"No, I do not. Will you sit here in the grass with me for a while?" He smiled and, after a moment, took a seat with his back against the trunk of the tree as Elizabeth gingerly lowered herself next to him, her back to his chest. She felt his arm snake around her middle and his hand protectively rest on the swell of her abdomen. She sighed contentedly.

"I find it hard to fathom, but we have yet to discuss a name for this little one," she began, covering his hand with her own. "I know you were named for your mother's family, but I do not wish to carry on that tradition."

"It would be to honour you, love, not your family," he said softly, nuzzling her temple.

"Nevertheless, while I appreciate the gesture, I would prefer to use a different name." She smiled as she turned to watch his profile. "We could name a boy Fitzwilliam," she mentioned lightly, giggling when he grimaced.

"I do not wish to do that to my child. For one, my aunt and uncle may look at it as if I am honouring my heritage. Other than the Darcy name, I have no desire to honour my family.

Elizabeth nodded and looked out over the lake. "Are there any names you are partial to?" she asked, as he furrowed his brow to think.

"I like my middle names, James Alexander, and I would not be averse to honouring Richard or your uncle, Edward."

Beaming, she turned to him. "You truly like my uncle."

"He is a good man, Elizabeth, and I am honestly glad that you did not lose the entirety of your family when you left Longbourn. I am happy to include them among my family."

"We could shorten Fitzwilliam to William," she suggested. She still hoped to somehow name a son after her husband. We would still be naming him after you, without the reference to your mother's family, William James Alexander Darcy."

"You really wish to name our first born son after me?"

"I do." He smiled and held her a bit closer.

"Well, since you picked out our son's name, I want our daughter to be called Grace," he said authoritatively, even though he was smiling.

She raised that one eyebrow and turned a bit more to truly see his face. "You certainly are resolute. May I ask why?"

Leaning forward so that his face was closer to hers, he claimed her lips softly before pulling back so that their foreheads were still touching. "Because it was by the grace of God that I found you that day in the rain."

Elizabeth could not help but feel the tears that came to her eyes as she took his face in her hands and gave him a short but passionate kiss. "Grace it is," she confirmed. She released his lips and settled her side against the strong wall of his chest. "But she needs at least one middle name."

"What about Madeleine for your aunt and then Rose for your middle name?"

"Grace Madeleine Rose Darcy," she whispered, testing it out on her tongue. "I think it sounds lovely." She had just leaned her head against his chest when they heard children's laughter. They both looked to find her aunt and uncle returning from their walk.

Greeting them, Darcy stood and aided Elizabeth to stand. "I believe you have become fatigued," he said softly.

"I am so tired of being tired," she laughed. "I suppose we should return to the house. It is such a pleasant day that I did not wish to miss all of it, confined indoors."

The children were rushed upstairs to the nursery as soon as they entered the house, and Mrs. Reynolds ushered them all to the drawing room where she soon had tea and other refreshments delivered. All partook of the small repast before the Gardiners excused themselves to call on a friend of Mrs. Gardiner in Lambton, and to visit a few special places around the area.

Darcy and Elizabeth spent the remainder of the day in the library, reading; although, Elizabeth fell asleep cuddled next to her husband on the sofa for several hours, until it was time to dress for dinner. The evening was very enjoyable, and since the Gardiners had plans to sightsee the following day, a picnic by the lake was discussed and agreed upon for two days hence.

~ * ~

Friday 7 August 1812

It was a beautiful day for a picnic, and Elizabeth was laughing merrily at the attempts of the Gardiner children to fly a kite with their father and her husband. Elizabeth had enjoyed seeing Darcy interact with her young cousins. He read to them and took young Edward for horseback rides, further convincing her that he would be a wonderful father.

Georgiana had even deigned to join the party, but she sat by herself under a tree, reading. There had been no further incidents with the young woman since she received her stinging rebuke, and Elizabeth was at least thankful for that. Darcy and the children had attempted to include Georgiana in their play, but she had declined. She had not been disdainful as she had in the past, which prompted Elizabeth to hope that they may have finally managed to make some progress. Sighing, she leaned back into the chaise her husband had had the servants bring outside, so that she would have a comfortable place to rest when she was in need of it. She was just about to fade to sleep when the sound of a rider startled her awake.

"Richard! Freshen up and come join us!" Darcy called when he saw the rider. Noticing his cousin's sombre expression, he strode forward while Richard dismounted. "Has something happened?"

"Philip passed last night," Richard imparted low enough so only the two of them could hear.

Darcy closed his eyes and exhaled before glancing back to his wife. "Allow me to introduce you to Elizabeth's relatives before we excuse ourselves and adjourn to my study." Richard nodded his agreement and politely greeted Mr. and Mrs. Gardiner as he made their acquaintance, apologizing for his untimely interruption. The two gentlemen excused themselves quickly, not saying a word until they were behind the closed doors of Darcy's study.

"I knew you said he was not expected to last much longer, but I did not anticipate it to be this quick," commented Darcy. "My assumption is that your father sent you to persuade me to attend Philip's funeral."

"Yes," confirmed Richard. "He does not wish for any gossip to arise from your failure to attend. With the warm weather, the burial will be the day after tomorrow; which is fortunate, as I understand that you do not wish to be away from Lizzy any longer than is necessary at this time."

"I do not wish to leave her at all, but the three of us did play together as boys," said Darcy, as he dropped into his seat. "I should attend, regardless of your father's wishes. When did you plan to return?"

Sitting in the chair in front of Darcy's desk, Richard ran his hand through his hair nervously. "I had hoped I could persuade you to let me ride one of your mounts for the return trip this evening," he replied warily. "I am without a steward at Ashworth at the moment."

"You released Mr. Morris?" Darcy asked, surprised.

"It was imperative," Richard confided. "Do you remember your offer to review the books with me?" He paused and exhaled heavily before continuing. "I sent to Ashworth for them, but received only delays and excuses for why they were not being messengered. I became suspicious and demanded them immediately upon my return." Darcy's eyebrows rose in surprise, yet he remained quiet, waiting for the drama to unfold. "Morris had been stealing money for years, only my brother was so busy with his other pursuits that he never paid attention to the expenditures listed in the accounts."

"I hope you turned him over to the magistrate." Darcy

frowned and leaned forward in his seat.

"I did, a week ago, and I have been attending to estate matters myself ever since," Richard sighed. "There is little hope of retrieving everything he stole, but I believe I have finally sorted through the mess he created. I had intended to write you regarding advice on a replacement, but I was never afforded the opportunity with Philip's illness progressing as it has this last week. I had to write Grey and inform him of certain details, since I could not travel to Briarwood."

"We can consult with Jacobs prior to our departure. He may know of a suitable replacement, but I should really speak to Elizabeth before we leave."

"Of course," sympathized Richard. He was still upset at his inability to visit Miss Grey since she had left Pemberley almost a fortnight ago.

Darcy rose from his seat and opened the door to his study, finding Mrs. Reynolds with a tray of refreshments for his cousin. "Thank you, Mrs. Reynolds. Please notify Evans that I will need him to pack enough clothing for a few days at Ashworth, which will include the funeral of Philip Fitzwilliam." Luckily, the housekeeper had placed the tray on the surface when he imparted the last bit of information since she abruptly stood up straight, turning to Richard.

"I am terribly sorry to hear of your loss, Mr. . . . . pardon me, Lord Ashworth," she stumbled.

"Thank you, Mrs. Reynolds," he replied. "Please do not make yourself uneasy. It will take me some time to become accustomed to it myself."

Nodding, she turned to Darcy. "I will let Evans know, and do not worry, we will take very good care of Mrs. Darcy."

He smiled in thanks at Mrs. Reynolds, and turned to go locate his wife.

~ * ~

Darcy glanced back as he rode away from Pemberley with

354

Richard at his side, seeing Elizabeth still standing in front of the large oak front doors as he departed. Though she understood that he needed to attend his cousin's funeral, she could not help but feel desolate at the thought of him being away for several days; his promise to return immediately should she need him did not comfort her.

In addition to Mrs. Reynolds's vow, he had extracted promises from the Gardiners and Claire to notify him immediately should he need to return early. Mr. Gardiner even chuckled as he patted him on the back and attempted to calm his worry about leaving. "She will be fine, and will be here waiting for you when you return—still large with child."

Elizabeth lifted her hand to wave one last time before he turned to urge his horse to a gallop, hoping to make Ashworth by nightfall.

~ * ~

Elizabeth awoke from a fitful slumber—she was exhausted. Darcy had left two days before, and she had not slept well since. She was reminded of the awful time after her husband had found the planted letter in her dressing room. Looking around the master's chambers, she sighed, not really wishing to rise for the day, but unable to ignore the baby's insistent pressing on her bladder and the ache in her hips from lying on her side for so long. As she rose to a sitting position, her attention was captured by a knock on the door that separated the sitting room from the master's room.

"Come in!" she called, as the door opened to admit Claire, followed by her aunt.

"How are you this morning, dear?" her aunt questioned, as she approached the bed with a concerned expression.

Madeleine Gardiner was aware of how little sleep her niece was getting, especially when the dark circles manifested under her eyes. She remembered well the later days of her own confinements, and sympathised with her niece.

"I am as well as can be expected, I suppose." Elizabeth

checked the clock on the mantle, realising the lateness of the hour. It was almost noon, which was unusual for her. She turned to put her legs over the side of the bed to discover Claire, who had exited upon showing in her aunt, had re-entered the room, holding what appeared to be the post.

"Pardon me, ma'am, but these just came express for Mrs. Gardiner."

Her aunt stepped forward to take the letters and furrowed her brow. "They are from Jane," she remarked almost absent-mindedly. "This one was misdirected at first, and it is no wonder, she wrote the direction remarkably ill."

Sitting on the bed next to Elizabeth, she placed an arm around her. "I will go read my letters in your sitting room while you attend to your toilette, and then I will have tea with you while you break your fast, if you would like. Oh, and your uncle and I do not expect you to keep us company today. We have planned to take the children into Lambton, so you might want to remain in your nightclothes, since you will have more time to rest in your rooms"

Elizabeth nodded, and slowly climbed out of the bed, frowning at not being able to see her feet. She crossed her chambers to her water closet and dressing room, where she allowed Claire to brush out and re-plait her hair. However, as she reached the door to her sitting room, she heard a muffled sob, and hastened through to find her beloved aunt with tears streaming down her face.

"Aunt Maddie, what is it?" she asked frantically, as she crossed the room to the settee. "Are you well?"

"Oh Lizzy," she replied, endeavouring to recover herself. "I am quite well; I am only distressed by some dreadful news, which I have received from Jane." Elizabeth took a seat next to her aunt, waiting with bated breath for her to compose herself enough to finish. "Your youngest sister has left all of her friends—has eloped; has thrown herself into the power of—of Mr. Wickham. They are gone off together from Brighton. You understand enough of his character to doubt the rest. She has no money, no connections, nothing that can tempt him to—she is lost forever."

356

Elizabeth closed her eyes in mortification over the impulsive and imprudent actions of her most ridiculous sister, feeling tears prick at her eyes. "What has been done to recover her?"

"It says here," she said, holding up the letter. "That upon hearing the news, your mother took to her rooms. Jane wrote to me instantly after receiving a letter from Mary. Mary had requested Mr. Mason's aid, since they were traced to London and not beyond. She begs our return in order to have Edward help locate them."

"She did not care to return to Longbourn. I am surprised she is concerning herself with this."

"Mr. Mason is very concerned with appearances and his reputation, Lizzy," her aunt explained. "I would imagine he is very worried about the scandal affecting him and his business."

Nodding, Elizabeth thought long and hard in the hopes of remembering something that might help her aunt and uncle locate Lydia. "Georgiana Darcy's last companion, Mrs. Younge, worked with Wickham," she divulged. "I remember Will saying that she has a boarding house in Saffron Hill."

"I will let Edward know," her aunt replied. "The weather does not look promising for travel, but we *must* leave. I will have the servants prepare for our departure while I acquaint your uncle with the particulars. I am hesitant to leave you though, Lizzy. We made a promise to your husband. But I do not see Mr. Mason accepting Lydia into his home after this, and I cannot leave Edward to deal with her on his own."

"He will understand. Now, do not fret if your trunks are not prepared when you are ready to leave, I will have them sent along as soon as they are packed." Mrs. Gardiner stood and Elizabeth followed her to the door. "I will dress and be downstairs to see you off as soon as I can."

"Dear Lizzy," her aunt cried, placing her hands on Elizabeth's cheeks. "Neither Edward nor I expect you to go to that trouble. The baby is supposed to arrive in a couple of weeks, but you never know when this little one will decide it is time." Mrs. Gardiner placed her hands on her niece's burgeoning belly. "You cannot deny that you have not been sleeping well since your husband left, and you will need your rest. We will come say our farewells before we leave. I assure you."

Teary eyed, Elizabeth nodded, and hugged her aunt quickly before Mrs. Gardiner departed, leaving Elizabeth alone once more. Her aunt and uncle came by her sitting room half an hour later with the children to say their goodbyes, and hastily departed as soon as they were loaded into the coach.

Elizabeth lay down in her husband's bed. Her mind was restless with the events of the morning; nevertheless, overwhelming fatigue claimed her soon after, and she remained in a sound sleep until she woke to a loud crack of thunder and rain pouring down the windows two hours later.

Rising from the bed, she took a seat in the window and stared into the rain. She had been disappointed with Jane's resentment, and mortified at her mother and Lydia's behaviour. However, over the last week, she had come to realise that while they were once her family, her family was now her husband and the child that rested within her. She had truly left everything at Longbourn behind when she fled that rainy November day, and while she had mourned them to an extent when she left, she had never really belonged there the way she did with Will. Love at Longbourn was fickle and had conditions—it was not true, not like the love of her husband. He would never disregard her or place conditions upon her as her mother and father did.

Darcy looked out of the study window at the pouring rain and clenched his fists at his sides. They had interred Philip that morning, and returned to Ashworth when the heavens opened and the deluge began, trapping him inside the house with his cousin and his uncle, the latter actually expressing his appreciation for helping Richard during Philip's convalescence. Darcy was stunned, and the earl excused himself to rest, which left the cousins to their pursuits.

Running his hand through his hair, he turned to glance at Richard, who was reviewing records with his new steward. Mr. Jacobs had sent the young man the previous day to interview for the position, and upon satisfying Richard of his competence, was swiftly employed. Darcy sighed, and turned to resume his vigil.

"Darce," Richard called from his desk. "Come away from the window. I know you wish to be at home with your wife, but you cannot leave in the midst of a storm." Darcy left the window and walked over to take a seat before the desk. He listened to his cousin's discussion as he ruminated on any method that could hasten his return to Pemberley.

Close to an hour later, a servant entered the room with a letter. "Pardon my intrusion, sir, but a messenger from Pemberley just arrived with an urgent message for Mr. Darcy." Leaping from his seat, he snatched the missive, mumbling his thanks while turning his back to Richard and his steward. He immediately noticed the writing did not belong to Elizabeth, which only fuelled his worry, and tore it open, quickly devouring its contents.

"Is there a problem, Darcy?" Richard asked, as he excused the steward from the room.

"Not with Elizabeth, thank God!" He reviewed the message once more to ensure he had not missed anything of importance, since receiving an express in the current weather had made him think something dire had occurred. He looked up to find themselves alone, and handed Richard the note.

"Wickham!" his cousin exclaimed upon reaching the explanation of the Gardiners' departure.

"Yes," confirmed Darcy. "I had asked the Gardiners to keep a close eye on Elizabeth while I was gone, but they had to begin their return to London this morning due to this . . . debacle. As soon as the weather clears, I am leaving for Pemberley. I do not like Elizabeth being there alone."

"You have an excellent staff, Darcy. They will care for her," Richard said with a furrowed brow. "I am more concerned with Georgiana."

"I do not understand why. Wickham is in London, and Georgiana is restricted to the house during my absence."

Richard began pacing back and forth, as Darcy had seen him do many times in the past when he was attempting to work out a dilemma in his mind. "Wickham was seen with Georgiana in Lambton, she has been receiving letters from him, and I am sure due to those factors, that he has not surrendered the idea of eloping with her and making a claim for her dowry."

"We told him in no uncertain terms that we would have to sanction my sister's marriage, which would never happen if she married him," Darcy stated. "I admit, I believe he is trying to get to me through Georgiana, but I do not see him attempting another elopement."

"I do not know what he has running through his twisted head; but I do not like this, at all." Richard turned his head to stare into the rain. "We need to get to Pemberley as soon as possible. Someone needs to keep an eye on Georgiana, and Lizzy is in no condition to do it."

Chapter 28

Sunday 9 August 1812

Elizabeth remained in her rooms for some time after the Gardiners departed. She thought about all that had occurred—Lydia, Georgiana and Wickham. Coming to a decision, she rose from where she was seated propped in the pillows, and rang for Claire, requesting to be dressed. Her maid, who, along with the housekeeper felt she should be keeping to her rooms, eyed her warily, but acquiesced; she planned to warn Mrs. Reynolds should they need to somehow try to force the mistress back to her chambers.

Once Elizabeth was dressed in one of her most lightweight gowns, she left her room and walked to the guest wing where Georgiana's room was located. Taking a deep breath, she steeled herself for what she felt would be an unpleasant encounter, and knocked upon the door while she listened to the rustling within. The door finally opened, and Elizabeth found Georgiana staring her down, an implacable expression upon her face.

"I need to have a word with you," said Elizabeth in a steady tone.

Georgiana exhaled heavily. "I am in no mood for a lecture today."

"I have something I need to tell you," began Elizabeth authoritatively, "and I hope that you will speak with me."

She observed Georgiana's facial expressions, wondering if the young woman would be averse to listening. She had a momentary feeling of victory when Georgiana moved and allowed Elizabeth into the room before closing the door. Elizabeth carefully regarded Georgiana as she took a seat, and the young woman turned to look at her expectantly.

"Well?"

"There is no easy way to say this, so I will just come out with it." Elizabeth mentally braced herself for the possible tempest the disclosure could bring. "My aunt received a letter this morning from my sister, Jane, in London. My youngest sister, Lydia, has eloped with George Wickham, which prompted the Gardiners' early return to London so my uncle can assist in the search."

"That is impossible," blurted Georgiana.

Elizabeth paused at the sudden shock and emotion that came over the young woman's face. She had expected Georgiana to be angry and to rail at her as she had in the past, but the distress and despair was a surprise.

"He would not do that to me!"

"I assure you, I have no reason to lie to you," Elizabeth said, watching Georgiana search her mind for anything to justify Wickham's actions.

"No, he loves me," she mumbled. "He. Loves. Me." Elizabeth looked on as Georgiana desperately attempted to compose herself. "He will come for me, and we will be married," she stated, almost as if it was a question.

"I know that this must come as quite a shock, so I apologize for asking this of you. However, I need to know anything you can tell me about him," Elizabeth said sympathetically. She suspected if she attempted to demand information, Georgiana would refuse vehemently. Of all people, the girl had chosen to love and care for Wickham, to pledge her allegiance to him, no matter how undeserving he was. "Anything . . . I am not here to criticize, and I will not lose my temper, but I think it will also help your brother to understand why you have betrayed him for someone who has only treated him ill."

"I do not understand."

Recognizing the lost tone of Georgiana's voice, she tried to nudge her to begin speaking. "You can start at the beginning. What you remember of him from when you were young, how you came to care for him, and then maybe

Ramsgate?"

"You just want your sister found and him made to marry her," Georgiana quickly accused, giving a response more akin to what Elizabeth expected. "You could save your family, ruin all of my hopes in one fell swoop, and you would finally have your retribution for the letter I placed in your dressing room."

"Georgiana, despite what you may think of me, I am not one to seek revenge. As for my family, with the exception of the Gardiners, I have had nothing to do with them since I left Longbourn," Elizabeth confided. "As you well know, I refused Mr. Collins, and my father attempted to force my hand. I have been told that he is still very angry at my defiance, and as for my mother, well, she always preferred Jane and Lydia."

"She did not like you?"

Noticing that Georgiana had her brow furrowed and seemed genuinely interested, she hoped confiding might spur the young woman into divulging the secrets she had kept so closely guarded. "She always said that I had no compassion for her nerves," said Elizabeth, with a small smile. "I was my father's favourite, and my mother did not think I was as pretty as Jane, nor did I have Lydia's lively personality. I spent all of my time rambling the countryside with my nose in a book, which she lamented would never attract a husband." She watched as Georgiana regarded her with a strange expression. "Why did you attempt to elope with George Wickham?"

"I never said I would talk," she said haughtily, as she fiddled with the pleats in her skirt, suddenly avoiding Elizabeth's steady gaze.

"Nevertheless, I am asking. I doubt your answer will betray him in any way," Elizabeth replied. "I responded to your question about my mother." She watched as the young woman closed her eyes and took a deep breath. "I will not leave until you speak to me, Georgiana." Sighing, the young girl looked back up from her lap.

"Since my father died, he is the only person who has truly cared for me," she returned, looking Elizabeth directly in the eye.

"You do not believe your brother cares for you?"

"I did not know Fitzwilliam until he returned during breaks from Cambridge," she responded disdainfully. "He had never returned before for holidays or when my mother died. He just appeared one day when he finally decided that I was worth his notice, and gave me a *book*, as if *that* was supposed to make up for everything."

"Georgiana, did you ever ask him why he did not visit you?" Elizabeth could not help but ask.

"No," she replied spitefully. "This was his home. He could have come when he wished, yet he did not, because he did not care."

"Your parents sent him to London during the holidays, where they employed tutors to further his education while he was not in school." Elizabeth watched as the young woman's face showed confusion.

"Father never mentioned that," Georgiana thought aloud, looking to the side before returning her gaze to Elizabeth. "Why would he not have Fitzwilliam come home for our mother's burial?"

"Will has told me that your father did not write him of her death until he was on holiday," she reasoned. "Perhaps your father did not think a twelve-year-old boy had a place there. He also may have delayed notifying him so the news did not interfere with school. I do not know. You were not old enough to remember, so where did you learn of it?"

"I have heard some of the older servants commenting on it over the years."

Nodding, Elizabeth thought for a moment. "Before we came to Pemberley, your brother told me about how accomplished you are at the pianoforte. He was very proud of you, although he could not understand why you behaved the way you did, as well as the manner in which you spend money," said Elizabeth, hoping she could make the girl understand. "Will and Richard were concerned about you— and despite everything you have done, he still worries about you." She could see indecision on Georgiana's face and prayed she was reaching her.

Georgiana, meanwhile, figured that it could not hurt to tell the story of her relationship with Wickham. She would never admit it to anyone, but ever since her brother had showed her Elizabeth's garnet cross, she had begun to wonder about George's loyalty to her. What if her brother's version of how George had obtained the necklace was correct, and she was being played for a fool? She had too many questions, too many doubts, and perhaps speaking of it all might allow for her to work through the muddle in her own mind.

"George Wickham came home to Pemberley during school holidays and breaks, and when he was at Cambridge, he would bring me a little trinket of some sort," she began cautiously. "I remember he would take me for walks in the gardens close to the house, and my father seemed to favour him."

"I am surprised your father did not object to him bringing you presents and taking you for walks."

She furrowed her brow and replied, "I am unsure if he ever knew. He was not around often. When my father died, George no longer visited, and I did not understand why he never came to see me. It was not long before Fitzwilliam and Richard decided they could not be bothered and sent me to school."

"I can assure you that was not the reason," Elizabeth declared, offended that the girl would believe that of her own brother.

"What other possible reason could they have had?" Georgiana asked with a challenging look upon her face.

"As I am sure you are aware, it is not unusual for a young woman of your station to go to school or have a companion. Your brother was a young man, who had just lost his father and had an extremely large responsibility dropped in his lap. I know he was very unsure of how to raise a young girl, and he thought it would do you good to be around others your own age."

"Well, he was wrong! I only had a few friends, and the girls from titled families would pick on me."

"That is ridiculous. Your grandfather was an earl, as is your uncle."

"It was the Darcy name that was not titled. They could care less who my grandfather and uncle were."

Sighing, Elizabeth shifted, trying to find a more comfortable position. "Georgiana, why did you not tell your brother? He would have done something about it."

"He left me there, and I believed he and Richard did not want to be bothered," she shrugged. "So I kept to myself. After a few years, Fitzwilliam removed me from school and hired Mrs. Younge."

Elizabeth observed her expressions carefully, yet for the first time, did not seem to detect any artifice in the young woman's demeanour. "He removed you from school because of how quiet you had become. He and Richard were concerned, and hoped Ramsgate would make you happy."

"It was then that George returned to my life," she said with a sad smile. "He told me that Fitzwilliam forbade him from visiting me, not to mention how he refused him the living my father promised in his will." She looked down at her skirts, avoiding Elizabeth's steady stare. "Since I have always believed that my brother did not want me around, it was easy to understand George's explanations. I already resented my brother, but after hearing George's version of events, I began to hate him."

Although she finished at a little more than a mumble, Elizabeth heard every word. "Your brother has proof," she said, prompting Georgiana to look up from her lap. "He has documents signed by Wickham, in which he relinquished his right to the living in exchange for three thousand pounds. He will happily show them to you whenever you wish." She watched as Georgiana nodded, once again avoiding her gaze.

"George warned me that if Fitzwilliam came to Ramsgate, he would not permit our marriage. He explained all of my brother's objections, and told me if he happened to visit, to confess to the elopement. You see, he had called upon me, so the servants could have exposed us. George felt that if I confessed, my brother would not be as harsh as he would if I concealed the truth. He was right. When I returned to London, he only restricted me from shopping. I could still take walks with a companion in the park, and go to the museums. I was to await George in London before my brother insisted on my return to Pemberley."

Elizabeth furrowed her brow. "Georgiana, why would he wait so long? If he truly wished to marry you above all else, why would you still be with your brother a year later? You were on your own in London for several months while Will was in Hertfordshire."

"He ran into some financial problems following Ramsgate," she explained. "He could not come, and then he joined the militia." Elizabeth had to feel some sympathy for the girl; she looked as if she was finally seeing things clearly for the first time.

"When you met him in Lambton, what did he say?"

Georgiana shrugged and her gaze returned to her lap. "He asked me how I was, and told me he would not be much longer—we would be together soon," she said, seeming to have trouble voicing the last.

"Do you know of any information that would help my uncle?" Elizabeth asked as she prayed the girl would continue to talk.

"Other than Mrs. Younge's boarding house in Saffron Hill, I cannot think of anything to help you," she said softly.

Elizabeth paused, giving thought to how best to phrase a question she had wanted the answer to for some time. "Georgiana," she observed the young woman steadily as she leaned forward as much as she was able, "you have been willing to throw everything away to marry the steward's son, yet you have treated me and others as if they are beneath you. Do you truly believe this? I do not understand your wish to marry someone who is by social standards considered inferior to someone you have ridiculed for their status." She watched as Georgiana turned a vibrant shade of red.

"When I confessed the planned elopement to my brother, he scolded me, saying George was beneath me, and I would ruin the family should I wed him," she revealed. "When I learned that you were none but a country gentleman's daughter from a small estate, I became angry with his hypocrisy. He denounced my choice, yet married someone who was considered beneath him. That was the only reason I said those things. I never would have been friends with Miss Bingley, if I truly believed what I was saying."

"May I ask why you spend money in the manner you do?"

Georgiana sighed. "I enjoyed myself when I was out in London at the shops. When my brother would come home and find the bills, he would become so frustrated. I hated him and he controlled everything and I enjoyed making things difficult for him."

Nodding, Elizabeth rose and began to walk to the door, when a small voice caught her attention prompting her to turn. "George never did love me, did he?" she asked pitifully.

"No, Georgiana," she replied. "I believe the only person George Wickham loves is himself."

~ * ~

Monday 10 August 1812

It was noon the next day, when Mrs. Reynolds watched two rain-soaked riders and their mounts gallop up to the front doors of Pemberley. Once they had dismounted and made it within the grand foyer, she was stunned to discover that they were none other than the master and his cousin, the new
Lord Ashworth.

"Mr. Darcy, Lord Ashworth, whatever were you thinking riding out in this rain?" she scolded. "You are sure to be wet through!" Reminded of their return to the house in the same state as boys, the two grown men smiled before tendering their unnecessary excuses.

"The rain had let up this morning before we left Ashworth, but it began again about an hour into the journey." He removed his great coat, and handed it over to the closest maid. "We were already halfway here, so we decided to continue. Where is Mrs. Darcy?"

Smiling at his question, Mrs. Reynolds gestured to their muddy boots, indicating that she wished for them to remove them. "She is within your chambers," she replied. "When I checked in on her an hour ago, she was well. Claire and I have both been keeping very close watch over her since you left. She has not slept well the last few days, and Mrs. Gardiner told her yesterday to rest as much as she can. However, she is tiring of remaining within the master and mistress's suite."

Darcy smiled, imagining his wife's growing impatience at being confined for even that short a period of time, while eagerly anticipating surprising her. He was so wrapped up in his thoughts that he almost missed Richard's question to Mrs. Reynolds.

"Has Miss Darcy behaved herself during our absence?" he asked, once he assured the maids had departed and there was no staff other than the housekeeper and butler close enough to hear.

"Yes, my lord," Roberts answered. "However, there is a letter which came for her two days ago in your study." He looked to Darcy. "I hope you do not mind, but I took the liberty of placing it in the top middle drawer of your desk, sir." He gave the master a meaningful look as he continued in a lower tone. "It would not be visible to anyone, say, cleaning the room in there."

"That is excellent, Roberts, thank you," stated Darcy appreciatively.

"Your baths are being warmed, and should be ready soon," Mrs. Reynolds interjected, hoping to hasten the two gentlemen up to their rooms where they could dry before they took ill.

"Thank you, Mrs. Reynolds." Darcy smiled as he passed her by, and strode directly to his study with Richard following in his wake. Opening the drawer his butler had indicated, he found the note in the same fluid female handwriting he had seen on all of Wickham's other messages, that was, until he broke the seal and checked inside. "It is from him," he indicated without even touching it, as if the slightest brush of his fingers would make it more tangible, more real; that without that sensation, the offending letter might just disappear as if it had never existed in the first place.

"Do not just stand there, Darcy! Open it!"

Gingerly, Darcy lifted the folded piece of paper and broke the seal, opening it to reveal the rather simple, yet cryptic message contained within.

G-

I am on my way. Be ready.

GW

He closed his eyes, exhaled heavily, and held it out for Richard to read.

"My God!" Richard exclaimed. "This is one time I wish my instinct was wrong. We need to find out exactly what the Gardiners were told about his elopement with their niece. Obviously he is coming here, so why would they travel to London?"

"Elizabeth will probably know. I cannot imagine the Gardiners just leaving without giving a reason, but I would like to refresh myself before I see her. She will worry if she finds me wet through, and she does not need that at the moment."

Nodding, Richard began moving towards the door. "I do not believe either of us can afford to become sick, and we will need our wits about us until we are unable to unearth Wickham's machinations."

"It should not be too difficult, Richard. He either wants money, revenge, or both."

~ * ~

Darcy bathed and dressed in breeches and a shirt as quickly as he could before quietly slipping into his rooms to find his wife; she was in the window seat of his room, napping quietly with a book in her lap. Smiling at the picture she presented, he gingerly placed a hand on her belly, in time to feel the baby move, giving him a profound sense of relief that at the very least they both were well. He had lost himself in his thoughts when he suddenly felt her hand cover his and a sleepy voice broke through the whirlwind in his mind.

"Will," she breathed, moving aside the book and carefully manoeuvring herself to face him. He captured her lips passionately, as he tried to convey how much he had dearly missed her. When they broke apart, she glanced outside before regarding him worriedly. "Please tell me you did not ride here from Ashworth in that." As she gestured outside at the weather, he chuckled.

"It was not raining when we departed this morning," he reasoned, hoping to allay her fears.

"Will!" she exclaimed. "You could take ill!"

"It is so warm outside, that I doubt I need to worry about that, besides we were protected by our great coats," he smiled, touched by her concern. "We received an express from your uncle yesterday, explaining their hasty departure." He showed her the letter and gave her a moment to read. "Is there anything other than what is in the express?"

Elizabeth closed her eyes, mortified by her family. "Stupid, stupid Lydia," she mumbled before sighing. "No, that sums up the situation as far as I am aware of. I told my aunt of Mrs. Younge's boarding house, but I could not be of any more help than that, I am afraid."

"It is the best place to begin," he agreed. "I hope he is prepared; she will require a hefty bribe."

Elizabeth smiled. "My uncle does fairly well," she responded. "His business is more profitable than most realise. He only lives in Cheapside to be close to his warehouses, which allows him to come home for meals and spend more time with his children." Darcy helped her to stand, and she made herself comfortable on the bed as he sat beside her.

"I spoke to Georgiana yesterday," she began cautiously, having moved in order to have a comfortable place to sit for the long discussion she was sure would follow.

"And I am sure she ignored you as she always does," he replied disdainfully. He was fed up with it all—Georgiana's attitude, Wickham's schemes, and he just wanted to leave the drama to someone else.

"Actually, Will, we conversed for some time," she responded. Turning to see the truth in her expression, he looked at her incredulously.

"How?" he declared. "We have been trying for months to no avail . . . why now?"

"I wonder if my garnet cross affected her so profoundly that day because it gave her a reason to doubt him," she claimed seriously. "Perhaps she doubted him before . . . I do not know. I simply informed her of Lydia's elopement, and asked for her to tell me the story of her relationship with Mr. Wickham." He was awed that his wife had finally managed to crack his sister's hard exterior. He knew she was an amazing woman, but he had either underestimated his wife in this matter, or he had overestimated his sister's recalcitrance. He listened intently as his wife explained why his sister had become the person she was, and why she had bestowed her loyalty to Wickham rather than her brother and Richard.

"So you see, you could not have predicted your father's actions would begin this," Elizabeth soothed. She knew he would still feel the sting of the predicament acutely.

372

"If I had not sent her to school . . ."

"Stop, Will," she interjected. "You only did what you thought was best for her. Pemberley had just been dropped into your lap, and you were learning how to assume your responsibilities." She looked into his eyes to ensure he understood the truth of her words. "It is not unusual for girls of her station to go off to school, and she was looking for reasons to dislike you. Her resentment was formed long before then."

"I will need to go speak with her." He ran his hand through his hair.

"Must you go now?" Elizabeth asked. "I have missed you."

Smiling, he took her in his arms. "No, I can wait, especially for a reason such as this." He held her close while he told her of the funeral and their hurried return, ending with the newest letter received from Wickham.

"Oh, Will," she exclaimed. "What does that mean? I am not sure she would go with him now, with her knowledge of his relationship with Lydia. She did not say as much, but I believe she is devastated. He is the one person she thought was constant in her life, and she was grossly mistaken in his character."

Sighing, he held her a bit closer. "I imagine she feels like I did when she planted that letter in your chambers. I do not have it in me to pity her though, Elizabeth."

"I know," she replied sympathetically. "I did not call her attention to it, as it might have prevented her from confiding in me further, yet I have no problem with you doing so." Hearing servants milling about in the sitting room, she noticed Darcy furrow his brow. "With the exception of my discussion with Georgiana yesterday, I passed the entirety of the day within these chambers. I would hazard a guess that Mrs. Reynolds is conspiring to keep me here again today, and has sent up some refreshments."

"Are you hungry?" he asked with concern.

"Not particularly, but Mrs. Reynolds will fuss if I do not eat something."

"Do you not feel well?"

"I am uncomfortable, hot, and I can only eat small amounts in a sitting, else I am so full. Mrs. Reynolds seems to want me to remain abed, yet I find that I am sore on days when I do so."

Rubbing his hand in large circles on her back, he kissed the crown of her head. "Has the midwife examined you since I left for Ashworth?"

"Yes," she replied. "She believes I increased so quickly because of my smaller stature." Chuckling, she looked at him mischievously. "There was also an interesting theory that I must be having a boy, since I am carrying everything all out in front. She was exceedingly insulted when I laughed."

He laughed as he remembered Mrs. Reynolds making a comment about that superstition earlier in her confinement. However, he was glad to have someone with experience confirm their health, as well as his suspicions as to why she had been so uncomfortable.

Holding out his hands, he helped her scoot to the edge of the bed and put on her dressing gown. "We will go have some refreshments, I will rub your feet, and back, and then while you nap, I will have a talk with my sister."

"Do you have a plan?"

"Honestly, no, I truly have no idea what to do," he confided. "I am sure Richard will wish to be a part of it—perhaps he will."

Nodding, Elizabeth began walking slowly toward the sitting room, her husband close by with his hand resting on the small of her back. "She has to talk this time, regardless of her wishes. There is too much at stake."

"I know, love . . . I know."

Chapter 29

Monday 10 August 1812

Richard indeed wished to be a part of Darcy's latest interrogation of Georgiana, deciding there would be no further avoidance on her part to answering their questions. Upon knocking, they were immediately granted entry, and requested that Amy and Mrs. Annesley leave them, in an attempt to keep the situation as private as possible.

"I told your wife essentially everything, and I really do not wish to discuss it any more," she replied, as humble as they had ever seen her.

Darcy took a seat so that he was facing his sister. "Before we discuss other matters, I would like to apologize for losing my temper so badly during our last argument." Georgiana's expression reflected her surprise. "I know it is no excuse and I should have done so sooner. For what it is worth, it was never my intention to strike you. While I know that the child Elizabeth carries is mine, the slanderous words coming from your mouth—well, it was all just too much."

Despite the apology, he held fast to the belief that he needed to be firm with his sister. He hoped that her loyalty to Wickham was not as steadfast as it had been, but he had learned over the past years to be wary. Seeing no response forthcoming from Georgiana, he continued. "As for Wickham, Elizabeth has already informed me of your conversation yesterday; however, there has been a new development, and I need a better knowledge of the situation than what you have already divulged," Darcy stated authoritatively, proffering Wickham's small note for her to view. He witnessed her blanch, and he could swear there were tears in her eyes as she closed them for a moment to compose herself.

"I do not wish to see him, and I will not go with him," she

stated simply, yet vehemently much to the relief of her guardians, who had been expecting an argument.

"Georgiana, was there a strategy in place to aid your flight with him, or do you know what he has planned?" Richard implored. "For once, think of your brother and his wife. Lizzy is close to the end of her confinement, and I am concerned Wickham could become dangerous should he not obtain what he wants. You must have a conscience, and at least consider the safety of the child."

She took a deep breath and sighed. "To the best of my knowledge, he has never had a definite plan. I truly have no idea of how he intends to contact me once he is near, but I believe he will send some instruction in the same manner he has been employing since Ramsgate."

"You no longer have any wish to leave with him—marry him?" her brother asked, still amazed at her sudden turnabout.

"Elizabeth claims you have documents to prove he lied about the living at Kympton?"

"Yes, I do," he replied. "I would be happy to provide them for you to view at your leisure. I can also introduce you to several former servants and merchants' daughters who have been ruined by him, some of whom have borne his children." Her eyes widened and she began frantically shaking her head.

"It is not necessary," she declared, visibly attempting to keep a tight control over her emotions. "I already feel enough of a fool, and I have no wish to pour salt in the wound."

Nodding his head, Darcy stood and moved beside his cousin where he turned to face Georgiana once more. "When I returned from Cambridge, I longed for a relationship with you. The only true familial bond I had was with Richard, who is essentially a brother in my eyes, and I dearly wished to have something similar with you." He took a deep breath and sighed. "I have attempted for years to reach you, and now, looking back at our past interactions, I can see that you never desired the same connection." He paused, attempting to collect his thoughts. "As long as you are pleasant and you do not cause further problems, you may remain at Pemberley. Eventually you will come out, and we will take things from there. If you do not find someone suitable, you may remain here, or if you desire to no longer live with us, you can live in the Dower's cottage. I will see to it that you have the appropriate servants, as well as everything you need. "However, I do not know if I will ever have the ability to trust you as I do Richard or Elizabeth, which is no one's fault but your own." He watched as she nodded meekly, bit her lip, and returned her eyes to her lap. Darcy looked to Richard, who shrugged at her lack of response. "We will expect you for dinner," he finally stated before they departed through the door.

~ * ~

Tuesday 11 August, 1812

Richard proved to be invaluable, ensuring footmen were posted where they were most important, and preparing pistols in the event they were needed. He even spoke to several of the more prominent store owners in Lambton, requesting word be sent to Pemberley if Wickham was noticed within the small village. Darcy was exceedingly thankful for his cousin's presence, and prayed fervently that should Wickham come, the situation could be managed without violence.

Everyone was on tenterhooks awaiting something, anything that might indicate Wickham's presence in the area. Then, finally, three days later, a letter for Georgiana arrived at Pemberley.

G,

In Lambton, meet me at the same place as last time, Friday 14 August, at 10:00 a.m.

G.W.

~ * ~

Friday 14 August 1812

Since they assumed Wickham was alluding to the smithy,

Darcy and Richard had their horses saddled, and promptly rode in to Lambton. They arrived a quarter-hour before the specified time, observing the green from the alley beside the chapel as they waited for the blackguard to show. They lingered for over an hour for their prey, but he never came, so when it began to rain, they turned back toward home. What they did not know was that Wickham had been there at the appointed time, but had been planning on making his approach from the very alley where they were lying in wait. He quickly realised they were aware of his meeting with Miss Darcy, and angrily set off towards Pemberley, determined to obtain what he had travelled to Derbyshire to retrieve.

~ * ~

Elizabeth was bored and fed up with remaining in her chambers, her only reprieve to go downstairs for dinner. So stealing away to her dressing room, she donned a dress before hastily exiting to the hall. However, it was not until she quietly closed the door that a sound suddenly echoing through the quiet corridor caused her to turn. She immediately recognised the figure of George Wickham emerging from Georgiana's former rooms, and found herself rooted to the spot in shock at the man's audacity. When he turned to creep down the hall where she was standing, she suddenly comprehended her mistake in not hastening back to her rooms.

Looking around frantically, she realised there was no footman in the hall. Richard had been insistent in his planning that no matter the circumstances, there was to be a manservant posted outside of any room the mistress occupied. What could have happened to whoever was in the corridor?

"Well well," Wickham said haughtily, as he came closer. "It is none other than the illustrious Mrs. Darcy. How are you, my dear?"

"Do not address me so informally," she replied with an edge to her voice, attempting to curb any nerves she might inadvertently reveal.

"No need to be offended, madam. We are good friends, you and I—are we not?"

"You, sir, are a liar, and no friend of mine!" Taking a step back, she found her back against the wall.

"I see," he sneered. "I believe I understand."

"Exactly what, pray tell, do you think you understand?" she asked. She hoped to give herself some time to determine the best method of escape, as she began to glance fleetingly around the hall. Her eyes glanced toward the direction of the stairs, and Wickham suddenly lunged forward, grabbing her painfully by the arm. She startled, and frantically attempted to pull back from him, crying out in pain at his fingers digging into the tender flesh of the inside of her arm.

"That your husband has informed you of the truth of our past."

"Of course he did," she replied. "What man would wish for his wife to think so poorly of him?"

"It matters not. I poisoned his sister against him years ago. At the time, that was my ultimate revenge. Now I have something much more satisfying in mind." She became frightened at the look in his eyes as he began to propel her down the hall.

"My husband has done nothing to deserve your retribution."

Stopping abruptly, Wickham whipped her around to look him in the eye. "His very existence has always plagued me." Wickham's teeth were clenched, giving him an almost sinister appearance as he turned and began once more dragging her toward the grand staircase.

"He was your childhood friend. How could someone as gentle as Will have angered you so?" she pled.

"Where is Georgiana?"

"I asked you first," declared Elizabeth bravely.

Digging his fingernails further into her arm, he pulled a pistol from where he had been hiding it within his coat. Elizabeth's eyes bulged as her arms instinctively moved to cradle her abdomen in an effort to protect her unborn child.

"I believe she is in the music room," she bluffed, hoping they would come into contact with a footman or someone who could free her from the wastrel.

Proceeding to pull her down the staircase at his side, Wickham began to rant. "Everyone *loved* the young master," he declared with disdain. "He could do no wrong. The servants, the tenants, even my own father could not stop singing his praises. I was ignored. I was as intelligent as he, the tutors said as much, but I never received the praise or credit he did. I hated Darcy for it, so I proceeded to steal anyone of consequence to him. The only person I was unable to sway was Colonel Fitzwilliam. I hear he has now inherited his brother's title. That bastard is just like Darcy—he has all the luck!"

"It would only be natural for the estate to be excited over an heir. His own father, the one person he wished to hear praise him, was perhaps the one person who never lauded his efforts—just like you. I do not see why that would make you detest him as you do." Elizabeth reasoned, as she prayed he would calm and not harm her or the babe.

"He had his own father, and it was not *my father!* My father was supposed to favour me! Not the master's son! Every day there would be some achievement that would give him cause to praise Darcy." Wickham grimaced before beginning in a mocking voice. *"The young master rode his new stallion out today. Young Darcy is reading a book of stories in French,"* he mocked. "If only he had jumped that new stallion off the ridge for what I cared of it! I could not stand him."

He paused for a moment as a sickening grin came over his face. "I used to do little things to hurt him—hitting him, stealing his belongings, getting him into trouble—to make him pay for stealing my father's attention from me, but it was never enough. Shortly before we both began school, I decided if he was going to take my father, I would take his. I

380

was always good at manipulating people, so I charmed the elder Mr. Darcy." The twisted grin became larger and he chuckled.

"I remember the look on the son's face when he would find me spending time with Mr. Darcy. When we left for school, his father placed his hand on Darcy's shoulder and told him to make the Darcy and Fitzwilliam families proud, not to disappoint him. He told *me* that he would miss my company." Wickham's puffed his chest in pride at his achievement. "Darcy's face was truly priceless."

"And now I have stolen his sister. She is truly an achievement—not that it was difficult—only in that it was something that took time, years, to accomplish. His father unwittingly aided me quite a bit by keeping Darcy in London during school holidays."

"That may be, but you will not receive her dowry, which I am sure was of consequence when you planned this, especially given the history between you and my husband. Both of Georgiana's guardians must release her fortune, and neither will willingly hand it over to you," Elizabeth interjected.

"It matters not," he replied. "The money was an added inducement, but not my main motivation. Even if they did relinquish the money, I would abandon her somewhere once I had my fill of her, preferably with my child in her womb. It would be a real coup to be the father of the next heir of Pemberley."

Elizabeth was disgusted, and desperately trying to think of how to be released from his tireless grip when she saw Georgiana behind Wickham. She was emerging from the music room, a footman in tow, with a stricken look upon her face, which was masked as quickly as it was noticed.

"As if I could spend my life with a bland little thing like her. Of course, I would have to return to be a proper father to my child, when they became the next in line to inherit." He laughed almost maniacally, and turned as he noticed Elizabeth staring at something over his shoulder. Seeing his prey, he plastered a sickly sweet smile upon his face. "Georgiana! I have been looking for you. Are you ready to become my wife, dearest?"

Wickham saw the guard behind Georgiana, and shifted Elizabeth so that the footman could see the pistol pressed against her abdomen. "Go back from whence you came, or I will finish her." The footman's eyes bulged, and he backed through the door. Elizabeth prayed he would bring help soon.

He set his sights on Georgiana and smirked. "Well, shall we go to Gretna Green?"

Watching the young woman's expression, Elizabeth felt his grip slacken a bit as he waited for Georgiana to answer his question.

"I will not marry you, George," she replied in a stronger tone than Elizabeth would have expected. "I know about Lydia Bennet, and I will not be made the fool any longer by you."

"That little twit!" he exclaimed incredulously. "I simply used her for the money to pay my travel to London, and then I sold her to a brothel for my passage here."

Georgiana paled and looked to Elizabeth, who closed her eyes tight, not only in mortification of her younger sister's actions, but also horror at the consequences, and prayed that her uncle and Mr. Mason found the stupid girl. Granted, there was not much that could be done for her or her reputation at this point. Nevertheless, her family could not just leave Lydia there.

"I heard what you were saying to Elizabeth about me, George. Even if you had not eloped with Lydia Bennet, I would not go." The words were stated simply. They were not emotional or pleading, and she stood straight as she said it. "I know the truth now. I should have never trusted you."

"It does not matter. I had my way with that little brat, but she was simply a means to an end. You will leave with me, Georgiana. You will do exactly as I say," he stated vindictively. "Or I will kill your new sister." The pistol in Wickham's hand moved closer to Elizabeth, causing her to flinch. Tears poured down her face while the pistol dug into the skin of her abdomen.

Georgiana was rooted to the spot. She had never tried to be friends with Elizabeth, yet Georgiana had actually found she had grudging respect for the woman. She was intelligent and caring, after all, how many women of the ton would have taken the time to try to reach someone who treated people the way Georgiana did. Her spite and malice had really been meant for her brother. Elizabeth had simply been a means to an end. Georgiana did not want his wife to be harmed for her own folly, and the last thing she wished was for an innocent child to be injured as well.

"George, do not hurt them," she pleaded. "What do you want me to do?"

"I want you to go and fetch anything we can sell, as well as some clothes, and return here as quickly as you can. If I find that you have told a footman or anyone, I will kill them," he threatened, gesturing towards Elizabeth's abdomen. "Do you understand?"

Georgiana nodded, and quickly raced up the stairs, while Elizabeth glanced around the great hall. She suddenly remembered that Roberts was meeting with some of the footmen this morning, and Mrs. Reynolds with the maids and kitchen staff. The meeting was something they did once monthly, but that it happened to fall on the day Wickham decided to enter Pemberley was bad luck indeed. She still wondered what had become of the footman who was supposed to be guarding her. Meeting or no meeting, he should have been at his post!

She found it even more odd that not one servant had come through the room since they had been there. Through her tears, she suddenly noticed Samuel peer through the door that led to the kitchens and servants' quarters; however, as Wickham surveyed the room, the footman backed to where he could not be seen. She felt Wickham relax his grip a bit more, and took a deep breath, attempting to calm her nerves in order to think clearly. If she could just get free of him, she could make it to the kitchens, where she was sure at least one of the male servants had brought a weapon with them.

"Well, Lizzy," Wickham said suddenly, drawing her attention back to him while he leered at her breasts. "I do believe you should come to Scotland and witness our nuptials."

"I do not believe Georgiana will marry you now that she is aware of the truth."

"It matters not. I will ruin her regardless, but I have yet to decide what to do with you."

"What do you mean?" Elizabeth asked, as she began to panic.

"Simply that I have left two people out of my retribution until now. Darcy would never have married you if he did not care for you, not with the way he feels about duty, and I can guarantee he does not want his child and only heir harmed. So you will be coming with us," he said, smiling in a disturbing manner. "I will figure out what to do with the two of you later."

Elizabeth turned away from him in order to hide her reaction to his disclosure. The glint in his eye terrified her, and she somehow knew that if he removed her from Pemberley, she and her unborn child would not survive. Not wishing for him to know that she found him unbalanced, and moreover, that she was afraid, she took a few deep breaths attempting to calm herself. Somehow she did not feel showing her nerves would be a prudent move; Wickham would not have much sympathy for her fear.

She remained facing away while Wickham had begun muttering to himself. For a short time, she tried to decipher what he was saying, only to find that the words were too jumbled, and abandoned the pursuit. She felt as if they had stood there for an eternity when Elizabeth heard the front doors open loudly, and turned toward the source of the noise. A profound sense of relief mixed with fear overcame her to find her husband enter from the rain, pulling a pistol from under his great coat where it was protected from the water. Everything seemed to move in slow motion as Wickham turned to point his gun toward Darcy, while she used the distraction to pull her arm free from his merciless grip. Moving as fast as her enlarged body would allow, she felt someone grab her around her waist, and began to struggle with all her might to free herself from the entrapment.

"Lizzy!"

In her frantic bid to escape, she did not register the call of her name, and continued to struggle until she heard the familiar male voice once more.

"Lizzy!" Following the sound of her name, she looked up to find she was trapped between Richard's body and one of his strong arms, the other holding a pistol directed at Wickham as well. He was not looking at her, but maintaining his aim at their mutual enemy.

"Are you well?" he asked, staring at his target, who was still aiming his weapon at Darcy.

"Yes, he has done nothing to permanently injure me."

"Good, now go to the kitchens. We will come and retrieve you when the situation has been resolved."

Elizabeth, for the first time since escaping Wickham's clutches, looked to find her husband and the intruder both standing with their weapons pointed directly at each other's hearts. Paralyzed at the scene before her, she froze in place, and did not move.

"Lizzy," Richard called. He waited a moment, but when he did not feel her move, he momentarily took his eyes from his target to find her wide eyed gaze riveted to the scene before her. Recognizing her condition from witnessing similar situations with young recruits in battle, he returned his sight to the intruder as he moved to place her behind him to protect her body with his own.

Richard turned his attention to the situation at hand, and heard Darcy ask, "What did you think you would accomplish by invading my home?"

"I came for your sister, Darcy. Did you not know that we are engaged?" Wickham stated in a sarcastic tone, while Darcy began to walk sideways toward the stairway; his opponent rotated his body to follow him, neither dropping his weapon or relinquishing his aim.

"She does not wish to marry you any longer, Wickham. Her eyes have been opened to your lies and manipulations, and she will no longer be your pawn." Wickham laughed maniacally and Darcy tried desperately to swallow his nerves, which were attempting to assert themselves.

"It does not matter what she wishes. She will leave with me regardless."

"Over my dead body, Wickham!"

"That can be arranged, Darcy!" he yelled in return. "I have always hoped to be there when you die; I only wished to take everything from you first. Then, as you are taking your last breath, you will know that as your sister's husband, I will have everything that is supposed to belong to you."

"Elizabeth is with child," Darcy replied smugly. "Do you think that I have not made arrangements for him or her to inherit Pemberley should I die before the birth? You presume too much."

Wickham laughed. "I do not presume anything. I said you would lose everything, which means you would part with them before you would leave this earth. I would leave no chance that your seed would remain. The next Darcy to take control of Pemberley would in actuality be a Wickham," he laughed savagely. Darcy suddenly understood that the boy he had played with as a child was not just scheming—he was truly insane.

"She fancied me first. Did you know that?" he taunted, as he gestured toward Elizabeth. "I will have to find something special for her before I dispatch her—perhaps once your brat is born and I have taken care of him." Wickham's eyes glazed and he chuckled. "Yes, Mrs. Elizabeth Darcy will truly be worthy of my individual and prolonged attentions."

Darcy was terrified. He was thankful that Matthew had found them at the stables, informing them that Wickham was within Pemberley, and that he had his wife. It allowed them to formulate a plan. Darcy entered from the front doors while Richard crept in from a hallway behind them, allowing his cousin to safely grab Elizabeth during Darcy's distraction, since they both believed that Wickham would immediately target Darcy. He had seen Richard pull Elizabeth behind him, to shield her with his body, and although he knew that his cousin would sacrifice his life to save his wife and child—he had endangered his life in battle protecting comrades he barely knew—Darcy wished her as far removed from the fray as possible. His life meant nothing if Elizabeth was killed in the altercation.

"Elizabeth," he called. "Love, please leave the room." Frightened Wickham would target her if she ventured from her cousin's protective stance, she remained where she was as she grasped the back of Richard's clothes.

Richard felt her burrow further into the back of his coat, and wrapped his one arm behind him to ensure she was completely blocked from Wickham's aim. "Darcy, I swear to you, she will be fine. *Concentrate on your task!*"

A sudden movement from the grand staircase drew the attention of the three men in the room as Georgiana came running, ceasing her descent a few steps from the bottom. She had heard her brother yelling from the hallway upstairs, and had hurried down as hastily as she was able.

"Where are your things?" Wickham roared, incensed when he noticed she had no burden in her arms.

"I told you I will not leave with you!" She had her fists clenched at her sides, her eyes darting from person to person, ending with her former betrothed's gun that was trained on her brother.

"She will not be leaving, Wickham!" Darcy yelled. "Servants have already been dispatched to fetch the magistrate. It is only a matter of time. The question is, do you leave Pemberley in a box, or will you die at the gallows? We both have you in our sights, and you have only one shot. If you fire at one of us, you will most assuredly die. You are very aware that Richard's aim has always been infallible."

"Then I will take you with me, Darcy!" bellowed Wickham, as he drew his finger back and pulled the trigger.

From that moment, everything was a blur, the sound of pistols discharging, the screams of two women, and the fall of bodies hitting the floor before silence descended upon Pemberley—for a few moments at least.

Chapter 30

Elizabeth was frantic. As she had stood behind Richard, she felt the jolt of his body recoiling from the force of him firing his weapon, immediately followed by him propelling her to the ground and covering her until the din had subsided. Needing to see if her husband was injured in the fray, she pushed with all her might at Richard's body, until she saw his face turn toward hers.

"Are you well?" he asked, the concern evident on his face.

"Yes," she replied. "Where is Will?" her frantic voice conveying her worry as he carefully lifted himself from where he was shielding her with his form. Richard offered her his hand to rise, which she took gratefully as she managed to get to her feet. Once he had ensured she was steady, she took in the scene before her. There was a light haze of smoke, and as she scanned the room, the unmoving form of a body near the foot of the grand staircase.

"Will!" Elizabeth screamed as she moved to his side as hastily as she was able. Running her hands over his chest and head, she noticed as he opened his eyes and raised his hand to her cheek.

"Elizabeth!" he exclaimed. "Thank God! Are you injured?" He rose to a seated position and began scanning her body, confirming with his hands what his eyes told him.

"Will, what happened? I could not see, and Richard forced me to the ground after he discharged his weapon."

He shook his head. "As I was taking my shot, I was shoved from the side which caused me to stumble and fall. I hit my head on the floor, but I am well," he said, touching his hand to the back of his head to find a small amount of blood staining his fingers. Grimacing, he glanced at the area around him. Wickham was directly across from him with a wound to his chest. His lifeless body lay sprawled across the marble floor in an oddly unnatural pose. Darcy knew it was impossible that his shot had hit Wickham, and thanked God for Richard's flawless aim as he turned behind him, where he found the crumpled, limp form of his sister on the floor, a crimson stain spreading from her pale body.

"Georgiana!"

~ * ~

Georgiana Darcy stood mesmerized at the foot of the stairs, frantically viewing the scene as it unfolded before her. She heard her brother's question,

"The question is, do you leave Pemberley in a pine box, or will you die at the gallows? We both have you in our sights, and you have only one shot. If you fire at one of us, you will most assuredly die. You are very aware that Richard's aim has always been infallible."

Georgiana watched with wide eyes, noticing the crazed look in Wickham's eye just before she recognized his trigger finger shifting.

"Then I will take you with me, Darcy!" he screamed, as his finger began to pull back.

She had no idea whether her brother was preparing to fire; her only thought was of preventing the innocent from being harmed when she charged at her brother, shoving him with all of her might. Feeling a burning sensation rip through her upper abdomen, she screamed in pain as she fell to the floor.

~ * ~

"Oh God!" cried Darcy, as he propelled himself to where she lie. Gently lifting her body and cradling it, he placed his hand on the side of her face. "Georgiana!" Her eyelids fluttered open to where she was focused on his face while a tear dropped down her temple and into her hair.

"I am sorry," she croaked, wincing in pain.

"Shhhh . . . it is not important."

"No!" she forcefully choked. "It is. I was gullible and naïve, and I fell for his lies. You were r . . . r . . . right." She struggled to catch her breath, her eyes closing for a moment until she was able to speak once more. "No matter what I said about her, Elizabeth loves you as you love her, and I could not allow your child to grow up without a father due to my mistake . . . my . . . my . . . " Crying out as her body tensed in agony, she glanced to where Richard and Elizabeth were knelt on her other side, looking on with horrified expressions.

"Richard," she breathed weakly. "I . . . I . . . I owe you . . . apology. Elizabeth . . ."

"Please do not stress yourself by speaking. I forgive you, Georgiana," Elizabeth soothed, recognizing that the young woman would most assuredly die, and despite their past relationship, wished to allow her some peace prior to her passing. Darcy glanced at her, the pain evident in his eyes as his dream of the little sister he had so wished to have emerging as her life dwindled before him. He looked back down, unaware of the servants who were bustling in and out, sending for the physician and dispatching someone to investigate why the magistrate had still not arrived.

Georgiana's eyes locked with her brother's once more. "I . . . am sorry," she forced out just before her eyes fluttered closed, never to reopen, and she took her last laboured breaths.

Darcy's head dropped as his body began to shake. Crawling around to his side, Elizabeth placed an arm around his shoulders and drew him closer. A tear escaped to roll down her cheek, not in mourning of a friend or someone who was cherished, but for the utter waste and tragedy that Georgiana's life had become, and the misery that had been born of a lie.

The three of them hovered over Georgiana's body for what seemed like an eternity before the voice of Mrs. Reynolds finally intruded. "Pardon me, Mr. Darcy, the magistrate is here, and wishes to speak with you and Lord Ashworth. We found Thomas, the footman who was supposed to be stationed outside of the master's suite, in Miss Darcy's old room. He has a nasty bump on his head, but he will be well." Mrs. Reynolds paused for a moment, and, in a very maternal type gesture, placed a hand on his shoulder. "Master Fitzwilliam," she said gently, calling him a name he had not heard since he was a boy. "Let us move Miss Darcy somewhere more private. Allow us to care for her, and then you can have as much time as you wish to say goodbye. I have taken the liberty of having her room prepared until we can make further arrangements."

Elizabeth had noticed her husband drying his eyes on his sleeve as he nodded in recognition. She looked up to find Richard with his hand held out to help her rise and, taking his hand, stood. Darcy cradled his sister in his arms as he rose from the floor and proceeded up the stairs. She, Richard and Mrs. Reynolds followed him while he quietly carried Georgiana to her room and laid her on the bed. Carefully, he placed her arms on her stomach and brushed a stray curl from her forehead as he choked back a sob before straightening his shoulders while turning to face the room.

"Elizabeth," Darcy breathed, as he laid eyes on her. Striding to where she was standing, he raised his clean hand to her face and touched his forehead to hers, so as not to cover her in Georgiana's blood, which saturated his chest and one arm. "Thank God you are well, love. I knew Richard would protect you to the best of his ability, but I still feared for you!" He felt her trembling, and opened his eyes to see hers welling with tears, beginning to sob as the events of the evening hit her with full force. "Mrs. Reynolds, I am going to escort Mrs. Darcy to her chambers. Please notify the magistrate that I will be right there, and send Mr. Hughes to the mistress's chambers. I would like him to examine Mrs. Darcy as soon as possible."

Richard cleared his throat, which prompted everyone but the sobbing Elizabeth to look in his direction. "I will go down and speak with the magistrate. I believe we should lead him to believe that Wickham intruded with the intention of stealing when he was happened upon and matters escalated." Darcy nodded his head in agreement, as Richard took a deep breath, turning to stride through the door with purpose.

392

"I will go and fetch Mr. Hughes then," Mrs. Reynolds stated, as she bustled through the door.

Darcy placed his arm around his wife, leading her as she continued to cry, to her chambers where Claire was awaiting them. Once she had calmed a bit, he kissed her on the temple, whispering that he would return as quickly as he was able, and left to join Richard in the great hall.

The magistrate, having dealt with Wickham in the past, made the assumption on his own that the miscreant had entered Pemberley with the intent of stealing. He had absolutely no problem believing that the man had not only unlawfully entered the great house, but had also left the tragic disaster in his wake. Since that was the story they had hoped to tell the magistrate, Darcy and Richard saw no reason to negate the man's conclusions. They had no desire to allow the truth of the matter to reach the public. There would be enough supposition and rumour as it was.

The rain had let up, and a cart was brought around to the doors allowing Wickham's body to be loaded and delivered to the undertakers—there were none within the great house that wanted the man there one minute longer than necessary, dead or alive. The magistrate departed soon after, leaving the remaining souls at Pemberley to clean the mess and attempt to recover from the horror which had occurred in their midst.

As soon as William exited the room, Claire ushered her mistress to take a seat upon the bed, as she hastily retrieved a shift from Elizabeth's dressing room. Once she was quickly changed and tucked into the bed, Claire remained holding her mistress's hand as she wept and sobbed, feeling completely helpless until the physician knocked upon the door.

After completely examining Mrs. Darcy, the physician could find nothing amiss, other than she was overwrought. He administered a small dose of laudanum, and remained long enough to ensure his patient had calmed before being escorted to the master's chambers, where he awaited Mr.

Darcy, who appeared almost a half hour later.

"Mr. Hughes, how is my wife?" he asked as soon as he laid eyes on the man in his rooms.

"She is well. I was concerned with how emotional she was, so close to her confinement; therefore, I administered some laudanum. I left instructions with her maid should she need another dose during the next week or so."

Nodding, Darcy scrutinized the old doctor. "Thank you for coming. I believe I would like to refresh myself and look in on Mrs. Darcy myself.

"Not so quick, young man. I checked Thomas before Mrs. Reynolds asked me to look in on Mrs. Darcy. Now I am going to ensure you and your cousin are also well before I return home."

If there was one thing Darcy knew of Mr. Hughes, who had been the local physician for the last twenty-five years, it was that the man could not be dissuaded. Therefore, once he bathed and dressed in clean breeches and shirt, he allowed the doctor to examine him, and finding nothing amiss other than the small cut to the back of his head, Mr. Hughes departed to pester Lord Ashworth. Darcy breathed a sigh of relief, quickly changed into a robe, and hastened to the door of the mistress's chambers. He entered to find Claire seated in a chair beside his wife's bed.

"How is she?" he asked, as she stood and curtsied.

"She has been sleeping quietly since the physician administered the laudanum."

"You may retire for the evening. I will remain with her." He watched while Claire nodded and quickly exited. Removing his robe, he carefully slipped into bed behind Elizabeth, spooning his chest to her back. He ran his hand over her swollen belly, and felt the babe give a small roll, not only reassuring him of their wellbeing, but also causing him to fret over the stress of the altercation, not to mention the possible future ramifications on their health. Finally, releasing the tight control he had been keeping on his

394

emotions since he had left Georgiana's room, he sobbed until he fell asleep, but slept fitfully, disturbed by nightmares until he finally awoke early the next morning.

~ * ~

Saturday 15 August 1812

Elizabeth fidgeted and whimpered in her sleep; the sheet, which had tangled around her legs, was preventing her from thrashing and moving as she was obviously trying to do. Placing his arms around her, Darcy began to speak in soft tones next to her ear.

"Shhhhh . . . Elizabeth, all is well. You are safe." Her eyes fluttered open and she turned her head to look into his eyes, tears forming in hers.

"Oh, Will," she cried. "He was here. You and Richard were lying beside Georgiana. You left me all alone with him."

"It is over. We are safe, and George Wickham can never hurt anyone ever again." She shuddered as he held her close while rubbing his hand up and down her back. "I am here, and I am not going anywhere." As she calmed, he placed small kisses to her hairline, eventually pulling back to look her in the eyes. "I will always protect you and our children."

She nodded and he smiled.

"I do not know what came over me yesterday, and I still cannot understand why I could not stop crying. It was as if everything suddenly bombarded me all at once."

"It is not uncommon in traumatic situations such as the one you endured, Elizabeth. Richard has told me stories of battles he has experienced, of soldiers who had similar responses. It can happen to anyone."

"Will?"

"Yes, love," he responded softly.

"How are you this morning?" she queried cautiously. She knew he would more than likely not wish to discuss the events of the previous day, and heard him sigh heavily as he clutched her a little tighter to his body. "Please confide in me if it is what you need." Drawing back, she gazed at him pleadingly.

He recognised the determination in her eyes and touched his forehead to hers. His hand found hers and they entwined their fingers. "I wish I could have done more. I feel as if I have failed."

She withdrew her hand, placing it on his cheek as she looked into his eyes with an earnest expression. "Georgiana made mistakes, and sacrificed herself so you would not pay the price for those errors. Do not punish yourself for what you feel you should have done; she would not want it—she did not give her life for that. She wished for you to live to be the father neither of you had. The father you both deserved to have."

Nodding, he understood the truth in her statement, not that it made things any easier, but he vowed to remember his wife's words should he begin to regret or question his actions where his sister was concerned. Not wishing to speak of it further, he brushed his lips against her forehead.

"I will ring for our meal to be delivered to the sitting room, so we can have some more time to ourselves. How does that sound?"

"Lovely," she replied, a small smile forming upon her lips. "I will refresh myself and join you as soon as I am able."

He smiled and rose, ringing the bell, only to have Mrs. Reynolds herself respond quickly. As she had anticipated his request, she informed him the meal would be served shortly, and he went to his dressing room for Evans to shave him before he walked back to the sitting room, finding his wife waiting for him.

Their food was soon laid out, and the post was set to the side of the table. Darcy, however, did not spare it a glance. They would be busy enough over the next few days with Georgiana's funeral, so he decided to put off the business of the day for a brief time in order to savour the peaceful moment with his wife.

~ * ~

Tuesday 18 August, 1812

Three days later, Darcy and Elizabeth were seated at the sitting room, breaking their fast when a knock sounded upon the door.

"Come in," called Darcy.

Mrs. Reynolds bustled into the room and placed a stack of letters on the table beside him. "The message on top was delivered by private courier early this morning," she explained, as he glanced at the top letter.

He picked up the note and hastily tore it open as he recognised Mr. Gardiner's handwriting.

13 August, 1812
Gracechurch St.
London

Darcy,

While it was difficult for the children, we travelled straight through to London without overnight stops, and arrived safely in the evening, the day after we left Pemberley. Everyone including the servants were exhausted, but I managed to drag myself out to search for my wayward niece.

Fortunately, the intelligence Lizzy provided, along with a healthy bribe, quickly provided Mr. Mason and myself with Lydia's location. The blackguard had sold her to one of the seediest brothels in Saffron Hill. I never thought I would see Lydia humble, but she was actually relieved when we arrived to take her home.

It is now impossible to return her to Longbourn, so Mr. Mason has made arrangements for her to become a companion to his elderly aunt in Scotland. We intend to have Lydia installed in the position as soon as possible, and she will be kept in seclusion until it is certain whether or not there are any consequences to her actions. If it is discovered she is indeed with child, she will be passed off as the young widow of an officer. She is surprisingly compliant, and I dread to think what she must have endured the last week (Despite the fact that it is her own doing.) to render her that way, although, I must say that it is a relief not to have to argue with her over the plans we have made.

I must warn you, Darcy. Mrs. Younge claimed to have no knowledge of Wickham's current location. But upon questioning Lydia, she told us she would periodically hear him mumble about making you pay, as well as causing harm to your sister and Lizzy. Please take every precaution to protect yourselves, as we have reason to believe Wickham is not completely sane.

Today Lydia is to depart for the north, and we, Mrs. Gardiner and I, will travel to Longbourn to acquaint my sister and brother of the necessary measures we have taken to secure Lydia's future and protect the reputation of the family. As long as Fanny was not so imprudent as to spread the elopement to the entire neighbourhood, we hope to claim she travelled to us due to a position we arranged for her. Only time will tell the true extent of Lydia's folly.

Yours, etc.

Edward Gardiner

Darcy sighed and passed the note to his wife upon her inquisitive look. Once she had read it, she exhaled heavily as she folded it and laid it next to the remainder of the post.

"Since the letter was addressed to you, do you wish to respond, or shall I?" asked Elizabeth. "I do understand that you will be very busy over the next week." Things had already been hectic since that fateful day. The funeral and internment had been the day before, and had been quite the event with most of the local gentry coming to pay their condolences, keeping both Darcy and Elizabeth excessively occupied.

Lord Matlock, whom Richard had notified by express the evening of the incident, arrived the morning of the funeral. He eyed Elizabeth strangely and made her uneasy. She was excessively thankful that he was only at

Pemberley for a short time before the service, only remaining long enough afterwards to attend the meal before returning to Matlock. Fortunately, without the knowledge of the true events of Georgiana's death, he openly blamed the elder Mr. Darcy for creating Wickham, and was sympathetic towards his son and nephew for their inability to save his young niece, which allowed them to breathe a little easier.

Mr. and Miss Grey came to Pemberley the morning of the service as well, allowing Richard and the latter to spend some time together, as they had been unable since her previous visit. Miss Grey also remained behind during the funeral to visit with Elizabeth, which relieved Darcy, since he did not like to leave her so soon after the incident. The brother and sister stayed at Pemberley for the night, before they returned home the next day, not wishing to impose on their friends during the difficult time.

Richard returned for two days to Ashworth after the internment, to ensure the new steward was performing adequately before returning to aid his cousin as much as possible, giving him more free time since the birth was drawing closer. Darcy, who had been extremely busy with the harvest, was still blaming himself for his sister's death. The midwife also seemed to think that Elizabeth would deliver any day, which all combined to put the father-to-be in a panic of gargantuan proportions.

~ * ~

Friday 21 August, 1812

Elizabeth awoke, and awkwardly rose to hurry to the water closet. Things seemed a bit off from the usual morning, but she was not sure if it was what she assumed. Returning to her bed, she spotted a note from her husband on his pillow.

Good morning, love,

I must ride out with Mr. Jacobs today, as Richard has gone to Briarwood to call on Miss Grey. Mrs. Reynolds and Evans know where to locate me should you have need of me.

I love you,

Sighing, she looked out of the window at the sun just peeking over the horizon.

"He must have just left," she spoke softly to herself. She was not hungry, and since it was still early, she decided to try to go back to sleep. She fell asleep quickly, only to wake up to the sensation of her abdominal muscles clenching. It did not last long, and was not painful, so she returned to sleep only to be awoken about an hour later to the same sensation, suddenly noticing that the sheets and her shift were damp. She sat up and removed herself from the bed, realising that her rush to the water closet must have indeed been her waters rupturing, and rang the bell to summon Claire. It did not take long for the maid to appear and help her into a clean shift and her dressing gown.

"Does it hurt much ma'am?" Claire asked curiously.

"Not yet, my stomach just gets tight. The midwife said I should walk, that the movement would help the pains to increase."

"Let me notify Mrs. Reynolds about what has occurred, and I will return to assist you," Claire explained before hastily rushing from the room.

Elizabeth laughed lightly. Claire had been excited about the idea of the babe, but as the birth neared, Elizabeth had noticed that she feared attending her mistress during the event. Claire was attempting to hide her nerves as best she was able, yet it was evident in her hurried manner and her wide eyes. Not one to be kept waiting, Elizabeth ventured into the hall and began waddling toward the end of the family wing, turning back at about the same moment Mrs. Reynolds came bustling down the corridor with Claire in tow.

"We have sent for the midwife, and I was hoping to discover how you are progressing before I begin preparations."

"Truly, Mrs. Reynolds," she smiled. "I think Claire is being a bit overzealous by sending for the midwife so soon. I believe

400

my waters broke a few hours ago, but I have had only two . . ." she paused as another somewhat stronger wave bore down on her stomach. "Make that three pains, and they really have not hurt as of yet."

"Well, the midwife will be notified at the very least. She may be delivering a baby on the other side of Lambton, for all we know."

"When do you expect my husband to return?" she asked, hoping she did not show the butterflies that suddenly fluttered within her at the idea that her husband was away from the house.

"I do not believe he will want to be out much longer. There looks to be a storm coming, and I do not think he will want to be caught in it." Mrs. Reynolds smiled and curtsied. "If you will excuse me, I will leave you with Claire, and I will return to my duties."

"Of course, Mrs. Reynolds," she responded, beginning to walk once more, her maid trailing behind.

Four laps through all of the upstairs wings, and Elizabeth was no longer smiling. She was tired, her feet hurt, and the pains had actually become painful. However, Elizabeth was thrilled that her maid was no longer as nervous as she was in the beginning. Claire had seemed to calm around the end of the first lap—apparently walking had done them both some good.

"I need to sit," she gritted out as the latest contraction subsided as she hobbled into her chambers and dropped onto the sofa. Leaning her head on the back of the seat, she closed her eyes and was wishing she could sleep, when she heard Mrs. Reynolds voice.

"There you are, ma'am," she began. "How are you feeling?"

Rubbing her belly, Elizabeth opened her eyes. "Tired. The pains are much more frequent, and they hurt." She took a deep breath and closed her eyes as the next came, attempting to breathe deeply until it was over.

"Well, ma'am," Mrs. Reynolds said sympathetically, "the midwife is delivering a baby about ten miles from here, and sends word that she will be here as soon as she is able."

Elizabeth nodded as she opened her eyes. "Mrs. Reynolds, can you *please* send for my husband," she pleaded with tears in her eyes. She watched as the older woman seemed to study her for a few moments.

"Yes, ma'am," answered Mrs. Reynolds before she hastened out of the door.

Taking another deep breath, Elizabeth stood and turned to Claire. "Things definitely began to progress when I walked. I think we should repeat our tours of the different wings of the house." Her maid looked at her oddly before taking her arm and escorting her back into the hall.

~ * ~

Close to an hour later, Elizabeth finally saw her husband come striding down the guest wing. "Elizabeth, I have been looking everywhere for you! What in blazes are you doing out of bed?" He stopped at her side and watched as she did not acknowledge him, but held on to a table that was against the wall. She was leaning and gripping it tightly, with her eyes clenched shut. "Elizabeth?"

A minute later, she turned and glanced at his attire. "You are filthy," she remarked, sounding rather out of breath.

"I just came in from the fields. I returned as soon as I received the message that you were preparing to deliver, and wished for me." He watched as she nodded and began to walk. "Elizabeth, why are you not in bed?"

"The midwife says walking helps the baby to come quicker, so I walk."

"I think it is time to return to your room, love. You can barely stand," he observed, as he leaned to lift her in his arms.

"Fitzwilliam Darcy!" she exclaimed, trying to push him

402

away.

"What?"

"You smell like horse, and you are dirty!" she cried. "I will walk. You get cleaned up, and I will see you when you no longer smell." Darcy looked taken aback and hurt, almost like a little boy. "Please, Will, just go take a bath." She glanced at him pleadingly before she continued to slowly lumber down the hall.

Quickly overtaking her, he hastened to his dressing room, where his tub was just being filled and Evans was waiting for him. He laughed as he understood that Mrs. Reynolds must have anticipated the situation in which he now found himself. Quickly, he divested himself of his clothes and sank into the warm water, scrubbing thoroughly from head to toe before emerging to dry and dress in the breeches and shirt Evans laid out for him.

As he hurriedly strode to the mistress's chambers, he heard Elizabeth crying and raced to her side. "Love, look at me," he pleaded, as she lifted her head and opened her eyes. She was in a seated position, leaning to the side, propped on one arm with her other hand clutching her belly and a tear rolling down her cheek.

"It hurts," she panted, the look in her eyes showing her pain.

"Breathe," he said, placing one hand on her cheek and the other atop hers, where it rested on her swollen abdomen. "Shhhhhh . . . relax." Although his hand was covering hers, parts of his fingers overlapped hers, and rested on her abdomen; he could feel when the tension eased as the pain released her from its grip. She dropped back into the pillows and clutched his hand.

"I am so glad you are here," she said softly, as her nerves subsided some with the help of his presence.

Darcy remained for the next several hours, as the intensity of her labour increased, praying for the arrival of the midwife before the rain that had been threatening began. Elizabeth was suffering with pains that were coming so close together, she was not having any kind of a respite and Mrs. Reynolds, worried the midwife would not arrive in time, sent for Samuel's mother, Mrs. Ellis. She had certainly birthed enough children and had been present at many of the lying-ins of the tenants' wives to know what to do.

Mrs. Ellis arrived swiftly and was shown into the room. She looked nervous and uncertain of being in the great house, but she seemed to lose her inhibitions when she saw Elizabeth panting on the bed. Once Claire had shown her where to wash her hands, she came to stand at their feet.

"Mrs. Darcy," she said, trying to get the mistress's attention. "I need to see where the babe is."

Elizabeth opened her eyes to see the older woman's kind face, and took a deep breath before she gingerly rolled to her back, crying out at the pain in the base of her spine. When Mrs. Ellis was finished, she said something Elizabeth did not understand, which prompted the housekeeper to hurry from the room.

"Ma'am, the babe is ready to come," she explained. "You might be more comfortable sitting up. If you would like him to stay, your husband can sit behind you, and you can lean back on him. It will help that pain in the lower part of your back."

Elizabeth caught the scandalized look on Claire's face, and could not help but laugh as she struggled to sit, since the pain had subsided. Her husband scooted behind her, with his legs on either side of her, and his hands spanning her abdomen. Mrs. Reynolds came bustling back into the room with an armful of towels and stopped short.

"Mrs. Ellis, she should be in the birthing chair," Mrs. Reynolds exclaimed, prompting the woman to glance over to the wooden chair placed in the corner of the room.

"Mrs. Darcy, do you want to use the birthing chair? I know I would not want to give birth in that thing."

Elizabeth could hear her husband chuckle as another pain came, and Mrs. Ellis began to tell her to bear down. She pushed for what seemed like hours before she was given a reprieve from the unbearable pressure, as a lusty wail echoed through the room. Elizabeth watched as the older woman lifted a wiggling and flailing baby with a head full of dark, curly hair. She vaguely heard Mrs. Ellis say it was a boy before the woman placed the wailing bundle on her chest. Mrs. Reynolds laid several towels over the child as Elizabeth's arms wrapped around her son and her tears began to fall. She felt her husband kiss her on the temple just before he placed one of his large hands on the babe's back.

"I love you, Elizabeth," he whispered in her ear. She glanced back and noticed tears running down his face as well. "Thank you."

"I love you, too," she smiled.

"Mrs. Darcy," said Mrs. Reynolds softly to gain her attention. "Let me take him and clean him up while you finish things here."

Elizabeth nodded as the housekeeper lifted him from her chest and took him to a table that had been set up for Mrs. Reynolds to tend to him. The afterbirth was delivered, and Mrs. Ellis was just finishing and cleaning up, when the midwife was shown into the room.

"Why is she not in the birthing chair?" she exclaimed. "This room is not dark enough, and there is a man in here! This is completely inappropriate!"

"Well, I would not want to sit in that hard chair, and I do not see what a darkened room is supposed to do. As for Mr. Darcy, he has been helping his wife," Mrs. Ellis responded defensively.

"You are not a midwife. What do you think you are doing?"

"Well, you were not here, and that babe was not inclined to wait for you," Mrs. Ellis retorted, gesturing towards where Mrs. Reynolds was tending to the newborn.

"Mr. Darcy, I will not work this way. Either you and that

woman vacate this room, or I will."

"Mrs. Owen," Darcy stated authoritatively, vexed at the woman's manner. "Mrs. Ellis, I believe, has delivered my son and served admirably as a midwife. As far as I can tell, your services are no longer required."

With a huff, the woman strode from the room, muttering as she left while Mrs. Ellis positively glowed at the master's praise. Mrs. Reynolds, a smug grin on her face, returned to the bed with their son in her arms.

"Mrs. Darcy, here he is. He sure is a handsome young man."

A wide smile on her face, Elizabeth radiated happiness as the housekeeper placed her son in her arms. Darcy shifted to the other side of the bed, lifting her off of the linens they had placed under her to protect the mattress so Claire could remove them, as everyone disappeared from the room, leaving the new family in peace.

"So, William James Alexander Darcy?" he asked.

"Yes," Elizabeth confirmed. "Unless you have an objection."

"No," he said softly, placing his hand under his child's head. "I am proud that you wish to name him for me." They continued to stare in awe as his eyes opened to reveal two brilliant blue eyes.

"He looks like you," Elizabeth exclaimed, before more tears streamed down her cheeks. "He is perfect." They smiled when suddenly a loud cry pierced the quiet of the room.

"I should try to feed him."

"Are you sure you do not wish for a wet nurse?" he questioned, unsure of his wife's decision to feed the baby herself.

"No, I want to nurse him. My aunt recommended it, and since we do not plan on travelling to London for the season, I see no reason why I cannot do it," she said softly. She opened her shift, exposed her breast, and helped the babe to latch on.

"Does it hurt?" he asked, watching her curiously.

"No," she smiled, as she ensured he was feeding as he should. "It is hard to explain, but it . . . it is special." She glanced up at him and cupped his cheek in her free hand, drawing his eyes back to her face. "Are you well?"

"Yes," he smiled. "Both of you are beautiful and healthy, and we have our whole lives before us." Kissing her softly on the lips, he pulled her closer to him and held her. "I am a very lucky man."

"Far be it for me to argue with you, husband, but I believe I am the fortunate one," she replied with that arch smile that he loved so much.

"Really, and why is that?"

"If you had not found me that day in the rain, who knows what would have become of me," she smiled.

"We would have found our way to each other," he stated assuredly, as she raised her eyebrow. "Of that I have no doubt."

"Mrs. Reynolds said it looked like rain earlier, yet I never heard it storm," she commented, peering out of the window.

"I think it passed us by, love . . . I think it passed us by.

The End

Acknowledgements

There are a few people who I'd like to recognize for their support or help while I was writing and editing this story.

I'd like to recognize Jane Austen for writing such amazing characters that two hundred years later we're still obsessed with them.

I'd like to thank my husband. When I was waivering about publishing, he kept saying that I should and has supported me as I get everything prepared .

My children have been amazing. They didn't complain when I was caught in a scene, but were so excited that mom was writing a book.

To be honest, I can't say enough to express my thanks to Lisa, Kristi, and DebraAnne. These women took time out of their lives to read and edit my story for nothing more than my thanks. My degrees are in Biology and Art, not English, so I appreciate their help sooooo much!!!

There are a group of ladies known as the Chat Chits. These ladies make me laugh so much. They are also some of the most supportive people I've had the pleasure of knowing. When I came up with the idea for a story, I had intended to pass it off to one of them to write. Instead they convinced me to do it and then when I had problems or became stuck, they were my cheerleaders. Thanks a bunch ladies!

I'd like to thank Regency Encyclopedia for their great website! You make research so much easier!

I'd lastly like to thank those who first read my stories and left me their comments! Comments may not seem like much when you're reading a new story, but they help us know that we're doing a good job! Thanks!

Want to know what I'm up to, follow me here -
https://www.facebook.com/LLDiamond

Made in the USA
San Bernardino, CA
26 February 2014